A MOMENT IN TIME:

The Train—Part 2

By

Keith Schafer

October - 2021
El Dorado County Library
345 Fair Lane
Placerville, CA 95667

Dedication

This book is dedicated to the people of Jadwin: past, present and future.

Acknowledgements

Without the thoughtful editing of my wonderful wife, Cathy, and my friend, Bob Bax, as well as the creative front and back cover illustrations and tireless encouragement of my son, Lance, this book's "Moment in Time" would not have occurred.

Also, my special thanks to my daughter-in-law, Tanvi, the first reader of a draft of this book, who gave me valuable feedback to revise one of the book's chapters to make it stronger.

And for all who supported me and encouraged me to write the rest of this story, I will always be grateful.

Chapter 1

She heard the wagon rattling down Lough Lane as she was tending to a flower bed in the front yard of her family's little rock house standing out on the point of the peninsula that dropped steeply to the wet weather creek in the valley below. She loved flowers of all kinds, but particularly the lilies and irises so notable in her yard at blooming time.

She'd been weeding for more than an hour. She groaned as she rose awkwardly from her kneeling position and arched her back, hands on hips, working out the kinks. Who would be coming unannounced at this hour of the day?

Food! She'd need more food, maybe a lot more depending on who and how many were on that wagon. She had a pot of stew simmering and bread in the oven, but that was barely enough for her own large family. And it sure wouldn't be fancy enough if it was somebody highfalutin, like the preacher or a school board member coming down to confer with Jess. It crossed her mind that it could be easy to resent the unannounced visit right at suppertime, but it wouldn't be Christian of her, so she drove that thought out of her mind.

Thank goodness she'd made a peach cobbler earlier in the afternoon! And Anna could make a wilted lettuce salad from the spring greens in the garden. Anna had become a good cook. A few of her dishes could even rival Bessie's, except maybe for the baked goods. It was widely recognized throughout Jadwin that nobody baked like Bessie.

Where was Anna? Maybe she'd hitched a ride on the wagon since it had to travel right past the school. Anna had usually finished her grading and the next day's lesson plans by this hour, and was home to help with supper. It was a little odd that she wasn't back yet.

The rattling grew louder as the wagon cleared the woods to the open area along the high meadow where the Lough cattle grazed. Bessie shaded her eyes to see who was on it. There were two men and no Anna. Bessie immediately recognized the familiar figure of Sam Kofahl, Jess's cousin from Rolla, and relaxed a little. The other man was bigger than Sam, and a stranger.

For a second, she worried that something might be wrong in Rolla, but then she saw Sam laughing and gesturing broadly to the man beside him, so he must not be bringing bad news. Still, it was unusual. Sam always alerted them in advance before he came down.

Sam saw Bessie and waved his hat in his patented broad-sweeping motion. The wagon was still a few hundred yards away. She saw him say something to the man next to him and heard him laugh loudly. The old rascal was probably telling the stranger something at her expense! She could make out the features of the stranger better now. He was young and his size definitely eclipsed Sam's.

When they reached the edge of the yard, Sam yelled, "Howdy do, Bessie! What's fer dinner?"

"Well it'd a'been a lot more if you'd just told me you was a'commin, you rascal!" She had her hands on her hips, feigning gruffness, but couldn't pull it off as she began to grin. "It's good to see you, Sam. Martha and the kids alright?"

6

"Fine; they're just fine, Bessie. Martha sends her love and looks forward to seein you at Jadwin on Memorial Day. And as for forewarning you, well, when these two boys showed up last night and I found out who they were, I thought I'd better git em down here to Jadwin as fast as I could or risk yer wrath."

Bessie was guessing that Jess had brought the man on business with Charlie Schafer and his sawmilling operations. But he would never bring a stranger to supper unannounced. Yet here he was, spouting something about how she'd be angry if he hadn't brought this one. And he'd said something about two boys? Where was the other one?

"Did you see Anna at the school? She must be running late. I'd have thought she would've hitched a ride with you if she'd seen you pass."

Sam grinned wickedly. "Well, I cain't honestly say that she seen me. She was what you'd call, 'otherwise engaged'."

"Alright, Sam Kofahl! Quit your evil grinning and your riddles and tell me what's going on. What do you mean by, 'she was otherwise engaged'?"

"I'll git to that, Bessie, I'll git to it, but where on earth have your manners gone? Wouldn't you like to meet this fine young gentleman that I've brung with me?"

Bessie's face colored a little and she gave Sam an evil look, and then addressed the stranger. "Why certainly, my apologies, sir. It's just that you're travelin in such bad company that I forgot my manners!"

The man smiled politely, stepping down off the wagon. He walked over and extended his hand. It was a very big hand, swallowing hers as she took it. They shook hands as she looked up at him inquisitively. "That's no problem, ma'am. I know Sam's just harassing you. My name is Christian Gunther and I'm particularly honored to meet you."

Christian Gunther? She knew that name but just couldn't quite place it. But she knew that she should remember—that it was important. And then suddenly, she did! She looked up at Christian and, almost in a whisper, asked, "Are you from New York?" He smiled and nodded. "Yes, ma'am. I'm Ben McDonald's friend."

Her face went pale and she felt a little faint. She looked over at Sam, who was grinning from ear to ear. Her mind raced. Sam had said Anna was "otherwise engaged" and that there were two boys who had showed up unexpectedly. Where was the other boy? Could it be Ben McDonald? Was he with Anna now? Is that why she hadn't ridden down from the schoolhouse with Sam?

She realized she was still holding the young man's hand. She blushed and let go. He smiled down at her and waited for the barrage of questions passing across her face. Sam, however, was not inclined to give her time to recover. He intended to milk this for all it was worth. "Hope you've got enough to eat for three more, Bessie! Guess who's coming fer supper?"

She looked at Sam and then back to Christian, her eyes wide. "You saved their lives! Anna wouldn't be here except for you." Before Christian could respond, she put her arms around his chest and squeezed tightly.

8

Christian hadn't expected that. He awkwardly leaned down to her to return her hug and patted her on the back. "I'm really honored to meet you, Bessie. Sam has told us all about you. If there's credit to be had for saving Anna, it goes to other people more than me, including Ben, you and your family."

Sam was touched, but slightly taken aback by Bessie's reaction to meeting Christian. He cleared his throat. "Okay then, you two newly met lovebirds; you should tear yourselves apart from each other before Jess sees you. I'm shocked at you, Bessie! In the arms of another man; you bein a Christian woman with children and all!"

Bessie laughed through tears and released Christian, but still held on to his hand and looked up at him with wide glistening eyes. "Oh, hush up, Sam Kofahl. If you were half as good lookin as him, and had done what he did, I'd hug you like that every time you came down this lane!" She addressed Christian. "I assume the 'other boy' Sam was talking about is Ben and that he's with Anna now?"

Before Christian could respond, Sam cackled. "That's right, old girl, and when we left them at the school, she was already startin a readin lesson. I'm not entirely sure when they'll come down, so you've got some time to fret over supper, like I know you will. Where's your uglier half? I want to see the look on his face when I tell him the news."

"You're enjoying this way too much, Sam Kofahl! Jess is down in the valley with the horses and wagon. Ring the dinner bell and he'll come. You men always come when there's food on the table. Christian, come talk to me while I make more supper; if that's alright with you."

Christian smiled and nodded. He immediately took to this good-hearted, straightforward woman, surprised at how comfortable he felt around her. They walked to the house with Bessie still holding his hand. Sam went around to the back of the house to ring the dinner bell.

He rang it loud and long—much louder and longer than Bessie normally did. In the field below, it scared Jess. Maybe one of the kids had gotten hurt! Jess hurried over to the wagon and turned the horses up the steep hill at double time. The wagon was loaded and heavy. He had pushed the horses halfway up the steep grade before he saw Sam sauntering out the back gate, a big grin on his face, waving broadly.

Jess immediately slowed Jim and Prince. They were already winded from the fast climb and swelled their bellies, blowing repeatedly through their noses to recover their wind. He stopped them for a few seconds to rest. They turned their heads back to give him cross looks, wondering what had gotten in to him. He apologized. "Sorry, old boys. It's just that rascal of a cousin of mine. You'll get double the grain for your effort when we get to the barn."

He started them up again, this time at a leisurely pace. The horses still had to strain to reach the top of the steep rise where the house stood. They were anxious to get on to the barn and free of their harnesses. They'd been worked all day. Jess always rewarded them with a little grain each time they made that arduous climb up from the valley, particularly if the wagon was loaded. As they reached the top, Jess stopped them beside the house to let them blow again. Sam sauntered over, grinning like a cat that'd swallowed the canary.

"Sam, you worthless old coot! You gave me a scare. I could've killed the horses coming up out of the valley that fast. I've half a mind to run you down that hill and back up again with you pushing a loaded wheel barrow to see how much you'd blow if it was done to you!"

Sam's grin didn't waiver. "Ah, well, maybe sometime, cousin, but not today. You won't be havin time for such drivel when you hear who's going to be at your supper table tonight."

"You don't say! And who, pray tell, might that be—the King of England? And what brings you here unannounced at suppertime, at least not to me, gloatin like you've got some big secret to tell? Maybe you're here to reveal some long lost uncle we never knowed that's died and left us a fortune. That'd be nice. Bessie and me'd like to travel a bit more afore we die—at least I would."

Sam laughed. "Ah, Jess, it's somethin much better than money. Go inside and get introduced to a man much younger and better lookin than you that your wife has already hugged and fallen in love with, even if she'd never met him afore, and is probly havin thoughts of replacing you as we speak. I'll take the horses to the barn and give em their grain."

Jess looked at Sam inquisitively but knew he'd get no more information. Sam was the big practical joker of the family and he definitely had something up his sleeve now. Jess handed over the reins, telling him to give each horse two full Folgers cans worth of grain for their unneeded exertion. He spoke to Jim and Prince, telling them that they could each step on Sam's feet for the misery he'd put em through coming up the hill. They nodded their heads up and down impatiently and looked at Sam out of the edges of their blinders.

11

That sobered Sam a little. It was widely known that Jess's two big work horses were the most intelligent around and had a special relationship with their master. "Now surely you don't think these two horses understood what you just said?"

Jess just laughed and said, "They know more'n you think, old bud. I'd walk careful around em if I was you."

Jess walked up the porch steps and on into the kitchen to the sound of frantically banging pans and the sight of a flustered wife rushing around. Sitting at the table was a young man Jess'd never seen before, a big, muscular guy, calmly peeling potatoes, just like he was family. That threw Jess a little. Normally Bessie would never let a stranger help prepare a meal. All the kids except Zach were gathered round the young man looking starry-eyed, like he was some famous somebody. Bessie saw Jess and ran over to him. "Jess! Did Sam tell you?"

"Tell me what? He was so full of himself that I couldn't get nothin from him except that you'd found a new love and are thinkin about trading me in." Jess looked over at the young stranger and grinned. The stranger smiled back. There was already a pile of peeled potatoes on the table in front of him.

Bessie took his arm and dragged him over to Christian, who wiped his hands on his trousers and stood up. "Well, Jess, Sam was right about one thing. I do already love him and you will too when I tell you who he is. Jess Lough, meet Christian Gunther!"

Jess had already stuck out his hand and taken Christian's, but he didn't connect with the name immediately. He looked puzzled for a second, and then he, too, remembered. His look of puzzlement changed to surprise. "Christian Gunther? The boy who led Anna and Ben McDonald out of Hell's Kitchen? You're that Christian Gunther?"

Christian laughed. "Yes, and it's an honor to meet you, Jess. Sam told us a lot about you on the way from Rolla. But my part in the Ben and Anna story didn't really amount to much."

Jess began pumping Christian's hand, squeezing it as hard as he could. He also slapped Christian on the back with his free hand and exclaimed, "That's not the story we git, young man! Anna told us that you gave up just about everythin important to you to save their lives. She said you were riskin your own life to boot. Next to Ben McDonald, there's not a bigger hero known to this family. I can't believe you're standing here, big as life, in our kitchen! Did you bring Ben with you?"

Christian smiled. "Actually, he brought me; and yes, he's here. He and Anna are probably still at the school, but I'm sure they'll get here soon and you'll get to meet the real hero in the story. I suspect you'll be seeing a lot of him in the future by the way Anna greeted him when she saw him."

Jess's eyes shone. "Well ain't this just somethin! Ain't this really somethin! It's hard to believe. I can't tell you how happy we are that you finally come. Anna's waited so long for this day. We'd begin to think it warn't never gonna happen."

"Well, you had pretty good reason to believe that. But it's ended well and I'm glad to be here to see it. Now, I'd better sit down and finish peeling these potatoes or Bessie may change her opinion of me pretty quick." He laughed and looked over at the potatoes. "In fact, she may anyway once she sees how bad I am at peeling. I'm afraid I've left almost as much of the potato on the peelings as in the pile."

Bessie laughed and picked up the potatoes he'd already peeled. "You're doin just fine. I'll eat potatoes peeled by your hand any day, Christian."

Jess started over to grab a kitchen knife to help Christian, but Bessie stopped him. "Jess, go out to the smokehouse and get that ham—the good one we were saving for a special occasion. Scrape off the salt outside and bring it in." Then go to the cellar and bring me three jars of green beans, and go to the garden and get whatever peas that are still there and some lettuce and green onions. It won't be the best dinner I'll ever prepare for em, but it'll have to do for tonight!"

Jess hurried out to complete his assignment. Sam came in from tending the horses and joined the general melee. The kids were swarming all over everybody, but mainly Christian—all except for Zachary, who held back. Christian noticed and looked over at him. "I'm guessing you're Zachary. It's nice to meet you."

Zachary frowned. "Were you really the head of the Bowery Boys?"

"For a while."

"I heard about you. You were supposed to be really mean." A sudden hush fell over the kitchen and everyone froze.

Christian turned to him, realizing that he'd just been called to account for his past. He stopped smiling, taking on a serious demeanor, and addressed Zach. "You heard right, Zachary; I was mean sometimes. I'm sorry to have to say that, but it's true."

"But you're not anymore?"

14

Zach's back was turned to Bessie and she began to move toward him, looking apologetically at Christian. He glanced at her and shook his head slightly. She stepped back. Christian looked back down at the little boy, who had now walked up right in front of him. It crossed Christian's mind that this was a bold little kid. How old would he be now? Eight maybe?

"Well, Zachary, I guess that might depend on who you talk to, but I'd say, for the most part, I wouldn't be considered mean anymore by the people who know me now, and certainly not to those I care about, like Ben, or Anna, or you and your family."

"Well, how can you be that mean and then become nice?"

Christian realized his inquisitor wasn't going to let up easily. "That's a good question, Zachary, one I've asked myself a lot in the last few years. When I led the Bowery Boys, I think I was mostly mean, or at least the things I did would be seen as mostly mean. Some of it was what I thought I should do to take care of my gang, which was like my family, and some of it was to let people know I was the boss. I did some good things too, but certainly a lot bad."

He paused, looking down at Zach. "Sometimes things happen that make us change. From what I hear, you've changed more than anybody since you came here. I hear that you're one of the healthiest, fastest and smartest guys around for your age. You weren't able to do those things in New York at the orphanage, were you? You're able to do them now because you've changed, right?"

Zachary nodded.

"Well, for you, changing may actually have been easier than for me. It just meant you had to get stronger in your body. Anna, Jess and Bessie helped you with that. You were already strong in your head and your heart. In my case, I was strong in my body but kind of shriveled up inside. For me, a guy named Bill Chambers, and then my friend Ben, helped me grow stronger inside. I began to see myself and other people differently. I may not have grown as much as you, but I'm pretty sure I'm not shriveled up anymore. I can't fix what I did before, and I still have a way to go, but with help from people like you, who care enough to tell me what you think about what I've done and what I should do differently, I think I'll be okay. You think you could help me with that?"

Zachary didn't respond for long seconds, mulling over the question. Bessie held her breath. The room was quiet enough to hear a pin drop. Then Zach's face brightened and he smiled. "Sure. Anna says we wouldn't be here without you. She says we owe you a lot and that nobody's all good or all bad. I guess we should help you if we can."

Christian smiled. "Well, thanks, Zachary. That means a lot to me. Orphans probably should stick together, don't you think? I suspect you and me could become good friends if we try."

Zachary walked over and stuck out his small hand. Christian shook it solemnly, looking down at this brave little kid. Zachary said, "Deal!" Christian responded in kind. "Deal!" Everyone else in the room let out a collective sigh and the noise started up again.

Jess and Sam had walked in the door just as Christian and Zachary were finishing the handshake. It was obvious that they'd missed something. Jess looked over at Bessie, who had tears in her eyes. She shook her head to let him know not to break the moment with his questions. He could quiz her tonight after they went to bed—assuming anybody would actually do that tonight. The conversation picked up again as everybody began talking at the same time, the typical conversational mode in the Lough household.

As the late afternoon light mellowed, Bessie started fidgeting. Anna and Ben had remained at the school for a long time. She thought that if they stayed much longer, it might be seen as unseemly by someone—she wasn't sure who—but someone. She also wanted to meet this boy whom she had heard about for so long.

But it began to turn dusk and they still didn't come. It wasn't a good idea to be walking down a dark, wooded lane with cougars and bears still known to be about. She told herself, "Those two have obviously faced far greater risks, and when they were much younger." She tried to tell herself that she was just fretting over nothing, but she'd be more comfortable when they showed up.

Supper was ready, but no one was going to eat till Anna and Ben arrived. Bessie edged over toward Christian and motioned him to join her in the living room. Jess and Sam were jawing and the kids had resumed their play, so no one paid much attention as they exited the kitchen. Bessie didn't quite know how to broach the subject. "Christian, I don't know exactly how to ask this, but….." She paused, feeling slightly embarrassed.

Christian grinned. "You're worried that Anna and Ben haven't come home yet and you're wondering what they're doing."

Bessie blushed, but looked relieved. He was also a mind reader! "Well, a little bit, I guess. It's nigh unto dark and it's a half mile through those woods."

Christian looked sympathetic. "I understand. I'll head up that way and let them know supper's ready. But, Bessie, I know Ben very well and I can assure you that Anna could never be as safe with anyone else as she is with him—in every way. He'd never let her be hurt or do anything that might bring embarrassment to her. He's as fierce a protector of her as anyone alive." I can personally attest to that." He smiled and touched his own arm that Ben had broken on the night he'd saved Anna from Christian's gang in Hell's Kitchen. "I'm sure the time has just gotten away from them. I'll bring them back. It'll just take a few minutes."

Bessie sighed and took his hand. "You're the most thoughtful man, Christian Gunther. We're so blessed to have you here." She turned and went back into the kitchen.

He smiled to himself as he turned toward the front door. This Bessie Lough was a really fine person! As he stepped out to the yard and looked up the lane, he saw them coming, not far away now, walking hand in hand. He slipped back into the house and into the kitchen. He went over to Bessie as she stood at the stove, stirring the beans. He whispered, "They're just about to arrive, Bessie."

She nodded and smiled at him, mouthing, "Thank you". He walked over to the table and sat down near Sam and Jess, looking forward to the excitement when Ben McDonald walked through that door.

In less than a minute, a jubilant Anna Murphy floated into the kitchen, holding Ben's hand, which shocked nobody. Sam looked up. "Well, here are the two love birds now! I figured

Bessie was goin to mount a search party at any minute." Bessie hit him on the arm for that, her face blushing a little with guilt, because she knew it was true.

"Anna laughed and guided Ben over to Bessie. "Sorry, Bessie. We just had some work to do with this guy's reading skills. I am pleased to say that he's teachable."

Ben grinned. "That remains to be seen. We'll soon learn how good a teacher she really is. It'll be more of a challenge than she thinks." Then Ben took Bessie's hands into his. "Hello, Bessie. I can't tell you how excited I am to meet you after all I've heard about you from Sam and Anna." As she looked up into those big blue, smiling eyes and that handsome face, just for once, Bessie Lough was flustered into silence. She blushed.

Any doubts that she might have harbored about Ben McDonald, or the worthiness of his intentions toward Anna disappeared like magic. He had a look of solemnity about him that seemed far beyond his age. She had noticed that same look in Christian, and even in Anna, for that matter. It must have been the trials they had faced as children. She supposed it had matured them beyond their years; but what a terrible price to pay for maturity! Ben was very tall, taller even than Christian, with broad shoulders that tapered to a thin waist. His face was expressive and his eyes—well those eyes could probably melt butter on a cold day!

She became even more flustered. Anna saw it and laughed. "Yes, Bessie, I think he's turned out pretty nicely since I saw him last."

Bessie laughed and found her voice. "Ben McDonald, you have no idea how many days and nights we've waited for your coming, wonderin how it'd be when you finally got here. And now that you have, and I see you two together….well, there's just no words to express how good it is to see you." She gave him a big hug and Ben reciprocated without the slightest hesitation.

"Thanks for all you and Jess have done for Anna, Bessie. We'll forever be in your debt."

Jess came rambling over and grabbed him by the arm and pumped his hand. "So you're actually real? We'd begin to think Anna'd just conjured you up in her mind like a ghost! Welcome home, son!" Ben laughed and put his arm around Jess' shoulders. Jess was delighted with this boy. He seemed every bit the match for Anna—and that was saying a lot!

Anna stood watching the people she loved most in the world— now all in the same room. Her face was beyond radiant. Bessie had believed there was nothing that could ever make that girl more beautiful, but as she watched her now, she knew that she hadn't even been close. How two such incredible young people had found each other, lost each other, and then came together again, with everything in the world stacked against them, would be unbelievable to most people. But Bessie Lough wasn't at all surprised. She was sure that it was just the way God intended it all along!

Chapter 2

Later that evening, long after the Lough children were finally corralled and coerced to bed, the adults sat around the kitchen table. Ben and Christian shared more about what had happened in New York after Anna left, including the sad circumstances of Bill Chamber's death, and of finding Ben's family again.

They talked until Bessie's grandfather clock—which really was her grandfather's clock—struck 2:00 a.m. Sam declared that he needed to get back to Rolla by the next afternoon and should get a little sleep before heading over for a quick meeting with Charlie Schafer early in the morning. Christian said that he'd go back with Sam to return to Indiana to tell Jake and Emily about Ben's and Anna's reunion, and to help Jake get through the rest of the planting season. Pallets were laid out in the parlor and living room for Ben, Sam and Christian, and everyone finally drifted off to bed.

Jess, who was president of the Jadwin Elementary School Board, anticipating Anna's desire to spend the next day with Ben, had already taken Sam along for company and ridden up to Hattie Jacobs' house earlier in the evening to get her to substitute for Anna the next day.

Before retiring, Christian took Ben aside and told him that he'd cover for him in Indiana until Ben and Anna decided what they were going to do. Then he'd make his own decision about his future plans. Ben hugged him. "Thanks for coming with me and for going back to help Jake and take care of my family while I'm gone. You'll never know how much your friendship means to me."

Christian smiled. "It works both ways, Ben. This Lough family is really something special! You're a lucky man to get to associate with them. And I'm guessing that I'll see you and Anna soon, no matter what our long-term plans turn out to be. Just relax and enjoy yourself. You've earned it."

There were more hugs all around as they left the next morning. The family stood out front of the house and waved until Sam's wagon disappeared up the lane. Then they went back into the house for more coffee and visiting.

After coffee, Anna took Ben up to sit under a massive oak tree, the centerpiece of the meadow that overlooked the house and valley below. It was Anna's favorite place on the farm. The tree was tall and stately, and at least fifteen feet in circumference. Its limbs branched out a good thirty feet on all sides. The cows and calves, grazing in the meadow, ambled over sociably for their friend Anna to scratch their ears. Prince and Jim decided to get in on the action too, nuzzling Anna and getting acquainted with the new stranger. After doing so, they and the cows went back to their grazing.

"This all still feels like a dream to me, Ben," she said as they sat on the velvety moss under the tree, she leaning back against his chest.

"Yea, it does. I'm almost afraid I'll wake up and still be in Indiana and realize that none of this is true."

She laughed, "Well, we're awake and we're together, and I'm counting on you not to send me away from you again anytime soon!"

He laughed. "Never again, Miss Murphy! That'll never happen unless you attempt an escape, and even then I'd try to catch you.

There's a big hole in my life when you're not around."

"I don't think you'll ever have much to worry about on that score. It took far too long for us to find each other again. It was a horrible wait and I almost lost hope. I don't want to go through that twice in my life. So you're going to be stuck with me a long time!" She leaned back and kissed him.

The next day was Saturday. Anna and the family packed a lunch and took Ben to Cedar Grove on the Current River, a popular recreation site only a few miles south of Jadwin. The Current River, one of Missouri's most beautiful streams, runs crystal clear and cold from the numerous springs that feed it as it meanders through 184 miles of southern Missouri and on into northern Arkansas, finally emptying into the Black River. The river's *Big Spring* at its lower reaches is one of the largest in the world. But Jadwin was near the headwaters, where the waters were much narrower and swifter.

At that time, the river originated from a single large spring near the mouth of Pigeon Creek. From there, it meandered through rugged hills covered by hardwood, cedar and pine trees. The river had created long, narrow valleys with soil for farming along its banks. But the hills closed in on the valleys quickly and were steep and rocky, with little topsoil and a lot of rock and clay, the perfect mix for the trees that covered the area.

Anna particularly loved the river. After spending a little time there, Ben could see why. It ran so clear and fast that, when he looked into its depths, it was like looking through glass at the river bottom. But he found it had a hard edge to it as well. It was so cold that it took his breath away when he waded into it. And Anna warned him to be careful. The depth of the water was deceptive. Whether knee-deep or over his head, it would look much the same to his untrained eye. While it was narrow at its upper reaches, a few novice swimmers drowned nearly every year as they misjudged those depths.

There were pathways all along the river. Some led to bluffs that gave climbers a panoramic view as the river meandered south. Anna had adopted one such bluff as her own, and she always went there when visiting the river. She led Ben there to take in the scenery.

The Lough kids, who had often accompanied Anna to her bluff on prior occasions, weren't overly impressed that Anna and Ben got to run off by themselves, but Bessie shushed them and told them to go play for an hour while she and Jess prepared lunch. She said that it would probably be best if they avoided drowning if they could. They were offended by her lack of faith, and told her so as they waded down the river in a bit of a huff.

After spending an hour on the bluff, Ben and Anna rejoined the family. By that time Bessie had laid out a large picnic lunch that always seemed to taste better at the edge of the river than at home. After lunch, the family again enjoyed the shallows, splashing one another with the cold water and watching lazy trout swim past.

Jess spent most of his time fishing and had some luck. By the time they were ready to head back toward Jadwin, he'd caught five nice trout, which he placed in a couple of Bessie's tubs that he'd brought, filling them with fresh river water and covering them with cloth to keep the fish alive until they reached home. They'd all enjoy fresh fish for supper that night!

On the next day, the family took Ben to church to show him off. The congregation was extremely friendly to him. The rumor had already gotten around that he'd finally arrived in Jadwin. Now that he was real and among them, he was a bit of a celebrity.

Anna took his arm and held it proudly throughout the church meeting and during all the introductions. She was ecstatic that he was there, believing that people who met Ben would now understand why she'd avoided taking a beau in Jadwin.

Ben met Charlie and Nellie Schafer for the first time, a very interesting couple, she at four feet eleven inches and he every bit of a lanky six feet five inches. He was the only person at the church taller than Ben. Charlie and Nellie already had six children and counting.

Charlie was a noted businessman in the area. Ben was impressed that Charlie had earned that reputation at a very young age. Charlie couldn't be much more than ten years older than him, if that. Both men sized each other up and liked what they saw. Each left that day thinking that they'd like to get to know each other better.

Late in the following week, Ben joined Jess as he did his evening chores. He was nervous, which soon became apparent to Jess. Guessing why, Jess grinned and got right to the point. "What's eatin on you, Ben?"

Ben laughed. "It's that apparent, huh?"

Jess grinned. "Yea, and you might as well spit it out so's it don't give you heartburn."

Ben smiled, embarrassed. "Yea, you're right. So here goes. I know Anna and I still look pretty young to most folks, but I don't feel that young and neither does she. We can't imagine our lives without each other. I'll be honest, I have no idea how to ask this properly, and I'm not even sure if you'll think that I should be asking you, but I'd like your blessing to ask for Anna's hand in marriage. And frankly, I need your help in figuring out how best to ask her."

Jess guffawed, then quickly caught himself, recognizing how important those questions were to Ben. "Well, Ben, first off, I appreciate that you're asking me, and I guess I'm the only one Anna's got left to be asked. You probably didn't have to, but it's respectful and it's much appreciated."

"Now, as for bein too young, that might be the case in New York, or even in Indiana, but it's not so much around here. In this neck of the woods, both of you are clear marryin age. And if you warn't thinkin about it, I'd be right disappointed in you. So for what it's worth, and I spect this'll go for Bessie too, you have our full blessins."

"Now, as for how best to ask the girl, I ain't offerin no advice t'all. Ever young buck has to figure that out for hisself. But you'll need a ring to do it, and if you got the money, you can probly get what you need in Salem. I'll take you there as soon as you say go."

"But in case you don't have no money, then I'll tell you this story. When I decided to ask Bessie for her hand, it all came on me in a flash. I knew a boy needed a ring to do it, but I decided I couldn't wait to make enough money for a store-bought ring. I had no money t'all at the time. I fretted about that fer a week, all the time just sure that she was like some big ol' trout in the Current River who'd likely swim away any second if I didn't git my line in the water."

"So I took me some horseshoe nails and spent a full half-a-day bendin em in a circle that I thought might fit her finger. I kept workin on a pattern, flattenin out the nail heads so they'd look prettier. I finally got one the way I wanted it by flattenin the head and then shaping a heart out of it. I was still guessin at the finger size but that'd be pretty easy to adjust if she liked the ring. Then I took it with me to ask her to marry me."

"I was all of seventeen at the time and she was fifteen." He grinned and reflected. "I was just scared to death that she'd get away from me if I waited a minute longer and I knowed I'd never find another like her!" He paused again, looking away, remembering.

"Well, anyway, I presented her that ring and asked for her hand. I felt sure that it was the lamest proposal any man ever made to a girl, but to my surprise, she took that bent horseshoe nail and looked at it like it was gold, and then she said yes."

"About five years ago, I scrounged up enough money to get her a real weddin ring as a Christmas present. Took a year's worth of work at the mills to afford it, but I was proud as peach to present it to her. On Christmas Eve, I slipped that horseshoe ring off her finger and told her I didn't want her wearin it no more. She was surprised, a'course, and started to protest. Right then, I handed her the new ring in its fancy velvet box. She opened it and started to cry. I told her that it sealed it for her; she'd never get away from me now!"

"She told me that the horseshoe nail ring had already done that, but that she loved this new ring as well. She put it on her finger and danced around with it. Then she surprised me. She asked for the old one back. You wouldn't notice this without my tellin ya, but she made me stretch it a little and she wears that old thing on her right hand now. She says it's as precious to her as the store-bought one. Cost less than a cent and the other one was over $50 dollars! Go figger! Women're just plain unpredictable." He looked away and Ben saw a tear leak out of his eye.

Ben put his hand on Jess' shoulder. "Thank you for telling me that story, Jess. I'm not sure why, but it makes it a lot easier for me to think about asking Anna. And I'd really appreciate going to Salem as soon as you can get away. If I don't like what they have there, you can show me how to make one of those horseshoe nail rings. I can see how Anna might like it just as much as Bessie did."

Jess nodded and reached out to shake Ben's hand. "You're a lucky man to have her love you like she does, Ben; but then, you already know that. But I want you to know that I think she's just as lucky to have you askin her. You've got my blessin, free and clear."

They traveled to Salem the next day after Jess made some lame excuse about needing supplies. They left early, right after the chores were done. Bessie had asked Jess what he needed in Salem, but he just hum-hawed around, so she let it go. She chalked it up to restlessness. When she found out Ben was going, she began to worry that maybe Jess's travelin malady might be rubbing off. Ben had stayed pretty close to Anna's side from the time he'd arrived, but now he was waltzing off for the day with Jess on some jaunt.

Jess and Ben arrived in Salem mid-morning. They walked down the street to the only jewelry store in town. A lady named Sally Buckhalter greeted them. "Why Jess Lough, I haven't seen you in a long while! How are Bessie and the children?"

"They're just fine, Sally. Bessie would have wanted me to say hello if she'd knowed I was a'comin here." Then he sort of whispered, "It's a bit of a secret, you see."

Sally joined the game and took a hushed tone while dramatically glancing around. "So, keeping secrets are we? Is it Bessie's birthday and you've finally decided to buy her that gift she so rightfully deserves for putting up with the likes of you?"

Jesse laughed. "You must think we're growin money on trees down Jadwin way, Sally! Actually, I'm not the customer today. My friend, Ben, here is."

Sally's attention shifted quickly. "So are you *that* Ben? Anna Murphy's Ben?" She'd already guessed, but she was going to play this to the hilt.

Ben laughed nervously. "News travels fast down here, doesn't it?"

Sally laughed. "Well, you're big news down in Jadwin, and from the looks of you, I can see why. The people from there already filled us in. Now, Ben, how exactly can I help you today?" She'd already guessed the answer and didn't even wait for him to respond, leaning down below the counter to bring up a display of rings. "Tell me your price range and I'll show you your options."

He grinned. "Well, I see that you've already figured out what I'm looking for. Unfortunately I'm limited to about $100 dollars. If that's not enough, maybe I can pay you that much now and more later?" On the way to town, it had occurred to him that he had no idea how much a ring might cost. When he'd

29

asked Jess, his only response was that it ranged all over the place and depended on how big a fool the man was.

Sally was empathetic and not at all intimidated by Ben's limit. "Actually, Ben, we have some very nice rings in that price range." She reached under the counter again and pulled out a rich-looking walnut box. She opened the lid to reveal a variety of pretty rings, some silver and some gold, held neatly in slats covered with red velvet lining.

Ben was unsure about which would be best and Jess was absolutely no help—in fact, he was the opposite of help, laughing and joking, and generally making the process harder. He refused to offer an opinion about silver or gold, or about any of the settings. He said that the selection of a woman's ring was one of a man's most perilous adventures, and that the poor sucker who was paying had to make his own choice.

But Sally was patient. She pulled a number of the rings out of their little sockets for Ben to hold in his hand. As he inspected them, she casually asked about the wedding plans and how he liked the Jadwin community.

Ben finally settled on a gold band with a curling leaf pattern on top. Sally took off her own wedding band and put it on her pinky finger to model it for him. Ben thought it quite attractive and hoped Anna would too. "Do you think Anna would like this, Mrs. Buckhalter?"

Sally smiled warmly and said, "Now, Ben, let me ask you something. Do you think there is any ring in this box that Anna Murphy wouldn't absolutely adore, knowing that you'd picked it out just for her?"

Ben looked relieved. "I see your point. Thanks. This is my favorite. I'll take it."

"Wonderful choice! Do you know the size of Anna's ring finger? If you can wait a couple of hours we can fit it, clean it and have it ready to go."

A panicked expression crossed Ben's face. "Oh, no! I'm afraid I don't." He wished now that he'd talked to Bessie. He was sure Jess wouldn't know. Now it might require another trip to Salem! He looked over at Jess, who just shrugged.

Sally smiled and patted Ben's hand. "Well, that's not unusual. Most men don't know the size of their girl's ring finger, and if you're going to surprise her, it's not as if you can ask her, is it. Let's just guess. We'll get pretty close and then you and Anna can come back if it needs refitting."

Sally asked Ben to guess the approximate size of Anna's hands by comparing them to hers. He said they were long and slender and that he thought Anna's ring finger would be about the size of Sally's pinky finger. He hoped that observation wouldn't offend Sally.

It didn't. Sally had met Anna a number of times when she'd come into the store on errands for Mrs. Steelman during the time Anna was attending school in Salem. Sally was an astute salesperson and always made a point of looking at the hands of young ladies who might someday become customers. She assured Ben that his guess would be close and that it wouldn't hurt to size a ring more than once if they missed it a little. She told them to come back in a couple of hours and she'd have the ring ready to go.

Jess and Ben walked around Salem to introduce Ben to the town, then had a little lunch at Jess's favorite diner and headed to the courthouse square to jaw with some of the old guys who often hung out there. At the appointed time, they picked up the ring in its beautiful velvet-covered box.

Ben took it out at least ten times on the ride home until Jess laughingly told him he'd better be careful not to wear the velvet out before Anna even saw it. Ben sheepishly put it back in his pocket and didn't take it out again, but he still touched the outside of his pocket from time to time to feel the lump and make sure it hadn't fallen out. It was the most expensive single thing he'd ever purchased, and definitely the most important. It made him nervous, just carrying it around.

On the way back to Jadwin, Jess asked, "So, how you gonna pop the question, Ben?"

"I'm not sure yet, but I do think I know *where* I'm going to pop the question, if you agree. I'd like to ask her on her favorite bluff overlooking the Current River if you can get us there on Saturday—assuming the weather's good."

"That'll be a good choice. She loves that place. It seems to set her at peace. Always did. I don't know why. It's pretty and all, but she just seems more connected to water and heights. We're good for a day at the river anytime. I'll tell Bessie that we're going on Saturday, although I'll not tell her why. It'll be almost as fun to surprise her as Anna! This time, I'll have her pack you a picnic lunch fer the bluff."

So the kit and caboodle of them hopped on the wagon on Saturday and headed back to Cedar Grove. To Ben's delight, it was a beautiful day weather-wise. When they arrived at the river, Anna wanted to head right for the bluff, as Ben suspected she would. Bessie handed them a wicker basket with a "light snack" since Jess told her they could benefit from a little more privacy and might be at the bluff longer. Ben kissed Bessie on the forehead as he took the basket. She looked at him quizzically, but said nothing.

Ben and Anna walked along the river for a little while and then climbed up the steep path to the bluff. Anna opened the basket and laid out one of Bessie's old quilts and plopped down on her stomach to take in the view. Ben pretended to do the same, but she caught him watching her out of the corner of his eye. They held hands but didn't talk. The pastoral scene below gave a wonderful sense of peace and quiet, broken only infrequently by canoeists floating down the river.

After a while, Anna rolled over onto her back to watch the puffy clouds float by. Then she dozed like a big cat in the warm sun. Ben couldn't, so he spent his time watching her peaceful sleep. He remembered the time at Central Park with her, one of their first times alone together that had not been filled with tension. She was older now, physically more mature, but her face was not that much different. She looked more sophisticated now, but he could still see that beautiful 13-year old girl he'd been so attracted to. How lucky he was to have found her again!

After a half hour or so, she stirred and opened one eye to locate him. He was right there, his head propped up on his elbow, looking at her. She was still a bit groggy. "The scenery's out that way, buster." She was pointing down toward the river.

He smiled. "It's pretty down there alright, but not quite as pretty as what I've been looking at the last half hour."

She smiled and sat up, straightening her dress and pulling on her bonnet. The sun was warmer now. "Really, I've been asleep for half an hour?" He reached over and took the bonnet off her head. She laughed. "So, you want a brown Indian girlfriend, huh? Well, I'm afraid you'll be disappointed and only get a freckled red-headed Irish one if you don't be careful."

He smiled and then his face grew serious. "Remember the question you asked me last week about our future?"

Anna looked out on the meandering river below. "Yes, I remember it. You said that you were going to be President and that I was to marry a Prince, wasn't I?"

"Those are good options, but I've considered it a bit more this week and I think there might be other choices."

"Okay, I'm always open to choices. What do you have in mind?" She looked over at him.

He hesitated a bit too long, and then shrugged. "I am not as good as you are with words and I still don't think I've figured out the right ones...." She sat up and faced him, realizing that this could be something special and that she needed to give him her full attention. He took her hands in his. "When I'm with you in a place like this, or like that time in Central Park, I can't really properly describe how I feel. It's a kind of peace that settles over me that sets everything right."

"I've had that same feeling every night before I went to sleep since I found you again. On that first night I thought I'd have a hard time sleeping knowing that I'd have to wait until the next morning to see you again, but then this feeling came over me and I just drifted right off."

"Every single evening since I've joined you here, I think, 'well that was the best day of my life!', but then I'm wrong every single time—the *next* day is. Every single day, it gets better. I tell myself it can't always be like that: it's just not practical, but then I realize the next day that I was wrong again, and can't wait to find out if that's true the following day."

"For way too long, I thought I'd lost you. I even tried hard to forget you, but couldn't. You haunted my thoughts every day and night. Now that we've found each other, I don't want to spend another day without you right here beside me, day and night. I love you more than I know how to say, and I know that will never, ever change. I don't know what our future holds, but it doesn't matter as long as we're facing it together."

"We're not kids anymore. We haven't been for a long time, I guess. The events in our lives made us grow up fast. There's nobody here who thinks we're too young, or that society won't approve. Our time has come. If you'll have me, I'd like to become your husband and create a future together with you."

He held out his hand and she saw the box. Her breath caught in her throat. That's why he and Jess had gone to Salem! Of course—she should have known! She reached out tentatively to touch it. He passed it to her, hesitantly, like it was a butterfly that might startle and fly away.

She opened it and saw the ring nestled in its red velvet holder. Great tears began to roll down her cheeks. The little diamonds sparkled as brightly as that beautiful river below and as clear as her tears. It was as though he had captured a piece of it and handed it to her.

He reached over and carefully pulled the ring from its perch, taking her hand and—holding his breath—slipped it on her ring finger. To his relief, it slid smoothly over her knuckle and fit perfectly, like it had been made just for her—like it had just found its home.

She held her hand up to eye level and then looked past the ring at his face. She nodded, at first slowly, and then faster. She reached for his neck and pulled him close, laughing and sobbing as she did. He held her and kissed her head. They sat there, swaying in the breeze, like the trees that surrounded them. They had roots now, too, and could weather whatever winds came their way.

Eventually, she spoke. "Ben McDonald, that's the most beautiful ring I've ever seen. If I live to be a hundred, I won't ever take it off my hand. Bessie always told me that God has a plan. I doubted her for such a long time. I half believed it when I became a teacher, but I still found it hard to fathom that the Creator of something as beautiful as that scene below had time to pay attention to the individual needs of people like you and me."

"We kept singing this song at church. It has a line that goes 'you'll understand it, all by and by'. Bessie's faith is far beyond mine. But now, I understand better what the song means. You rescued me in Hell's Kitchen but I lost you, and then you found me again. Those are my miracles. No matter what happens in the future, those miracles will always be mine."

"But I'll admit that I'm getting greedy now. I want more miracles. I want to know that you'll be the last person I talk to before I sleep and the first person I see when I wake up for as long as I live. Yes, Ben McDonald, I'll be your wife, and I'll wear this beautiful ring proudly. I can think of no greater honor on this earth."

He swallowed hard and held her close. Time slipped by as smoothly as the crystal water below. For just a little while, no one else existed—the universe was all there just for them.

Later they ate their "snacks" that Bessie had prepared, which was actually a full-fledged meal. As they finished, Anna asked, "Does Bessie know you were going to do this?"

He chuckled, "I can never be sure what Bessie knows. She seems to know what I'm thinking before I know it. She and Christian are kindred spirits in that regard. But, no, I don't think Jess told her. He wants to see how she'll react when she sees the ring."

"Well then, let's not keep her waiting any longer!" They descended and returned to share the news with the family. But before leaving their bluff, they promised each other that they'd come back on that date every year to remember the commitment they'd made to one another.

Bessie was the first to see them coming; Jess was napping. As they approached from a distance, it occurred to her that she'd never seen two people who fit together as well as this tall, handsome boy and spectacularly beautiful girl. Anna walked up to Bessie, smiling mischievously. Bessie looked at her questioningly. Then, in a flourish, Anna pulled her hand from behind her back and held it up right in front of Bessie's eyes.

Bessie's scream woke Jess up with a start. He saw his wife hugging Anna, dancing her in a circle, and realized what had happened. He grinned and looked over at Ben, who stood watching the women. Jess got up to kiss Anna and shake Ben's hand, congratulating them both over and over, pumping Ben's hand until it hurt. "How'd you do with the question, boy?"

Ben laughed. "To tell you the truth, I have no idea. I'm numb; but the girl said yes and that's all that matters, isn't it?"

Jess laughed and nodded, "Yep, that's the prize alright. You're a lucky man and she's a lucky girl. I hope you're as happy together as me and Bessie through the years. If you are, you'll understand a little better what the preacher means when he describes heaven."

Bessie walked over to her husband, taking his arm and leaning close. "Why Jess Lough, you may become a poet yet!"

Other folks who'd come to the river that day, hearing the commotion, strolled over to offer warm congratulations. Anna twirled slowly in their midst like a dancer, holding up her ring hand. They laughed and applauded. By the time they were finished congratulating the couple, Ben's shoulder felt dislocated, and he suspected that he'd never be hugged again by so many excited women. He kidded Anna. "If this is how all the women are going to react when they hear the news, we should go on a tour."

She punched him on his sore arm and told him that if he got to liking that too much, his quota of hugs would forthwith be limited to a single source. He was okay with the message.

The kids danced around Ben and Anna chanting until they were hoarse. Zachary shook Ben's hand solemnly and told him that he should have been consulted in advance, but that he still approved of the engagement. Ben told Zach that he was truly sorry for the oversight, because his approval was especially important to him and Anna. Zach said he could forgive the oversight but that, on matters relating to his sister, Ben shouldn't make that mistake again. Ben apologized again and agreed.

After they had tired themselves in the waters of the Current River until late in the day, the Lough family and its newly engaged couple, packed up and headed Jim and Prince back toward their little Jadwin home.

Chapter 3

When Sam and Christian left the Lough home on the day after Ben and Christian arrived in Jadwin, they made their way to Charlie Schafer's office. Charlie had ordered some equipment and Sam wanted to give him a shipment update while he was in the neighborhood. Charlie's company was growing rapidly and Sam wanted to become a regular supplier.

Charlie Schafer had grown up in the Dent County area, as had his father, Jacob. He was one of the large Schafer clan along the upper Current River about five miles from the Jadwin community. He already owned a number of lumber mills and had contracts with other independent saw millers. He was rumored to be thinking about starting a flooring operation. He also owned a lot of land, much of it bordering the river.

Charlie's grandparents had moved into the area from Indiana around 1853. The matriarch and true head of the family was Charlie's grandmother, Mary Elizabeth Mattern Schafer, born in 1809 somewhere around Darmstadt, Germany. Mary was a phenomenally accomplished woman by any standard and in any age, but particularly so in the early to mid 19th century. She held a medical degree in Obstetrics and Home and Family Care from the University of Heidelberg, one of the world's foremost medical schools. It was exceptionally rare for a woman anywhere in the world to have obtained such a degree in those days. She'd done it before reaching age 30.

Mary Mattern had married Johann Christian Schafer in 1830; both of them were age 21 at the time. As brilliant as Mary was, she made a poor decision in choosing a marriage partner. Johann probably had positive attributes, but they weren't easily apparent to those who met him.

He was tall, which was usually a good thing, but not so much in his case since he was *too* tall. He stood a full seven feet from head to toe, and might have better fit as a circus performer than the husband of an ambitious, woman physician. But Mary was not an attractive lady—actually, she was extremely homely-looking—which may have limited her matrimonial options.

Charlie never knew whether his grandfather developed his drinking problem before or after his marriage to Mary. He suspected it was before, but such things were not discussed in this reserved German family. Either way, along with being very tall, Christian's reputation was formed by two traits: he was a heavy drinker and he had a very bad temper. These were not compatible and didn't portend success for either him or his wife.

Mary and Christian migrated from Germany to Franklin County Indiana sometime around 1840. It was rumored that Christian's drink and temper outbursts had forced the move. Mary attempted to get her medical credentials recognized in the United States, but America was unprepared for a female doctor from Germany, or from anywhere else for that matter. Her application was denied. It was a bitter pill to swallow. Had she been able to remain in her homeland, she would likely have made major contributions to the practice of medicine and to medical research.

Johan Schafer's bad temper didn't improve in Indiana, but they stayed there for thirteen years. It was there that most of their eight children were born. Charlie's dad, Jacob, was the last of those children.

The family then moved west to the wild, rural environs of Dent County, Missouri. There, Mary became known as "the best midwife Dent county has ever seen", which shouldn't have surprised anyone who knew her history, since she her medical training exceeded the vast majority of physicians in America.

Mary's bitterness over the rejection of her credentials soured her attitude toward the American education system in general. She considered it far inferior to that of Germany—which it was—so she decided to home-school her children. While they benefitted greatly from her exceptional instruction, she also passed along her disdain for American education, which they also assimilated and passed along to their children. But unlike Mary, they were not as vigilant about the home schooling part of the equation. Formal education in the Schafer clan had seriously eroded by the time Charlie came along.

This fact didn't seem to deter the Schafer clan's business acumen. They were some of the brightest and most astute people in southern Missouri. Jacob, Charlie's dad, had inherited his mother's brilliant mind and his father's inclination for alcohol addiction and bad temper.

After buying land along the Current River, Jacob decided to build a grist mill to convert wheat, oats and corn to meal and flour. His problem was that he needed a source of running water for the water wheel that would provide the necessary power for his stone grinder.

Jacob's land included creeks that flowed into the Current River but not at the right location to intersect with the roads that would bring customers. So he diverted a fast-flowing stream by digging a six-foot wide canal for more than a quarter-mile to bring it to his mill site. Naturally, Charlie and his other three sons did the digging.

Jacob was nearly as tall as his dad, at 6 feet 7 inches, and was slump shouldered, in part because he was ashamed of his father and embarrassed about his own height. Charlie, two inches shorter and not at all embarrassed about his height, still developed the slump.

Charlie's relationship with Jacob was always strained due to Jacob's heavy drinking and volatile temper. Charlie didn't allow his own kids to spend unsupervised time at their grandfather's house, even though Jacob lived close by. They feared Jacob and never came to know him well.

Charlie was a good horseman and handy with a rifle, like most other young men in rural southern Missouri at the time. But he was also a noted pistol shot, which was unusual in that neck of the woods. He could repeatedly center a hole in a one inch circle at ten paces.

In his teen years, he followed the rodeo circuit, giving him an opportunity to travel to the western states, but he never became a major winner. His rodeo adventures continued until age 21, at which time, he was, himself, corralled and hogtied by a beautiful little 4 foot 11 inch girl named Nellie Asbridge. After that, his vagabond days were over.

In rural Dent and surrounding counties, the land is hilly and rocky except in the narrow valleys created by the rivers or creeks. The soil has heavy clay content and is not deep, making it good for growing timber, but not much else. That made the land cheap. Eventually, Charlie and a man named Taylor Spencer came to own over 12,000 acres along the Current River, including much of what would later become Montauk State Park.

As Charlie began to think about how to make a living, he knew that he didn't want to work for someone else. He'd take his chances at developing his own business. And he thought that the lumber industry was ripe for expansion. There were a few small sawmills around, but nothing of the scope that he had in mind. He believed that the markets in the state would support a more robust operation.

Many farmers in Dent and Shannon counties had properties that included good stands of hardwood trees, and even some uncut stands of bull pine for framing lumber for home construction, but most farmers saw trees as the enemies of their farming operations and failed to recognize their economic value.

Charlie, with backing from his dad, convinced the Salem bank to stake him to the startup costs for his new forestry business. He talked the local farmers that he knew into letting him harvest the mature trees off their land with the promise of future payment once he produced the lumber. They trusted Charlie, knowing him to be honest, ambitious and hard-working. Even if Charlie's business venture failed, he would have removed unwanted trees to open more pasture land.

He had plenty of labor at his disposal. The area had a high unemployment rate. There were men all over Dent and Shannon counties needing work, some who owned draft horses for skidding logs out of the woods and pulling loaded wagons to Charlie's mills. Charlie knew nearly every family in the area and picked workers from the steadiest families.

From the beginning, he was a stickler for precision. In the first years, he personally chose which trees to harvest, saving those not fully grown for later harvest and avoiding those with visible rot or insect infestation. He purchased the best sawmill equipment and dry-kiln furnaces on the market for accurate cuts and to assure proper moisture levels in his lumber to avoid

44

warping.

Within two years, Charlie was turning a profit. He and Nellie plowed every dollar they didn't need to live on back into the business.

He began to buy his own forest tracts. At first, he bought tracts containing only a few acres, which was all he could afford at the time, but that soon changed. The Salem bank was comfortable with loaning money to him because he never overreached, and the loans were backed by the land itself.

Charlie would cut off the trees he wanted and then subdivide the land, clearing smaller tracts along established roads for new home sites, selling them off and keeping the backwoods land for future harvest. He almost always sold the sub-tracts for more than he paid for the entire tract, so the harvested trees were essentially free. Within five years, he had opened three sawmills and was now buying thousand-acre timber tracts.

His lumber products buyers in St. Louis and Kansas City liked him and began telling him how much trouble they were having in obtaining good quality flooring products. They were forced to import the flooring from eastern states at high transportation costs. They ask him to consider expanding his business to that line. He traveled to a couple of good flooring plants in Georgia to see what that would entail.

He came back enthused. He researched flooring equipment and knew what kind of shapers and planers he wanted. But he had a problem. He needed a couple of strong leaders to share the management responsibility for his growing business. He'd learned early on that those kinds of men were hard to come by. He wanted men who could think strategically, communicate, and who weren't afraid to take calculated risks. He knew that he had to find them soon, because even his current level of the business was outstripping his ability to keep up.

When Sam came by that day, he updated Charlie on the status of the equipment and introduced Christian Gunther, explaining that he and Ben McDonald had just arrived in the Jadwin area. Charlie was delighted to hear it. He admired Anna and knew about her affection for the mysterious Ben McDonald.

"So, Christian, you came out of New York. This area must look pretty backwoods compared to there."

Christian laughed. "Well, it's certainly different, but I don't know if I'd characterize it as backward. If I had to make a choice between Hell's Kitchen, where I grew up, and this area, I'd choose here, hands down. That wasn't a very healthy place to live."

Charlie nodded. "Yea, from what I've heard about Anna's story, I'm sure that's true. So how'd you come to know Anna?"

Before Christian could answer, Sam butted in. "This boy saved Anna's life in New York City a few years back, and Ben McDonald's too. Christian was a gang leader at the time. From what I hear tell from Anna and Ben, he ran the most powerful youth gang on the streets, and done it well. They said there was nobody tougher or smarter."

Charlie paused, taking the information in, then said. "Are you sticking around this area?"

Christian shook his head. "No, I'm headed back to Bloomington, Indiana tomorrow. I'm working for Ben's father, Jake, who owns a large feed and implements business there. Since Ben may not be going back soon, I'll need to cover for him for a while."

Charlie nodded. "Well, I spect Ben's daddy's lucky to have you. Nice to meet ya. Hope you come back down this way again."

Christian smiled. "Thanks. I hear you've built an impressive business here. It was good to meet you, too."

Sam and Christian departed for Rolla. After they left his office, Charlie sighed. He'd like to have learned more about this Christian Gunther. Something told him that this guy was special. But the really good ones just never seemed to be available.

Chapter 4

Ben and Anna set their wedding date for late June, which Bessie thought a bit precipitous considering the amount of preparation necessary. But the kids had waited long enough and would have gone to the justice of the peace the week after Ben proposed if they hadn't been aware that their wedding was important to more people than just them. Ben wanted Christian to be his best man and he hoped that his mother, father, sisters and brother could be there as well. Anna still hadn't met his family and he was anxious for her to do so as soon as possible.

Ben sent a telegram to Jake and got a quick response indicating that nothing would stop them from being at the wedding short of a catastrophe. He also invited Ben and Anna to Bloomington for a visit to become accustomed to the town, as soon as their honeymoon week was over. Jake assumed that the newlyweds would return to Bloomington so that Ben could remain in the family business.

But the decision about where they would live was complicated. Making their home in Bloomington guaranteed the couple a good living with meaningful work for Ben. It also meant that he could watch out for his family in case John McDonald ever returned. John was a dangerous, vengeful man and Ben wasn't sure that Christian Gunther's threats when he ran John out of Bloomington were enough to keep him away. While it had been many months since Christian had loaded John onto that cattle car and he'd disappeared, Emily and the children still lived in fear that he'd return.

Ben suspected that the real reason Christian had chosen to go back to Bloomington was to protect Ben's family in his absence. Christian's loyalty to Ben and his family seemed limitless. Ben was deeply grateful, but he felt guilty that Christian kept subordinating his life to help him. He was long past ever being able to repay what he owed to Christian for all that he'd done.

Despite all that, taking Anna back to Bloomington might not be in her best interest, especially in the near term. She was closely attached to the Loughs, Zachary, her job and her friends in Jadwin. If she moved to Indiana, she would have to seek teaching credentials in that state, which might be more stringent than those in Missouri. He knew she could eventually meet Indiana teaching requirements, but what if that required additional schooling?

Even if she already met Indiana's requirements, she'd likely not find a teaching job there immediately. And leaving Jadwin now meant that a new teacher would have to be found quickly for the coming school year, something both she and Ben regretted doing to Jess and other school board members on short notice.

Ben and Anna were up in the meadow under the big oak tree when they discussed it. "Ben, my place is with you. I'll go wherever you need to go. It's true that I'll miss the Loughs and Jadwin, particularly Bessie and Zachary, but it's not that far by train from there to Jadwin. We can come to visit every summer."

Her offer was tempting, but he still worried that it was not fair to her. Anna loved her Missouri family as much as he loved his own, and she took great pride in her job. "Thanks for saying that, and I know you mean it, but whatever decision we make has to be best for both of us. It's true that I'd like to be near Mom, Dad and the kids to help protect them, but Christian and Dad are there. I love my family, but I really don't have any real responsibilities or strong ties to Bloomington. It's different for you here."

49

"I just need to know that my family is safe. With Dad and Christian there, I doubt if there's much more I could do. If it weren't for the threat of John, I'd frankly rather remain here. I really like the people and the geography! I don't yet understand why, but it feels more like home to me than anyplace I've ever lived. My dad's business is well-established. I know that he'd be delighted if I came back, and is probably expecting it, but he doesn't really need me there. Christian or my little brother could become just as important to him as I could."

"I don't know what to say, Ben. I know I'll be happy with you, wherever we go. Bloomington might be more comfortable than here, and I'd get to know your family better, but I'll admit that I'd really miss this place."

He nodded. "Well, tell you what. I think we should make a go of it here for a little while and then see what happens. Let's stay here at least through another school year and decide during that time. I'll look for a job and you can continue to teach. Then, if we decide to go back, it won't be so hard for the school board to find a new teacher. As long as Christian stays in Bloomington, my family's as safe as anyone could make them."

Anna still looked conflicted. She worried that Ben would feel guilty about not going back if something happened to his family or Christian. "Ok, Ben, but if you change your mind, we can leave at any time. Nothing's more important than your family's safety."

Ben smiled. "You're my family too, Miss Murphy, and this isn't an either-or choice. It'll be the best of both worlds and it'll be an adventure. Let's run on Bessie's faith and see what happens."

Anna put her arms around him and squeezed. "Ben McDonald, you are such a special man to give your life up for me!" She nestled her head against his chest.

Ben laughed. "Glad you think that. I'll keep trying to fool you as long as I can."

He wrote a long letter to his parents that night explaining their decision. He received a letter back from Emily indicating that, while she and Jake were disappointed, they understood and would look forward to frequent visits. They'd see them soon at the wedding to meet Anna and learn more about these wonderful Jadwin people.

So it was settled. Now all Ben had to do was to find a job. And he had a good idea where to start looking. He went the next day to see Charlie Schafer. When he showed up at Charlie's office, Charlie greeted him warmly and seemed anxious to chat. "Ben McDonald! Glad you stopped by. I been a'meanin to talk to you. You want a tour of the place?"

Ben indicated that he'd like that. Charlie took him around, explaining the operation, including the latest technologies he employed in his milling and dry-kiln operations. When they finished touring, they headed back to Charlie's office.

"So, Ben, I hear yer tyin the knot with Anna in a few weeks. She's really something special. You two are fortunate to have found each other agin. I guess you'll be takin her back to yer family's business in Indiana?"

"Actually, Charlie, that's why I'm here. Anna and I have decided to stay in Jadwin for a while. She has too many responsibilities at the school for us to leave right now and I'm not sure I want to take her away from a community that she loves, and one that loves her back."

Charlie nodded approvingly. "That's good of ya, Ben, and I know the community'll be happy to hear it. The Jadwin families with school-age kids will be excited fer sure. But it sounds like yer givin up a lot in Indiana with your dad."

"Maybe, but my dad's business is well-established. He's been at it a long time. I know he'd like to have me back, but the business will be good whether I'm there or not. I'd like to try to make it on my own for a while."

"So what do ya have in mind to do?" Charlie's mind was already racing toward possibilities.

"I'm not sure yet. I was hoping I might work for you. I'd be glad to start as a timber or milling hand if you think I can hold my own."

Charlie chuckled. "Well, it'd fool me if you couldn't. I'd certainly be interested in ya workin with me, but bein a timber or millin hand may not be the company's best option. Tell me a little more about what kind of work ya did in New York and Bloomington."

Ben described his work at the Simmons warehouse with Bill Chambers, and how he'd been promoted to supervisor and his later work at his father's business. When he finished, Charlie said, "Well, now, here's the deal, Ben. My business is growin fast enough that it's about to outpace my ability to handle it by myself. I'm lookin fer some management help. The company has three lines a'work right now."

"I buy timber tracts, cuttin off the good trees and getting them to the mills. Once the logs are harvested and brought in, we cut em into green lumber to stack fer a while, and then dry it some more in our kilns. That avoids warping. Then we finish the lumber to precision grades for sellin."

"Another line a'work is developin the markets and make sure the lumber is delivered to the satisfaction of the buyers. That involves quite a bit of travel and findin new customers."

"The final piece is re-sellin the land after the timber's cut off. I do that to git money for the next land purchase, unless there's a maturin stand of timber on a piece of land we've already harvested that'll be ready for cuttin in ten years or less. In that case, I tend to hold on to the land. If not, I subdivide it, improve it a little for home sites, and then sell it off. So the business has a real estate piece as well as manufacturin."

"Now here's the thing. There's a potential fourth line a'business that I'm thinkin about, and it could be big. It's the floorin business, includin interior trim and other finished wood products. Some retailers in St. Louis and Kansas City are askin that I take it up. It'd probly double the company's profit margin pretty quick. It could even do better than that, dependin on the markets."

"But, there's a problem. I got opportunities to expand, but right now I'm havin to spend all my time managin what I'm already doin, and even that's gittin to be too much. If I expand, I have to make sure that the front end of the business, the timber harvestin and the sawmillin, stays solid. If that slips, then I cain't expand and my business falls back."

"In fact, I suspect it may already be slippin. When I inspect the land that we jest cut, sometimes I see trees that should 'a been harvested still standin and stumps of trees that shouldn't a'been cut. And in the sawmill operations, I'm always havin to check the lumber and waste. When trees ain't cut right, they're lost for scrap. If poor-cut green lumber gits into the kilns for drying and then we have to cull it, that's even more costly."

"You see my problem here? I need a couple of strong managers that I kin trust to take over some of the stuff I'm havin to do all by myself and that sure has to be done if we expand. You might be able to help in that regard. If yer interested in tryin it out, we'll give er a shot."

As Ben listened, his excitement grew. The opportunity was far beyond anything he'd envisioned in Jadwin. "Charlie, I don't know your business yet, but that sounds like an exciting opportunity, and I understand why you need the people you're looking for. We had the same problem in the warehouse operation in New York."

"I don't know whether I'm good enough to help you manage your business, but I'd sure be willing to try. If it doesn't work out, I'd be glad to drop down to a regular worker slot. I know that I could do that. Or I can always go back to Bloomington and work in my dad's business."

Charlie laughed. "Well, we won't be happy to see either you or Anna leave the area, so let's see if we kin make it work. But some would think yer crazy not to step into an established business like yer dad's."

Ben nodded. "Yes, I understand that, and I admit that it's tempting, but I don't think it's the best option for Anna right now, and it might be a little too easy for me if I did it. I'd like to test myself first."

"Well then, let's try er out. At first the pay won't be that much, but that'll change when you prove yourself. What I'd like you to do first is study the current operation. Go spend a week or two in the loggin sites. Go spend another couple a'weeks at a sawmill. Help me put together a timber purchase, includin the bank loans, the sale contracts and so on. I've also got some land for resale. I can show you how I do that."

"Then, what I really want is fer you to get familiar with floorin production. I may want to send ya to Georgia and to another production site in a state that I ain't yet visited. Once you've done all that, we'll talk about where you can help the most. That okay with you?"

"That sounds terrific! When do I start?"

Charlie chuckled. "I admire your enthusiasm, but as I recall, you got a weddin to go to and then maybe a honeymoon. Why don't we give ya the time to do that and then start when all that's done."

Ben laughed, "Well now that I think of it, I will be a little tied up for a while. Thanks for reminding me. I'll be here first thing in August. Thanks for giving me this chance, Charlie. I'll try not to disappoint you, or embarrass myself."

Charlie laughed. "Well, I doubt you'll disappoint me, but you should embarrass yourself a few times. I do it weekly. That's one of the best ways I learn. Go tend to that weddin and we'll start when that's all done."

Ben couldn't wait to get home and tell Anna and the family

about the new opportunity. When he briefed them on what he might be doing for Charlie, his enthusiasm caught them too. People around the Jadwin area believed that Charlie's business was destined to become a major industry leader.

Anna was the most excited for Ben and relieved that he'd found work that appealed to him. She hated to think that he would have to settle for menial labor, although she knew he'd have done it without complaint for her sake.

Charlie was also enthused by the conversation and told Nellie so that evening, "Everythin about that guy looks good to me, Nellie. If my hunch is right, he's goin to become a big part of the business. I'm a little worried that I'll train him and then he'll go back to his dad, but that's a chance worth takin."

Nellie smiled. "Well, you're seldom wrong about what people are made of, and fer sure, you're not likely to be wrong in this case. After all, somebody of the likes of Anna Murphy waited a long time fer him to come. He has to be good to merit that kind of loyalty from a girl like her. I'll wager that you made a big catch today."

Chapter 5

The first big news to come out of Bloomington in May was about John McDonald. Jake was not willing to leave his family in dread about when John might show up or what he might do if he returned, so he talked to the county sheriff, explaining the situation and asking if he thought there was a possible resolution.

Emily had filed for divorce shortly after John left, and it had been conditionally granted, once Emily could show reasonable proof that John was dead or after a period of seven years without hearing from him; or if he was still alive and they could find him, he would have to provide written consent to the divorce. Since no one knew where he was, divorce papers couldn't be served and Jake wasn't happy about the idea of waiting seven years. He planned to rectify his mistake of long ago and marry Emily as soon as legitimately possible.

The sheriff was sympathetic and indicated that it would first be important to know where the train was headed that John was on when he left town. He told Jake that he'd check into the destination and then they'd talk some more. Finding that out was relatively easy, given the fact that they knew John's exact date and time of departure from information that Christian provided. The records showed only one train pulling livestock leaving Bloomington early in the morning on that day. As usual, it was headed to the Chicago stockyards.

Given that information, the sheriff suggested one of two options. The first was for the sheriff to contact his law enforcement colleagues at the Chicago police department and ask them to investigate. But he warned Jake that they ran into a lot of drunks and might not remember him. They also had little authority to spend time on a missing person unless he or she was a minor, a criminal, or the known victim of a crime.

The second option, that the Sheriff thought might yield better results, involved the Pinkerton Detective agency, which happened to be headquartered in Chicago. It wouldn't be cheap, but if Jake was willing to pay the price, there was a high likelihood that the Pinkertons could find out what happened to John McDonald and where he was. The sheriff gave Jake the Agency's contact information.

Jake chose the second option and hired the Pinkerton detectives a month before Ben and Christian left for Jadwin. He didn't tell Emily or Ben because he wasn't sure it would lead to any resolution and he didn't want to get their hopes up unnecessarily. The Pinkerton man with whom he spoke took detailed information about John, including his age and physical build, when he should have arrived in Chicago, his history of alcoholism and distinguishing features. With that information, he was optimistic that they could find out what had happened to John in Chicago, but he warned Jake that the agency was extremely busy at that time and wouldn't be able to work the case immediately. And in fact, it was six weeks later before they got to the case, but they resolved it in less than a week.

Yes, the people at the stockyards unloading the cattle that came up from Bloomington that day had been surprised when a disheveled man clambered out of one of the cars—very drunk, as they recalled—hideous looking, with a long scar on his face.

Yes, the Chicago police in that precinct came to know this man as one of the homeless street people in their area. They said that he was a mean son of a bitch, constantly causing trouble and arguing with the cops on the beat. In fact, they'd been called frequently when he got into fights with other homeless men at a local shelter, until that shelter had finally kicked him out.

No, the police didn't know where he was now. He was either gone or dead. They guessed dead because it had been an extremely cold winter that year and the guy made enough enemies that it was doubtful that he would be allowed in any of the remaining shelters. They knew of at least two shelters that had banned him. Word usually got around quickly among the shelters, so the rest probably banned him too.

Yes, in fact, the city morgue did have records of a deceased John Doe fitting that description, including his age and size, and that the emaciated body had a long scar on the face from the edge of the mouth to the eye. No one had claimed the body and there was no identification on him when found. The coroner's report, a copy of which was sent to Jake, confirmed all that.

Jake felt sadness and emptiness at his brother's death, but also relief at the resolution. His attorney filed the Pinkerton report with the court, also attaching the coroner's report. Within the week, the judge, a friend of Jake's, ruled that Emily McDonald was officially a widow and entitled to the estate of John McDonald, which was worth a grand total of nothing, except the absolution of her fear and her freedom to move on—which was the best thing John ever gave her. A week later, Jake McDonald fixed his historical error and asked Emily to marry him.

Jake allowed Christian the honor of informing Ben. Somehow that seemed right, since it was Christian that had sent John on his way to Chicago to avoid Ben killing John for his terrible abuse to Ben's mother and siblings. When Ben heard it, he just felt hollow, and couldn't bring himself to feel any sympathy for the man that had forced him onto the streets of Hell's Kitchen.

The second piece of news coming out of Bloomington again came from Christian, but secretly this time. Jake McDonald had proposed to Emily and she'd said yes! They were to be married in late May before traveling to Missouri for Ben and Anna's wedding, so their nuptials wouldn't become a distraction to Ben and Anna's. It was to be a small, intimate ceremony, attended by the family and a few close friends in Bloomington. Jake asked Christian to be his best man, along with Matthew. Christian had initially demurred, thinking he should just be a spectator until Jake insisted that he stand beside him, reminding him that none of this would be possible had he not saved Ben's life and brought him home to Bloomington.

What Jake and Emily didn't know was that they would have two surprise guests at the ceremony. They hadn't told Ben and Anna in fear that it might cause them to set aside their own wedding preparations to rush to Bloomington. But Christian thought Ben and Anna would want to know, so he secretly alerted them. He told them why they hadn't been invited.

Ben was ecstatic. No matter what it took, that was one wedding he wasn't going to miss! He and Anna scheduled the trip and alerted Christian to their arrival schedule on the evening before the wedding. Christian got them to the hotel without being discovered, and the next morning, five minutes before the ceremony was to start, they entered the church, planning to slip quietly into one of the pews and then let Jake and Emily know once the ceremony was over.

But Emily saw them enter and she gasped. Jake, alarmed, looked back and saw who was there. His face broke into a wide grin and he rushed back to bring them forward. He looked at the beautiful young woman beside Ben. "You can't be anybody but Anna! " She smiled and nodded. He won her respect by taking her arm and leading her up to stand beside Emily, Julie and Alyssa. Ben followed and took his place next to Jake, Matthew and Christian.

Before the wedding began, Jake addressed the small audience to introduce Anna. While he was doing that, Emily, Julie and Alyssa were quietly hugging Anna and welcoming her into their family. After all the commotion settled, the ceremony proceeded.

Ben and Anna stayed for a week in Bloomington, allowing Anna get to know the McDonald family. Ben's sisters were awed by this beautiful young woman who'd been saved by their brother. It was like a real life fairy tale. Ben excitedly described his work opportunity with Charlie Schafer. Everybody was happy for him.

Their time in Bloomington flashed by and before they knew it they were boarding the train for Rolla. There were a few tears as they departed, but not too many. They'd be seeing each other very soon to celebrate yet another wedding in the family.

Three days before Ben and Anna's wedding, the entourage from Bloomington came down to Jadwin to meet the people important to Anna's and Ben's life and help with the wedding preparations.

Jake had rented a large buggy, drawn by fine-looking horses, to travel from Rolla to Jadwin. Jess, Bessie, and the Lough children, along with Ben and Anna, met them in Salem, to accompany them the rest of the way. Ben and Anna rode with Jake and Emily, and Christian and Ben's siblings rode on the Lough Wagon.

Everybody was impressed with the fancy buggy and the handsome horses—except for Jim and Prince. The fancy horses pranced out toward Salem first. But Jim and Prince didn't like following them. Despite Jess's best efforts to calm them down, they kept snorting their disgust and trying to pass the buggy. He'd never seen them act that way. He would have thought it funny except that it was getting a little dangerous.

The problem was finally resolved by letting the Lough wagon lead the way with the fine horses trudging behind. Upon arrival, Jim and Prince continued to act out, nipping at the other horses when they were let out into the meadow together, forcing Jess and Jake to watch them a little while to make sure they didn't hurt each other. Within a few minutes, however they'd all settled down and were grazing peacefully.

Ben, Jess and Christian bunked in the barn while the McDonalds were there and Bessie slept in the parlor, giving up hers and Jess's bed to Jake and Emily. They protested, but to no avail.

The next day, Anna and Bessie showed Jake, Emily and the kids the school and the church. They experienced one of Bessie's scrumptious meals at lunch, with the remaining food left on the table all afternoon and into the evening for anyone who wanted to graze as they visited. Ben's brother and sisters quickly became fast friends and co-conspirators with the Lough kids. It was one continuous rowdy party with little sleep to be had by anybody.

Very late, when Emily and Jake were finally in bed, she reflected. "Wow! Isn't this an interesting little community with such wonderful people! I don't think I have ever met a more hospitable group. Anna was fortunate to have landed here."

Jake responded. "Yep, and this community was lucky to have her come its way. You're right, these people are easy to like.

They're a lot like our folks in Bloomington, but they seem a little more trusting, and maybe a little more close-knit. I guess that comes from living in such a small community. Ben'll be happy here. I'd liked to have seen him come home, but I understand better now why he's staying, particularly seeing how this community treats Anna. She's already become a big part of them. I think Ben made the right decision." He kissed her and they drifted off to sleep.

On the next day, they visited Charlie's operation. Ben proudly introduced them and Charlie took them on a tour. When they returned to his office, he talked about his vision for the company. Jake was impressed.

Later, Charlie pulled Christian aside and asked him if he'd decided whether or not he was staying in Bloomington. Christian said he would for a while, but wasn't sure how long. "Well, if you're lookin fer a place to land, don't forget about us. I'd love to talk to you about workin with my company if you was ever of a mind to consider it." Christian thanked him and said he'd think about it if he decided to leave Bloomington.

Bessie and Emily hosted the women of Jadwin to a wedding shower for Anna. Since Anna and Ben's story was now well-known throughout Jadwin and the surrounding area, no self-respecting woman wanted to be left off the guest list. The number of women and girls indicating they wanted to come caused Bessie to move the shower to the Jadwin community center, which was good, since more than a hundred women and girls attended. Of course, all the men and boys were barred, which was also a good thing. The bantering and jokes at those showers would have made more than a few men blush.

Anna was amazed by the shower gifts. They ranged from the

practical (sheets, pillowcases and towels) to the exotic, including a beautiful hand-made quilt made by Bessie's mother and handed down to Bessie when her mom died. It had been carefully preserved and treated reverently. Anna had seen Bessie bring it out for showing only on rare occasions. She was shocked when she opened the present. "Bessie, I can't take your mom's quilt! It's far too precious!"

Bessie smiled and took Anna's hand. "My mother would've wanted you to have this, Anna, if she'd known you. It *is* precious and that's exactly why it's coming to you. It's my gift, and her gift, to you. Someday you'll pass it on to one of my grandchildren and our memory will live through it."

"But, Bessie, this should have gone to one of your daughters!"

"It did, Anna. It's going to my firstborn daughter. That's the tradition."

Anna thought about that statement for long seconds. Tears came to her eyes. She nodded, unable to speak, then gave Bessie a long hug.

Emily had brought a beautiful traveling dress for Anna, with matching hat and gloves. The card that accompanied the gift indicated there would be something else waiting for her and Ben when they visited Bloomington after the honeymoon.

After all the gifts had been opened and the party was over, Jess and Jake had to make two trips from the community center with the wagon and buggy to carry all the gifts home. Each was carefully stored away until Ben and Anna found a place to live at the end of the summer. They spent the next day writing thank you notes.

Bessie had suggested that the wedding take place at the church on Sunday, June 24th at 2:00 p.m. to allow the completion of the Sunday morning services, after which people who planned to attend the wedding could eat a light snack to tide them over until the reception after the wedding, which would include a late afternoon potluck meal on the church grounds.

Jadwinites loved potluck meals at the Church of Christ grounds, whether they were members of the church or not. There was a rambling outdoor "table" on the west side of the church, shaded by some large oak trees, made from rough-sawn oak 2" x 6" lumber that sat on a scaffolding of posts and crossbeams. The table top was three feet wide and at least thirty feet long.

The wedding ceremony would also be outdoors on the east side of the church to accommodate the large crowd. Since the wedding was by open invitation, Jess and Bessie guessed that there would be a lot of people attending. It had been announced at all the churches around the area and advertised on the community notice boards at the Jadwin post office and community center.

Bessie and Jess had also sent invitations to Sam and his family in Rolla, and Mrs. Steelman in Salem. On the Thursday before the wedding, the Salem paper made it headline news, along with a story of how Anna and Ben had met and then been reunited.

Jess and Herman Lough had built a temporary platform for the wedding, including wide steps for easy access, which Bessie had insisted on due to Anna's dress. The preacher, bride and groom would stand on the platform during the ceremony so everyone could see them, and the groomsmen and bridesmaids would stand on the steps.

To Bessie's relief, the day turned out bright and clear. Early on, in the planning, it had dawned on her no building in Jadwin would hold all the guests if there was rain. Anna didn't seem worried about it. For days, Bessie had nightmares about what they'd do if three-hundred or more people showed up on a stormy day at a little church building that held 60 people, assuming they all scrunched in and hadn't eaten too much that morning.

When she asked Anna, Ben and Jess what great ideas they had for handling a downpour, they all said, "Umbrellas". Then they had the audacity to turn her faith back on her, smiling sweetly and saying that "The Lord will provide"! Well, she guessed that He had, and so they were going to have a nice wedding outside.

It was high season for flowers in Jadwin. Early that Sunday afternoon, large quantities of flower arrangements, picked from gardens all over Jadwin, were brought to the church grounds and positioned by the ladies that Bessie had assigned to that task.

By 1:45 p.m. the 300 people Jess and Bessie had planned for had already shown up, with more still coming. The women deposited their dishes in various places along the outdoor table and hurried to find a seat, either on folding chairs as long as they lasted, or the church pews moved outside for the wedding, and even on thick board planks placed on wooden blocks that Jess and some of the men had set up the day before to try to handle the overflow.

The guests who arrived in time for a seat crowded in close, but there still wasn't enough room. About 100 people were left standing in the back and around the sides. To Bessie's consternation, there was still a line of wagons coming down the church lane at 2:00 p.m. She hated to see late comers because it

66

reflected on their time management skills and delayed the ceremony.

At 2:15 p.m., Ben, Christian and the preacher finally came out from around the back of the church building and climbed the podium steps. The groom and his party had been stuck out back because the inside of the building was the domain of Anna and her entourage.

Ben hadn't been allowed to see or talk to her all day. They weren't even permitted to sit together in the Church services that morning. He thought that a bit silly, but tradition was tradition.

The preacher, Brad Smith, was a charismatic young man, 25 years old, and originally from the Jadwin area. He'd returned to preach there after his schooling at a Bible College in Tennessee. Everyone figured that he wouldn't remain at Jadwin long; he was too dynamic, but they were happy to have him there as long as it lasted. It had been a harmonious year since he'd come, rare for a church full of opinionated people, many who thought that arguing about religious matters was the sign of a true Christian. Brad was particularly good at special events, like weddings or funerals. This certainly fit that billing.

Zachary, the proud usher for the Lough side of the family, had already escorted Bessie to her seat up front. Ben's little brother had just as proudly ushered Emily and Jake up to their seats. Then the little flower children were released by their mothers up the aisle. The little girl came in leisurely fashion, dropping flower petals from her basket just as she'd been instructed, but the little boy was not inclined to that protocol. He saw it more as a race, reaching Ben's group before the little girl had really even begun, which didn't bother her at all. She wasn't fond of him anyway and was glad she had the aisle to herself.

The bridesmaids came out of the church and walked up the aisle through a crowd that hadn't quite hushed yet. There were four bridesmaids in all, Emily's two girls and two of Bessie's. But by the time they'd reached the front, the crowd hushed in anticipation of the bride's grand entrance.

At last, the fiddler played the wedding march and all eyes turned back to get their first glimpse of Anna. Ben was anxious to see her. Bessie had sowed frantically for the last three weeks to make the wedding dress, but of course, he'd been barred from a preview.

As Anna finally came into view, women of the audience oohed and awed while a few of the young men in the audience, who'd carried crushes on Anna, sat somberly, their hopes dashed. She was so beautiful, this tall slender girl who had so effortlessly won them over. Her dress, made of white satin with a delicate embroidered outer shell, flowed gracefully with her body. She had a lace veil that only partially obscured her long auburn hair cascading down her shoulders with its hint of red to affirm her Irish roots.

She carried the cedar comb that Ben had carved for her in the mausoleum as the *"something old"*. Bessie had provided a blue garter for the *"borrowed and blue"*. Although bunches of cut roses were scattered all around the podium, Anna had chosen to carry a simple bouquet of wildflowers held by a large yellow ribbon. The most prominent flowers were the large yellow daisies with their black centers, her mother's favorite, that Zach had picked a little more than an hour prior to the ceremony.

Ben's knees trembled slightly when he saw her. He wasn't really nervous about the wedding ceremony or large crowd, but seeing this spectacular woman walking down that aisle toward him, caused him to doubt himself just for a second. How in the world could he ever have been so lucky! But the anxiety passed quickly. They'd been thrown together by some mysterious force that wouldn't be defeated. She'd waited for him. He'd waited for her. This was meant to be.

She came up the aisle with her eyes only on Ben. She could just as easily have been alone with him and the preacher. She only had only one regret. She wished that her father and mother were there to share the day with her. Jess walked along beside her in measured steps, worried about tripping over the skirt of her dress as he tried to keep centered between the sea of people on either side.

Bessie, eyes shining, sat there remembering—the first time she'd seen Anna in Rolla and decided that she must help this sad, lovely girl and the little boy that she now cared more about than herself; the day Anna took her test for high school; the day she became Jadwin's elementary teacher; and the day that Ben, along with Christian came home to Jadwin to claim her. How very lucky she and Jess were that God had made them part of this marvelous story. How blessed they were to have this girl in their lives!

Emily, watching Anna walk down that aisle, came to the sudden, peaceful realization that she'd probably never again have to worry about life being unfair to Ben McDonald. He'd gone through hell, literally, to get here. But if he hadn't, this moment might never have happened. Everything in his life was just a rehearsal for this day and the life that would follow. She pried her eyes from Anna and looked up at him. His face was shining. Emily could tell that he was mesmerized as Anna drew near. She smiled and whisked away a tear. Her lost orphan had finally found his home.

When Anna and Jess reached the podium, Brad asked. "Who gives this woman in marriage?"

Jess squeezed Anna's arm a little tighter as he spoke, surprising her with his words. "My wife Bessie and I are standin in for Anna's mother and father, who are surely the proudest people in heaven today." Anna reached over to give him a hug before he turned back to Bessie. When he did, Bessie took his arm and snuggled close, letting him know that he'd done good.

Brad didn't begin the wedding ceremony in the usual way. "Friends and neighbors, we're gathered here today on what is probably the most unique occasion I've ever officiated."

"Now, all weddings are very special, of course. But this one is transcendent. Those of us who have heard her story know that it's a miracle that Anna is here today. Actually, it's a combination of many miracles. First, it's a miracle that she's even alive. For that matter, the same can be said of Ben. He single-handedly challenged the most powerful youth gang in Hell's Kitchen to save her, making himself a marked man. But he survived against all odds, with some very unusual assistance."

"Remember the parable of the Good Samaritan in Luke 10: 25-37. A living example of that parable stands before us now; except, I respectfully submit that it was harder for this Samaritan to do what he did than the one in Luke's parable."

"That Biblical Samaritan had come upon the victim of the crime after the bad guys had already left. This Samaritan came on the scene as the crime was occurring. That Biblical Samaritan had the resources to purchase assistance for the victim at a nearby town so he could go on his way. This Samaritan didn't dare ask anyone for help because he knew he'd die if he did, and he had nowhere to go for safety."

"Actually, from what Ben told me, he never intended to be a Good Samaritan. He knew it was a fool's errand. But for reasons that even he didn't understand, that time, he couldn't turn away. He was a reluctant Samaritan, but he was a courageous one. He put his life on the line for her, the most precious gift anyone can ever give another person. And he did it believing that she was already dying and had little chance for recovery."

"And then, when things couldn't seem to get any bleaker, he got the help he needed from a most unusual source. It came from the fearsome leader of the very gang that Ben had attacked to save Anna's life, the toughest guy on the streets, and one of the gang members that Ben had injured in the attack to save Anna."

"And that guy is the next miracle in a story stranger than fiction. He gave up everything important to him at the time to help them, even to the point of risking his own life. He had more to lose than Ben. He had status and prestige and what he thought was a future in an adult New York gang awaiting him. He threw that all away in one valiant act. And, unbelievably, that guy is with us today; he's Ben's best man, standing here proudly beside him. I told you this story is stranger than fiction."

"But at that time, the story didn't have a fairy tale ending. Almost as soon as Ben saved Anna, they were separated—she to an unknown destination, and he, forced to remain in New York. He had no idea where she'd been taken on that Orphan Train to the west. It was at tragic love story that their friends said just wasn't meant to be. The people who cared the most about them said they were just too young and that they had to move on separately with their lives."

"So, they tried—but they couldn't. The bond wouldn't break. We, here in Jadwin, watched Anna struggle with the sadness of her loss. I suspect Ben's friends did too. This is a day no one thought would ever occur." Brad paused for long seconds, looking out at the sky, over the heads of the crowd. Then he looked down at the crowd and smiled. "Well…that's not exactly right, is it? Someone did. Someone knew. Someone planned for this magic day all along. Someone who sees things that we simply cannot see."

"We sing that wonderful hymn, *God Moves in a Mysterious Way*. I've always known that song was special, but I'll be the first to tell you that seldom grasp its full meaning. I take it for granted. But then, something like this happens, and I am reminded what it's really telling us."

"The presence of these young people here today defies human logic. We have to look elsewhere to make sense of it. Because, you see, Anna and Ben are more than just two young people who have decided to spend their lives together in marriage. They're Jadwin's own miracles."

"Anna, I don't know why God saw fit to set you down in this small, backwoods community with us. He could have taken you anywhere, but He chose here, and we are so grateful that He did. Through yours and Ben's story, our faith is renewed."

"So let's not delay the inevitable any longer. Now, I am aware that wedding protocol suggests that I ask anyone to speak up if they know a valid reason why these two people shouldn't be joined in marriage. But I'll not bother with that today. Who would dare challenge God's own will?"

"Ben McDonald, do you take this woman, Anna Murphy to become your lawful wedded wife, to have and to hold, to love and to cherish, for richer or for poorer, in sickness and in health, for as long as you both shall live?"

Ben smiled at Anna and answered Brad's question with the most important words of his life. "With all my heart, I do."

The audience clapped and cheered when the new married couple walked off that podium that day. The radiance on their faces would never be forgotten by those lucky enough to attend that ceremony at the little rural church in southern Missouri.

Chapter 6

After the wedding and reception, Anna and Ben changed clothes in the church building, got an enthusiastic sendoff from the large crowd and headed to a secluded cabin on the Current River that Charlie had arranged as a gift to them for a week long honeymoon.

After they'd gone, Jess and Jake asked Charlie to stick around for a few minutes for a talk. Jake kicked off the conversation. "Charlie, we'd like to help Ben and Anna get started here by building a house for em. Jess has 10 acres of land just east of the school he's giving the kids for a home site, and Emily and I want to purchase the building materials from you and Sam, and pay for the cost of the labor. We want it to be a surprise for the kids. We'd like to get the construction underway while the kids are visiting us in Bloomington."

Charlie chuckled. "That's a right nice surprise, Jake! Sure, I'll be glad to furnish the lumber. Who you contractin with to build the house?"

Jess answered. "Hermann said he'd take on the project. We'll arrange some house buildin parties on the weekends while the kids are away to help him. If we all pitch in, we should be able to move it along pretty good. With volunteer help, Herman thinks he can finish it by the end of October. Ben and Anna can stay with Bessie and me till then."

"Bessie's got a book that shows house plans that start modest but can be expanded as a family grows. The later additions look like they was all part of the original plan."

Charlie nodded. "Herman's a good builder. Get me a copy of

those plans as soon as you can and I'll get my boys pullin the lumber together. We'll deliver whatever Herman needs as soon as Anna and Ben head out toward Bloomington. I'll also send a few guys over to help clear and level the building site and pour the footings and foundation. Ben and Anna'll be in fer a big surprise when they get back! How long they stayin in Bloomington?"

"About a month. Then Anna's got to get back to prepare for the school year and Ben's anxious to get on with his work with you."

"Well, with that kind of time, if we all pitch in, we'll have their house framed and roofed and maybe even a little further along than that. Tell Herman to come by my office in the next few days for a little scheemin."

Ben and Anna had a mostly peaceful honeymoon on the river. The humans in the area knew they were newlyweds and left them alone. The animals hadn't gotten the message. Late on the first night, after they'd drifted off to sleep, both of them were awakened by the rattling of the cabin's door. It was noisy and it didn't stop. Luckily, they'd bolted the door when they came in, but whoever was outside just kept turning the doorknob and banging on the door.

Ben had no weapon in the cabin. He quickly pulled on his trousers and picked up a metal poker from the fireplace. He went to the door and yelled. "Who's there?" No one answered, but the noise stopped. Ben looked out the front window to see who was on the porch, but saw no one. He came back to the bed, where Anna sat against the headboard, holding the covers tightly around her. He sat down on the edge of the bed, still holding the poker. Hopefully, it was just a drunk or a vagabond who was gone now.

But they were not so lucky. Soon the noise began again and the door knob started turning even more rapidly than before. Ben told Anna to crouch between the wall and the bed and then went back to the door. "Who are you and what do you want! There are people in here! If you're looking for a place to sleep, this isn't it!"

This time the noise didn't stop. Ben became angry. He didn't know if this was a practical joke—he'd heard about some of the chivalry stories where the bride and groom were harassed on their wedding night for fun—but this wasn't funny. Holding the poker in his right hand, he jerked the door open with his left.

A furry form flew into the room, landing heavily and sliding across the floor. Whatever it was started chattering loudly, picked itself up and moved over to the stuffed chair in the corner, staring at them and still scolding as it went,. It climbed into the chair and plopped down and finally stopped chattering.

In the dim light Ben wasn't sure what kind of animal it was. He moved between it and the bed where Anna still crouched on the other side. He held the poker ready, but the animal didn't seem at all intimidated and was now ignoring him.

Suddenly Anna stood up and began to laugh. The animal looked up at her, seemingly interested. She came around the bed and walked over to the chair, kneeling down in front of it.

"Anna, get back, that thing might be dangerous!"

Anna laughed again. "Hi there Rascal! Charlie told me you might visit us, but he didn't say you'd be sleeping in here with us."

"Ben, meet Rascal, the cabin mascot. I forgot to tell you about Charlie's warning. He was brought here as a baby by some hunters. Charlie said he's perfectly friendly and nearly always shows up when the cabin is in use. In the excitement of the wedding, it slipped my mind, but it's kind of nice that he's joined us."

Ben came over cautiously. "Is that thing safe?"

"Of course he is! Raccoons are intelligent, friendly animals unless threatened. They even wash their food before they eat. They're also very brave. Rascal looks tired. I'd suggest that we all get some sleep and get to know him better in the morning."

So they did—at least she and Rascal did. Ben, still uncertain about sharing his honeymoon suite with a raccoon, didn't get to sleep until it was almost morning.

Anna was the first one up. Rascal, still in his easy chair, opened his eyes and watched her. She walked over and sat on the floor beside the chair and started to talk to him. He was a handsome little guy with his built-in bandit mask on his face and his bright eyes. He wasn't big, probably only about ten pounds or so in weight. "So, how are you this morning, Rascal? Did you sleep well?"

He chattered back in friendly fashion and got up from his reclining position, arching his back like a cat. He climbed down to the floor and hopped onto Anna's lap, looking up at her, clearly waiting to be petted. She began scratching his back gently. He arched it, inviting her to scratch all along the top. As she did, he chattered happily. Ben watched all this from the safety of the bed, somewhat amused, but still a little worried that

Anna was so close to a wild animal.

"Let's go out to the porch, Rascal, and let brave old Ben get his pants on." She set Rascal down, got up and walked out the door to the porch swing, still in her nightgown. Rascal sauntered along after her. She patted the seat of the swing and he hopped up beside her, sprawling out on what was left of the seat.

Ben came to the door and watched Anna slowly swinging back and forth, her hand on Rascal's back, looking out over the river. It was a beautiful, early summer morning. No one would likely be floating yet on the river. It was obvious that Rascal had taken to Anna. Ben came out and sat in the rocking chair on the other side of the porch. "Pushy little guy, isn't he."

Anna giggled. "He probably thinks the same about you. Remember, he believes he owns the place. He probably sleeps under this porch, or on it, when nobody's around, and then takes over the cabin whenever anyone shows up to let him in."

And that's exactly what Rascal did for the entire time they were there. Anna left the door open a crack so he could go in and out whenever he chose. When they ate, he watched them expectantly. Anna got the message and set him a plate on the floor each time, along with a bowl of water.

Ben, who hadn't fully warmed to Rascal yet, did get a kick out of watching him fret over every morsel of food he ate, inspecting it, washing it, then inspecting it again before putting it into his mouth. His paws looked like puffy little human hands with long, roundish fingernails. After going through that ritual, he'd start all over again with his next morsel.

Rascal slept in the cabin every night they were there. Ben

already knew that Anna was an animal lover by the way she treated the Lough pets. But he didn't share her enthusiasm about Rascal joining them every night in the easy chair. Anna, not at all embarrassed, teased Ben. Rascal paid no attention whatsoever to their extracurricular activities each night before sleeping and he showed no interest in joining them in the bed. He liked his chair just fine, thank you very much! Early each morning, Rascal and Anna went through their petting ritual and then made their way to the porch.

When their week was over, Anna carried out the remaining food and set it on the porch. She showed it to Rascal, talking to him all the while, as though he understood what she was saying. By the way he chattered back at all the appropriate times, Ben couldn't be absolutely sure that he didn't. He'd grown comfortable enough with Rascal to pet him a little and tell him goodbye. Rascal tolerated this good naturedly, although he didn't arch his back the way he did when Anna petted him.

As they were riding back to Jadwin, Anna said, "I'll miss Rascal. When we return from Bloomington and find a home to rent, maybe we could invite him to stay with us. I'm worried that some hunter might shoot him down here, not knowing he's tame. I'd like to put a collar on him." She looked out the side of her eyes over at Ben, waiting for his reaction.

Ben laughed. "That'd be fine, Mrs. McDonald. Far be it from me to ever try to stand in the way of one of the men you shared your honeymoon with." She smacked him on the arm for that— hard—and told him to stop being jealous, that she had enough love for the both of them.

They returned to Jess and Bessie's house for one night before leaving early to catch a train at Rolla. They'd decided to stay in

St. Louis near Union Station for a couple of days to see the city before heading on to Bloomington.

Within an hour after they'd gone, Charlie's men delivered the building materials to the new home site for Herman. It had been the original homestead site on Jess's land and was still a good place for a new home, situated on the county road. Jess and Bessie had contemplated building there but ultimately chose the seclusion of the peninsula. Jess, at varying times, had toyed with selling it to raise money, but never got around to it. Anna had liked this site when they showed it to her, and he thought she, or one of the other kids, might want it someday. It was still mostly clear, with only sparse brush and a couple of massive old shade trees that had once protected the old homestead. They'd do it again for the new one.

On that first day, Herman and Charlie's men cleared and leveled the building site and poured the footings. Three days later, the foundation was set and the construction began. They built the floor and framed the walls by the end of the first week.

Most of Jadwin's men had either built their own homes or helped someone else do it, so roughing in a house was a familiar task. Herman demanded precision, and a few of the volunteers grumbled, but Herman knew that would pay off in a thousand little ways as the construction proceeded. Plus, it was just the principle of the thing.

In only two weeks, the walls were completed and the roof trusses built and set in place. By the middle of the third week, the house was under roof, the outer walls boarded and the new windows that Sam brought up from Rolla were installed. Then Herman began his interior work.

Meanwhile, Jess, who'd committed to laying stone on the front and halfway up the sides of the house, and to making a rock walkway, went at it with a vengeance. Neighbors showed him good rock in easily accessible creeks on their land and some even helped him harvest it. Each morning, Jim and Prince were used to haul the stone to the home site so Jess could cut and set it in the afternoon.

The well diggers came and commenced their work. In addition to building the well, they also laid a sewer line and built a septic tank. Ben and Anna would have an indoor bathroom, unusual for that area in those days. A small hand pump in the bathroom provided water for filling the holding tank on the wall above the commode and for bathing. While filling the commode's tank after each use was an inconvenience, it was infinitely better than an outhouse, still common in Jadwin, including the one at Jess's and Bessie's house.

Herman would have one more weekend of free labor from the men of the community before Ben and Anna returned. He was confident that he could finish the interior walls, the stairs, the main floor ceilings and upstairs floor. Sam had ordered hardwood flooring, which was featured throughout the house. Basically, everything would be done but the finish work and the kitchen and bathroom cabinets by the time the kids returned to Jadwin.

Herman was the most talented cabinet maker in the area. He decided to use walnut in the bathroom and maple in the kitchen. He also lined all the closets with native cedar from Charlie's mills, both for its pleasant smell and for protection from moths.

While the construction progressed in Jadwin, an unsuspecting Ben and Anna were enjoying a relaxing month in Bloomington.

One day, as Christian and Ben were traveling to inspect a new project, Ben asked, "Are you any closer to making a decision about where you want to settle?"

"Not really. Jake's made me a good offer and it'd be better than anything I'd get back in New York, but I'm still not sure what I want to do. Your family's great and they try hard to include me, but I really don't think Jake needs me in his business that much. He already has good managers. I'll stay a while longer and then decide. Someday I might go out West and see what that's like."

Ben nodded. "Well, Charlie's business is growing fast, and it's a little rough around the edges. You never know when he might have need for a thug like you to keep everybody in line!"

Christian smiled but didn't respond. Time would tell. He was just glad to have options. He knew that he'd never return to New York. He felt no ties there anymore.

Shortly after Ben and Anna arrived in Bloomington, Jake and Emily took them for a carriage ride, allegedly to show them one of Jake's new Reeves and Company steam-powered farm tractors. Jake knew that Charlie was already using steam power to operate his sawmills. They arrived at one of Jake's big warehouses and went in to inspect the powerful-looking tractor. After spending a few minutes explaining how it worked, Jake and Emily said they had something else to show them in a back room.

When they entered the room it was like walking into a small furniture store. There were two bedroom suites, one made of rich cherry and the other of walnut, including mattresses, dressers and matching wash stands. There was also a stately oak dining table and six matching chairs. Another section of the room held attractive parlor furniture, including sitting chairs and a divan. Ornate picture frames hung from the walls, with art reproductions of pastoral scenes, including one from Central Park in New York City. Jake said, "Take a look at this furniture. We think it'd fit nicely in a house in Missouri."

Ben looked shocked. He turned to his mother. She smiled and nodded. Anna exclaimed, *"What have you two done?"*

Emily giggled excitedly. "Don't you remember at your wedding shower, your card from us said that Jake and I had something for you and Ben that you'd see when you came to Bloomington?"

"Yes, I remember, but we never dreamed it'd be this much!"

"Well, Jake and I have dreamed of doing this for you from the moment we found out you'd been reunited. We've had great fun piecing this furniture together. We hope you like it."

Anna's eyes misted as she went to Emily to embrace her, then turned and hugged Jake. "You two are far too kind to us."

Jake laughed. "Nonsense, young lady; it's the least we could do to give you a good start out there."

Ben gulped. "Mom, Dad, I don't know what to say. There aren't enough words to thank you for all this. You do realize we haven't even looked for a place yet? I don't even know whether we can afford anything large enough to hold all this beautiful stuff." He, too, hugged Emily and Jake.

Emily laughed and said, "Oh, Ben, I wouldn't worry about that too much. We're sure that you'll find a good place; and we'll keep the furniture here until you're ready for us to ship it. I bet that'll happen quicker than you think."

They spent the next couple of hours inspecting the furniture—sitting in the chairs, opening drawers and laying on the comfortable mattresses. Jake and Emily enthusiastically described the qualities of each piece. It was obvious that they'd spent a lot of time researching their purchases. When they finished, Ben said, "These are wonderful gifts, but far too expensive!"

Jake shook his head. "Ben, you and Anna literally went through hell and back to get where you are today. You deserve far more than what you see in this room. Emily and I are busting with pride for both of you. When you use this furniture, it'll just be a small reminder of how much we love you. Besides, when we come to visit, we want to sleep on one of those good beds!"

Anna laughed. "Well, we'd actually envisioned a tent for you, but I think we can accommodate you now—assuming we can find a place to hold all this. I bet the furniture will be worth more than the house we live in!"

Emily responded. "Remember what Bessie always says. God provides."

"You know, Emily, I'm coming to appreciate that more each day. Thank you for all of these wonderful gifts. We'll cherish them as long as we live."

In the second week in August, the newlyweds returned to Rolla where they spent the night with Sam and Martha. Jess was there too, waiting to take them back to Jadwin. They left early and made good time, arriving late that afternoon, weary, but happy to be home to start their new life together.

But Jess, chattering away, somehow missed the turn down Lough Lane, to the frustration of Jim and Prince. Jess had a little trouble keeping his team from trying to turn around in the middle of the road. Anna laughed and admonished him, "Jess, how could you miss the turnoff to your own house!"

"Well, sure as shootin, I did, didn't I! Sorry 'bout that. I wasn't payin good attention. We'll just go down a little and turn around."

They passed the school and began to see horses standing in harness, hitched to wagons, along the side of the road and some sort of commotion up ahead. Children, many of them Anna's pupils, were playing in the road or alongside it, waved as they went by.

Anna looked over at Jess suspiciously but he didn't seem to notice. He just stared straight ahead, urging his unhappy horses forward. But even Jim and Prince became inquisitive as they continued to pass more wagons with hitched teams standing on both sides of the road, the horse's heads down, their tails lazily swishing at the swarming horseflies. The going was getting tight and they wouldn't be able to turn around until they got past all the commotion. Anna wondered what in the world all these people were doing!

Then she looked up ahead and realized something was very different. To the left, she saw the roofline of a new building that hadn't existed before she and Ben left for Bloomington, less than five weeks ago. She turned to Jess. "Okay, so who's building the new house? That sure went up fast!"

"Yep, it shore did. I thought we'd be able to turn here, but looks like some kind of shindig going on. We'll just stop by a minute and see. Must be a house warmin party."

They pulled into a new driveway, where there was only one parking spot available. Anna muttered, "How in the world did they raise that house so fast?" She was sure that something wasn't right about all this and Jess was acting far too coy.

Then she remembered that this was the old homestead site on the southeast corner of Jess and Bessie's land! She saw Bessie in the yard, waving excitedly and the puzzle fell in place. "Jess Lough, what's going on here!? This is your land!"

"Oh, no, it's not no more Anna. I deeded it over recently, just before this house construction got underway. Didn't I tell you? Must've slipped my mind! Come on up and I'll introduce you to the new owners."

As they traversed the pretty new stone walkway to the front porch everybody suddenly stopped milling and began to gather behind them—even the children—looking at them expectantly. Ben, who still didn't realize what was happening, stopped to say hello and shake hands with some of the people he remembered, but Anna just gave them suspicious looks and began to shake her head at them. They all laughed at her.

Herman Lough and Charlie Schafer were standing on the porch. Jess led them up close. The crowd waited in anticipation. Then Jess said, "If you wanna go in, you'll meet the new owners."

Ben said, "Sure", and stepped up onto the porch, preparing to enter the house. But he was holding Anna's hand and she held back from going in for some reason. Charlie walked over to him.

"Hey, Ben, I know yor not from here, but we got a tradition fer such occasions. The bridegroom always carries his bride across the threshold. Assumin she's not too heavy, you might want to do that; or if she is, you just grab her arms and I'll grab her feet and help you." The crowd started hee-hawing at that.

Ben looked confused. "Charlie, I know the tradition, but isn't that supposed to happen at the place they live?"—And then it finally hit him and he felt like an incredible fool. "You all didn't! You couldn't have done this!"

Herman grinned. "Oh, yes we could, boy! We're faster around these parts than you might think. When you carry your bride through that door, you'll be enterin your new house, thanks to Jake and Emily, Jess and Bessie, and a whole bunch of people who worked like dogs to get it this far along before you got back."

"It ain't done yet on the inside, but it'll not take much longer. The design's Bessie's, but the sweat came from all your friends out there watchin you from the yard, awaitin for you to go in there so's they can follow!"

Anna turned around and looked at the crowd below her. She couldn't speak from the lump in her throat. A tear rolled down her cheek. She raised her hand to her heart and tapped it, then threw them all a kiss as they smiled up at her, the pride showing in all their faces.

She looked back at Ben. He looked at her. Neither was sure what to do. Then, he shook his head, incredulous. A huge smile came on his face and, in a flash, before she could protest, he picked up his girl and carried her, light as a feather, across the threshold into her new home.

87

Chapter 7

Ben spent that autumn orienting himself to Charlie's business. He soon came to learn how brilliant a businessman Charlie Schafer really was. As Charlie had suggested, Ben spent a couple of weeks in the logging operation and another two weeks working at two sawmills. He joined Charlie on timber purchasing trips and watched as Charlie prepared and sold land that he had previously purchased.

Charlie was discriminating in the land that he sold and what he kept. He'd already kept over 5,000 acres of choice land along the Current River. It was land that he knew would increase in value, or it had a second good timber harvest maturing in only a few years.

Charlie sent Ben to Georgia for two weeks to look at the flooring mills he'd previously visited, and then on to a couple of plants in Michigan that Charlie had not had time to see. Ben talked to the owners of those plants about the problems they'd encountered in setting up their operations and what they'd do differently if they had the chance to start again.

Ben researched flooring production equipment, particularly the latest shapers to make the precision cuts and the big planers for making the flooring silky smooth. Ben checked with the managers of flooring companies already using the equipment to see which lived up to its reputation and which did not.

He finished his apprenticeship by mid-October, after which he and Charlie sat down to see what he'd learned. "So, Ben, will it be a smart thing for us to enter the floorin business?"

"Yes, I'm convinced that it will be. There's a good market and it'll open a large new use for our lumber. We should be able to recover our startup costs pretty quickly. We'll need to install new kilns, as well as the new shapers and planers, but that'll increase our quality for both the lumber products as well as our new flooring line. It'll set us apart from the rest of the wood companies in Missouri."

Charlie nodded. "That's my thinkin too. I'm ready to get goin as soon as we can. I'd want you to help oversee the expansion of the floorin line."

"So, now that you've seen the whole operation, where's our greatest risk?"

Ben thought a minute. "I think it's on the front end. The men in the timber crews are generally independent and bull-headed. There's a lot of inconsistency in how they do their jobs. There's a little more conformity at the mills, but there's still a lot of wasted lumber from poor cuts. We don't have enough backup for the timber bosses and the head sawyers when they get sick or hurt. The turnover among the men, particularly among the timber crews, is high from burnout and injury. There seems to be a kind of a culture that's sprung up among them that safety is for sissies."

"Each timber crew I visit is sure they're smarter than anybody else in the woods. It'll take some doing to win their respect to make changes. I think we need somebody who spends full time supervising the front end of the operation. Whoever does that will have to handle tough, stubborn men."

Charlie chuckled. "You know anybody around here that can do that?"

Ben shook his head. "Not around here, but I know a guy who could do it. He's in Indiana."

"You mean Gunther?"

"Yes, Gunther. He's used to handling people like your crews. I'd be very surprised if he couldn't do it."

"He's impressive alright. I talked to him a couple of times hoping he'd stick around. But he's helpin your dad."

"Yes, but I'm not sure for how long. He's thought about going out West, but he doesn't exactly know what he'd do there."

"Why would he consider comin here?"

"If he has a close friend in the world, I'm it. He likes you and what you're up to. He'd thrive on the challenge. He's one of the strongest leaders you'll ever meet, but right now he doesn't have anyone to lead."

"You think your dad would feel slighted?"

"I don't think so. I'd talk to him first before I talked to Christian."

"Well, do it then. I really like Gunther. Whatever it'd take to get him here, you do it as long as it doesn't put you crossways with your dad."

So Ben did. He and Anna traveled to Bloomington for a week over the Christmas holidays and Ben talked to Jake. "Dad, I need to ask you how you'd feel about losing Christian."

Jake was a little surprised at the question. "Well, I'd hate it, of course. People like Christian don't grow on trees. On the other hand, Emily and I worry about how happy he is here. It's nothing he's said or done, mind you. But I think he's restless, and he probably misses having you around. I'd like to see him happy wherever he decides to go. You got something in mind for him?"

"Yea, the reason I'm asking is that Charlie and I have a big need for a guy with his skills. Charlie didn't want me to approach Christian unless you were okay with it."

"Well, if that's all that's holdin you back, talk to him. We owe Christian more than we'd ever be able to repay. If he'd be happier with you and Charlie in Missouri, I'd be the first to encourage him to go."

"Thanks, Dad, I appreciate it. I'll talk to him."

Ben talked to Christian that night. "Charlie and I need a person like you to manage the timber crews and sawmills. I talked to Jake and he said he'd hate to lose you here but that he wants what's best for you. Would you consider coming to Missouri?"

Christian reflected a second and then said, "Tell me more about the job."

Ben filled him in. "It's tough, hard work, Christian, and the guys doing it could make some of the Bowery Boys look tame. But it's critical to the business. If that domino doesn't fall right, everything on down the line suffers."

Christian nodded. "You really think your dad would be okay with this?"

"Yep, but you can talk with him about it yourself if you decide to come with Charlie and me. Jake just wants you to be happy and to stay connected with the family, wherever you go. None of us want to lose you. You mean too much to us."

Christian smiled. "You won't. Let me think about it and talk to Jake. I'll let you know before you and Anna leave for Jadwin."

A couple of nights later, Christian pulled Ben aside. "I'm interested, but there are conditions that you may need to run by Charlie. I'd like to come in as a logger for six weeks or so with one of Charlie's crews without them knowing that I might manage them in the future. Then I'd like to do the same at one of the mills. After that, I'll tell you and Charlie if I'm interested."

Ben grinned. "Sure, that's easy to arrange, but you do know that Missouri weather is really cold in the winter. Think you're up to it?"

Christian laughed. "Remember where I came from?"

Ben sobered a little and nodded. "Yea, I guess we've dealt with bad weather before, haven't we. I don't need to talk to Charlie. He told me to do whatever it takes to get you to Missouri. You've got a deal. It'll give you a good lay of the land. If you don't like it, I know Dad would take you back in a heartbeat. Charlie will hook you up with his most experienced timber boss. When do you want to come?"

"Give me a month here to finish up with Jake. Let me know where to show up and who to talk to."

"We'll do that. It'd be great having you there, Christian! You'll like Charlie, and Anna and I will be happier to have you closer. We'll cross our fingers until you decide whether it's the kind of work you'd like."

Chapter 8

Christian Gunther arrived at Eminence, Missouri in Shannon County on a cold day in late January 1889. Eminence was a small town with an economy based largely on the timber industry and people floating or fishing on the Jack's Fork and Current Rivers that converged near the town. At the time of Christian's arrival, the town had a few homes, a boarding house, two stores, two churches, a cafe and, of course, two drinking establishments.

Christian had been directed to meet Jim Lane, Charlie's best logging boss, at the Eminence cafe to talk about work. Charlie had told Jim that Christian would be a good man for his crew and that he'd cover the cost of training him if Jim liked him.

Jim was good with trying out anybody Charlie Schafer vouched for. But he reminded Charlie that it wasn't a "picking-daisies kind of job" and that he hoped the guy was tough. Charlie chuckled a little in that unique little tee-hee-hee laugh of his and said there was a pretty good chance that the guy was tough enough. By the way Charlie said it, Jim figured that the guy came with a reputation that Charlie knew about, but wasn't telling.

Jim Lane was a grizzled old veteran of the woods whose family had migrated to the area from eastern Kentucky. He'd been in the timber business one way or another for more than 30 years now. It showed. At 53, he was the elder statesman among the timber men who'd survived the rigors of the work.

He knew that he couldn't continue it much longer. He had scars on top of scars from logs that had rolled on him, axes that had slipped; arthritis from smashed knuckles and other damaged joints; and sore legs and feet from mules that'd kicked him or stepped on him as they slid on muddy slopes pulling a big log.

Despite it all, this was the work that he knew and it gave him the freedom he cherished. And he was a very good timber boss. His men, a bunch of rough, red-neck boys from the back country, liked and respected him. He was fair and he cared about them and their families.

He'd first become a personal friend of Charlie's dad, Jacob—one of the few Jacob ever had. They'd been drinkin buddies in their early years. But Jim was milder in personality than Jacob. He'd seen, and even experienced, the temper that accompanied Jacob's drinking. Despite that, Jim still believed there was a good, smart man under all that. Jim was the only one who could talk Jacob down when he became belligerent—he'd done it many times over the years.

He watched Jacob's kids grow up and was like a second father to most of them, especially Charlie. In Charlie, Jim saw Jacob's considerable talents without the meanness. He'd taken Charlie under his wing at a young age.

Charlie didn't really like his dad because of the temper and all the abuse he meted out to his kids. Jim understood that and didn't pretend that Charlie should feel otherwise. Instead, he let him vent about his dad, trying to help him understand that it was the drink more than the man that Charlie didn't like, and always, always advising him never to take up drinking himself.

Jim would've walked through fire for either of them, father or son. But he saw Jacob less frequently now. Jacob was already a broken man. He still lived up at Schafer's Landing, but he was almost a recluse, and sickly. His drink had made him weak and old before his time and he'd become meaner and more bitter, even when sober. It was Charlie that had picked up the mantle as the business leader of the family. And he was infinitely better than his father when it came to working with people.

When Christian walked through the door of the cafe in Eminence that day, Jim knew who he was. There weren't many strangers coming through Eminence at this time of the year. And he was definitely big enough to do the job, assuming that he was tough enough. Just the physical appearance alone made Jim understand why Charlie had laughed when questioned about whether the new guy could handle the work.

Jim immediately sensed something special about the way the man carried himself, but couldn't quite put his finger on it. He motioned Christian over to his table. "Howdy stranger. I guess your name'd be Christian. I'm Jim Lane." As they shook hands, Jim tested the boy's grip. The hand was big and strong.

"Yes, I'm Christian Gunther. Thanks for meeting me and giving me a chance for the job."

"Glad to do it. You come recommended by one of the best. Where ya from?"

"Lately, Bloomington, Indiana."

Jim looked a little puzzled. "Can't say as I know the place, but I do know that Indiana's a fer piece from here. Why'd you migrated all the way down heer?"

"I heard of the area from a friend of mine named Ben McDonald. He's working with Charlie now. Ben knew I was looking for scenery a little less tame and a job that lets me work outside. I worked for a farm implements and feed company in

Bloomington, mostly inside. It was a good job, but pretty laid back. Ben thought this might fit me better. He said you're good at what you do and that I'd learn something."

"You get in trouble in Bloomington? That why you come this way?"

Christian smiled. "No. I left in good standing. I'm just looking for something different."

"Well, you're big enough and it ain't laid back down this way, that's fer sure; maybe a little tamer than when I started, but it's still plenty rough. This ain't easy work, to say the least. You'll git hot in summer and cold in winter. Specially bad in summer though. The ticks'll bother you something fierce and they'll get regular help from the mosquiters. It's genly better if you sweat a lot. Ticks don't like that so much, but then the mosquiters and flies do. It's sort of a trade-off."

"You also got to watch out for the copperheads, timber rattlers and the occasional bear and panther, though they don't come around when we're workin because of the commotion. You'll tend to work on the sides of steep hills where it's hard to plant your feet and you'll have to learn to deal with an ornery mule or two. You ever worked with horses or mules?"

"Not much."

"You ever used a canhook, cross cut or an axe?"

"No."

"You know what a singletree is, or a skid."

Christian grinned. "I have no idea."

"Well, damn, boy! You're as green as the trees we cut! What makes you think you're qualified to take on this job?"

"I'm good with my hands, Mr. Lane, and I learn fast. I have a good head on me and I'm steady. I don't drink much and I keep my word. I don't tire easy. I can carry my load."

Jim stared at Christian for a second. "Well, them's right commendable traits and not overly easy to find round here. Charlie thinks you'll be good, so let's find out. Meet me here in the morning at daylight. I'll buy you breakfast once and last, and then we'll go to the woods to see what yer made of. You got some good work clothes?"

"What you see on me."

"Well, that'll do I guess. You got a place to stay?"

"Yep, just took a room at the boarding house across the street."

"Well, okay then. See you in the morning, Gunther. Oh, and I should warn you that the boys in the crew can be a little rough on new guys—in particular, new greenhorns. They usually don't mean nothin by it, but they'll probly rub you a little raw for a few days. My suggestion to you is to take it and act like you like it, even when you don't. It'll end quicker."

Christian smiled. "Thanks for the advice. I'll take it to heart. See you in the morning."

Jim left the meeting not entirely sure what all he'd learned. It now made sense why Gunther had come. Jim had met Ben

McDonald when he was down getting familiar with Charlie's operations. Jim appreciated that they'd sent Christian to him, but still, there was something that was a little off—something a little more than Charlie or Gunther was saying. And why would Charlie pay the boy's wages?

To Jim, Gunther seemed above a regular job in the woods, although he couldn't exactly put his finger on the reason he had that impression. So why would a guy as smooth as him come way down to the sticks for low pay and hard labor he hadn't done before unless he was running from something or somebody? Jim shrugged and decided that it wasn't really his business, and he didn't give a damn about the reasons if the guy could work.

And by gum, the guy could work! He showed that in spades the next day in the woods. He was raw, like he said, but he caught on real quick, and he didn't shy away from his share of the load—and then some. He only had to be told once how to do something. And man, the guy was quick and smooth!

He didn't talk much and the razzing from the crew just seemed to roll off his back. By the end of the day, Jim could tell that the other boys were impressed. In fact, it was a little surprising how quick they'd cottoned to him. The boy had passed the greenhorn harassment stage by noon. And he didn't look like he was that much worse for wear when the day ended, which surprised Jim. This was hard work and there weren't many men that could put in a whole day at the beginning and not look pure beat at the end. This guy looked like he could've put in a few more hours and still be good for wear.

By the end of the first week, Jim decided that he was dang near in love with the boy! Christian had mastered the basic woodsman skills, including how to tell which way a tree would fall on a hillside and how to fell it without getting a crosscut blade stuck. That took both skill and a knack that came from instinct. He just didn't seem to make as many mistakes as he should have. If Jim hadn't known how green he was on the first day, he wouldn't have believed the progress he'd made! It caused him to wonder if Gunther was really as green as he said.

One of the most surprising things about that first week was how quick the mules took to the new guy. Mules were independent, smart-alecky, cantankerous cusses, and condescending to humans. Jim was pretty sure that the mules thought they were smarter than people. Christian didn't say much to them, and when he did, he talked quiet. But they responded to him in ways that were just plain unusual. He'd either been around animals a lot more than he admitted, or he had a knack. The boy had somehow let them know that he respected them and they seemed to respond in kind.

During the whole week, Jim never saw Christian curse or raise his voice to a mule. He let them pick their own way when pulling a log up steep slopes to the logging wagon. Most guys didn't trust an animal to do that and constantly corrected them when they wanted to go their own direction. Christian allowed it and watched their choices closely, like he was learning from them! If they got stuck, he never reprimanded them. He just moved the log a little or cut out a sapling, and then he walked up beside the mule and put his hand on his shoulder to let him know he could go on, talking low and walking beside him until he was in the clear again. It didn't hurt that Christian fed each animal a sugar cube when they did something he liked.

It went on six weeks that way. By that time, everybody considered the new guy one of them. But still, no one felt that they'd really learned much about him personally. He did his job exceedingly well, he was friendly and respectful, and that was all.

The crew was cutting off the old Simmons tract. It was around a thousand acres, with good hardwood, but hilly terrain with steep slopes. From what the stumps told, almost all the old growth pines had been cut off long ago. But some younger pines had matured during that time, and there was still a lot of old-growth hardwood on the hillsides that no one had bothered to cut. There was plenty of work yet to be done on this tract. Jim's crew wasn't even a fourth through it yet.

Charlie came down for a visit one day. He'd been coming down less often now. They all liked it when he did. He always remembered to ask after their families and knew the names of each one's wife and kids. He always had funny stories and jokes to tell. He ate lunch with them sitting on a stump, just like everybody else, and they noticed he was still eating the same old egg sandwiches.

They knew that his business was growing bigger by the day, so it was a pleasant surprise nowadays when he had time to come down. On this particular day, they figured he just needed to get away because he didn't seem to have any new ideas to tell them, and he didn't ask them to do anything different. He even pitched in with the work a little when he could be helpful, but mainly he just watched.

But at the end of the day Charlie called Jim and Christian Gunther aside. "Say, Jim, I lost a good hand at one of my mills up in Gladden. I need a guy up there fer a few weeks. Christian, you look like you caught on pretty quick down here. You want to learn a little how the millin end works? If you don't like it, you can move back down here if you choose."

Before Christian could answer, Jim swore. "Now con sarn it, Charlie, I just got the boy trained good and I ain't hankerin to lose him! Leave him be! Why don't I give you old Jody? He's done that work before."

Charlie tee-heed a little. "Nice try, Jim, but I know your boy Jody. If it's all the same with you, I'd like to see how Christian here takes to the millin side of the business. He seems to have done pretty good endearin himself to you timber rats."

Jim frowned and his neck reddened. "Well, you're the boss. But I don't like you stealin my people on your whim. He can do what he wants, I guess."

Charlie faked shock. "Why Jim, I think you've got attached! I really do preciate you accommodatin me though. What about it, Mr. Gunther? Can I steal you for a little while?"

Christian laughed. "Sorry, Jim, but it's hard to say no to the boss. I have a feeling we'll see each other again. When do you want me up there, Charlie?"

"How soon can you break loose from your housin down here?"

"Anytime; I paid by the week because I wasn't sure Jim would tolerate me long. I can be up there tomorrow afternoon if need be."

"Okay, good. Come up to Gladden Road and take a left. Ask for the Schafer mill. It's just a quarter-mile off the main road. You'll not miss it. Don't worry about a place to stay. I'll have some people in the area put you up for no longer than you'll be there." Christian nodded and headed off to settle up with his landlady.

"Thanks again, Jim. I ought to come down more often, I know. You mad at me for takin the new guy?"

Jim was still pouting. "If it's the same result as today, I'd just as soon you didn't drop by, and yes, I'm still a little pissed. You know how hard it is down here to find good men, Charlie? It's dang near impossible! Those that are available are the kind I generally don't want. And if me and a few other loggin bosses don't hold it together, you won't have them good logs to make all your fancy produce."

"That boy was really good! I don't mean, just normal good for a greenhorn, I mean really good! I never see'd a guy learn so fast at everthin he took up to do. I could see that he watched everthin close and he figgered it out quicker'n than anybody I ever worked with. He'd a made you a good loggin boss hisself in a year. Our producin went up a lot with him around, along with our morale. Now I've gotta replace him and I'm tellin you, I won't find another like him who'll stand to his level of work."

Charlie grinned sheepishly and slapped Jim on the back. "I know, Jim, but I've got my reasons."

Jim spat sideways, his face red. "Well, the Lord giveth and the Lord taketh away. I guess yer playin the Lord in this deal, ain't ya. Just don't send me more people like him that I can git my heart set on and then take em away agin. That's not good for my indegestun."

Then he sighed and his shoulders slumped. "Truth is, I'm gettin tired, Charlie. I don't know how much longer I can stand up to this kind of work. Most men my age have quit and long gone to somethin lighter. My body started complainin a few years back. I thought maybe Gunther could replace me and I could just stick around part-time and be paid a while to help him learn the ropes at bein a loggin boss."

Charlie nodded sympathetically. "I understand, Jim. You're the best I ever saw at handlin a loggin crew and I know that you cain't go on forever with this kind a'work. When that day comes, I'll be sorry to lose your skill in the timber, but I'll bring you up to one of the mills for trainin and make you a head sawyer when you git ready to hang it up down here. I need an extra head sawyer ready to step in when someone's sick or needs time off. The work's not as strenuous as you have now and I know you'd be one of the best with a little trainin and experience at the cut. You just say the word when you're ready and we'll do it. Now as far as Gunther's concerned, just be patient with me and that which is seen thru a glass dimly will become clearer later on."

Jim laughed and slapped Charlie on the shoulder. "Don't spout your First Corinthians chapter and verse to me, Charlie Schafer!" You and me both know that wasn't referrin to loggin when old Paul writ it. I guess I ain't got much choice about Gunther, now do I? You're still the boss and I know you got your reasons. You're too smart not to. We'll make do."

"I know a big bruiser of a boy down here named Hoak Beasley who keeps buggin me for a job. I been holdin out on him cause he's got sech a bad reputation—probly well earned. I think he's a bully, and he's from a family of no-goods; but maybe I'll have to give him a try and hope he reforms hisself. With all his faults, they say this Hoak boy's smart. Maybe I can straighten him out a little."

Charlie frowned and shook his head. "Be real careful, Jim. Them Beasleys is hard cases. I'd steer clear of em if I could. It's your call, a'course. I know the boys who work for you now—all good boys. I suppose nobody's ready to take over the crew from that group yet. But before you jump to Beasley, think about it and see if you can come up with somebody else you already have faith in. If you cain't and you want to take Beasley, I'll back you. I just hope you can handle him."

"I'll mull it over some more, Charlie, but I don't got a'lotta choices down this way. I gotta make do with what I can. This ain't exactly a luxury job we're offerin, you know. We're deep in the boonies, and if you ain't from round here, you genly don't want the work. I still cain't figger why Gunther came all the way down heer to do it."

Charlie nodded and wished him luck. He apologized again for stealing Christian and headed north.

Christian was at Charlie's mill early the next morning. Charlie introduced him to the head sawyer, Harold James, a droll, lanky man who chewed tobacco, spitting often and saying little. Charlie explained to Harold that he wanted Christian schooled in mill work, including a little head sawing practice when Harold had the time to teach him. All this was to be done in a few weeks.

After Charlie left, Christian waited for Harold to quiz him on what he knew, but Harold never asked him anything. He just put Christian to work with the canhook to roll the logs onto the saw carriage, the iron-wheeled carrier on which a log was secured for cutting it into planks and then into boards if the plank was of high enough quality. Otherwise, the plank became a railroad tie or pallet material.

Logs were placed on a long wooden trestle whose top was even with the saw carriage. The logs were rolled along the trestle and secured on the carriage for cutting. The carriage itself moved back and forth on metal rails, much like mini railroad tracks. The carriage's movement was controlled by the head sawyer by pushing or pulling a lever. That placed tension on wide rotating belts connected to a pulley on a steam engine and to the underbelly of the carriage.

The log to be cut was placed on the carriage so it stuck out beyond the edge of the carriage far enough to be passed through a large circular saw. The saw blade was also turned by other belts driven by pulleys on the same steam engine.

The head sawyer controlled the movement of the carriage in such a way as to make a first pass through the blade to cut off the bark and to create a flat side on the log. Then the sawyer backed up the carriage and flipped the log down with his canhook onto its flat side and ran the log through the saw again. When he had done this on three sides, the cut log was called a "cant" from which boards could be cut if the log was good enough quality.

By comparing the small end of the log to its larger end, a good sawyer could determine in a split second how much to cut off on the first pass through the saw to create the three-sided cant without wasting potential board. Then he could cut the appropriate number of boards of varying widths from the cant with greater precision. A bad head sawyer could diminish the log's value by cutting an initial cant too deep or slicing the boards too thick or too thin.

Christian spent six weeks at the mill, learning quickly, remaining quiet, watching how the operation worked. It took him only two days to master the head sawing skill to an acceptable level, which even shocked Harold. He'd seen some men take months to catch on as quickly as Christian did.

Once Christian's work at the mill was finished, Charlie called him and Ben to the headquarters office to confer. The meeting between them occurred in late April, with spring in full bloom in the Ozarks. All three had been looking forward to the meeting since it was the first time they had a chance to sit down together since Christian had come to Missouri to work. Ben had also been keeping a furious pace as he and Charlie prepared to open the flooring operation.

Charlie chuckled. "Well, Christian, you've earned respect everwhere you went. I swear, I've had to fight people off to git you away from em, and it tested the good will of a few old friends!"

Christian smiled. "It's been an interesting orientation, Charlie. I learned a lot and liked the work. I suspect it'd be harder in the heat though."

"Yea that it is. All the seasons have their challenges. Spring's usually wet and that hampers us on the roads. Winter's cold, and the frozen ground makes the work slippery. Summer's hardest though. When it's hot, everythin slows down some. So, tell Ben and me about what you learned during your sojourn in the wilderness."

"From what you and Ben told me already, I think you have a pretty good handle on the problems. It's mostly about finding the right men and animals and training them properly. I have a few additional thoughts, though."

We probably should give the crews some incentive to spur their production. I'd give a bonus every six months to the crew whose logs created the highest number of board feet of lumber produced at the best quality. That should cause them to want to cut the largest and best timber and get it to your mills. That assumes all five crews have comparable timber tracts to cut on. If not, other measures need to be considered."

"With Jim Lane, I didn't see that he missed any trees that I would've cut, and he surprised me with a few that I would've passed up. In fact, I learned a lot by watching which trees he left standing. I doubt if all the timber crews pay that much attention, though."

The bonus doesn't have to be that much—these guys don't make a lot—but it ought to be enough that they see the value of competing for it. That'll also make them want to use the best equipment and mules or horses, and to keep their tools sharp. Using dull saws was a problem the whole time I worked with Jim Lane, and it was the same at the mills with the head saws."

"I think that I agree with Ben when he says that we should probably own the horses or mules, but that presents another problem. If it's not their teams, the timber crews may not take care of them as they should, and some of the men may even be inclined to abuse them. If we do decide to use our own animals, we should test a team with the timber crew that's steadiest and see how it works. Also, people like Jim Lane are proud of their own animals and get paid more when we use them. Most owners like Jim pay a lot of attention to their animals and how the men treat them, so we need to move carefully if we make that change."

"Another thing to consider, I don't know about the other timber bosses, but Jim clearly doesn't have anybody to hand off to when he has to be away from the woods for a day. That's a big problem. We should set up a pay scale for an assistant timber boss in each crew for backup and to take over when the timber boss leaves or retires."

"Jim has some rough guys working with him, but that's just Shannon County. It may be better with the crews up here in Dent, nearer Salem. The sawmill down in Shannon also had pretty rough men, prone to drink. I'm not sure how to fix that. I've got to think more about it."

Ben spoke up. "So, I take it that you're okay with taking on management of the timber operation and mills, Christian?"

Christian smiled. "You know, I kind of like that part of the operation best. It'll be a challenge but I can relate to the characters that are doing the work. They're actually not too different from the gangs in New York. I just have to figure out how to train them and keep them motivated. If Charlie gives me the latitude and a little money for bonuses, I think I can do that."

"Done!" Charlie exclaimed, "and I'm grateful to have your idees. It'll be a hard job ridin herd on that part of the business. That's a tough group of boys you'll be workin with. I notice you don't seem to rely on a weapon of any kind. You might want to think about that. You're gonna be spending a lot of your time in some rough territory. You ever used a pistol?"

"No, I've never relied on a gun. To tell you the truth, I'm afraid I might use it too quickly. I may change my mind at some point. If I do, I understand you have skills in using a pistol, and I may need some lessons."

Charlie chuckled. "I'll be glad to give you pointers if it comes to that. I admire your decision, but be real careful. This is the world I grew up in and know well, but I still get nervous sometimes when I'm dealin with some of these boys. Most are good unless drinkin, but a few are just bad and won't ever be anythin else. Them's the ones to watch out for."

"Now boys, let's talk about how we make this worthwhile for the three of us. I'll give you a monthly salary to live on and each of you 10% of the profits at the end of the year. You'll be junior partners in the company. The better the operation works, the more we benefit. Are you in it with me on this?"

Ben gulped. "Wow, Charlie, I'd have done it for the salary alone and felt blessed. Sure I'm in."

Christian nodded. "That's generous, Charlie, but it's good strategy too. We'd bust our butts to make this work in any case, but it's nice to know we have a personal stake in it. I feel privileged to be on the team."

And so the three young men, joined together by mission and mutual respect, proceeded to build themselves an empire in the backwoods of southern Missouri.

Chapter 9

On August 12, 1890 Emma Mason, of the New York Children's Aid Society, sent a telegram to Ben and Anna McDonald. The telegraph operator, realizing its urgency, sent a carrier to Jadwin. Anna got the telegram late that afternoon. The Reverend Charles Loring Brace had died the 11th of August. It was the end of an era for the Children's Aid Society of New York.

Anna had heard that he was ill and had sent him a long letter wishing him a speedy recovery. When Emma looked into the middle drawer of Reverend Brace's desk early on the morning after he died, she saw Anna's letter. When she read it, she immediately understood why he'd kept it. It was wonderfully written, full of gratitude, hope and optimism. From that letter, Emma learned that Anna had become a teacher, and that she and Ben McDonald had been reunited. The letter also told about how little Zachary had thrived in his new environment.

Emma realized that Anna and Zachary were the living epitome of Reverend Brace's life's work. And she needed an epitome more than ever now, because things could quickly change for the worse as a result of Charles' death unless she prevented that from happening.

Emma had already decided to use Charles' memory as a lever. She proposed a memorial ceremony for Brace in October, convincing her Board that it would be the right venue to honor him and further the goals he had pioneered. She was confident that she could get numerous state and federal dignitaries to attend. She even wanted President Harrison's daughter, Mamie, to come if he'd allow it. Emma was a friend of Mamie's and knew of her passion for lost children.

Emma decided that Anna and Zachary's story could be a poignant centerpiece to memorialize her friend and mentor, assuming, of course, that they had the personalities to carry it off. She needed real-life examples of orphans who had ridden the train to a better life and who could speak articulately about it. These former orphans from Missouri might be just the ones to do it.

Emma knew that Anna was not a typical orphan train child, being much older when she was placed. But that, too, could speak to Brace's innovative vision, and besides, Anna's story was uniquely fascinating. Here was a young teenage girl who had been saved from horror on the streets by an orphan boy that she would ultimately marry. In turn, he'd escaped with Anna only because of the help of one of the most notorious gang leaders that Hell's Kitchen had ever produced.

Both of those boys had become close to and deeply respected by Bill Chambers, the highest commendation she believed anyone could attain. Apparently the young gang leader, named Gunther, had paid a high price for helping Anna and Ben. No one in New York knew where he was now. Brace had told her he'd left town with Ben McDonald after Bill Chamber's death, making the story even more titillating.

And then there was young Zachary, that frail, crippled little orphan boy with no hope, who, according to Anna, had blossomed into a brilliant, healthy youth. He was a perfect example of the success of Brace's policies! How old would he be now, maybe 11 or 12? If he had really progressed as much as Anna said, he'd be a true representative for the many thousands of lost and fragile young children that Brace had helped.

Among other notable skills, Emma Mason was a marketing

genius, and she instantly recognized that Anna's and Zach's stories were a marketer's dream. And there'd be no bigger stage for telling those stories than at a New York memorial ceremony for Reverend Brace. The question was, could Anna and Zachary live up to the hype? She knew that she had to find that out before introducing them to the general public.

Emma's vision was much broader than Brace's. He'd wanted to help individual kids, using the voluntary resources of the philanthropic agency that he had created. She, on the other hand, wanted to engage large and powerful government systems that should be helping kids, but weren't. She believed that cities, states and the federal government had to assume more responsibility for America's struggling children. Voluntary agencies like the Society, no matter how resourceful, simply didn't have the resources or authority to serve and protect the overwhelming number of abused and abandoned children in America.

Anna was saddened by the news of Brace's death, but couldn't help smiling at Emma's telegram. It was all business, short and to the point. It read:

REVEREND BRACE DIED AUGUST 11. *STOP.* **COMMITMENT TO HIS WORK MUST NOT BE LOST.** *STOP.* **I NEED YOUR HELP IN FURTHERING THE CAUSE.** *STOP.* **COME TO NEW YORK AS SOON AS POSSIBLE.** STOP. **ALL TRAVEL EXPENSES COVERED.** *STOP.* **BRING ZACHARY.** *STOP.* **NEED YOU, ZACHARY AND YOUR HUSBAND FOR A WEEK.** *STOP.* **HOW SOON CAN YOU GET HERE?** *STOP. STOP*

That night, she and Ben talked it over. Anna was reluctant to go. She was in the early stages of pregnancy with their first child and was experiencing nausea every day. Her school would start in less than a month. She had already prepared, but she wanted a quiet month to relax and get healthier. She no longer feared New York as she once had, but it still held many painful memories. She had no desire to go back.

Ben listened as she expressed her concerns about the trip. When she finished, he said. "I understand. I worry about you having to ride that far on a moving train with a queasy stomach. I'm afraid it'll drain your energy and might even threaten yours or the baby's health. I wish we had a better idea what Emma wants from us and why we can't help her from here. And I wonder why she wants us to bring Zachary?"

"I'm guessing she's considering using us as poster children for Reverend Brace's work. If that's the case, she'd need to know how good we'd be in that role."

"Yea, that'd make sense; you and Zach would be great examples. Let's sleep on it and decide in the morning."

But Anna had nightmares that troubled her sleep. In her first dream, she was trying to get to Ben, who'd been beaten by a gang of young thugs and lay crumpled on the ground. She was being held back by the gang, who were laughing and taunting her. The nightmare was so real that she awoke gasping for breath and in a deep sweat, her heart racing. She lay awake, trying to shake it off, and then gradually drifted off again, only to have another dream. This time there were hundreds of little children all around her, pleading for help. All their faces looked just like Zachary's when she'd first met him.

She awoke again and refused to go back to sleep. She got up and went to the parlor to avoid disturbing Ben. When she returned an hour later, he was sitting in a chair, looking out the window into the darkness. "What's wrong, Ben?"

"Do you remember when Bill bought us all those clothes?"

She nodded, fearful of what he'd say next, anticipating it.

"While you were in the bedroom dressing that day, I told Bill that we didn't have any money to pay for the clothes. He just smiled and said we should take them, and that we'd know how and when to repay the debt at some future time. I asked him how we'd know, and he said we'd just know when the right time came along. I think this is what he was talking about."

She sighed and walked over, leaning down to put her arms around his neck. He reached up and held her arms, leaning his head back to her chest. She kissed the top of his head and decided not to mention her nightmares. "You're right, of course. I know that we have to do this. Tempting as it is, we can't duck this responsibility because it's inconvenient. I think this kind of thing would always be inconvenient, no matter when the request comes. We're being selfish."

He didn't answer at first and continued staring out the window at the darkness, holding on to her. Finally he leaned his head back again, looking up at her. "Yea, a little, I guess. I don't think we'd forgive ourselves if we didn't go. It'd be about like all those good New York citizens who tried to pretend that we didn't exist when we were in Hell's Kitchen. Let's take a trip to New York, Mrs. McDonald! You left as Anna Murphy, the beautiful, sad orphan girl. You're returning as Anna McDonald, the beautiful, successful woman with a man who adores you and who'll always be at your side to protect you. Don't forget that. I'll always be here for you."

She smiled. "How could I ever forget that, Mr. McDonald? You're my own personal knight in shining armor! You owe fealty to me for as long as I live! What more protection could a fair damsel ever need?"

Chapter 10

They arrived in New York City on Tuesday afternoon, August 19, 1890. The weather was terrible. They'd traveled through severe thunderstorms in Pennsylvania that had followed them into New York. Emma Mason met them at the station and hustled them over to the Gilsey House at 29th and Broadway. It was a luxury hotel but Emma knew the owners and got the rooms free for Children's Aid Society guests as a contribution to support the Society's efforts. She'd booked two adjoining rooms, one for Zachary and one for Ben and Anna. "You all can relax for a few hours and then we'll meet for dinner in the lobby at 7:00 p.m. We can talk a little about tomorrow's agenda then."

They said that'd be fine and Emma rushed back to the office. She was now the Acting Director of the Society, with pressing matters to attend. And, although she hadn't informed them yet, she'd called a special meeting of her Board the next day to début her Missouri guests.

Anna was tired and decided to rest before dinner. Ben and Zach walked up Broadway to take in the sights. Ben would've liked to go on up to the Simmons Warehouse to see old friends and take Zach on a quick jag through Central Park but decided against it, since he didn't want to leave Anna alone that long. She'd become nauseated on the train and was exhausted.

Anyway, they'd have a chance to tour over the weekend since Emma had given them time to get reacquainted with the City. She'd been thoughtful in other ways too. Her agency had solicited complementary tickets to a Broadway show on Saturday afternoon. If Anna felt like it, they'd go up to the Park early on Saturday morning and then take in the show that afternoon.

Emma was in the hotel lobby at 7:00 p.m. sharp, and was pleased to see that Anna, Ben and Zach were already there awaiting her arrival. The weather had finally calmed and the evening had turned cooler. Anna, feeling better after her rest, asked Emma if they could walk to the restaurant.

Over dinner, they filled Emma in on what had happened after Anna and Zachary were taken in by Jess and Bessie Lough in late November 1884. Emma laughed heartily remembering her suspicion about Jess possibly wanting Anna as a second wife. Anna giggled and indicated that Jess had never fully forgiven Emma for that and still grumbled about it.

Emma inquired about how Anna and Ben were reunited, and about the wedding. They told her of Ben's work, and Zach reported his progress in school. From his animated, articulate responses, Zach struck her as a marvelously talented youth. He summed it all up succinctly. "So, you see, Mrs. Mason, I'm doing very well now. I really enjoy learning and I've had a great teacher for the last five years." Zach looked over at Anna and grinned. "I get to go to Salem high school next year. I may not fare as well there without her."

Anna laughed. "You know perfectly well, Zach Lough, that you surpassed my ability to teach you anything new over two years ago. Mrs. Mason, my 'great teaching' as far as Zach is concerned consists of desperately trying to locate enough books and materials on subjects far beyond his age level to keep him entertained. We could open a library with the books we've purchased for Zach's education."

Emma said that was wonderful to hear. She meant it, too. "Zachary, have you decided whether you'll pursue your education beyond high school and what profession you'll take up when you're older?"

"I hope I have a chance to go to a university somewhere. I'd either like to go into medicine or the law. I know I could be helpful as a doctor in rural Missouri, but I'd prefer to be a lawyer. My hero is President Lincoln. You probably already know that he trained himself as an attorney, so even if I can't go to college, maybe I can prepare myself to pass the law bar exam, like he did. A medical degree would definitely require a full university education and that may be out of our reach financially."

"Well, I believe you would be spectacular in either of those professions and you should pursue one of them. A boy of your abilities must not waste his talents." Zach smiled and thanked her for her encouragement.

Emma changed the subject to the activities of the next day. She had worried that what she had in mind might spook them, but after talking with them, she doubted if any of them would be intimidated. "I've arranged for a gathering of my Board tomorrow morning to meet you. I hope you don't mind. I know they'll be excited to talk with you. They'll want your perspective on the program and whether it needs refinement now that the Reverend Brace is gone."

"The Board's comprised of some of the most influential people in New York. They're committed to Charles' vision but they don't always agree on the best pathways to get there. Some don't see any need for change. Others believe the world is growing more complex, and that no single private philanthropic organization is capable of addressing the needs of all our homeless children. It'll require more money than the private sector can contribute, and regulatory powers that we don't have, particularly as it relates to family abuse, the operation of orphanages and child labor laws."

"Some, including me, believe that this calls for a more active role for governments, but others on the Board don't support the expansion of government institutions into family matters. All those differing opinions will come to a head now that Charles is gone." He was a master at deflecting conflict." She smiled, somewhat sardonically. "I'm not known for that ability."
"As for your contribution tomorrow, I just want you to tell your stories. My Board will love to hear them because they so seldom get to see living examples of the success of their work. They may also ask you what you think of the Society's goals and activities and how they could be made better."

"Say whatever you want, whether it sheds a positive or troubling light on what we do. I'm very comfortable with you stating your candid opinions. We'll just see where the conversation goes. I assume you know of your Missouri State Senator Percival Webster and his positions regarding the Society's orphan train program?"

Ben looked at Anna. They both seemed puzzled. They shook their heads simultaneously. They'd not heard what Senator Webster thought. Anna responded. "We've heard of Senator Webster, of course, but not met him. He represents the western part of our state. I wasn't aware that he has a position on the Society's efforts."

Emma smiled sardonically. "Oh yes, the good Senator is our greatest critic. He believes we have corrupted your state with our placement of orphan children from New York City. He's written to us repeatedly and posted editorials in the New York Times. He detests our work and has petitioned federal legislators, and even the Office of the President, to bring a halt to the orphan trains. I'm surprised that you haven't heard his criticisms."

Anna shook her head. "I'm afraid we haven't. We're pretty far removed from the political center of our state where we live. Our Salem and Rolla newspapers haven't covered anything about the Senator's positions on the placement process."

Emma's face showed a little disdain. Keeping current on the political winds that blew up and down the Atlantic Coast, and even in the larger Midwestern urban centers like Chicago and St. Louis, was like life's breath to her. She assumed that the same would be true for anyone who followed current affairs, particularly a teacher. Her response was slightly patronizing. "Well, that's too bad, dear. I suspect you'll personally hear from the Senator at some future time."

"Now, you should also know that we plan a memorial to Reverend Brace later this year that will also include remembrance of the work of our mutual friend, Bill Chambers. We haven't yet decided exactly how the memorial will be structured. Let's see how tomorrow goes and then we can talk more about that afterward. I promise to set you free to explore the city and relax by no later than Friday noon. I'm sure you'll want to see the some of the sights and renew old acquaintances. You certainly deserve that opportunity."

Anna didn't have any old acquaintances to renew. All she really wanted to do was visit the graves of her mother and father. She would have been happy to do that and then take the first train home. But Zach and Ben were excited about the Broadway play, and Ben really wanted to see Central Park in the summer. So she'd humor them. She knew that Ben had a different perspective on the city from his time with Bill.

The Children's Aid Society Board was comprised of some of the elite movers and shakers of New York City in the late 19th century. Some members were prominent business people; others were the wives of wealthy entrepreneurs; still others were noted members of the clergy. Among them was the wife of the owner of the New York Times. The Mayor's Deputy Chief of Staff was also there because of the mayor's sincere concern about the plight of the city's orphan children, but also to deflect criticism from the Mayor's office for not doing enough to solve the street urchin problem in Hell's Kitchen.

Placing prominent New Yorkers on the Board had been Bill Chambers' idea to broaden support for the Society's efforts. Brace had not initially warmed to it. He, like many visionaries, didn't like to be second-guessed by a bunch of meddling do-gooders, particularly those who stood on the sidelines criticizing but doing little else. But Chambers believed that the way to get them off the sidelines was to co-opt them into joining the cause.

The Board met every third Wednesday of each month. This meeting was more exciting than most. By this time, nearly every Board member was familiar with the Anna and Ben story, and anxious to meet the saga's main characters. Mrs. Mason had also informed them of Zachary's successes. They would be glad to meet him, too, but it was Anna and Ben that they really wanted to see. After opening formalities, Mrs. Mason got right to it.

"You all know our organization has come under increasing criticism, both in New York and in the West, due to the placements of orphan children. While I have no doubt that we've done immeasurable good, the Board seldom gets the opportunity to see, firsthand, the living examples of your efforts. Today, you'll have that chance."

"This is a crucial meeting. Charles has passed. Some of the Children's Aid Society's long term supporters are asking if we should consider changing our strategies. I understand that it's an appropriate time for introspection."

"I, too, am concerned about the growing criticism in the western states to our placement policies. I also realize that all it would take is just one or two sensational cases in which children have not fared well, or have broken the law, to negate thousands of our successes in the minds of our critics."

She paused, letting the Board reflect. She knew they were all anxious to talk to Anna, Ben and Zachary, but she wanted to set the context for *why* it was important to showcase their success, not just their notoriety.

"Politicians in the western States, biased against immigrant families of all kinds, view the placement of orphaned immigrant children as a symptom of our country's broader problems. Conversely, New Yorkers have supported our efforts, in large part, because they fail to accept immigrant street urchins as their own problem. These are, after all, the orphan children of immigrants, whose thwarted intentions were to simply pass through this city on their way to a better life, often in the same western states who now despise their coming. If we don't find a way to change attitudes on both sides, we're at risk."

"I'm particularly concerned about Missouri, the very state from which our guests hail, and where we have placed a large number of our children in past years. I understand from our sources there that State Senator Percival Webster is looking for national attention. He has certainly obtained the attention of this Board—but not favorably. He has been extraordinarily vocal in his attacks on our work. As you are already aware, he's written long, loud letters of complaint to our Governor, the Mayor, and even to the White House. As a result, we've received 'inquiries' from the press asking for response. Charles chose to ignore them. I'm not sure we can continue to do so."

"Now I know you're all excited about talking with our guests, and after visiting with them myself, I know their stories will be inspiring. They're phenomenal young people. But I also think that we need their perspectives about how to strengthen our program and fend off unwarranted criticism. I'd like at least part of the conversation to focus on that. Now, let me introduce you."

Emma turned to Ben and Anna, asking each of them to take some time to explain what caused them to become homeless on the streets of Hell's Kitchen and what that experience was like. Most of the Board members had never interacted directly with Street Urchins. Emma saw the rapt attention of the Board as Anna began to speak and made a mental note that she must create more such opportunities in the future.

Anna began with the story of her mother and father, their deaths, and her confusion on the streets. She stopped at the point of the attack by the Dragons and turned to Ben. He began with the story of his family; describing the nature of the man that he thought was his father and the efforts of his mother to protect him and his brother and sisters from abuse. He described his feelings of abandonment when they left him and talked about what he saw in his three years on the streets, particularly the plight of the younger children.

Then he introduced them to a side of Christian Gunther that

they'd never heard. They certainly had heard of Christian Gunther, one of the most notorious youth gang leaders ever to come through Hell's Kitchen, but they had no idea of his role in saving Ben and Anna, or his collaboration with Bill Chambers.

The wife of the owner of the Times made a mental note that this would be extremely attractive story for her paper's readers if the Society, Ben and Anna would allow it. But it would be complicated. The story could still cause trouble for the Society since it had protected Ben and Anna, and it might even put Gunther at risk if he ever returned to New York. She didn't want that and decided to defer to Emma's best judgment on the matter.

Ben continued his story. He related how he had tried to avoid confrontation with the Dragons until that fateful night of Anna's rescue. He told them about the mausoleum where he'd taken her. He described the time with Bill prior to, and after, Anna's departure. He struggled with his emotions as he described his feelings at Bill's death.

He stopped there and turned to Anna to discuss her ride on the train. Emma, who'd traveled as the supervisor on that train, was embarrassed at some of Anna's observations. She realized that she'd appeared callous in her all-consuming goal to get the children placed, ignoring what they were feeling as they traveled to unknown destinations to be taken away by people they'd never met. She decided that she and the Society's staff needed sensitivity training from the perspective of the children riding the trains. Anna could help her with that.

When it came Zachary's turn to speak, he effortlessly mesmerized the Board with his story. He was obviously a boy of great intelligence, articulate and funny, and not the least intimidated by them. There were tears in the eyes of some of the

Board members when he talked about how it felt to be the kid that no one wanted, rejected repeatedly at every placement stop.

When he saw that, he was surprised and a little embarrassed. He paused in his narrative. "I'm so sorry if that is maudlin or depressing. Let me try to explain it better. I believe every kid is frightened when he or she gets on those trains, no matter how he might be acting. Then, if a kid gets rejected at every stop, that just adds to the anxiety and makes it hard to try to stay positive. It's tempting to pretty much give up on life."

"I decided that I was of no value to anyone. I'd lost hope. I was just lucky that Jess and Bessie Lough adopted me anyway, and I know they wouldn't have except for my sister Anna." He looked over at Anna and smiled. She returned his smile, pride clearly showing on her face.

When Zach finished, Benjamin Waters, Chairman of the Society's Board, spoke. Waters was the venerable President of the Bank of New York, the city's premier banking establishment, founded 100 years earlier by none other than Alexander Hamilton himself. "Mr. Lough, I know that I speak for the rest of the members of this Board when I tell you that there is nothing for which you need to apologize. We must learn to see the world from the eyes of the children we're trying to help. You've done us a great service by what you've told us here today."

Zach responded by telling the Board that his orphan placement ride had a very happy ending, and he suspected that there were thousands of untold positive outcomes just like his. They all applauded.

The stories had already consumed two hours of the agenda. That was how long the entire meeting was to have lasted, but

Chairman Waters said, "Let's take a short break. I'm exhausted just listening and I can only imagine how Anna, Ben and Zach must feel. But I think that we need to extend this meeting and not lose the opportunity to obtain their insights on how we can make our program better. Fifteen minutes and then please return promptly. Any of you that must leave because of your schedule, feel free to do so."

When they broke, not one Board member headed toward the exit. They all gathered around Anna, Ben and Zach to shake their hands and tell them how grateful they were for their presentations. Emma Mason stood back and watched, exceedingly pleased with herself that she had called these young people in to visit with her Board.

Shortly before they reconvened, Benjamin Waters pulled Zachary aside. "Mr. Lough, I assume you are going to college when you finish your preparatory schooling?"

"I hope to sir, if I can find a way. It's very expensive and I don't know if we can afford it. My dad and mom don't make much money and they have lots of other children. It'll be a sacrifice for them just to send me to high school in Salem. I think I may need to do what Anna did and teach a while first. That might give me a chance to save some money to pay my tuition to a university. That way, I might be able to afford at least a couple years of higher education. It's my dream, but I can't ask my mom and dad to do something for me that they can't do for my brothers and sisters."

"I see. But if you could attend a university, what would you study?"

Zach's eyes lit up. "Oh, I'd like to study the law and sit for the law bar exams in Missouri someday. I admire what President Lincoln did. He's my favorite historical figure. He was exceptional in his self-education."

Waters smiled. "Yes he was, Zach. That he was. I had the privilege of meeting President Lincoln a few times and he's a very good example for you to emulate, both in his legal work and his service to his country. Law is a noble profession. Would you mind giving me your mailing address at home? I might like to keep up with your progress in school."

Zach was flattered. "Certainly sir, thank you!" He wrote his Jadwin address on the back of the fancy card that Mr. Waters provided.

Chairman Waters reconvened the meeting. "Mr. and Mrs. McDonald and Mr. Lough, your observations are astute and valuable. So let me ask you to address the following question in our remaining time together. If you were responsible for administering the Orphan Train program, what would you do differently?"

Ben looked at Anna and nodded. He knew that she'd thought about that question often, and the three of them had discussed it on the way to New York. She addressed Chairman Waters. "Thank you for asking. Actually, we do have a few suggestions. We offer them knowing that that our perspectives are limited to our personal experiences and ask you to consider them in that light."

"First, we believe that brothers and sisters should never be separated when placed if at all avoidable. I remember, very painfully, the separation of the Stewart twins on the train that Zachary and I rode. They were a young brother and sister whom

I supervised during the trip. They were placed in different states. Their respective families seemed nice, but I often wonder if they will ever have a chance to see each other again. It's horrible to lose your parents. It would be nearly as painful to think that you might never see your brother or sister again."

"Second, we believe that each child's placement should be carefully documented, with the names and addresses of the parents and the name of the child recorded into a master file. Forms recording the age at placement, gender, prior schooling and special health conditions a child should be developed before the child is placed. The information should be given to the family taking the child. These forms could be in duplicate and could include a section for information to be completed by the family that could include the town or rural location, the mailing address and other pertinent information of the host family."

Emma blushed. She remembered the difficulty that Ben and Anna had experienced in corresponding while Ben was still in New York and Anna was at some undocumented site in southern Missouri with a family whose name and location she didn't remember accurately.

"Third, it would be nice to know something in advance about the families interested in taking the children. Perhaps someone locally could interview prospective parents, help them complete an application, and ask them to obtain references from their church, local police officers, court officials or community leaders. The interested families could bring this information with them to a placement event."

"And if they come not intending to take a child, as was the case with Jess and Bessie Lough, should a family spontaneously change their minds, they could be asked to complete the information there and send references to the society shortly after the placement. If they fail to do so, they could be visited by a Children's Aid Society representative."

"Finally, we suggest that there be designated representatives for the Children's Aid Society in each state in which children are placed, even if they are only volunteers. Perhaps it could be local ministers, or even orphans, now grown and in good standing in their communities."

"We suggest that you tell each family that takes a child, that it might be visited on a random basis to check on the status of the placement. By indicating that the visits will be randomly selected, all families will know that they could be visited."

"Even if they are not visited, they should be told that they can still contact the in-state representative if problems arise or they have questions. This could give you better information about how well the program is working and perhaps avoid some children remaining in troubled environments. I know that Ben and I would gladly participate if called upon for such a monitoring role"

As Emma listened, her first reaction to Anna's suggestions was defensive. Surely these ideas weren't realistic! But Emma loved innovation, something Brace generally resisted, and as she continued to mull over Anna's ideas, she began to wonder about possibilities that she'd never considered.

It struck her that Anna might be right. A monitoring program *could* provide critical feedback for program improvement, and it might go a long way toward solving some of the Society's most pressing public relations problems. If there were reputable local representatives in each state, they could become the antidote to local critics, or at least they'd be better positioned to counteract criticism than an easterner like her. And if they could collect enough data, even if only randomly, on how placed children were doing—well, that could be an extremely powerful tool to refute unfounded criticism!

She almost spoke out at that point, but a glance at the faces of the Board members assured her that it wasn't necessary. So she waited for their reaction. Waters opened the floor for clarifying questions. At first the Board members sat silently, thinking. The silence continued so long that Anna began to worry that her ideas might not be as good as she thought. She glanced over at Emma, who gave her a little smile and nodded. Then the hands began to shoot up and the discussion became animated.

A few Board members thought that interviewing prospective families and monitoring child placements might be too time consuming and could dampen family participation. Emma was asked how many children had been placed in Missouri. She estimated about 10,000 in the last ten years, although she had no way of accurately knowing because they hadn't collected the very data Anna was suggesting.

Anna and Ben were shocked at the number. They'd been clueless as to the magnitude of the placements. If that was just in Missouri, how many total children had been placed in all the states?

But Emma had a broader view and didn't want the Board to give up on the idea too quickly. "I'll admit that I was initially intimidated by Anna's proposal. I agree that it would take greater resources than the Society currently has, but she's certainly correct about one important thing: should we choose to use them, we have an army of untapped volunteers out there in those states, both among the children we've placed over the years, now grown, and from members of the many churches we work with. We've never even considered giving them that kind of opportunity to help us."

"As I listened to Anna speak, I'm frankly embarrassed. I can't imagine why we haven't thought about these ideas. It wouldn't be easy. It would involve training to assure consistency. I know our resources are limited, but as I think about what Anna's suggesting, I can see a way to do it."

A number of the Board members nodded as she spoke. She continued, "Such a strategy could partially pay for itself. It's likely to lessen the number of children who must be returned to New York because of a failed placement. And Zachary was certainly right. Not being chosen by a family destroys a child's self-confidence. When that child must be brought back, we have a big problem. We have to place them back into an orphanage, and none of us believe that's a good solution for any child at this time in our city."

"And while we've seldom revealed it, sometimes, we can't even find an orphanage that will take a child back, so we have to consign him or her to a gang on the streets. The process absolutely crushes the spirits of everyone involved. I can tell you personally, since I was the sponsor on Anna's train, that's what I expected to happen to Zachary before the Loughs took him in. I don't think I could have gotten him replaced into his orphanage. They were afraid of his health condition, which is why they referred him to us to begin with."

Anna had never considered that possibility before and shuddered at the thought. Zachary frowned and looked down at the floor.

Mrs. Mason continued, "Now, as to monitoring the homes once future children are placed, I admit that could be a daunting task. But if, as Anna suggests, we randomly select the children to be monitored, then it's feasible. Even tracking a random sample of ten percent or so of the placed children in each state would tell us volumes."

"We might get help from some of the research students at Columbia University to process the data, or we could ask a university in each state to do it. That would lend local objectivity to the study. We need data to overcome the increasing criticism we're facing in the states. This could be an important vehicle for that."

"As I see it now, our primary costs would be the travel involved for the volunteers. We'd need to at least cover those expenses. I'll have our staff estimate that and report to you."

The Board liked Emma's strategy and asked her to report back as soon as she could. As the discussion wound down, Chairman Waters summarized the day, "I must say that the personal stories and the suggestions of our guests today are some of the most interesting I've heard in my time on this Board. I admire their courage and intelligence and their wonderful personal successes thus far in their lives. They are the stellar examples of why we're committed to this work."

He turned to Anna, Ben and Zachary. "I assume that Mrs. Mason has briefed you on the memorial we're planning sometime in October for Reverend Brace to honor his landmark achievements. I realize that it's a major inconvenience to ask, but I really hope the three of you will come back to New York to play a role in that." Ben, Zach and Anna all nodded to his request.

Emma smiled and said. "My thoughts exactly, Mr. Chairman; I'll do my very best to make that happen." Anna frowned just a little, realizing that they'd be visiting New York City at least one more time, and even sooner than she would have preferred.

A reporter from the New York Times had been quietly taking notes throughout the entire meeting at the request of wife of the Times' owner, once a journalist herself. She'd also brought a Times photographer with her. Emma never told her guests about that because she thought it might offend or intimidate them. While Anna, Ben and Zach spoke to the board, the photographer had been taking pictures. Anna and Ben assumed it was just for use by the Board. But on the weekend after the meeting, the Times ran a front-page story about the meeting, telling the stories of Ben, Anna and Zach in detail, but leaving out the details about the role of Bill Chambers and Christian Gunther in saving their lives.

In following days, the Times ran five more articles highlighting the plight of orphaned children in Hell's Kitchen, always linking the stories back to the initial article about Anna and Ben and their recommendations for improving the orphan placement process. Every article was positively received by Times readers, with many complimentary editorial comments. With each article, the fame of the two former orphans, now a successful married couple in Missouri grew exponentially. By the time the October memorial for Charles Brace rolled around, New York's citizenry was anxious to see and hear more from these famous orphans.

The articles were also read by prominent individuals in other parts of the country, including one Percival Webster, who had never previously heard of Jadwin, Missouri, or of Ben or Anna McDonald. He made a mental note to remember those names and to find out whether they really were such wonderful young people, should he ever have the opportunity. He would enjoy exposing them if they were charlatans. But until then, he wouldn't acknowledge them. The Senator was wily and his time as an attorney had taught him not to play a card without knowing what was in his opponent's hand. Anna, Ben and Zach never saw the New York Times articles and remained unaware of them or of their growing notoriety.

The Children's Aid Society staff, riding the wave of enthusiasm, frantically prepared for the Brace memorial. They arranged for the return of their three, now-famous, friends from Missouri, despite the fact that Anna would be farther along in her pregnancy by that time.

The Board also arranged for a significant financial grant from the Astor Family Foundation to be used to promote Anna's ideas, and instructed Emma to notify Anna and Ben that the Board wanted to develop a demonstration model in Missouri.

Emma indicated to Anna that she was willing to wait to start the program until Anna took a sabbatical from teaching during the spring semester of the coming school-year, when her pregnancy would preclude her from being in the classroom anyway. She offered her a lucrative annual stipend for the next five years, more than triple her salary at Jadwin. Emma wanted to make it as difficult as possible for her to say no. She knew that if they hooked Anna, Ben would come along for the ride. That strategy was effective.

Anna, Ben and Zach returned for the Brace memorial in October and, as expected, were a highlight of the ceremonies, although Anna didn't speak publicly due to her pregnancy. But Zachary Lough held the audience of over 5,000 people mesmerized as he described the conditions of the orphanage where he spent the first five years of his life, his experiences on the orphan train and his adoration for the girl and family who saved his life. He received a standing ovation when he finished.

Ben and Anna, watching him speak, realized that he was even more exceptional than even they had ever imagined. To them, he was just Zach, but to everyone else in that crowded memorial hall, this youth carried a mantle of future greatness.

Also attending the memorial that day was Ira Hyde, a former member of Congress from the state of Missouri. He was the father of 13-year-old Arthur M. Hyde, who accompanied his dad that day and met, Ben and Zach. The elder Hyde was in New York on business and had brought his son along to see the big city. They happened to read in the New York Times about the memorial event that would feature young speakers from Missouri, so, on a whim, they attended.

Young Arthur Hyde was no slouch himself. He would ultimately be in the public eye as well, becoming the Governor of Missouri in 1921. But on that particular day, he was just a gangly youth with stars in his eyes. The star that nearly blinded him was Anna McDonald. When Anna spoke to him, he thought she was the most beautiful woman he'd ever seen. In later years, after he became good friends with both the McDonalds and Zach, he laughingly told Ben, "Your wife was my first real crush and I have idolized her ever since!" Ben smiled and told him that he had good taste.

He and his father—primarily his father, since Arthur was struck speechless—congratulated Anna, Ben and Zach on their amazing histories. In the future, Arthur Hyde would ask Anna to help him frame a strong vision for services for Missouri's children and families.

Emma held her three young celebrities in New York for a day beyond the ceremony to talk about the new Missouri monitoring project, patterned almost exactly after Anna's original suggestions. Anna viewed her involvement in the project as temporary, but would eventually realize that this was not to be the case. While she would have mourned had she known it at the time, Anna McDonald's days as the regular teacher in the one-room schoolhouse in Jadwin were all but over.

Chapter 11

By the winter of 1890, Charlie had given the company a new name, Missouri Hardwoods, Inc., and Christian Gunther was busily reshaping its timber harvesting and sawmilling operations. In late November, Christian decided to go down to Shannon County to spend a couple of days with Jim Lane, who was reportedly having trouble handling a new guy he'd hired.

When Christian arrived at Jim's logging site, no work was being done. Jim was sitting on a stump with his mules standing beside him, and something was definitely wrong. Jim's clothes were torn and he was nursing the makings of a black eye and a large bruise on his left cheek. There was also dried blood on his nose. He was hunched over, obviously in some pain. Nobody else was around.

"What happened, Jim?"

"That damn Hoak Beasley finally crossed the line and beat the hell outa me, that's what happened! He'd been gittin more belligerent by the day, intimidatin my boys and sassin back at me. I warned him privately a number of times about his attitude, but he just sneered and laughed in my face."

"He came saunterin in this afternoon. By the smell of him, he'd been drinkin and feelin his oats. He lit into me as soon as he got here—embarrassed me in front of my boys. I tried to fire him. He laughed in my face and said that warn't happenin."

"I'd been careful with him before, but he pushed the wrong button today and I lost my head. I went after him. He reminded me with his fists that I'm not the man I used to be, and that he's a lot stronger man than I ever was."

"After showin me up, he laughed and hopped on the wagon we'd loaded this afternoon. Said he was headed to the mill. Told me he'd see me tomorrow so's I could apologize and hire him back. Said he'd take his good old time about gittin in, too, and that there'd be some changes around here so's I'd be more respectful of a hard-workin man like him. He said it was time for me to hang it up—that he'd be takin over."

"He cowed me, Christian! I just sent my boys home a few minutes ago. I didn't know what else to do. I think I've lost em. They won't respect me no more. Hell, I won't respect me no more! I'm too old and worn out to handle this job! I just pretended that warn't true till today." Jim looked down at the ground, disgusted.

Christian put his hand on Jim's shoulder. "Okay, let's think this through a little, Jim. I get how you feel right now, but you're not in position to make decisions about the future until the dust settles. I heard that Beasley is a big man physically and that all he knows is bullying. He's probably been getting under your craw ever since you hired him and so you finally lost it. Anybody would. It was a mistake to play into his hand, but that doesn't mean that you're washed up as a logging boss. You're still the best we've got, by a long stretch. How many men do you know over age 50 still leading a crew and working beside them in the woods every day?"

"Beasley presents a different challenge than you've faced. He'd have done the same to you whether you were thirty or seventy. I know you've been thinking about getting out of the woods and this feels like the time to go, but I guarantee you, it's not. You'll do that when it's right, not because some big dumb hulk drove you out. How bad are you hurt?"

"Aw, not that bad; I got sore ribs and a face that'll heal. It's my pride and my reputation I'm concerned with. I'm not so sure the damage can be fixed there. It feels real bad to me right now."

Christian nodded. "Yea, well this doesn't affect your reputation with me or the boys. You've already earned our respect for all the good years you put in. The boys know what Beasley's like. Your pride's important, but that's just a matter of perspective. Did you really expect to win a fight with a guy almost 30 years younger and eight inches taller, with a longer reach and fifty pounds heavier? Hoak isn't the better man; he's just the bigger, younger man. When it comes to managing a timber crew, he wouldn't have a clue and couldn't do it if his life depended on it. Do I need to get you to a doctor?"

"Hell no! I've had mules do me more damage than this. I'll be fine. I just need to go home and nurse my pride a little. I ain't drank in years, but I may do a little a that tonight. I'll tell ya though, Charlie's offer to move me to sawmillin looks right attractive to me now. But I admit that I hate lettin my boys down like this. I know they count on me. I don't want em to think that I'm walkin out on em."

"You don't need to do that, Jim. If you did, then I'd even be disappointed in you. We can fix this, and easier than you think. As for you transferring to a mill, we can choose somebody for you to train to take your place. This time next year, this incident will be long forgotten and you'll be able to leave the woods on your own terms, if you still choose to do that."

"I promise you that your boys haven't lost respect for you, Jim. They'll loathe Beasley for what he did and are ashamed of themselves for not helping you. I'm going to find Hoak and let him know that I'm backing you."

"And by the way, I think your guy Mullins might not be a bad successor if he had some training. He's been with you awhile, and he's still young and has some time left in the woods. He knows the ropes and he's steady with the boys and good with the animals. He'd probably have stepped up already if you'd let him. I think you can make him a good timber boss if you set your mind to it. We'll talk more about that later. How much of a head start does Beasley have?"

"An hour maybe; but be real careful of him Christian. He's a big, fast, mean dude."

Christian nodded. "Thanks, Jim, I'll be careful. I've dealt with his kind before. You can make it home okay, right?"

"Sure, no problem there; thanks, I feel a little better now."

Christian had already mounted his horse. He looked down at Jim. "You're a good man, Jim Lane, and you've been a strong friend to Charlie and his dad. You've nothing to thank me for. You didn't deserve what you got today. We'll make sure it doesn't happen again. I'll see Beasley and get the logs to the mill if he hasn't done it already."

It took less than a half-hour for Christian to catch up to the wagon on the rough logging road. His saddle horse had a smooth, fast gait and Beasley hadn't made good time. Christian guessed that he'd stopped to drink frequently along the way. He sighted the wagon and reined in his horse. The draft horses were standing at ease, still hitched to the wagon, and he didn't see Beasley anywhere near the wagon.

The horses had obviously been standing there for some time. They'd pulled the wagon into a bit of a ditch at the side of the road as they reached for tufts of grass and tender leaves on the low-hanging branches. Beasley must have left the wagon in a hurry. He hadn't bothered to tie the horses. Christian wondered what had distracted him.

He got off his horse and tied him to the wagon. There was an open gallon jug on the driver's seat, reeking of cheap whiskey. He saw Hoak's big footprints leading down a side-trail. He took the team's lead rope and tied the horses to a sapling. Then he followed the footprints, wondering what Beasley was up to. It didn't take him long to find out.

Up ahead, the path crossed a steep hollow and then climbed to a ridge. Just below the top of that ridge, Christian saw and heard Beasley arguing with two people. One had white hair and was obviously old. The other appeared to be a woman.

As Christian began to move toward them, he saw Beasley strike the old man and knock him to the ground. The old man rolled a few feet and lay prone. Beasley walked down and kicked him hard in the stomach. The old man let out a short grunting sound but said nothing. Christian moved faster, crossing the hollow, proceeding stealthily from tree to tree at the edges of the path.

As he drew near, he saw that the other person was, in fact, a woman in a dress and ragged jacket. She had long ebony hair tied in braids. She'd picked up a thick, dead limb about three feet in length. Beasley, still focused on the old man on the ground, had his back turned to her. She approached him quietly, and then, with all the force she could muster, smashed her makeshift club against Beasley's back. It splintered into little pieces. He only staggered a little with the blow.

Christian was still twenty feet away and downhill from Beasley and the girl. He knew he couldn't reach them before Beasley reacted. He moved into the middle of the pathway just above a steep drop in the path that had eroded, leaving exposed rocks below. He started to yell at Hoak to distract him, but it was too late.

Beasley cursed and turned on the woman like a cat. He was quick, even if he had been drinking. He backhanded her viciously across the mouth with his right hand, snapping her head around and knocking her off her feet. She lay on the ground, looking up at her assailant, her hand raised to her face as the blood began to flow from her lip.

Beasley laughed when he saw the blood. "Serves you right, squaw! You really think you can hurt me, you red whore! I'll show you how a bitch like you should be treated so she respects a white man." He reached down and yanked her up by her coat as easily if she were a rag doll.

From below, it crossed Christian's mind that Beasley looked monstrous, with arms that bulged under his sleeves and tree limbs for legs. He was well over six feet, probably even taller than Ben McDonald. "Let her go, Beasley."

Hoak startled at the voice and turned his head to look back down the path, still holding the woman up until she was nearly dangling in the air. He'd never seen the guy below him and didn't recognize the voice. It irritated him that somebody had come up that close without him noticing.

The stranger had spoken quietly, almost casually, and seemed in no hurry to rush up to interfere. Hoak knew that he had the higher ground. He dropped the girl in a heap and turned around. "Who the hell are you?"

"The name's Christian Gunther. Jim said he fired you, Hoak. I've come to tell you that you're through with the logging crew and you're done here. Leave these people be and start walking."

Beasley strutted down a little closer to Gunther, stopping about ten feet away. His face was red and he was slightly unsteady on his feet. He sneered. "So you're the famous Christian Gunther! The boys told me about you. They thought you was hot shit! They said they'd heard rumors you were out of Nu Yoak City— that you was some kind of gang leader there and a big fighter— somebody not to fool with. And now you've finally come down here to bless us with your presence, huh? I been awaitin a while to meet you, Gunther, just to see fer myself how tough you really be. Too bad the boys ain't here to see me do it."

Christian smiled. "I'll tell them about it Hoak."

Hoak's face froze, but then he guffawed loudly. "No need, Gunther. I'll tell em. You won't be feelin like seein em agin when I git done with you."

Christian hadn't moved from where he stood. "You can still walk, Beasley. You're mostly stupid drunk and unsteady. You probably can't even get down to me without tripping and falling on your ass. You were disrespectful to Jim, and normally I'd hurt you badly for that, not to mention what you just did to that old man and girl. You seem to like picking on old people and women. I'm guessing that's a habit. It usually is for a coward. You should listen to what the boys said and get out while you can."

144

He smiled up at Hoak. "Now, just tell these folks you're deeply sorry for being such an asshole, and I'll give Jim your apologies tomorrow. I'll see to it that you're paid what the company owes you. I'll even let you go without pressing charges against you."

Christian's face turned hard. "But, if you're thinking about taking me on, Hoak—and I know you're stupid enough to be thinking that—it'll be a mistake that you might not live to regret. I'm not Jim, or that elderly gentleman or girl up there. You're done here. Go crawl into your hole and sober up. We're done talking. Leave if you've got enough brains left to do it."

Hoak spat down toward Christian. "You don't know who you're dealin with city boy! You may've been cock-a-the-walk back where you came from, but we grow'm bigger down here than the scrawny-assed street boys you played with. It'll be you that's feelin the pain when we're done, and then I'll let you watch me take care of these dirty Injuns. I'm thinkin about takin a little pleasure with that pretty little squaw over there. It'll be good fer you to watch how a real Missouri man tames a woman. If yer not hurt too bad when I'm done, I might even let you have seconds. We could even become buds if you put up a decent fight aforehand."

"I don't play seconds to scum like you Beasley. I have better taste in choosing my friends. You'll not be bothering the old man and girl again."

Hoak's face turned purple. He decided that he was done talking with this uppity, smartass son of a bitch. He didn't look like much from where Hoak stood. "You think you can dance, hotshot? Then let's dance!" He made his move.

Christian let him come. The path was slippery with loose rocks and slick clay. Hoak was building up speed with his big body. Christian wasn't sure he'd make it down to him without falling, but he did.

At the last second, just as Hoak was about to barrel into him, Christian crouched low and in a single motion, jammed his left arm between Hoak's legs and lifted him up into the air and over his head.

Hoak was shocked to find himself soaring through the air. He looked to see where he would come down and realized it would be a rough landing. The path dropped off steeply, and he'd be skidding down a steep slope on exposed rocks. He wondered if Gunther had actually planned it that way. Surely not!

He tried to break his fall, instinctively reaching out to protect his face. He succeeded in that but at a high cost. He landed first on his hands, jamming his wrists back painfully and slicing away the skin from his palms all the way to his elbows. Then his knees hit and he felt his pants tear. He cursed as he landed, skidding at least ten feet down the sloping path until his momentum slowed.

He lay there for a second, dazed, and then remembered that he was in a fight. He tried to get his feet under him but his butt was uphill and it was awkward. He had reached a half crouch when a flashing motion appeared in his peripheral vision on his right. He felt a powerful, hammer-like blow to the back of his neck just above his shoulder. It sent him down again into the sharp rocks, and further down the path.

The pain from the rocks and gravel began to set in. On this fall, his face had smashed directly into the gravel and rocks. His eyes began to sting and his vision became blurred. He tried to get up again, slower this time, looking around as he did, expecting another attack. He was right.

Again, Gunther was beside him, ready to strike. Hoak decided to roll left; but before he could, he felt a fierce tug on his hair that jerked his head back violently, his body following in an awkward, painful arc. He saw another blow coming through his blurred vision, but he was powerless to stop it. Christian's knuckles slammed into the big man's throat, squarely on the Adam's apple. Hoak's windpipe constricted and he began to make a strange gurgling sound.

Christian continued to pull Hoak's head back, more slowly now, until his feet were pinned under his legs, his upper body arched backward until his head hit rock. Christian let go of Hoak's hair and drove his fist into the bridge of Hoak's nose. Hoak saw stars and heard a loud ringing sound in his ears. He was laid out like a chicken for the kill and there was absolutely nothing he could do about it. He stopped struggling and raised his right arm toward Christian for mercy. It was a mistake.

Christian calmly took hold of Hoak's wrist with his right hand and placed his left hand behind Hoak's elbow. For a second Hoak thought Christian was trying to help him up. But then he saw Christian's eyes focus on Hoak's right arm.

Hoak tried to yell, "No!" but he didn't have time.

Christian suddenly kneeled, to put his leg below Hoak's arm. Then with massive force, he slammed Hoak's forearm down unto the bent leg. Hoak watched it all happened, unable to do anything to stop it. He felt muscle and cartilage give way in his elbow. He yelled in surprise, and then the pain came. His yell ended in a long scream.

Gunther let go of Hoak's arm, now bent backward at a strange angle. Hoak reached over with his left hand to try to pull the arm up to his body to protect it, but it was too painful and he left off reaching for it. He looked up at Christian in time to see the boot coming toward the side of his face. He felt the bones in his cheek give way and tasted the warm, salty liquid in his mouth. His head fell back on the path and he resigned himself to his death. The woods and sky above him were swirling.

It was such an odd thing. He hadn't even hit this guy once! Never in his lifetime had he been in a fight where he hadn't landed blows. Usually, it took only one. He'd never lost—never even come close to losing. But here he was, lying on a rock-strewn path with no help likely from anywhere, his body screaming with pain—and he'd never even touched the guy.

He was certain that he was going to die. It made him feel weak and nauseated. The ringing sound was still loud in his ears. He decided it would just be good to have it over. That would end the pain. Gunther would kill him; he knew that. He knew it because that's what he'd do if he were Gunther.

The boys had been right. Gunther was dangerous. He hadn't shown any inclination for mercy, even when Hoak was clearly incapacitated and helpless. Gunther had just kept attacking. That was the signature of a killer. Hoak knew that to be true because he was one too. He'd always enjoyed hurting living things, either people or animals, inflicting as much pain as he could before finishing them off. It occurred to him that he and the man about to kill him were cut from the same cloth. But it didn't make him feel better about what was going to happen next.

He felt his hair being tugged again, this time with less force, commanding him to sit up. Then the boot came again, smashing into his ribs. He felt something give way in his chest. He vomited whiskey. Gunther let go of him and stepped back to let Hoak puke between his legs. The pain of the broken ribs didn't allow him to lean over far enough, so he vomited in his own lap.

Finally, Christian spoke. It seemed odd to Hoak that the bastard's voice never changed its inflection. But Hoak could see the intense hatred on Gunther's face and in those cold grey eyes. "Now, Beasley, you should feel lucky today. I should kill you. I'd like to. The world would be better for it. But that would probably raise too many questions. So I'm gonna leave you here and take care of the people you just molested. I'll be sure to tell the boys that your day wasn't entirely lost—that you were able to beat up a woman and an old man before I got to you."

He paused, staring down at Beasley. Hoak knew Gunther was struggling with himself not to finish him off. Christian's voice turned colder, sending shivers down Hoak's spine. "Now listen carefully, Beasley, before I put you out. If you ever come back to cause trouble for my company, any kind of trouble at all, I'll hunt you down. Or if I find that you've done serious damage to that old man or girl up there, you're done; somebody will eventually find your rotting body off in the woods near here."

"If I let you live, your body should eventually heal, but I know you won't forget this day. Any little excuse I can find in the future, Hoak, just any at all, will bring me back to you. That's what I'll be looking forward to."

Hoak stared at Gunther through watering eyes that begged for mercy. He realized that it was probably just like his own victims had looked at him before he killed them. He'd seen the fear in their eyes that he now felt, and for the first time in his life, he empathized with them. It was such an awful, helpless feeling. It filled him with humiliation and dread. He released his bladder.

He needed to communicate to Gunther somehow. He tried, but could produce only a gurgling sound from his throat. He wanted to tell Gunther that he understood what he was feeling—that if Gunther would spare him, he'd leave and never cause him trouble. But he couldn't form the words. That was the last thing he remembered thinking before Gunther's knee smashed into the side of his head, sending him into blessed darkness.

Christian gathered himself and remembered that he was being watched. He turned toward the two people above him. They were staring down with guarded eyes. He assumed that he'd see fear or revulsion, but their faces were impassive.

The old man was sitting up. That was a good sign. Christian saw great dignity on that aged face. He glanced at the woman standing beside the old man. She stood erect, looking taller on the uphill slope than she probably was. Her skin was bronze, but lighter and smoother than the old man's.

She was young. Except for the cut on the lip, her face was flawless—thin, with high cheekbones, and luminous brown eyes that stared at him without blinking. No fear in those eyes. Odd, given what had just happened to her and what she'd just seen. Her body was very thin—he guessed thinner than it should be. She held his gaze.

He started up the path toward them. She didn't back away, remaining beside the old man. Christian reached them and spoke quietly, wondering if they spoke English. "Did he hurt either of you badly?"

She looked down at the old man. "I think his ankle may be broken, but I'm not hurt." Her voice had a strange melodious sound with a slight sing-song accent that he couldn't quite place. She obviously had excellent command of English.

He looked more closely at her mouth. Her lip had burst open and was swelling. "You're brave, but I'm sure that lip hurts. Where do you live? I'll help you get him home."

He saw a slight flicker of concern cross her face. "It isn't necessary. I will find a branch that he can lean on and take him home. We must not bother you further."

Christian smiled. "It's no bother. I'm sorry you were attacked by one of my company's men and for the violence you just witnessed. I insist on helping you home. It's the least I can do. First, though, let's see if we can splint his ankle."

Christian took out his pocket knife and searched for a straight sapling. He found a young cedar, about two inches in diameter. It would make a good splint, flexible and light. He whittled at its base until he broke it off, and then whittled again about three feet up on the trunk. When he finished cutting the length, he found a rock and used it to tap the blade of his knife down through the center of the cedar. It split easily. The blade was strong with a flat back, allowing him to hammer it down through the heart of the wood.

As he worked, he saw the woman turn away and heard the sound of cloth ripping. When she turned back, she held a strand of her dress, which she ripped again into four thin lengths for tying the splint. He couldn't help but notice the long, shapely leg showing through the torn area of the dress, but it didn't seem to concern her.

He went over where the old man sat, watching them both closely as they were making the splints and ties. He nodded at Christian and moved his leg out toward him. Christian placed the splints on each side of the leg, with the bottom of the splints level with the soles of the old man's moccasin. As Christian held them in place, the woman quickly tied the splints onto the leg a few inches above the ankle, at the calf, and above his knee. Her motions were smooth and efficient and she knew how to tie a good knot.

Christian took the fourth, wider piece of the cloth and ran it under the old man's foot, spreading the cloth to its full width. He fastened one end of the cloth to the tie that she had circled around the calf. He carefully pulled the cloth tight, watching the old man's face, and then, to help brace the ankle, tied the other end to the other side of same tie circling the old man's calf.

The expression on the old man's face never changed. If he was in pain, he didn't show it. Christian glanced at the woman and nodded. She returned his glance and then looked down at the splint. "You will move easier now, Grandfather."

He smiled and thanked her.

The old man reached up to Christian, who helped him rise and balance. Again, there was no expression of pain on the old man's face, although Christian knew the movement had to hurt. The old man spoke. "I'm James Ridge and this is my granddaughter, Susanna. We're honored to meet you and appreciate your help. Thank you for taking care of that man. I feared we would have a very bad time with him. You are a strong warrior. And your name is Christian. That is a good name."

Christian shifted over to the old man's left side. "Thank you, Mr. Ridge. Now put your arm around my shoulder." Christian was surprised to find that the old man was taller than he was. He placed his right arm around the old man's waist. The woman moved to her grandfather's right side to help support him. They began to move slowly up the trail, allowing James to become accustomed to his splint. He leaned on Christian's shoulder and was soon moving in rhythmic fashion, placing very little weight on his injured foot. There was sweat on his forehead, but his face was stoic.

They traversed the path about 500 yards to where it began to run parallel with the ridge, but on the opposite side. Christian halted and set the man down to rest on a stump. Once James was settled, he spoke. "What is your company?"

"It's called Missouri Hardwoods. The primary owner is Charlie Schafer, from Gladden. My friend Ben McDonald and I each own a small part as well."

"We know of your company. You recently bought this land?"

"Yes, we're cutting off the timber and then we'll eventually sell it."

He saw the old man glance at the girl, but neither said anything. After a few seconds, Christian said. "Are you ready to go again?"

The old man nodded and they proceeded. After a few minutes, they came upon a faint side path. She motioned that they should take it. The going got tougher, with lots of intruding limbs and bushes. Shortly after they turned onto it, Christian saw an old hunting cabin below them about 200 yards ahead. It sat on a little knoll, halfway down the ridge with a sloping meadow below it.

The cabin was small—probably no more than fifteen feet long. It had a thick wooden door with heavy crossbeams. Beside the door was a small shuttered window. A lean-to was attached to the cabin's west side, likely a shelter for horses. A rough stone fireplace was attached to the cabin's east side. The roof sagged badly and the cedar shingles were very old with lots of gray-green lichen. Christian could hear water running over rocks below the cabin in the meadow below.

They entered the cabin. It had a single room with a beamed and boarded ceiling, covering about three quarters of the cabin's main area. A ladder ran up through the opening near the east wall to an attic. The fireplace had a grate in its firebox and a thick metal hook hanging down for a cooking pot. There was a rusty metal poker leaning against the hearth and an armload of broken kindling piled next to it.

A sitting bench that doubled as a single bed was built onto the side of the cabin wall opposite the fireplace. There was a rustic table at the end of the bench that could be moved in front of it for eating. There was no other furniture. The bench's thin bedding was covered with a blanket. Surprisingly, the cabin was relatively warm.

Christian helped lower Mr. Ridge onto the bench. Susanna went to the fireplace and added a few pieces of wood to stoke the coals. Christian glanced at the pile of wood. "You'll need more wood. Do you have an axe?" She shook her head no.

"Ah, well I'll gather more kindling and bring it in." He walked outside to the woods and began to break dead saplings. When he had an arm load, he brought it in. He did that four times. By then the fire was building and the cabin was toasty.

He saw her pour water from an old, dented bucket into the cooking pot. She took some small leaves from a pocket in her dress and put them into the pot. She then went outside. He could hear her rummaging around at the side of the cabin where the lean-to stood.

The old man had closed his eyes and was near sleep. Christian took the opportunity to look around more closely. There was a sack in the corner that looked like it held clothing. There were three roughly carved wooden plates and spoons, along with a couple of tin cans on the table. These people had very few possessions. He saw no food anywhere inside the cabin.

The girl came in quietly. She carried a small, skinned animal without a head that he guessed to be a young rabbit. She carried it to the pot and placed it in carefully to avoid being splashed by the water that had already heated to a boil. "If you have time to join us, we would be honored to share supper with you."

He hesitated a moment, thinking he should be going. Beasley would probably have regained consciousness by now and gotten back to the wagon. If so, the odds were high that Christian would no longer have a saddle horse. And he was sure that there wasn't enough meat on that small carcass to satiate the hunger of any one of them, much less three. She stared at him, awaiting an answer. He couldn't insult her by saying no, so he nodded. "Thank you; that would be nice."

When the meat was boiled and falling off the bones, she took it out with two forked sticks and laid it on some large leaves at the edge of the hearth. After it had cooled, she separated one of the larger back legs from the carcass and gingerly handed it to him. She pulled off a small front leg for herself. "If you don't mind, I'll keep the remainder and the broth for my grandfather. He'll need his strength to mend."

"Of course, that's fine." He tore off a little meat and ate it as slowly as possible. When finished, he said. "I have to go now, but I'll be back tomorrow to see how he is."

"That isn't necessary. I can take care of him."

"It's no bother. I'll be coming back by this way again anyway."

"She hesitated and then spoke cautiously. "Will you be coming alone?"

"Yes. I'll be alone."

He saw a flicker of relief pass across her face. She walked to the door with him. "Thank you, Mr. Gunther for all you did today."

"It was no problem. I'm just glad I came when I did. Again, I'm sorry for what Beasley did to you and your grandfather, and I'm sorry you had to witness the fight."

She wanted to tell him that the fight didn't disturb her, but she feared he might misunderstand, so she just nodded and watched as he walked up the narrow path and out of sight.

Chapter 12

Daylight waned as Christian moved quickly up the main path toward the log road. He hoped he'd find Hoak still passed out on the pathway, but wasn't surprised when he didn't. Then he hoped he'd find all three horses when he got back to the logging road, but that wasn't the case either. His smooth-gaited saddle horse that Charlie had given him as a birthday gift was gone.

The wagon and draft horses were still there. He walked around the wagon to see if Hoak had sabotaged it. He'd tried. The chains and their ratchet binders holding the logs in place had been loosened, but Hoak's injuries had prevented him from pulling out the side stakes.

He'd also tried to unhitch the horses but hadn't fully succeeded getting that done either. Christian pulled the ratchet handles back down to tighten the load and made sure that the horses were properly hitched. He loosened the lead rope and climbed onto the wagon, slapping the reins to get the horses moving. They were stiff from standing so long and pulled grudgingly against the weight of the wagon. But once moving, they sped up, anxious to get to the mill and then on to their stalls to be fed.

Christian wanted to get there quickly too. He'd heard that Beasley had family living only a mile or so from the mill. He feared an ambush if Beasley had made it home and rounded up reinforcements. On the other hand, if Beasley headed straight for a doctor, as Christian hoped, an ambush was unlikely this quickly.

He reached the mill without incident. No one was there at that late hour. He unloaded the logs and headed for Jim Lane's house to stable the horses and consult with Jim about the next day. He also needed to borrow a saddle horse.

Jim was home and glad to see him. He'd grown increasingly anxious after repeatedly going to the mill and not finding Christian or the team. Christian seemed to be no worse for wear. "Did you catch up with em?"

"Yes, but unfortunately he'd run across an old man and his granddaughter on the logging road and was assaulting them on a path leading to their cabin. I reminded him he was fired and sent him on his way, but he'd already injured the old man and backhanded the woman."

"Which old man was that?"

"James Ridge and his granddaughter Susanna."

"You mean that old Injun guy?"

Christian nodded.

"Sad story there. Charlie bought the acreage from the Simmons boys after their dad died. They sold the land off quick at a discounted price and took the money and run for better pastures. Simmons had owned it forever, at least as long as I remember. I don't know how he got it exactly. Charlie'd tried to buy it numerous times before from old man Simmons hisself, and at a better price than the boys finally asked for it, but the old man always refused to sell."

"He must'a had a soft heart for James Ridge and his family. There was an old homestead on the place—not a bad old house actually. Simmons and his family lived in it when his kids were young, before he built his fancy house around 1840. I was too young then to remember anything about why Simmons took the Injun family in, but I heard my folks talking about the big stir it caused."

"Ridge's pa died just after the family'd come to the area and so Simmons let James and his family live on the old homestead. I don't know what they'd a'done otherwise. Nobody'd give Ridge a job to take care of his family because he was an Injun and all."

"I don't know exactly how Simmons met the Injun family. That kind'a seemed to be hush-hush among the Simmons people. Some say the Ridges migrated over from somewheres east when James was real young—probably still in his teens. His wife was brand new then, but she got old and died not too long ago. They'd been in that homestead since I could remember until the boys sold out to Charlie."

"Young Ridge and his wife had a son after they got here. I don't know why they didn't go on west like all the other Injuns did. There was a lot of prejudice agin em here. Still is. Some said the boy and his young wife was real sickly when they got here, just like their pap, but they managed to survive."

"James may've had more kids than just the boy, I don't know, but only the boy growed up. When the boy was at marryin age, Ridge sent him out to Oklahoma among his own people to find a wife. He sure as shootin wouldn't get any white girl from here to marry him."

"We all figured the boy would stay out there and maybe call them out to him, but a little later he came back with a squaw—a right pretty young thing. A couple a years later, they had the baby, but the mother had a hard pregnancy and died givin birth. That caused a stir, too. From what I was told, they'd asked for

159

help from doctors around here and all the way to Salem, but none would come to treat her."

"Then, a little later, Ridge's boy got shot by somebody while he was fishin on the Jacks Fork. It was cold-blooded murder. He was killed at close range with a shotgun blast to the back. They found the body in the boat after it'd floated on down the river. They pulled him out and took him to Ridge and his wife. Nobody ever found out who did it. Old James is all the family the girl's got left now, as fer as I know."

"They avoid white people as much as they can. People ain't been nice to em here. Merchants would never sell em much of anything. Simmons bought what they needed and took it out to em while he was alive."

"James kept up the homestead and helped old man Simmons with his bigger place. There was a pretty good sized orchard on the homestead property and a new one that Simmons planted at his place. The old one apparently hadn't been kept up before Ridge came. James brought it back to life. Simmons made some money off both of em."

"It was always a sore point with the Simmons boys that their pa didn't run Ridge and his family off. They made it clear to everbody they knew that they thought he was too soft. They're among the people down here who think Injuns and blacks are all the same—not quite human—and not as good as white people, no matter how poor or cussed those white people might be. But fer as long as Simmons lived, the Ridges had a home."

"The week after their dad died, the Simmons boys evicted old James and his family. That was about a year ago. I hear tell that the old squaw died a few weeks later, although I didn't hear it from James hisself. They'd disappeared by that time. When the Simmons boys kicked em out, they did it fast—just rode up and threw em to the wolves—without given em time to get anythin out except just a few clothes and such."

"The Simmons family'd come out of northern Georgia and they thought all Injuns either should be shot or moved outa the way of whites. They've always made Andy Jackson out a hero for seein to it that all those Injuns was pushed out of Tennessee and Georgia. Big bunches of em came through Missouri purtnear here on the way to Oklahoma. I heard tell that a lotta Injuns got sick and died along the way."

"When they kicked James and his family out, the Simmons boys beat the old man a little for good measure and pushed the old squaw and the girl around some, but didn't really hurt em too much—or at least so they thought. That might have contributed to the old woman's death; who knows? Then they made em watch as they set the old homestead afire and burned everythin to the ground. I'm sure that didn't help the ole woman's health any to see that happen. I doubt they had much, but whatever it was, they lost it all. Then they scooted em on their way."

"We all thought it a sad state of affairs, but assumed Ridge would finally head west to be with his kin. Instead, I guess they found that old rotten huntin cabin on the back of the land we're cuttin off. We wouldn't a got over that far for at least six more months. I'd guess it's been a hard living for em there without supplies."

Jim paused, staring out the window, remembering something and looking a little distracted. Then he turned back to Christian. "Now let me git this straight. You found Beasley and just told him he was fired and he up and agreed and left?"

Christian smiled a little. "Well, not exactly. There was a little excitement. But I don't think he'll be around again. If he does, you need to send one of your men and get word to me. I'm going to go over and help the Ridges out for a day or two."

"But you don't look banged up any?"

"No, he didn't hurt me. But he did steal that good horse Charlie gave me while I was helping James and Susanna Ridge get home. I'm sorry, but I need to borrow a saddle horse if I can, and we need to feed and brush down the draft horses. They've been standing in one place way too long today."

"I'll take care of em, and gladly. You can borrow one of my saddle horses. Are you headed back to that cabin tonight yet?"

"No, I'm going back to the mill. I'll sleep in the shack there just in case Beasley's family decides to stir up some trouble. I've got some purchases to make before I go out to the cabin. I doubt that Hoak will be around tomorrow, and maybe not for a good while, if he ever does. If you hear anything about my horse, let me know. It was a good one and a gift from Charlie."

Jim shook his head. "That horse'll be over the line and sold in Arkansas in a couple of days if I don't miss my guess. You can kiss him goodbye. Why don't you think Hoak'll stay true to his threat and come back to harass me and my crew?"

"He won't be up to it for a while. But I don't know about his clan—how spiteful they might be. Have your boys keep an eye out."

"Shore nough. I'll help you saddle up and git you some grub for tonight. I'll git you a blanket, too, to take with you out to the huntin cabin or leave in the shed at the mill—either way. If it's there when we take in the next load, we'll retrieve it."

"Say, you want me to tell the old Injun and the girl to git off the land and move on west?"

Christian stared at Jim a long minute until it made him nervous. He began to feel bad that he'd said anything about it, but he needed to know. "I'm just sayin, if you or Charlie think they'll be trouble, I'll talk to em."

"No thanks. They're allowed to stay there at least through the winter. Then we'll think of something better for them. I'll talk to Charlie and we'll decide about it when we can. Make sure nobody messes with them between now and then." Jim looked a little surprised but nodded his head.

Jim saddled a big, young, raw-boned gelding that he warned was still only half-broke. Christian mounted and headed to the mill. The gelding was still learning to neck rein, but didn't have a mean disposition, so Christian managed him easily. He wasn't nearly as fine as the horse Hoak had taken but he looked like he had stamina and would be good for a while.

Early the next morning, Christian headed over to Eminence. He bought a small crosscut saw and an axe. He also bought a tin wash pan, some dish rags and towels and a good amount of soap, along with a hammer and some nails. He talked the merchant out of a used over-and-under combination twenty gauge shotgun that he'd just traded for. The upper barrel had a .22 rifle bore. He bought an ample supply of ammunition for both barrels of the combination gun. He bought salt and flour, a bag of potatoes and twenty cans of vegetables. That cleaned out his cash and he still needed one more thing.

The merchant, who knew Christian from when he'd originally worked with Jim, looked at him, grinning. "You settin up house somewhere around here, Christian?"

"Christian laughed. "Na, but there's a hunting cabin out on the land we're cutting on, and I thought I'd do some hunting when I'm down here on business."

"Well, there's plenty a game, that's for sure. Have fun."

"I'll try to do that. By the way, do you know of anybody around here who has a gentle horse that doesn't mind packing gear. I may use it for my hunting and to carry more items down this way from Salem."

"Well, old Stark's got a little mare that's got a gentle disposition. I think he's used her for such purposes. She's a bit too small for much else and a little sway-backed. He said, the other day, that he didn't have much use for her no more and needed to git rid of her."

"That sounds just about what I'm looking for. Thanks for the tip and the goods. See you next time."

"Yep, be careful out there. There's some lowlifes down this way'd skin you for a dollar if they could."

Christian nodded. "Thanks, Jeb. I'll watch out. Speaking of trouble, have you seen Hoak Beasley yesterday or today?"

"No, haven't seen that worthless son of a gun for over a week."

"Well, thanks again." Christian headed over to try to deal with Joe Stark.

She was, in fact, a little mare—not pretty, but gentle and friendly. Christian agreed to the asking price, which was too much, without haggling, on the condition that Joe would let him bring the money next time he was down that way. Joe knew Christian was good for it, and even if he wasn't, he knew he'd get it from Charlie without fail, so he was glad to make the deal and get the little mare off his hands for a better price than he expected.

Christian packed the goods and laid them across an old saddle that Joe had thrown in, along with the halter, bridle and some grain. He tied the load down. It was a bit awkward on the mare, but she didn't make a fuss or seem to mind. It helped that he gave her a couple of sugar cubes. He put the gun in the sheath on the gelding's saddle and headed out to the cabin, reaching it by mid-morning.

The girl was watchful of any movement along the path and saw him coming long before he reached the cabin. She was standing at the open door when he arrived. He began to unload the supplies and set them in front of the doorway. She looked at the gear cautiously and then helped him unload the remainder. When he was done, he said, "Just a little something that may help while your grandfather is healing."

"It's kind of you."

He shrugged. "My company owes you for the damage our former worker did. How's your grandfather?"

"He's sore and his ankle is swollen and blue, but it may not be broken, only sprained. He can move it."

"I'm glad to hear that. Is it okay if I help you bring the supplies into the cabin?"

She smiled and nodded. He pulled the gun out of the saddle sheath and saw her freeze in place for a second. He apologized. "It's for you. It's an old gun but good for hunting. It's a combination shotgun and small-bore rifle. I brought you some ammunition."

"It is a lot and we have no money."

"That's okay. It's a gift. I'll show you how to use it if you like."

Her face brightened a little and she said. "I know how. We had a gun once but it was lost in a fire."

They moved the items into the cabin. James Ridge greeted him warmly. "Mr. Gunther. It's very good to see you again! You are kind to check on us and bring these things."

"It's the least I could do, Mr. Ridge. If you don't mind I'll go out and show your granddaughter how to use this gun, so don't be alarmed if you hear shooting outside." He and Susanna walked a few yards from the cabin. He noticed that she carried the gun comfortably. She'd been around one at least. They reached the edge of the woods.

"Miss Ridge, this is called a combination gun because it is really two guns in one. It's made by the Merkel Company and is useful for hunting small game. With certain shells, called slugs, it can even bring down a deer if you're a good enough shot. The top barrel's a .22 rifle and the bottom is a 20-gauge shotgun. I'll show you how to use both. If the small game, like a squirrel or rabbit is standing still, the rifle is useful. If it is moving, the shotgun will be better. Which would you like to try first?"

"I'll shoot the rifle first. The rifle we lost was a .22."

She inspected the gun as he showed her how to break open the barrel to load the shells. It clicked shut with a solid sound, seemingly in good shape. Christian had worried that it might be defective and spit powder when fired, but it seemed tight. She looked up at him and he nodded.

"This is the safety. As long as it's to the left, the gun won't fire. On the side here is another lever. That lets you choose either the .22 rifle, by flipping the lever up, or the 20 gauge, down. You probably already know this, but it's good to always keep the safety on until you're ready to shoot." She nodded, smiling brightly.

"You can see that the top barrel is flat and ridged. It's more like a shotgun sight in that way. At the front of the barrel is that small bead, painted gold. Here's how you hold and point the gun. You sight along the top and align the bead on whatever you're shooting."

He handed it to her. "Give it a try. See that bright knot halfway up on that tree over there. Let's see if you can hit it. When you are ready to shoot, pull back this hammer."

She raised the gun comfortably to her shoulder. He stood slightly behind her and watched her right elbow. It was even with the gun and parallel to the ground, just as it should be. She'd been trained to use a gun before. She fired and hit the outer edge of the knot. "Good shooting!" And he meant it. He was surprised she could shoot that well. She broke it open, placed another .22 rifle shell into the upper hole, and snapped it shut. This time, she came within an inch of the center of the notch.

"Wow!"

She turned and laughed at him for the first time. "I've shot many times before."

He nodded and smiled back. "You want to try the 20-gauge?"

"Yes, I have never fired a shotgun."

"Okay, this type of shell that you'll shoot first has a number six load. That refers to the size of the shot in the shell. They're a bunch of small round metal balls and they scatter in a pattern. That's why it's easier to hit moving game. It'd be particularly good for big birds, like turkeys. It requires quite a bit more powder than a .22 rifle shell, so it'll kick back against your shoulder when you shoot. Hold it tight against your shoulder and aim it just like you did the .22 rifle."

She aimed, and let out a small exclamation as she pulled the trigger and the gun kicked. They went over to the knot. There were pellet marks all over the knot and six inches around it. Her look of surprise turned to elation. "Oh, I see the pattern. I understand why it's better for game that moves!"

"Okay, it's obvious that you don't need my training. You already shoot as well or better than me. We'll shoot one more type of shell. It's called a slug, and it's loaded with a lot of powder because it shoots one big ball. Think of it as a very big .22 shell. Now, if you're hunting larger game, like a deer, for instance, you'd use this shell, but you have to be close, maybe twenty steps or so away from an animal. Notice that the shell cover is green and the other shell is red. Hold the gun tightly against your shoulder because it'll kick harder and could bruise you. Also, it'll be louder. Are you ready?"

She looked slightly apprehensive but nodded. She put the shell into the lower chamber, aimed carefully and fired. It kicked her shoulder backward, but she didn't complain. She'd hit the knot again and it no longer existed.

Her eyes were wide as she looked at him. He couldn't help but laugh. She blushed and then began laughing as well. They carried the gun back to the cabin and she jabbered to her grandfather in a language he did not know. Her grandfather laughed and clapped. Then he looked at Christian. "We thank you, Christian. It was very hard to hit the game with the miserable bow and arrows I made. I'm afraid I lost my bow-making skill over the years. We've mostly been kept alive because of the traps that Susanna has built. This will make our lives much easier."

"You're welcome, sir. It was fun to watch your granddaughter shoot. She's very good at it. Now, if you don't mind, I'm going to take the axe and saw to cut some wood. Susanna, let's see if you are a huntress and can scare up some game for a meal."

She smiled and nodded. She picked up the gun and some shells and disappeared out the door. After she left, James looked at Christian. "Thank you, Christian. She has been very sad since my wife died. I haven't seen her smile in a long time."

Christian nodded. "She has a pretty smile. She should do it more often." Then he realized how stupid that sounded under the circumstances and he went outside to the woods. In two hours, there was wood of all sizes along the back of the lean-to.

He'd just carried his last load from the woods when he saw her coming along a pathway in the open meadow below the house. He'd heard only one shot while he was working and it had been the shotgun. He worried that she hadn't been successful. But as she got closer, he saw that she was carrying a large black object. Closer still and he realized that they'd have turkey that night for dinner. She reached the cabin and stared thankfully at the large pile of wood. She smiled and held up the bird.

Christian laughed and nodded. "Congratulations! I guess we'd better heat some water and pluck that bird. I'll make a fire out here and heat the water while you gut it. Do you have a knife?" She pulled out a short butcher knife from a pocket of her dress. "Okay, then! I'll get that water ready."

He cobbled some large stones into a circle and found some dead cedar in his woodpile, splitting chips off for kindling. In no more than 10 minutes, he had a hot fire. He carried water from the spring at the bottom of the meadow to fill the pot. He'd rigged a crossbar system with two stakes with y-shaped branches at their tops, driving the stakes into the ground on each side of the circle of stones. Then he placed a heavy green sapling across the top as a crossbar to hang the pot over the fire. He filled the pot with water and waited for it to heat up.

He silently thanked Bessie, with whom he'd help kill and clean some chickens in the spring. He assumed that de-feathering a turkey would be a similar process, only a bit more difficult. Bessie had stressed that the hotter the water, the easier the task.

When Susanna returned with the gutted turkey, he dipped it

repeatedly into the hot water, creating a strong, pungent smell of wet feathers. He held up the turkey and let the water drain away from the body. He tried to pull some of the feathers out, but they were still too hot to the touch, so he waited. She came over as he held the turkey up and she carefully pulled out the tail feathers. "For arrows," she explained. He nodded. Old habits obviously died hard with her.

He dipped the turkey in the boiling water again and waited for it to cool. The feathers came out easier this time. He repeated the process a few more times before the carcass was clean. He handed her the turkey. "Your turkey, Susanna. It'll take a while to cook. Do you want to cook it over this fire or in the fireplace? We can cut it up if you like, so it'll cook quicker."

"I'd like to cut it up and cook it in the pot if you don't mind. The broth it creates will be very healthy for my grandfather. Do you have time to stay until it is done?"

"Yes, I'll sleep in the shed with the horses tonight. There are a few more things I'd like to do tomorrow before I head back. I'll cut some cedar and see if I can make you a corral attached to the lean-to so you can keep the mare close at night."

"The mare?"

"Yes, the little pack horse I brought. I'm leaving her here in case you need to take your grandfather somewhere. She's gentle and easy to manage. I think she'd also skid small logs for you if you wanted her to. I saw an old horse collar and a harness in the lean-to that somebody left. If we take it up a little and clean it, it'll fit her good enough for light work. It'll be easier if you pull small logs to the cabin before you cut them up. I'll make saw horses for you in the morning while I'm doing the corral."

She was still stuck on the horse. "You're leaving us a horse?"

He grinned at her. "Yep, a cowgirl has to have a horse, you know."

She looked thoughtful. "I can take my grandfather riding if he can get up on the horse. He'll like that."

"With you helping him, I think you can get him on the mare. She's small and real gentle. She'll be patient with him while he's mounting. We can try it tomorrow if you like."

She turned away for a second and looked out on the meadow. He saw her rub the back of her sleeve across her eyes. She gathered herself and turned back to him. "You will not sleep in the lean-to tonight. You will sleep in the attic and I will sleep downstairs with my grandfather."

He hesitated and then shrugged. "Okay, thanks. I guess it'll be warmer that way."

She nodded and went off to cut up the turkey for the first good meal that she and her grandfather had experienced in a long time. There would be potatoes, beans, biscuits and turkey. It was like Christmas again!

Earlier that day Christian had hobbled the horses and turned them loose in the meadow. He'd been careful because he didn't know if either horse had been hobbled before. The gelding was skittish at first, so he stayed near and talked to him until the horse put his head down and began to graze. The little mare must have been hobbled before. She was calm and made no fuss. He'd glanced at them occasionally during the day. They had wandered only as far as the spring at the lower end of the meadow to drink, then turned back and grazed in the high meadow near the house.

Late that afternoon, he took a little feed and went to retrieve them. They smelled the grain and came willingly. Even the gelding had learned how to move around in his hobble. Christian fed each a handful, took their hobbles off and led them to the shed to close them in. They'd become quite comfortable with each other. The gelding laid his head across the top of the mare's neck and they settled in for the night.

At daylight the next morning, Christian quietly made his way down the attic ladder, but she was already up and the fire was going. She'd warmed the leftover biscuits and heated the pieces of turkey and some broth. She opened a couple of biscuits and dipped out a larger piece of turkey to place it on top of the bread. Then she ladled enough broth to soak the biscuits. She handed him the plate. It smelled good. He smiled and thanked her. She'd also made coffee, an incredible luxury for her and her grandfather that Christian had brought, along with the other supplies.

Christian worked hard all morning cutting cedar poles and dragging them up to the lean-to. By noon, he had fifty of them, each about 12 feet long. He laid the poles in an overlapping "v" shape to create a rough corral about 20 feet in diameter, attaching the two ends of the corral to the lean-to with some of the nails he'd brought. He used the axe, which had a single bit and a flat head, to drive four posts at the midpoint of the corral to allow him to make a gate. He debarked the cross poles so they'd slide easily. When he finished, he inspected his work and was pleased with it.

Susanna came out frequently during the day to watch the progress. She came up beside him now. "It's nice. I like the gate."

He smiled. "Thank you. The fence is not too high, but the mare won't try to get out. On bad days, you can keep her around the lean-to, but she can still get a little exercise in the corral. You can leave the lean-to gate open at night and just put her in the corral. She'll go into the lean-to when she feels like it."

"Let's go get the horses so I can show you how to hobble the mare when you want to let her out of the corral, so she won't wander. I doubt that you'll have to do that for long. I brought a 20 pound sack of feed. Take a handful out with you each time you go to get her. Before long, she'll be at the corral waiting for it in the evening. When she does, you don't need to hobble her. She'll stay nearby."

Susanna nodded. During the day, she'd cut part of the turkey into strips and built a slow fire in the pit Christian had made for her. She had the luxury of plentiful wood now. She had built up a large bed of hot coals and hung the meat over the cross pole to dry and smoke the turkey strips, turning them every half-hour. She'd worked all morning to dry the extra meat, which she'd ultimately hang at the far end of the attic, where it was cooler.

They ate more leftovers for lunch. Christian cut additional wood in the afternoon to replenish the pile. By late afternoon, he realized that he had to go. He said goodbye to James.

Susanna walked with him up the narrow trail until they reached the main path. He turned back to her and pulled a piece of paper from his coat. "I almost forgot this." He handed it to her. "It's a letter on my company's stationary that authorizes you and your grandfather to stay here. I doubt that anyone will challenge you anyway, but if someone does, show them this. I signed it on the bottom. Do you read?"

She smiled. "Yes, both James and I read well. We used to have books, but they were lost in a fire. We read in both English and the Cherokee language."

"The Cherokee have a written language?"

"Yes, we do. It was created by one of our people. The whites called him George Gist. My grandfather knew him as Sequoyah in Tennessee."

"You are Cherokee?"

"Yes, I am of the Principle People."

"Principle People?"

"Yes, there were five eastern tribes. We were considered the Principle People."

"I see. I'm afraid I don't know much of your history."

"No wonder. It is a vanishing history, I think." She placed her hand timidly on his arm and looked up at him. "Thank you, Christian Gunther, for all you did for us."

His body tingled at her touch. "Whatever little I've done, it wasn't enough."

"Will you return?"

"Yes, whenever I get the chance, but it'll be a little while. If you don't mind, keep the gun loaded when you're at home, and carry it with you when you're out. I don't think Beasley will be back, but I don't know that for sure, and there are others like him in the area."

She nodded and smiled. "We will keep it loaded, thanks to you, and we will be okay."

He looked at her a little too long and then cleared his throat. "Okay then. Well, I'll see you when I get down this way again."

She nodded. "We will see you then. Please be careful Christian Gunther."

He smiled. "I always am, Susanna." He turned and walked down the main path. He didn't look back, but he felt her watching him until he was out of sight.

Chapter 13

After checking in with Jim and his crew at the close of their workday, Christian made it back to Gladden late that night. He'd been thinking long and hard on the ride. First thing the next morning, he was in Charlie's office, waiting for him. Charlie came sauntering in about 7:30 a.m. and was startled to see Christian there.

"Well, howdy stranger! I thought you were down Eminence way?"

"I was."

"How is it down there? I heard Jim's been havin some trouble."

"He has—may still have, but I doubt it. I think it's over. We'll have to see. He hired a man named Hoak Beasley…"

Charlie interrupted Christian as he swore, which was very unusual for him. "I told Jim not to hire that boy! I told him it'd be nothing but trouble! He's as stubborn as my dad! So what happened?"

"Hoak behaved for a few weeks and then started to try to take over. He insulted Jim whenever he could and intimidated the men. Things went downhill. I finally heard about it from one of the men who'd come up to Gladden for something. I headed down that way as soon as I could. I got there a little too late. Hoak had beaten Jim up and embarrassed him in front of his men. Jim thought he'd failed and was ready to quit. He's reconsidered now though."

"I went in search for Hoak to back Jim up. When I found him, he was on one of our log roads beating up an old Indian man and his granddaughter. We had a tussle. Hoak was down for a while. I took the old man and his granddaughter to their cabin. When I got back, Hoak had regained consciousness and stolen the horse you gave me. That makes me sick. That was a really good horse and I miss him. I'm riding a borrowed horse from Jim."

"Was the old Injun named James Ridge?"

"Yea, you know him?"

"I met him a couple of times. Very dignified old guy, even if he's as poor as a church mouse. I saw the girl too. She was real purty. They're not treated real good down there by the locals. Last I heard, they was a'livin on the old Simmons homestead."

"Not anymore. When Simmons died and we bought the land, his kids ran them out and burned the house down with everything in it."

Charlie shook his head, disgusted. "Sounds like the Simmons boys. If I'd a'known that, I'd a'made it a condition that they could stay before I bought the place. I'm right sorry to hear about it. I liked old James, but I was in the minority. Where they livin now?"

Christian smiled. "In an old hunting cabin on the back of the land you bought. I gave them a letter on our stationary that they could stay there."

Charlie chuckled. "Good for you! They can stay there until we're done cutting the timber. That'll take a while yet. Will Jim hold up till it's done?"

"Probably not. I'd give him another six to twelve months. You told him that he could move to sawmilling when he was done with the woods. That still hold?"

"Sure. Jim'll do fine at that and he's a good friend. Anytime he's ready to make the change."

"I told him I'd help him pick a timber boss to replace him. He's got a guy working for him named Mullins. With a little training, I think he can take over for Jim. You okay with that?"

"Sure. Mullins is from a solid family. How long you think it'll take to make the switch?"

"Let's give it a year. It could be sooner, but Jim shouldn't let this incident hurry him."

"How do you know Beasley won't make more trouble for him in the meantime?"

"I don't, but he won't do it soon. He won't be up to it for a while."

"You hurt him some?"

"Some."

"Well, I guess he deserved it. I do feel sorry for old James Ridge though. Life hasn't been kind to him and his family. I think I've been to that cabin. It ain't much. I guess it'll buy him some time though. Then, who knows what'll come at him next."

"That's why I came in. I want to talk about that."

179

"Talk away."

"You remember the Coyney place we bought over near Jadwin?"

"Sure, 80 acres. It warn't much land to buy but it had some good old growth timber on it, and it was about all I could afford at the time. I didn't git around to sellin it because I liked the lay of it and it's close to Ben and Anna now, in case they ever decide to expand. I should git rid of it, though. I've got no use for it and Ben don't seem much interested in it. Coyney was a good carpenter in his day and the old house and barn are solid. There used to be a good orchard on it too. And there's a good spring on the land if it was cleaned out."

"I'd like to buy it."

That gave Charlie pause. He looked at Christian. "You wanna buy it? It's a little distant to work every day?"

"Don't plan on living there now. It'd just be an investment."

"And?"

"I'll ask James and Susanna Ridge to live there and keep it up for me."

A big grin crossed Charlie's face. "Is there something you're not tellin me about that girl, Christian?"

Christian's face reddened. "No. It's just a good investment and they deserve a break. It'd be good all around. Now what do you want for the place, Charlie?"

Charlie kept his wicked grin. "Yer bonus for this year."

"Done."

"Done. Why don't you have Bessie and Anna help you clean it up and git it ready for these new caretakers of yers."

Christian grinned. "Good idea, Charlie….and thanks. I know the worth of the property is more than my bonus."

"To you, maybe, but I think I just made a really good deal. If I'm guessin right, I may've just grounded one of my partners into this part of the country fer a spell."

Christian shook his head disgustedly. "You think too much, Charlie. Have your boys draw up the papers so I can become a landowner." He walked out on Charlie before he could harass him anymore.

On Sunday afternoon, Christian went down to visit Anna and Ben. Bessie and Jess were there too. They hadn't seen him in a while and were anxious to catch up. In fact, Anna and Bessie seldom saw him anymore at all except on holidays. Christian didn't attend church, which Bessie was still working on, but hadn't yet broken down his defenses. They caught up on all the news at Jadwin and in Christian's world.

But Bessie could tell that Christian had something else on his mind. She could read Christian better than anybody else. He actually seemed a bit nervous. She thought about just asking him what the matter was, but decided to wait for him to tell them at his own pace. Finally, he came out with it. "Anna, you know anything about the Cherokees?"

Anna was surprised by the question. She thought a bit. "Well, a little. I've read a book about their forced migration out of the Southeastern states. It was sometime in the late 1830s, as I recall. The Cherokees were the strongest of the five Eastern Tribes. Some of them were well educated and even owned plantations and had slaves. But they were pushed out by the whites who wanted their land. Gold was found in the mountains somewhere around Chattanooga, Tennessee shortly before that time. The states, particularly Tennessee and Georgia, were aggressive in confiscating Cherokee land."

"It was a very dark blemish on our history—very shameful. Apparently thousands of the Cherokees died in the migration to Oklahoma. Many of them actually came across Missouri, not far north of here. They called it 'The Trail of Tears'. I have a book in the library upstairs that provides a pretty good historical analysis of the events leading up to the migration."

"May I borrow it?"

"Sure, but why the interest?"

"I met an Indian family down in Shannon County. The man is old now and might have been in the migration. He has a granddaughter. They've been treated badly. His name is James Ridge and hers is Susanna."

"Really? That's interesting. One of the most affluent of the Cherokees was a man named Major Ridge. He had a son named John who also became a major leader. Both he and Major Ridge fought the extradition of the Cherokees until they realized it was hopeless. John Ridge agreed to an extradition treaty and his father supported him and signed it. Both were murdered in Oklahoma by an angry non-treaty faction of Cherokees led by a man named Ross. Let me get the book." She left the room and came back a few minutes later. "Here it is. It's old, but still in good condition. Take it and keep it. It's a sobering account."

Christian turned toward Bessie. "There's something else."

Bessie looked intrigued. "Sure, what is it, Christian?"

Christian's face reddened a little. "I just bought the old Coyney place from Charlie. I'm going to bring James and his granddaughter up to take care of it for me. I'm just buying the place as an investment."

Ben began to grin and Christian's face reddened even more. "How old is this granddaughter, Christian?"

Christian scowled at him. "I don't know. Probably in her early twenties. Why?"

"Oh, no reason. Just curiosity."

"Well, keep your curiosity to yourself, McDonald."

"Oh, absolutely, Gunther. Absolutely! That Coyney place is solid! It won't take much to fix it up. The house and barn were built with care. I guess Charlie held you up on the price?"

Christian grinned. "Well, I'm not sure. He didn't ask for much money but he mumbled something about trapping one of his partners into staying in Missouri. I guess he thinks I won't sell it again."

"The man is smart. We've always known that. It's a good deal all around."

Christian turned to Bessie. "Bessie, I haven't seen the place yet, but Charlie gave me a key. I was wondering if you'd like to go look it over. If all goes well, I'll bring Mr. Ridge and his granddaughter up at Christmas time. Do you think we can get it ready by then?"

Bessie's eyes twinkled. "Well, let's go find out."

So they did. And Christian had no doubt at all that it would be as ready as it could be by Christmas if Bessie Lough was in control.

Chapter 14

Very early on Christmas Eve morning, Christian Gunther left Gladden with a wagon and team, and Jim's gelding tied to the back. He was headed south. Shortly after noon, he made it down to where the timber crew was cutting. Jim was pleased to see him, rushing over to shake his hand and thump him on the back.

Christian gave Jim back his horse and thanked him. "Everything okay, Jim?"

"It's right as rain, Christian! It's all real good."

"Hoak or his family didn't come back to bother you?"

Jim actually snorted as he laughed. "Naw, he's long gone. After his little session with you, he went straight to old doc Matthews to be patched up. Doc said he was a mess; like he'd been in a train wreck, or worse. He told doc that he'd been drinkin too much and fell off a cliff down near where we was a cuttin, and that I'd sent him to get fixed up. Doc was skeptical right off cause he knew I'd come personally with any of my boys who was hurt as bad as he was."

"He said Hoak's face was cut up bad and had gravel and mud stuck in a lot of the cuts. His wrists were sprained. He had badly dislocated right elbow, sore ribs, a broken nose and a fractured jaw. My God, Christian, what you must have done to him, and how I'd like to have been there to see it!"

Christian smiled. "He did a lot of that to himself. I just helped him along a little. What did he do after getting fixed up?"

"I heered he went home and told the same lame story to his folks. He was apparently too embarrassed to tell em the truth. They asked him where the horse'd come from and he told em he'd won it off somebody in a poker game the night before. They probably thought that was fishy, too, since he's not known around these parts to be a good poker player. He stayed home a couple of days but the family said that he was real restless and nervous-like. Then he told em he'd had enough of this miserable place and lit out for Arkansas—or at least that's where he told em he was a'goin. I'm a'feered yer good horse is gone permanent."

"Yea, I was pretty sure of that already, Jim. I guess it's a fair price to pay. How'd the boys take it?"

"Come to find out, they was as delighted as me! They're still laughin about the cliff story. They're callin it the 'Christian cliff'."

Christian chuckled. "So everything's okay down here?"

"Right as rain, thanks to you. And I've been tryin Mullins out some. He's gonna be fine, like you said. It'll take some time till he's ready, but it'll come, and then I'll call in the cards from Charlie and go up to the easier life!"

Christian laughed. "Well, I wouldn't exactly call sawmilling the easy life, but I'll admit it's better than what you do now."

"What's the wagon for, Christian?"

"I'm delivering a few presents to you and the boys from Charlie. There's a big ham for each man and a ham and turkey for you, Jim. I've also got a few things for James Ridge and his granddaughter. I plan to move them up to Jadwin if they'll go."

186

"Really? Well good fer em! I hope they will. It's time they got a break."

"Can a couple of your boys ride their horses down with me to the path that runs to their cabin and widen it a little so I can get the wagon back there?"

"Why, shore! We'll do better than that; we'll all go. I think I'll just send the boys home early after that. It won't take us all long to widen that path and then they can go to their families and Santy Claus."

Christian smiled. "Good idea, Jim. I'll head on down that way and you can catch up when you get things in shape here. Loan me an axe and crosscut and I'll go get started."

Working together, it took the crew only half an hour to widen the main path. They reached the narrower side path to the cabin and widened it quickly as well, working around the bigger timber and cutting out saplings. They were noisy at their work, yelling good-naturedly and jostling one another, excited to be getting off early on Christmas Eve.

Susanna was on the porch watching them, her gun in hand. Christian walked down to greet her. "It's okay, Susanna. The boys are just making the path wide enough to get a wagon in here."

She nodded and kept watching.

When it was done, Jim and the boys wished them a Merry Christmas and headed out, singing Christmas carols as they went. "Is it Christmas?" she asked.

Christian, standing beside her and watching them go, nodded. After they were gone, he went in to greet James.

He didn't unload the wagon that night; but very early the next morning, before daylight, he slipped out of the cabin. He thought he'd been quiet, but she was standing just inside the door when he returned. She'd stoked the fire and it cast a flickering light reflecting on the packages he was holding in his arms. He laid them to the side of the fireplace and went out for more. Then he brought in the ham and the rest of the groceries that he'd also brought.

Her hands were over her mouth when he returned with the last load. James was sitting on his bunk, smiling. Christian walked over to the fireplace. "When it's light, we'll open the presents."

She looked at him, and despite trying not to, she began to cry. He took her in his arms and patted her back. James, watching them, said, "Merry Christmas!"

Christian, still holding Susanna, her face hidden against his chest, smiled at James. "Merry Christmas to you, too, James."

On December 26th, Charlie's wagon started north again. Susanna rode proudly up front with Christian in her new dress and coat. James rode on a pallet in the back, attired in his new clothes and a warm coat as well. The path was rough and it was still tricky getting back out to the log road, but they managed. Soon, they turned onto the main road and headed north. Susanna never looked back. There was nothing in the area she'd miss.

By that evening, they were in Jadwin, in the snuggly-built house that was to be their new home, already warmed by the fire that

188

Jess had started in the stove earlier that day. James and Susanna met Bessie and Jess, Ben and Anna, and all the children.

Zach, particularly, was in awe of Susanna and James. He'd read about the Cherokees and had heard that the tribe was comprised of intelligent, charismatic people, with many great warriors among them. He could hardly contain himself. He had a thousand questions for James, who just smiled and said he'd tell them all the story of his homeland and the Trail of Tears someday, but not on Christmas because this was supposed to be a happy day. Christian mentioned that Charlie Schafer was reading the Trail of Tears book now and would be very interested in hearing James' stories when he felt like sharing them.

Bessie and Anna had already cooked a big Christmas meal. It was all nearly overwhelming for Susanna. She was shy at first, but it didn't take long for her to warm to Christian's friends. Before the party broke up that night, she, Anna and Bessie were friends. She hadn't had a woman friend since her grandmother died. She couldn't get over how happy and nice they all were. She'd never been around happy people who had included her as one of them. She caught herself laughing often and realized it had been a very long time since she'd done that.

She glanced at Christian frequently. He smiled at her when he caught her doing it, and she was embarrassed. She had so many feelings about him that she hadn't yet sorted out. She told herself that she really didn't know this man yet—but she did.

Chapter 15

The lumber business got hectic and it was mid-February before
they all could find the time to get together again to hear James'
stories. Charlie had insisted on being there and he'd been
traveling throughout January and needed the first two weeks of
February to catch up before he could join the group. Zach came
down from high school to hear the stories.

They all got together on a Saturday for a noonday potluck dinner.
This time it featured some special Cherokee dishes that Susanna
had made. After they ate and the kitchen was tidied up, they
gathered in the parlor. James Ridge began his stories of the
Cherokees and the Trail of Tears.

"I am of the Principle People, as my father was, and his, and his
before him. You call us the Cherokees. For as long as our
stories were told around our campfires, my tribe lived in the
beautiful mountains of what you call eastern Tennessee and
western North Carolina. But my ancestors hunted across much
of the land that now includes parts of the states of North
Carolina, Tennessee, Georgia and Alabama."

"My tribe occasionally warred with other tribes for protection of
our homelands, for our honor, to steal horses and obtain hostages
for slaves. That was common then among Indian tribes in those
days. We were a strong people among all the tribes. We were
known to have many great warriors. Some, like Major Ridge and
Stand Watie, were even as strong and brave as our friend
Christian here." He smiled and glanced over at Christian. "The
Principle People once lived on a very large area of land. Not all
of us were wealthy, but we were fiercely proud of our heritage."

"Over 200 years ago, the Europeans came. They wanted our

land. At first, there were not so many of them, but more kept coming. There were wars between the Americans and the British. We sided with the British and lost much land when the British were defeated by the Americans."

"Then many more Americans began pushing west, always looking for land. We told them they could not have our land, but that there was plenty of land around for everyone to live in peace. But soon we came to realize that was not true. Too many of them kept coming, and they were greedy for our land to farm and build their towns. We fought them for many years before we realized that they were so many that we could not prevail. There was great bitterness and hatred on both sides, and terrible atrocities occurred."

"We had wise men in our tribe. One of the best was a man named Ridge, born in 1771, who was a distant relative of ours. He realized that the white man was as numerous as the stars in the heavens and that they had knowledge beyond our capabilities. He believed that we had to gain the white man's knowledge or risk losing everything. He particularly wanted the white man's education for our children."

"The only way to obtain the white man's education in those days was to invite their missionaries to come teach us. So we did, and some came. The early ones were the Moravians and then later, the Baptists. They taught us English and math and science, but they also wanted to teach us their religion. Many of us came to believe as they did. Some did not. Major Ridge's wife became a Christian, but Major Ridge did not."

"My own father was taught from his childhood by very skilled missionaries, and he learned quickly. The missionaries believed the Cherokee children were the best to teach because they had a strong interest in learning and carried themselves with dignity. They also liked that we were clean Indians who believed in bathing regularly"...James smiled mischievously..."unlike many Europeans who did not do so in earlier days and often smelled bad to the Cherokee." The audience laughed. "My entire family became Christians of the Baptist faith."

Anna glanced at Bessie, knowing that statement would excite her. She saw a gleam in Bessie's eye.

James continued. "After the wars between the American Colonies and the British, and when your great leader, Washington, became your chief, he was a good friend of the Cherokee. He thought that our tribe should learn to farm and be assimilated into the white culture. We embraced his vision. He sent money, supplies and teachers from his government to us. He especially chose our tribe among the five because we showed the most interest in learning; and already, some of our people could speak and write English fluently, thanks to the missionary schools."

"A number of our people became very successful at agriculture, including Major Ridge, who was perhaps the most successful, as was his son, John. They owned and farmed much land and became very wealthy. They also owned slaves, which was common with both the whites and Cherokees in those days."

"Then your Chief Jefferson came to power and thought differently than Washington. He decided that Indians and white people could not co-exist and suggested that we trade our homelands for lands in the west, where we could return to our life of hunting if we chose, or grow crops if we chose."

"But we told Jefferson that we wanted to keep our own

homelands where the bones of our ancestors lay at rest. He, and your succeeding chiefs, like Monroe and Madison indicated that we had too much land and did not need it all, and that we must give the whites more of it so they would have enough land also."

"We met with each of these chiefs in their time in New York and Washington D.C. Major Ridge, John Ridge, John Ross, James Van and others of our leaders pled our case. Major Ridge and his son John were considered the most eloquent and were highly respected by your chiefs and your Congress."

"We gave up more of our land to live in peace, but still the whites would not be satisfied. There was periodic violence and grave injustices on both sides, but overall we tried to live in harmony. We continued to teach our children the white man's language and increase our skills at agriculture."

"One of your generals, a man named Andrew Jackson, who was from Tennessee, had asked us to fight with him against his enemies, including some other, less civilized Indian tribes. Major Ridge took thousands of Cherokees and fought alongside General Jackson, who lauded him for his courage."

"But when General Jackson became your great chief in Washington, he told us that we must move to the West and give up all our homelands, or they would be taken from us. We appealed to him, reminding him how we had supported him, but he didn't care."

"His people got a few of our Cherokee leaders drunk and promised them guns and booty if they would sign away our homeland. They did and he had the United States Senate ratify it. But when Major Ridge and John heard about it, they went and explained what had happened to the Senators and they nullified the treaty, enraging President Jackson."

"Another of your chiefs came after Jackson. We met with him too, but he was cold to our entreaties and indicated that Georgia and Tennessee would take the land and give us nothing in return if we did not deed all of it over and migrate west."

"We were told that Jackson, now back in Tennessee and sickly, said to leaders in Tennessee and Georgia, 'If you squeeze them hard enough, they will ultimately have no choice but to move'. So, to make it harder for us, each of the states passed laws indicating that Indians could not enter contracts, vote, own land, serve on juries or have other benefits that white citizens had.

"By the late 1830s, John Ridge decided that our cause was hopeless and that we must take whatever land was offered in the west and move there. He told his father this, along with Stand Watie and other of our leaders. Major Ridge said that if he signed such a treaty and gave away the Cherokee land, it would be like signing his own death warrant; but then he came to understand what his son was saying was true and agreed to sign."

"John and Major Ridge, and their supporters, were opposed by another leader of our tribe, named John Ross, and also by the Vann family and its faction. Major Ridge tried to make them understand that it was hopeless to hold out, but John Ross and his people still blindly opposed any land swap, saying that ancient Cherokee law required that if a man gave up Cherokee land, he must die."

"In 1838 the federal government finally decided that it was time to move our tribe. The American General Wool was to guide us. He was our friend and he tried to round us all up gently, without using force. For that reason, he was considered too friendly to the Indians and was replaced with General Scott, who was later famous in your Civil War."

"General Scott was a fair man, but strict, and he began to round us up into large camps for the migration. Some or our wealthier people went by boat, such as Major Ridge and his family, but most of us were to go by land. That was a sad mistake."

"The summer of 1838 was very hot and many of our people become sick with contagious diseases and died after they were rounded up and taken to the camps, particularly the elders and the young children. My mother, father, fiancé and I were among those rounded up. My mother and father became very ill in the camps. We all appealed to General Scott to wait for cooler weather before pushing on and he agreed to do so."

"While we were waiting, John Ross offered to contract with the powers in Washington, D.C. to supervise the Cherokees migration under his direction, instead of being led by the American military. We did not know he was doing this. We would have preferred to be under the protection of General Scott."

"John Ross offered to take the Cherokees to the West at a very low price. The leaders in Washington and General Scott were happy to take him up on the offer. So in late September, we were again put on the march westward. My father and mother continued to be ill from the coughing disease and were very weak. The trip was extremely hard on them."

"My father was a proud and brave man. He had owned over 200 acres of prime land in Tennessee, where he grew tobacco and had great orchards. He had taught me how to care for fruit trees and had told me that I would inherit the orchards someday. He also had many animals. We lived in a large plantation house and all of us children were well-schooled."

"Shortly before that time one of our Cherokee scribes, Sequoyah, had created the Cherokee alphabet. It was patterned after the white man's alphabet but with different symbols that were based on the sounds of our own language. We learned to speak, read and write English, but we also learned to write and read in our own language. We were very proud of that. It preserved many of our traditions and allowed us to communicate better with one another."

"When my father's property was confiscated, he obtained only about one-fifth of the value of his holdings, only $5,000, with which to relocate to lands in Oklahoma; but he hoped that would be enough for a good start there. I do not know why we did not go by boat, which would have been easier, but I think my mother was terribly afraid of the big boats and unknown rivers. We were allowed to take very few possessions with us by land. John Ross had limited the Cherokee to one wagon for every 17 families because of the cheap deal he made with the whites."

"When our first camp moved west, my mother was too sick to travel so we waited there for the next caravan of Cherokee to come through. During that time I married my betrothed, Sarah, who is Susanna's grandmother. My father felt there was no longer any reason for us to wait. Both she and I were allowed to remain with my father and mother to care for them. That was unusual. In most cases, sons had to leave their parents if they could not travel, but my father talked to someone in power about it, and it was so."

"My parents felt better by the time the next migration came through. We began westward travel in October. Soon after, though, it began to rain and become cold. The Ross guides organized the days poorly and failed to protect us adequately from the weather. Because of this, we moved slowly, sometimes only four or five miles a day. Sometimes, when bad weather hit us, we didn't move at all. We just sat in the cold rain or snow and got sicker."

"People began to die. My mother became even sicker. It was early December by the time we came to the Kentucky border. She was running a high fever and coughing up blood. She died just past the border. We buried her in a shallow grave. It was so cold that the ground was frozen and we were too weak to dig a grave of normal depth."

"We had no casket or materials to make one with, so we buried her in her blanket. There was a lot of argument about that blanket. Some people in our party were freezing and wanted it even if it had been used by a very sick woman whose illness would have contaminated it. We were all heartbroken to lose my mother. My father was becoming very ill again too."

"We reached the Ohio River at the Illinois border and had to be ferried across. We heard that we were charged five times the normal fee for crossing, but we had no choice. The Ross people didn't care. They just shrugged and said we'd have to pay the charges if we wanted to cross. I think they may have received money from the ferry boats as a bribe."

"The day before Christmas, we finally reached the Mississippi, on the Illinois side. The land around the ferry crossing was a swamp. Everyone was coughing badly by this time, including my wife Sarah. We had been eating only salt pork and cornmeal for a long time. The meat was gristly and terrible; the cornmeal was soggy. We were becoming weaker by the day. Our older

people were increasingly disoriented. Many of us had open
lesions on our hands and arms from the poor food and our fevers.
It was a very bleak Christmas."

"At the Mississippi River crossing point, we were told that the
ferry was backed up. We also heard the costs of crossing this
ferry were even higher than the price for crossing the Ohio River.
My father still had money. I have no idea how some of the
poorer people paid."

"The weather turned bitterly cold as we waited. There was no
shelter. We were in a frozen swamp along the river for days. I
am surprised that any of us survived. There were burial details
daily. Digging graves was excruciating with our hands and arms
full of sores."

"It took them two weeks to get everyone across the Mississippi.
By then, my father's health was failing badly. We managed to
get a spot for him in one of the wagons and the weather became
milder. We made better time. We were into Missouri and not
that far north of this area when the Ross people discovered that
our name was Ridge and they made their threats. They came to
talk to my father and told him that Major Ridge and his family
were traitors and would die. They asked him if he agreed with
Major Ridge and he said yes, that there was no hope to remain in
our homeland. That made them very angry and they beat him
and threatened all of us with violence. They came by every day
thereafter to harass my father. If they saw that he was riding in
the wagon, they jerked him out and forced him to walk."

"My father was afraid that he would die and leave us to the
mercy of the Ross men. The three of us decided to try to escape.
We left one night and headed south. Late the next day, we were
traveling along a rutted road when a man came by in his wagon.

My father was very near death. I asked the man if he could give us a ride on the wagon. At first he said no, but then he said he would do so for money. My father reached into his money belt and gave the man $20. That man was Mr. Simmons."

"He took us to his house and fed us. He put my father to bed and cared for him after he and my father had talked privately. Two days later my father called me in. He told me that Mr. Simmons would take care of Sarah and me and that we should stay with him. Then he died."

"Mr. Simmons helped bury him. I looked through my father's effects, including the money belt that he always kept with him close at hand. There was only $200 left. Mr. Simmons said I could keep the money. He was kind to us and allowed us to stay in a shed behind his house to keep out of sight. We were still afraid some of the Ross men might come for us. We stayed hidden for a few weeks. Then Mr. Simmons heard that the migration had moved on toward Springfield. Our health finally began to improve."

"Mr. Simmons decided to buy some land to build a new house. He allowed us to stay in the little house he and his family had been living in. There were fruit trees there that had not been kept up. I knew how to maintain an orchard, so I helped Mr. Simmons bring it back to good production and helped him plant an orchard at his new home site. I also worked for him on projects around the homestead or at his new home. In return, he provided the food that we needed and a little money over the years for basic necessities."

"Sometimes I thought about going on to Oklahoma with Sarah to be with my people, but I heard from a Cherokee man traveling back to North Carolina that Major Ridge and John, along with others who supported them, had been murdered by Ross's men, so I feared it was no longer safe for us."

"My son, John, was born in 1846. Sarah and I worried about having children because we had nothing and I couldn't find a job in the area because people were not friendly to us. But God has his ways and we were blessed with a baby boy. I named him John in honor of John Ridge."

"Unfortunately, Mr. Simmons' wife and children never liked us. They believed Mr. Simmons should kick us out and sell the homestead for the money it would bring. Mr. Simmons refused and said we could remain as long as we wished. He knew that we had nowhere to go."

"The years went by and Sarah and I grew older. We sometimes fantasized about traveling on to Oklahoma, but worried that we would still be outcasts there. My son reached his 20s and had no one but us who cared about him. He was lonely and wanted a wife, but no white woman his age would associate with him."

"One day he asked us to borrow our horse and said he was traveling to Oklahoma. We understood and allowed him to go, although we feared we would never see him again. We assumed that if he found a wife, he would stay there."

"He met a wonderful girl there named Alice Watie. Stand Watie was her grandfather. To our surprise, John and Alice came back to Missouri because John was worried about us. John had not been as grateful to Mr. Simmons as Sarah and I, and he did not get along well with Mr. Simmons' children. He felt that Mr. Simmons had somehow taken advantage of us. He had not lived through the Trail of Tears and did not know how close to death we had been when Mr. Simmons saved us."

"In 1869, Susanna was born. She was a wonderful blessing and gave hope for the future to our family. Sadly, Alice died giving birth, which caused our son a great sadness, from which he never recovered. He began to drink, although I do not know where he got the whiskey. He relied on us to take care of Susanna."

"John sought jobs wherever he could. He got a few, including the times he worked with Jim Lane. But the jobs never lasted long. People called him a dirty Injun, even though he was cleaner, and could write and speak English better than most of them. He began to disappear for days at a time, hunting and fishing. He always brought us back what he caught or killed. Then one day, Mr. Simmons came to tell us that John had been shot while fishing on the river. He helped us bury him. It was a very sad day."

"Mr. Simmons recently died and his sons evicted us. They beat us and then, out of spite, burned the homestead we had lived in for so many years, telling us that they couldn't sell it because no one wanted to live where dirty Injuns had lived. They forced us to watch as our possessions burned."

"After that, we went quietly to the cabin in the woods. We were lucky to find it when we did. We had not known what to do and thought we might have to try to walk to Oklahoma. But I knew that Sarah could not make it."

James paused, the emotion evident on his face, then went on. "As you probably know, Sarah died. It's very lonely without her. There are many sad things about that, not the least of which is that she would have been so happy to have met all of you."

"Then Christian came to save us from another evil man and now we are grateful to be here with you. That is our story."

There was rapt silence in the room after he finished. Charlie finally cleared his throat, walked over and put his hand on James' shoulder. "Thank you, Mr. Ridge, for tellin yer story to us. We're lucky to have the chance to get to know you and Susanna. I want you to know that I feel bad about my part in buyin the Simmons land and causin you to be kicked outa yer home. If I'd a'knowed what the Simmons boys was up to, I'd a'put a stop to it."

"And I'm real sorry about Sarah and yer son. I'd like to have met em and have em safe here with us. I'm real honored to learn more about your people, and to meet a man who survived the Trail o Tears. I'm embarrassed at what my people did to yorn."

James looked up at Charlie, that tall, lanky, slump shouldered young man with his sincere eyes. He nodded his appreciation. He was deeply grateful that Susanna was now connected with these families. When his time came, he knew he could now die in peace. He'd been haunted by what would happen to her after he was gone. Now she'd be with these good families and that quiet young warrior who had rescued them. He wasn't sure either Christian or Susanna knew it yet, but he suspected they'd be together a long time. It brought great peace to a grandfather's heart to know that. If ever a white man could be reincarnated as a Cherokee warrior, Christian Gunther would probably be the one.

Chapter 16

On the day after James told his story, Bessie decided that she and Jess needed to invite James and Susanna to church, and she told Jess so. He looked a little taken aback. "Now, Bessie, I got a bad feelin about that. I think we should leave well enough alone a little while and let folks get used to em up here. Remember, James said people didn't cotton to em down Eminence way and I'm not sure they're much more enlightened up here. There's still old people in the Church who talk about a time when their families were threatened by maraudin Injuns, either in this area or in other states they come from. A few of the oldest ones had even lost close relatives through Injun raids. They still talk bad about all Injuns and they may not be willin to give James and Susanna a chance to prove em wrong."

Bessie's eyes sparked a little fire. "Well Jess, they'd be wrong, and I doubt that James and Susanna will try to scalp anyone during the church services. They're as civilized as me and you are, maybe more so." He was a little offended but was hesitant to point that out at that very moment. "And you heard James say that they're Christians. We're invitin them and never you mind about your bad feelin!"

He retreated, but his 'bad feelin' didn't. It would be embarrassing if the membership treated James and Susanna badly, and he was pretty sure that was how it was going to be.

So they went over Saturday evening to pay a visit to James and Susanna for Bessie to extend the invitation. "James and Susanna, we're a hopin that you'll let us pick you up in the mornin to attend worship services with us and introduce you to members of the church."

James looked cautious. "Thank you for the invitation, Bessie. Of course we'd enjoy the opportunity, but do you think it might be a little too soon? Perhaps we should meet a few of your friends more casually and see how comfortable they are around us before we attend your services."

Bessie, the eternal optimist, responded enthusiastically. "Now James, it's time you have a chance to practice your religion again and I know that the members of our church will welcome you with open arms once they get to know you!"

But they didn't. There were audible gasps when James and Susanna walked into the Sunday services, followed by loud whispering, lots of stares and even a little finger pointing from some of the old maids. James and Susanna pretended not to notice. But Bessie did and she was shocked. Her face turned crimson, and then took on a look that Jess could only describe as "her fightin face". Her eyes began to snap and she refused to look at Jess, who was pretty sure that they'd be traveling down their own warpath now.

At the close of the services, the women began to huddle in groups outside the building and whisper. Bessie made a point of dragging Susanna and James around to every one of those groups to introduce them, but some of the families deliberately snubbed her and walked away as she approached, without so much as a goodbye! The preacher, standing at the front door to shake everybody's hand, had halfheartedly welcomed Bessie's guests, but even he was a little too reserved for her liking.

Of course, there were a few members who were warm and friendly, going out of their way to tell James and Susanna how pleased they were that they were there and asking them to come back again. Bessie definitely put them on her Christmas card list, at the same speed as she removed others who'd deliberately shunned her guests.

Jess, guessing what she was thinking, figured that there was at least one tiny bit of good coming out of all this. They'd need to buy a lot fewer Christmas cards next year! It was always a sore point with him—the cost of all those store-bought Christmas cards that she always insisted on mailing—and they'd had an argument about that just last Christmas.

Charlie and Nellie were gracious and tried hard to make James and Susanna feel at ease. And surprisingly, among the friendliest of the churchgoers were Billy Scruggs and his family, all of whom crowded around James and Susanna to shake hands and offer their warm welcome. It was sincere, too. And it wasn't because Billy was drunk that Sunday either—because he wasn't. He just felt empathy with these two strangers who were looked down on by some of the more "righteous" of the brethren of the church.

On the trip home after church, everybody was silent at first. Jess was grateful for that. But then James broke the tension by saying, with a twinkle in his eye, "Thank you Bessie. You were gracious to have invited us, and maybe even a little bit courageous." He grinned. "It's been a long time since I was in a place of worship, and never with a bunch of nice white people."

Bessie sniffed. "Well, some of the members were a little stand-offish, but they'll get over it. We're picking you up every Sunday and Wednesday nights too, if you'd like. They'll warm up once they get to know you better." Her lips were set in a tight line and her eyes were still flashing. She was looking straight ahead and even James and Susannah were nervous about challenging her judgment.

Jess's shoulders slumped. Susanna tried to offer a dignified exit. "You know, Bessie, we could wait a little longer before we go back, just to give the people time to think about it and get a little more accustomed to us. We don't want to cause you and Jess any trouble or offend your friends."

Bessie snapped back a bit too quickly. "Friends huh! They need to remember what Christ's Church is all about. We're a pickin you up next Sunday and we're takin you with us!"

James looked over at Jess and grinned. Susanna looked over at Jess for help. Bessie kept looking straight ahead with an expression that said the war was on and they were going to be her righteous soldiers whether they liked it or not. Jess shrugged and winked at Susanna. She put her hand to her mouth to keep from laughing even though she knew this wasn't going to be funny.

James said, "Well, Bessie, you'd make our best warriors proud. If you want to fight this battle, then we'll be ready for church next Sunday!" It was an old battle for him and he'd seen very few victories in his long lifetime. But he knew that the battle was fresh for her and he doubted if she'd experienced many defeats before. He figured it was a losing cause, but then he'd seldom had allies of the quality of Bessie, and that felt pretty good to him!

Led by Bessie, their fierce champion, they all marched into the church on the next two Sundays with shoulders back, like they owned the place. The battle lines had been clearly drawn. The pro-Bessie forces sat on one side of the aisle and those opposed on the other—which was terribly disruptive for almost every member of the church—except Bessie's family.

Humans, like most animals, are creatures of habit, including the pews where they sat every Sunday morning—especially the pews they sat in every Sunday morning! Now, nearly everybody in the church except Bessie and Jess, along with Anna and Ben, were displaced.

Even Charlie had to move because he and Nellie normally sat on the other side of the aisle. It felt weird in their new locations for both those on the pro and those on the con side of the question. *And Bessie liked that more than anything!* She felt that it was time to shake this church up a little! And by golly, shake it up, she had.

The poor preacher, who'd recently replaced Brad, was beside himself. He stuttered through his sermon like a zombie. He always prided himself at looking into the eyes of the people sitting on both sides of the aisle, making contact with each member in the audience, watching for the snoozers so he could say something witty as they walked out of the building after services, but now he was scared to look either way.

Only about a fourth of the congregation sat in Bessie's army on his right, leaving about three-quarters of the membership to crowd uncomfortably into the pews on the left. Everybody squirmed in their seats like they needed to use the outhouse. So he avoided eye contact with anyone and looked straight down the narrow aisle, trying desperately to remember his prepared sermon, which unfortunately was on compassion and forgiveness—not really relevant subjects for the day.

Thankfully, at the end, when he gave a half-hearted invitation, the song leader, on his own volition, chose to sing only one verse of the hymn asking the poor sinners to come home, and gratefully, nobody came on that day. The closing prayer, traditionally uttered by Brother Leotus Jadwin, the dean of long closing prayers, whose very ancestors had started this church, was mercifully short. In fact, it was the shortest prayer he had ever uttered in his life at the church, and it came out so fast it was like one long, windy word.

"Bewithusinourtravelsandforgiveusoursinstillwemeetagaininyour Son'sholynamewepray.Amen!"

The kids, squirming in those extra tight pews on the right and expecting a ten minute sermonette from Brother Leotus, were so shocked that they almost forgot their solemn duty to escape from the church as fast as possible, running over a couple of crabby old people on the way, to conspire with their friends on how to con their parents into letting them go home with their buddies to spend Sunday afternoon playing together.

It had never occurred to them that the con was on them, since most of the parents were more than happy to trade their rambunctious little angels for a blessed Sunday afternoon respite, while the unlucky parents would get their respite the following week. Parental protocol demanded, however, that this must appear to be a parental sacrifice.

The infamous Jadwin church war continued for three Sundays, finally coming to a head on the fourth week, at which time a *MEETING OF THE MEN* had been announced to follow the Sunday night service.

Now, for those not familiar with rural church politics, suffice it to say that such a meeting was serious stuff! Since it wasn't the usual quarterly business meeting to review the church's meager finances—which was serious stuff in itself—it meant that something was rotten in Denmark—or in this case, Jadwin. No subject was given for the special meeting but everybody in the congregation, even the kids, knew exactly what the topic would be.

The women of the church weren't allowed to attend a men's meeting—hence the name—which was unfortunate, since they widely considered themselves the stronger sex, cerebrally speaking; so all that week they practiced points and counterpoints with the poor soldiers they would send into battle.

Many of the women groomed their men relentlessly, to the point that it might have been considered by some as nagging. But they did it out of the justified fear that their men were prone to compromise too quickly in such crucial matters.

Poor Jess was the one who received the most instruction. Nellie, a gentler spirit, gave her opinion briefly on the salient points to Charlie but otherwise, left him alone, assuming that he wouldn't speak publicly anyway. Anna and Ben discussed it briefly, but it never occurred to her to tell him what to say. All the same, everybody felt the pressure. It was hell week for most of the men of the Jadwin church.

By tradition, the preacher was to start the meeting. He did so with noticeable timidity, indicating that a solution of this magnitude, whatever it might be, would not come from his personal wisdom but from the sound judgment of the elders and deacons of the church. And then he sat down quickly.

Jess was not impressed. He thought, "Way to go, preacher! You're teeterin on a tall fence and afraid to fall either way." He stood to speak, as was his expected duty, since it was his wife that started the ruckus in the first place.

"This all seems to come down to two concerns about James Ridge and his granddaughter attendin church. First, they are Injuns, and somewhere, at some time, some Injuns may have hurt a few of our ancestors. Not James or Susanna, mind you, and maybe not no Cherokees, but some kind of Injuns done such things way in our past. Second, some of us ain't sure that we want certain kinds of people worshipin at our church—such as people who have a different color of skin ..."

Tom Smith had enough of that nonsense. He jumped up and interrupted. "Don't be tryin to make *us* out as prejudiced here, Jess Lough! If your grandma or grandpa had been scalped by heathens, you wouldn't be so high and mighty about sharing a pew with redskins either!"

"And last I heard, we still live in America, the land of the free, and have got a right to decide who we want to worship with. My family and me don't cotton to worshipin with Injuns, and neither does a largest majority of this congregation! I guess you'd even let niggers in here if they talked nice to yor wife!"

Jess almost came over the pews to get to Smith, whom he'd never liked anyway, but Ben jumped up and held his arm until he could control himself. Jess finally sat down, and contented himself with glaring at Smith.

Ben took up the cause. "I know I'm pretty new to the church here, but I remember how warmly you received me and how much I appreciated that. I thought I'd never met a group of people as friendly as you. I understand that losing ancestors in Indian raids could make this hard for some of you, and that you have a right to worship among the people you're comfortable with. But James Ridge, or his family, never harmed anyone."

"James' father was a well-educated man who owned property and farmed in Tennessee. He embraced Christianity, as did James and his wife; maybe of a different denomination than you, but still the same God. They speak and write English better than I can. I'm sure that James' dad planted his fields and prayed for a good harvest, just like you do. They raised their children in the Christian faith and hoped for something better for them, just like you do."

"Among the civilized Indian tribes in the Eastern states, the Cherokee people were considered the most enlightened. They embraced changes to fit into the new order dictated by the white settlers around them and excelled at it. And despite all that, their lands were confiscated by the government for payments that were far below their value. James' family was displaced and forced out unfairly and at great personal loss. "Some of you may have read about that forced march. Some of you, who are older, may have been around when it happened. It was called the Trail of Tears. Some historians say over 2,000 Cherokee died on that march; others even say up to 4,000, mostly old people and children.""

"When the Cherokees came through Missouri in 1838 and 1839, did they commit any atrocities that you heard of? To any Missourian? Did any of you lose any members of your family by the hand of a Cherokee in those days? Over 12,000 of them started this way. While many died before they even got to Missouri, thousands still passed through. And it wasn't the United States army that brought them, either. They were escorted by other Cherokees who were contracted by the federal government to move them to Oklahoma. James Ridge was 16 years old on that march. James" dad and mom were two of the people who died on the march."

"James and his family have lived in Missouri for more than 50 years now. They haven't harmed one soul during that time. If they were a threat to any of us, we would have known it a long time ago."

"These are people just like you and me. They want the same things. They'd like to worship God in peace. They aren't a threat. They have interesting histories and traditions. I believe the members of the church will lose a great opportunity to get to know them by denying their membership." He sat down and all was silent for a few seconds.

Then Mace Thomas got up. "Ben, you painted a pretty picture of the old man and his granddaughter, but I knew of em from down Eminence way, and I knew old Simmons who took care of em, and I'm friends with the Simmons boys who kicked em out. James and his family were moochers. They ain't ambitious. They took handouts all their lives from Simmons. That don't seem to fit your upstanding picture to me."

But even before Mace finished speaking, Charlie Schafer stood up. Now *that* was surprising! Charlie Schafer never spoke publicly in a church meeting. He never led a prayer. He never passed out communion. All of that despite the fact that he was known to be a brilliant businessman and a good boss to a number of the men sitting in the room. So when he stood up, everything got real quiet.

Charlie's voice tended to go too high when he tried to speak in public. He cleared his throat and took his time starting. He was holding his Bible open, like he was going to give a sermon, and he looked down at it as he began to talk.

"Funny thing about old Simmons takin care of James and his family. James' daddy and his family got run off from the caravan of migratin Injuns because one of their relatives, a man named Major Ridge, was unpopular with the Injun group who was leadin the caravan across Missouri."

"This Major Ridge, a widely respected Cherokee leader, who'd negotiated with multiple Presidents and members of the Congress, finally realized just how greedy our good forefathers were when it came to land. Both the federal government and the states of Tennessee, Georgia, and Alabama made it clear they were gonna confiscate the Indian land, no matter what, so Major

Ridge signed the treaty to move, gittin what he could fer his people."

"Another Cherokee man, named Ross, was the enemy of Major Ridge because he felt that Ridge should never agree to the move, even if it meant war. But once Ridge signed the treaty, Ross was shrewd and made a deal with the federal government to move the Cherokees for a fee. It was the Ross men that was a'leadin the caravan that James Ridge and his daddy was on."

Charlie spoke slow, still looking at his bible, almost like he was talking to himself, trying to keep his voice low. "Right at the Missouri border, the Ross boys found out that there was Ridges in their caravan. So they began persecutin em. It got real bad for James' group, in particlur his daddy. They realized they had to get away or die. They escaped from the caravan as it was passin through near here and went south through the backwoods, down toward Eminence. They had no idee where they was a'goin."

"They wound up on a little back road, and lo and behold, who comes by but old man Simmons—young Simmons then— remember it's 1839. They paid him $20 to take em somewheres warm and to bring them food. James' old dad pulled that $20 bill out of a money belt and gave it to Simmons, who'd refused to help em until he saw the $20."

"He hid em in his shed behind his house and fed em. Now, at the time, Simmons wasn't livin in that nice house that he built in 1840. That's certainly a great home—better'n mine and Nellie's now for sure. No, at that time Simmons and his family lived in a little, run down homestead on the land that I eventually bought. They may a'been rentin it, or who knows, squattin maybe. I know all this cause Jim Lane's people knows the Simmons family well and the stories involved, and Jim Lane's purtnear as reliable as daylight."

"Anyways, Simmons takes em in and old Mr. Ridge succumbs to his illness. But before he dies, he tells his 16 year old boy, James, 'Now you stay here with Mr. Simmons. He'll take care of you as long as you need. Don't try to go on to Oklahoma and don't make no noise for a while. Those Ross boys might come lookin and try to kill you if you do.' James stays put just like his daddy told him."

"And by the way, James' daddy was right. The Ross boys killed Major Ridge and his son and some of their allies soon after they all got to Oklahoma; assassinated em in cold blood. It's writ down in history books."

"Something else you need to know about James' old daddy. He was a big farmer in Tennessee. Owned 200 acres, a fine house, lots of animals, had a big orchard, and even had slaves. When the state took everythin, it paid only $5,000 for James' family's holdins, slaves, animals and fine house. It was worth five times that, but James' daddy was glad to git anything he could to start over with in Oklahoma. They probably would have done alright if they'd a made it out there safe."

"As best as I can tell from what I read"—and they all knew Charlie read a lot more than them— "and from James' own story, his daddy had to spend a little money on the trail before makin it to Missouri, but not much. They were gypped at the ferry crossins at both the Ohio and Mississippi rivers and had to pay a lot mor'n any white man ever did, despite how sick they were, but even that was probly less'n $30 dollars apiece."

"The federal government allegedly paid Ross for the food, sech as it was, and the few wagons they had on the caravan. There's lots of speculation in one of the books that I read that they fed the folks on the caravan bad and made off with lots a money. That may be true. Ross built this big mansion when he got to

Oklahoma and was rich the rest of his life. There's a pretty picture of it in a history book that I saw."

"Anyways, back to our little story here. When Simmons gives James his father's e-fects, the money belt has $200 in it. Now James was just a kid at the time and his daddy hadn't involved him much in the finances. James just assumed the rest of the money got lost on the way, or maybe his daddy had to pay more than he knew to keep em alive." Charlie paused, personally contemplating. "Well, maybe he did, but we'll never really know, I guess."

"But now you see, here's where it gits real interestin down Eminence way. Simmons, from all the old timers that Jim Lane ever knowed, was poorer than a three-legged dog. He was livin from hand to mouth and not doing well at all before the Ridges came along. But then, all of a sudden like, within a month after old man Ridge dies, Simmons up and buys mor'n a thousand acres of land down there! It was real good land too. I know cause I bought it a year ago from the Simmons boys. The pine had mostly been cut off it, but the hardwoods were still there. I suspect old man Simmons made a lot a'money off those pine trees over the years. I'm sure he got a lot more out of em than he paid for the land. Pine's real valuable for house buildin, as you know."

"Anyway, I wonder how Simmons, all of a sudden, found the money to buy that land. Then shortly thereafter, he builds that nice big house for his family on a place over by Eminence, and he leaves the two Injun kids over at the old homestead he'd lived on before."

"I had Jim ask around of the old people down around Eminence. Old man Simmons hisself apparently told the story in them days that a long lost relative from the East had left him $4,500. Other than that, the Simmons family wouldn't say much about it. A'course, nobody would've ever thought that he got the money from poor Injuns traipsin across Missouri, now would they?"

Charlie paused a long time, looking down at his Bible. "Well maybe it's true. Maybe he had a rich relative. We all pine for one when times get rough. But people who knowed Simmons was surprised at that story because the only Simmons clan they'd ever heered about was from down Arkansas way, and all of em lived like poor rats, just like old man Simmons had before he struck pay dirt."

"I'll give him this. Simmons kept his word to old Mr. Ridge, despite how unhappy it made his own family. He took care of James and his family pretty good."

"But his boys didn't do so good in that regard after their daddy died. They ran James and his wife and granddaughter—whose daddy had already died mysteriously by gunshot to the back on the Eleven Point River—off'a the old homestead only a week after Simmons was buried. First, though, they burned the homestead James'd lived in for 30 years with everythin they owned in it, makin em watch before scootin em on their way. James' wife, Sarah, died soon after—maybe from old age, maybe from illness—or maybe from the beatin they gave her afore they sent em on their way."

"It's just interestin to me that Simmons helps out a desperate sick Cherokee family, supposedly carryin somewheres around $5,000 from Tennessee, and then there was almost nothing left in the Indian's money belt when he died. And just after that, Simmons buys a lot of land and builds his house."

"Well, good fer him. He was a good Christian man, from what I hear. And wasn't he kind to James and his family for all those years!"

216

Charlie paused a very long time, again looking down at his Bible. The audience cleared their throats and shifted in their seats. They wondered if he was done. He wasn't.

"Now why'd I tell you this story here today? Doesn't really relate to what we're supposed to be solvin, does it? Cause if it did, one of our own—somebody who lived nearby—either took a lot of money that wasn't his, or got real lucky from a timely inheritance, and just happened to help a strugglin Injun family for nearly fifty years outa the kindness in his heart. Could have been one of those things, or two of those things maybe. But I doubt it was all three."

"Maybe we should be at least as kind as Simmons was; don't ya think? Maybe we should take what's left of this Injun family in. Sort of like that Good Samaritan we read about in this here Bible." He held it up and then made like he was going to sit down, but then remembered one more thing.

"Oh, and by the way, just so's you know. Christian Gunther and me is transferrin the title of the old Coyney place over to James and Susanna Ridge. We decided on that cause I think I may've paid the wrong man for some land down Eminence way. So James and Susannah is land owners around here now, if that makes a difference in their desirability to the church."

Charlie finally looked up and stared into the eyes of each and every man in attendance, long and hard. Nobody said anything or wanted to ask him any questions, and for sure, nobody wanted to talk next. Most of them looked down at their laps. A few nodded at Charlie.

All the men guessed that the meeting would be over after Charlie sat down. They wanted it to be over and done with so they could go home to tell the bad news, or the good news, whichever side of the pews they'd been sitting on, to their wives. But it wasn't over. Just as the preacher started to stand up to dismiss them, Billy Scruggs came forward. There were audible groans from the audience.

Billy smiled when he heard the groans and said, "I'm not here to confess tonight boys and I won't keep you long. And just in case you think I'm drunk right now, I'm not." He paused and looked at the audience.

"But I am a drunk.....You know it. My family knows it. And I know it too, just in case you thought otherwise. I wish I weren't, but I am. And I know that when I drink, I sometimes make a fool of myself and shame my family." His face was red and he swallowed hard, then ploughed on.

"Now why am I telling you this tonight? It's because, despite how weak or bad I am, you still keep me and my family as members of your church, don't you. Maybe it's because you feel sorry for me and my family—particularly them. And by the way, I'm very grateful to you for that. I'm grateful for the sake of my family. I suspect you do it mostly because you care for them, and just because you're good people at heart. Good Christian people."

"Now, James and Susanna Ridge have come to join us—and as far as I know, neither of them drink." There was a little nervous laughter in the room. "And in talking with em, I already know they are better educated than most of us in this room." He paused.

"But, of course, their skin's darker than ours, isn't it. That does make a difference, right? It must, because that's about all that's left when you get right down to it. Their skin's a different color than ours. And I do admit, that copper color on them looks much nicer than my pasty-looking white. And I bet James doesn't worry too much about gettin sunburned on the Current when he goes fishing."

"So, you'll fold a drunk and his family in your arms and try not to embarrass them any more than you have to, but you're thinking about denying membership to a good man and woman because their skins are a little darker than ours? Am I sayin that right?" He stared at them, but nobody nodded, or even moved.

"I know I shouldn't remind you of this, but from my research in the Bible commentaries that the preacher's always quotin, that picture over there on the wall of Jesus isn't quite right. Take a close look at it. It's a nice picture—inspiring with the bright light highlighting his head and face. And of course, he's white in the picture, just like us, so that makes it comfortable, right?"

"Well, we've got some Bible scholars here tonight; some a lot more well-read than me. Some of you have your Bible commentaries with you even now, written by scholars that give us a lot of details about the mysteries of God's Word that we might not otherwise know unless we went to a Bible college to study. And we all believe that the Bible's true—every single word of it. Right?"

"Well, the Bible tells us that Jesus' mother, Mary, was a Jew, and that Jesus lineage stretched all the way back to King David, the greatest of the Jewish kings? Now every picture I ever saw of a Jewish man living over there in Judea at that time had darker skin than mine. And in the pictures I see in the journals about that part of the world nowadays, most of the men still have darker skin than mine. And I'm pretty sure that the great King David had darker skin than mine."

"Maybe we'll be more blessed when we invite James and Susanna to join us. You scholars can tell me if I'm wrong, but from what I've read and seen, James' skin is probably a lot closer to Jesus' color than ours. We could point that out to our kids, maybe. I hope we do, because I can't think of one other reason why we shouldn't welcome them into this church. Can you, when it really comes down to it?"

Finally—finally—Billy sat down and the preacher dismissed the meeting quickly before anyone else could take the floor. He didn't want to embarrass them with a vote.

Everybody was real quiet as they left the building.

Later that week, the preacher, making his rounds, stopped by James' and Susanna's house. He told them that if they were interested in attending the church and even becoming members, the elders would welcome them doing so. James politely thanked him and told him they appreciated the invitation more than he would ever know.

After the preacher left, James looked at Susanna in amazement. "What happened?"

Susanna responded quietly, "I don't know, grandfather. Jess came by earlier this week and told me we'd be getting a visit from the preacher that we'd like. When I asked him what he'd say, Jess just got that mischievous grin on his face and said, 'God moves in mysterious ways, Susanna!' That's all I could get from him."

They rode to church that next Sunday with Jess and Bessie, as usual. Bessie walked into the building with her head held high and a spring in her step. All the men were very cordial to James and Susanna ...and some of the women were too. And they all went back to their usual pews in the Jadwin Church of Christ on that Sunday morning.

Chapter 17

It was a little over three months later, on a warm spring day in southern Missouri, when Christian Gunther came into the Jadwin post office to see Billy. They'd met before, but never really talked.

"Hello, Billy. Charlie tells me you know the Current River like the back of your hand and where all the big fish hide. I'm wondering if you'd consider taking me on a fishing trip for a few days. Jess promised me he'd cover at the post office if you're willing."

Billy was surprised and a little nervous at the request. Christian Gunther was mysterious and a little intimidating to him. But Billy was also flattered that Christian had sought him out and that Charlie had told Christian about his fishing skills.

Gunther had already become a bit of a legend in the area. Everyone who knew him said that he was a fine man, but could be dangerous when crossed. Billy didn't know why Christian would ask him to take him down the river. Truth be told, a lot of people in the area, including Charlie himself, knew the upper Current River at least as well as he. But it was all very intriguing, and he really did love to fish!

"If Jess'll cover for me, why not? I'll be glad to take you, Mr. Gunther....but you should be aware that my old boat's pretty leaky and my tent and gear's not the best. I've been meaning to repair em but I've been so busy lately, you know, and I just haven't had the time."

"Well, actually, Billy, I've never gone on a fishing trip before, so I asked Charlie to advise me on a good canoe and gear. I think I have enough gear for both of us. It's down at Schafer's Landing ready to go, so if it's okay with you, we'll just use that. If you can tell me what to get for bait and lures, we should be set. I've also arranged for food to be delivered to us at points along the way if that's okay with you."

That was more than okay with Billy. He was downright delighted, but he tried not to act overly enthusiastic. "Well, I guess that'd be fine, Christian. Maybe I should just bring the liquor."

"Sure, Billy. Whatever you want, but don't worry about bringing any for me. I probably won't drink on the river."

Billy's face fell a little. "Well, I probably shouldn't either, but I may bring a nip or two just to tide me over."

"No problem, Billy. I don't mind either way."

They met at Schafer's Landing the following Friday morning. When Billy saw the canoe and fishing gear he whistled. "Wow, this is top-of-the line stuff! You have to order away to get gear like this. Charlie advised you good!"

"Great, I hoped you'd like it. I know you've been on the river a long time and have probably seen better."

"Well, frankly, Christian, people don't have gear this good around here. That canoe and tent, and those rods and reels are the best out. I've never used anything like this before."

"Then let's go try em out. Just show me what to do and I'll give it my best, Billy."

Billy put Christian at the front of the canoe for better fishing, and because the front man didn't have to know much to handle the rapids. The weather stayed nice and the trip was pleasant. Billy really did have a lot of fishing acumen and they caught some nice trout to eat each day. Christian cooked the fish every evening and did a good job of it.

Christian was quiet and Billy was a chatterer, but the men grew more comfortable with each other as the four day excursion progressed. Every evening, Billy would offer Christian liquor, but Christian always politely declined. Billy drank a little, but not that much. It just didn't seem right when your partner was staying sober.

On the third night out, as Billy poured himself a drink, he said, "You probably know that I drink too much."

Christian nodded. "I've heard you struggle with that."

"I don't mean too. It just sneaks up on me and I feel better when I'm drinkin. Life doesn't seem quite as hard to take when I've had a few drinks, and I feel more confident."

"What makes life hard for you, Billy?"

"Well, frankly, I'm not very good at what I do. I never have been. The only really good thing I ever did was to get Martha to marry me. To this day, I don't know why she did it. She was from a lot better family than me. Maybe she felt sorry for me, I don't know. Then, her brother gave me my postmaster job. I know he did it for Martha. He looks down on me and thinks she's too good for me. He's right, of course."

"At first I drank to bolster my confidence, but then I began to drink for the pleasure of it, and now, when I'm sober, I dislike myself even more because I know I'm addicted to the drink. I'm disappointing Martha, and my kids are old enough for me to embarrass them now. I love her and the kids more than anything and I know I'm making life hard for them. They'd be better off without me, I'm afraid."

Christian remained silent and Billy began to feel embarrassed and wished he hadn't started the conversation. "I shouldn't have brought up all my troubles Christian. You came out here to relax and have some fun. I'm sorry. Let's talk about something else."

"It's okay Billy. I've had friends and family who drank too much. They were good people too, but their goodness got lost in the drink. You ever considered stopping drinking?"

Billy looked mournful. "Yep, I've tried over and over and failed every time. Now I'm afraid to try anymore because I look like a fool when I commit to my family and everybody that I've sworn off the liquor, and then they see me drunk a few days later. I'm a coward, Christian. I should be able to quit, but I can't."

Christian smiled. "I don't see you as a coward, Billy. I heard how you stood up in church for   James and Susanna Ridge. Charlie and Ben said it was one of the bravest things they'd ever seen. Why do you think your wife and kids put up with you?"

"She thought that I was a good man when she married me."

"And now?"

"I don't know how she could with my drinkin."

"You say that you still love her and your kids?"

Billy looked shocked and defensive. "Of course I do! Like I told you, more than anything in the world."

"But you tell me that your drinking hurts and embarrasses them. It looks like you love your drinking more than anything in the world"

Billy's anger flared. "Well yes, but I can't help that!"

"Why not. You're the one doin the drinking, aren't you?"

"I can't stand myself! I'm a failure! That's why I drink. If I didn't drink, I'd want to die!"

"Getting addicted to liquor to forget your troubles isn't hard, Billy. It doesn't take courage to do that. Stopping, and living with who you really are—now that takes some courage. The people around you apparently think a lot more of you than you do of yourself. I wonder who's right. What if you did stop?"

"What do you mean?"

"I mean, how would your family feel about you if you whipped it and stopped? How would you feel about yourself if you could do that?"

"They'd like it, I know. They'd think more of me."

"Yep, I think you're right. Long after you die, they'd probably be still talking about how their dad had the courage to beat the drink and turn himself around for them. I'm guessing they'd help you if you told them that you obviously can't do it alone? You'd have to stop feeling sorry for yourself and think more

225

about your family, I guess."

Billy looked angry again.

"What makes you dislike yourself so much, Billy? From where I stand, you're a nice guy, you married a good wife, you have kids who love you despite your drink, you have a job that you do well enough when you don't drink, and you have a lot of friends who care about you. You even have some influence around here. Most men would take that life anytime. Why is it so hard to accept yourself for who you are instead of who you think you aren't?"

"I don't know, Christian! I don't know."

"Well, give it some thought, Billy. You might just be confused about how you see yourself, although, I admit that it'd take some strong nerve to break your habit."

Billy didn't drink at all on the fourth night. He wanted to, but what Christian said kept recurring in his mind. Throughout the day he kept coming back to one thought. "Christian Gunther thinks I'm ok, and that I was brave to take James Ridge's side! Imagine that! They say that Christian Gunther isn't afraid of anybody or anything, and he said that I had guts!"

When their trip ended, some of the company's men met them and took them and the gear back up to Schafer's Landing. Christian and Billy shook hands as they prepared to leave. "Thanks for spending the time with me, Billy. I really appreciate what you taught me."

Billy's face brightened. "It was my honor to spend the time with you, Christian. Thanks for what you said to me and for letting me use all your terrific gear."

"Well, about that, Billy. I did enjoy the fishing, but I won't have much time to pursue it, I'm afraid. It'd be a shame to see all this good equipment go to waste. I'd like for you to keep it and use it if you don't mind. When we get customers down this way who want to fish, I'll know who to contact to take them out, assuming that you have the time, of course. You can store the gear in our facilities here so it'll not get stolen or damaged, and it'll be out of the weather. Here's a key to the shed."

Billy was floored. "You're giving me all this equipment! Including the canoe?"

Christian nodded.

Billy's emotions overcame him and he had to turn away. As he spoke with his back to Christian, his voice was tremulous. "Thank you, Christian. I'd be glad to take your friends out. And I'll do my best not to disappoint them—or you."

"I'm counting on that Billy." Christian walked away.

Billy watched him go, and thought, "What kind of a man gives away good gear like this!"

But he already knew the answer to his question. A man who rewards his friends for their courage to do the right thing and encourages them to be better than they think they are. That's the kind of man who would do something like this.

Chapter 18

In November 1890, shortly after Ben, Anna and Zachary had returned from the New York City dedication ceremony, Zachary received a letter from Benjamin Waters on very rich-looking stationary of the Bank of New York. He wrote:

Dear Zachary:

It was a distinct pleasure to meet you, Anna and Ben last August, and to visit with you again at the ceremony for the Reverend Brace in October. Each of you has made a lasting impression on all of us fortunate enough to meet you. The Children's Aid Society owes you a great debt for showing the world living evidence of the value of our work.

It was particularly inspiring for me to hear of your interest in pursuing your education in the field of law. I believe you could make a major contribution to any community in which you work, and perhaps on a broader stage of state or national leadership. We'd like to help you attain those goals.

The Bank of New York has a long history of furthering the careers of special young people through our philanthropic BNY Foundation. Normally, we make scholarship awards to students residing in the state of New York. However, since you originated from our city, I asked that the Foundation make an exception and consider you for a full scholarship to support both your secondary and post-secondary academic work, assuming that your secondary school achievements justify it.

I realize that it might be more convenient for you to pursue your secondary work at Salem to be near your family. However, I have taken the liberty of contacting the Acting President of the

University of Missouri, Dr. R. H. Jesse, whom I have known for some time. Dr. Jesse suggests that, in light of your high interest in the field of law, he'd like you to consider coming to the University's Secondary Preparatory School on the Columbia, Missouri campus for your high school years. He may also be able to provide you internship opportunities at the State Capitol in Jefferson City.

He agrees that this will not necessarily commit you to post-secondary work at his institution. Should you excel at the MU Preparatory School, I would like to talk with you after the first semester of your eleventh grade about suitable universities for your post-secondary work. Certainly MU might be one of them, but there may be others as well.

I realize that this will create some hardship in terms of being away from your family, including extra travel costs. Therefore, the BNY Foundation is prepared to offer you a full financial package that includes tuition, room and board on campus, and an ample monthly stipend to cover your incidental costs and travel to and from your home. The details of this offer are described in the attached documents.

The offer begins in the spring semester of 1891. President Jesse suggests that you and your family visit the MU campus in December, where you can meet with him personally, as well as the MU Preparatory School Director and some of its teachers and students.

I realize that this is short notice, but I do believe this course of effort will be valuable for your development. I have every faith that you will excel and make all of us at the Bank of New York deeply proud that we had the opportunity to sponsor you.

Should you choose to accept this offer, please complete the enclosed application forms and return them as soon as possible to the listed address.

Sincerely,

Benjamin Waters

Benjamin Waters,
President and Chief Executive Officer
The Bank of New York

When Zach read the letter, his heart began to race. He ran to show it to Jess and Bessie, and then rushed over to Anna's house to discuss it with her. She, too, was elated and encouraged him to complete the application immediately. Despite having to be away from the family, it was a phenomenal opportunity that he simply couldn't pass up.

He sent in the application papers and received a quick response regarding the requirements to hold the scholarship—primarily good grades, character references from his instructors, and continued exemplary behavior.

He, Jess, Bessie and Anna traveled to Columbia in December to meet with Dr. Jesse and the staff at the MU Preparatory School. Zach took a number of tests to determine the appropriate academic level in which he should begin his work. They told him that he should meet with his advisor as soon as he arrived on campus in early January to be informed of the test results and what they meant.

In January 1891, upon arriving at MU, he was told that he had tested very high, but that due to his age, and a desire not to rush his social development, they recommended that he begin classes at the sophomore level. He was happy to comply. He had assumed he would begin with freshman-level classes.

While Zachary missed his raucous family and the simpler life at Jadwin, the MU environment was highly stimulating for him, both academically and socially. Despite his age, he quickly showed that he could excel in both arenas. He was elected to key posts in student government and was president of the debate club for two of his three years at the school. He was also active in many other social clubs. And of course, he joined the track team and lettered every school year, breaking some of the school's sprint records.

MU's prep school was a good one and it opened a broader world to Zach than he could ever have experienced at Salem. He traveled to Jefferson City, St. Louis and Kansas City as a member of the school's debate team, had frequent opportunities to meet and talk with elected officials from Jefferson City, and excelled in state track championship meets all three years he competed.

He came home on holidays and for a couple of weeks each summer. He cherished this time with his family, but it was apparent to all of them that this young man had outgrown his rural roots and was destined for broader horizons.

Waters kept in regular touch with him and received reports on his progress from Dr. Jesse. All reports offered high praise and optimism about the exceptional talents of young Zachary Lough. Dr. Jesse indicated to Waters that they would love to have Zachary enroll at the University of Missouri for his post-secondary work, but Waters had other ideas.

He discussed them with Zachary over a new phone system that now connected the University of Missouri with the outside world. The sound was a bit scratchy, but it was incredibly exciting for Zach to be able to use this marvelous new communication technology to talk person-to-person with Dr. Waters a thousand miles away.

Waters:

"Hello Zachary. How well can you hear me out in central Missouri?"

Zachary:

"I can hear you pretty well, sir! Wow! It's really exciting to be talking by phone. Can you hear me okay?"

Waters:

"I certainly can. This technology will open many doors in the future. I've been hearing great things about your progress from Dr. Jesse, and I know your work there will be completed soon. Have you thought more about where you want to do your post-secondary work?"

Zachary:

"I've looked at some universities in the Midwest that have good undergraduate and graduate work in law, such as Washington University in St. Louis. And naturally, I like MU, but thought I'd wait until I could obtain additional advice from you."

Waters:

"Well, certainly MU is a good school, and Washington University's even better, but I think you should consider broadening your geographic horizons. I've talked to my friends at Harvard and Yale, here in the East and, upon the Foundation's recommendation, both of them are interested in receiving an application from you. Under the best scenario, I'd recommend that you attend Harvard for your undergraduate degree and then go to Yale Law School. Would you be interested in that combination?"

There was a moment of silence on the other end of the phone and Waters became concerned that they'd lost their connection.

"Zachary, are we still connected?"

Zachary:

"Oh, yes, sorry sir! I was just a little floored with your offer. Obviously I know of those schools but never thought that they might be options for me. I know they're considered the best in the nation, but they're very expensive. I hadn't dared hope for an opportunity like that. But if the Foundation is offering, I'd love to do that."

Waters: (Laughing).

"Well Zachary, we can afford it, and since we're investing in your future and ours, we'd like the best possible opportunity for you. I'll have the folks at Harvard send you an application that your advisors at MU can help you fill out, and then we'll get the process rolling. Good to talk to you Zachary. I look forward to visiting with you personally when you come this way."

Zachary:

"It's great to talk with you, Chairman Waters. Thanks for the advice and for all you've done for me. Sometimes I think I'm living in a dream!"

Waters:

"You're welcome, Zachary. It's no dream. You've already rewarded our trust by the quality of your work thus far, and I know that will only get better as you proceed further in your academic career. Talk to you soon. Goodbye."

And so Zachary Lough, that little, seemingly crippled orphan kid that nobody wanted, went to *both* Harvard and Yale, and as usual, succeeded with honors. Upon graduation from Yale in 1899, he passed his law bar exams and was credentialed in the states of Missouri, New Jersey New York and Massachusetts as a full-fledged attorney at law.

He was slightly tempted to remain on the east coast, but in his heart, he knew where he was called to practice, and that was in Missouri. Waters encouraged him to follow his heart. So he hung out his shingle for the first time in Rolla, Missouri in the fall of 1899. He was all of 21 years old.

Chapter 19

In 1892, Christian Gunther paid a visit to Susanna Ridge and her grandfather at their home in Jadwin. With the help of Anna and Zachary, who was still at the University of Missouri Preparatory School at the time, Christian had read as much as he could about the Cherokee nation and its traditions. He had also spent a lot of time quizzing James.

One intriguing thing he'd learned from James was that a Cherokee man of old could bring a gift of meat and other foodstuffs to the home of the girl he wanted to marry and present it to her parents, asking if they would allow her to cook a meal for him. If the parents approved, they gave the girl the food and asked if she wanted to cook it. If she agreed to do so, it meant that she became betrothed to the suitor. If she demurred, the suitor was rejected. And of course, the parents could simply refuse to give the food to their daughter, deflecting the question before it was asked.

Cherokee culture and traditions gave Cherokee women much more formal power than the white people granted their women in the 18th and early19th centuries. For example, in the old days, the Cherokee woman was the one who owned all the property in a marriage. When children were born, the brothers and cousins of the wife were the ones who provided their education and mentoring.

When Christian and Charlie decided that the family's inheritance had been usurped by Simmons, they had deeded the property and house in Jadwin to Susanna. They had actually intended to deed it to James, assuming that he would leave it to Susanna when he died, but he had insisted that the deed go directly to Susanna immediately. He already had an idea how Susanna's marital relations might eventually turn out.

By the 1890s, times had changed. Neither James, nor Christian knew whether the "cooking of the meal" tradition still held among members of the tribe, now scattered across the United States. And in Susanna's case, she had no parents for the suitor to present the question, and no brothers or cousins to mentor her children should she have them. But Christian still liked the idea that a Cherokee woman was a powerful partner in a marriage, so he decided to honor the ritual.

On that beautiful late-spring day, he brought fresh beef, potatoes, onions, some carrots and green beans, along with a gallon bucket of freshly picked strawberries. He worried that it might not be enough. He surprised himself by becoming nervous.

He presented the food to James in a formal manner and asked him if he would request that Susanna prepare the food. James immediately realized what Christian was up to and a broad grin broke across his face. Christian appreciated the reaction. At least he wouldn't be barred at the door! James called Susanna into the front room and said, "Susanna Ridge, Christian Gunther has presented me this food and requested that I ask you to cook it for him. Are you prepared to do so?"

Susanna, a little confused by the formality, looked at James and Christian quizzically. Was there some kind of joke going on at her expense? But she just smiled and said, "Sure, Christian. I'll be glad to cook for you. Thanks for bringing the food, but you really didn't have to. I could have prepared you something from what we have on hand."

"Are you certain that you want to prepare this meal for me?"

It crossed her mind that he might have been drinking, but he certainly looked sober. "Of course, Christian. I'm always happy to prepare a meal for you. We don't see you enough as it is."

James, who was watching all this with a mischievous look on his face said, "That's not exactly how it works, Granddaughter."

She looked at James, now utterly befuddled. James reminded her. "Think back to the story your grandmother told you about the first time I brought food to be cooked at her house and the question that came with it."

She thought back, trying to remember, wondering what it had to do with Christian's request. Her face held its puzzled expression for long seconds. They waited. She noticed that Christian's face seemed a little redder than usual. Then suddenly, she remembered the story and her look turned to astonishment. The bronze of her face took on a blush. "Ooh!"

She looked at her grandfather and he smiled. She looked over at Christian and he smiled. Then *she* smiled and got her own mischievous look on her face. "Well, actually, I am pretty busy right now." She put her finger to her cheek and looked up at the ceiling, feigning contemplation. She sighed loudly. "Well, Christian, considering that it's *you*, I guess I have time to cook the meal. You two get out of the kitchen and I'll call you when it's prepared."

Christian and James departed— and waited—for what seemed like forever to Christian. James just sat grinning contentedly and occasionally tried to engage Christian in trivial conversation, but Christian was distracted. There were long silences, which Christian was usually comfortable with, but somehow, this time, it was awkward. And of course, James didn't really try to help much. He just sat there grinning, sometimes even closing his eyes, pretending to be napping, obviously enjoying Christian's anxiety.

Susanna bustled around the kitchen like a dervish, seemingly in all directions at once, worried that she was getting nowhere with the meal. Her mind just wasn't working right. She tried to do three things at once and lost track of where she was with each of them. How should she garnish the meat? How should she cook it? Should she cook the vegetables separately or with the meat? What if the meal turned out badly! How would he interpret that? Her hands were shaking and she fumbled and dropped more pans and dishes in an hour than she had in her whole lifetime. She mumbled and chastised herself. "At this rate, you're never gonna get this meal prepared. He'll think you're totally inept!"

All the while, she was trying to get used to the idea. She had avoided allowing herself to think too much about Christian in a romantic way, although she couldn't control her dreams at night. She'd convinced herself that, as a very successful white man, he couldn't afford to marry an Indian woman. He'd be criticized— she wasn't sure by whom—probably everybody—well probably not Bessie, Jess, Ben, Anna, Charlie or Nellie—and certainly not by her grandfather, who she could tell, thought Christian was a reincarnation of his most illustrious warrior ancestors. But there would be others, probably many, who would never approve of a mixed marriage. She wondered what her mother and father would have thought. She wondered if Christian had really thought all this through.

But then she realized that Christian Gunther wouldn't care one whit what others thought. She wasn't sure if that was good or bad. If she married him, would she be hurting him in ways that he didn't foresee or would refuse to acknowledge? Would that make him bitter toward her later?

And beyond all that, Christian Gunther was still an enigma to her. He was always considerate and gentle with her and her grandfather, but he had been brutal with that man Beasley, nearly killing him. She'd watched the fight closely—if it could be called a fight, since it was so one-sided—and she'd seen Christian continue to beat Beasley mercilessly, even after he was clearly defeated and broken. By the expression on his face, Christian really seemed to want to destroy the man. Did he have a predilection toward violence? Would that affect their children if they had any?

Yet, she knew that he was caring, and even passionate, in his own quiet way. But that "quiet way" was not always easy to read. While polite, he sometimes seemed distant. And always, always, he was under control, as if that was his most cherished value. She'd never heard him raise his voice to any man or animal, yet he made many people anxious, as though they wanted to please him, but were afraid they might not, and weren't sure what would happen if they didn't. Yet she never heard or saw him say or do anything deliberately to leave that impression. It just hung in the air, and either he didn't recognize it, or he didn't care.

James, speculating on this one day, said that Christian just felt no need to prove anything to anyone. He believed that was the mark of the great warriors of the past—that quiet self-assurance that drew people to him, even when he didn't ask for the attention. It reminded James of Major Ridge, except that he was a great orator while Christian Gunther shunned the limelight. James suspected that Christian could be eloquent if he desired to do so. He just seemed disinterested in that kind of power.

Christian didn't smile much and perhaps was inclined toward melancholy. He must have a past that caused that, but he'd never told her about it. She'd only heard snippets of his time in New York from Anna and Ben, who obviously worshiped the ground he walked on. Surely their regard for him had to count for something!

The only time she ever saw him let down his guard, even a little, was around Ben, Anna and Zachary, and occasionally Bessie. She'd wanted to talk to Anna about what made him tick but she had felt it could be seen as unseemly to do so. Someone might think she was too interested. She didn't know how he'd feel about it if he were told about her questions. Now, though, she wished she'd asked.

Almost from the first, she could sense that Christian liked her—was attracted to her as a woman—but she never dared believe that he'd consider her as a wife. He was a white man; she was an Indian woman. She had thought it inappropriate to speculate about such things, and he'd never really given her a reason to think he was romantically inclined toward her.

She and James had ultimately come to feel welcomed at the church and she cherished that avenue for experiencing spirituality. But Christian had never shown interest in the church, or talked about his religious beliefs, despite Bessie's best efforts. Bessie had finally given up. Susanna had known that it was futile effort on Bessie's part from the beginning, although she wasn't sure how she knew that. How would she and Christian reconcile their differences in their need for spirituality?

Was he loyal? Yes, of that she was certain. He was incredibly loyal to those he cared about, whether it be Ben and Anna, or her and James. That was important, right?

It had better be, because, even with her uncertainties, she knew that she could never say no to this man, no matter how complicated their lives might be—no matter how much stigma they might face together. There was a greatness about him that drew her like a magnet. And now he was choosing her! She had seen how other single, eligible white women, and even some of the married ones, looked at him. He could have any woman he wanted. But he'd chosen her! She shook her head to clear it and sped up the preparation of the meal.

When she'd done the best she could, she called them to the table. Actually, she was proud of what she'd done. She thought the food and the presentation of it looked appealing. She stood at the foot of the table, waiting for him to say something, or at least to sit down, but he didn't. Instead he walked around to where she stood, with her knees trembling and took her hand. He looked into her eyes and smiled, a twinkle in his eye. "I like this Cherokee tradition. It gives a man an opportunity to see if the woman can cook." He looked over at James. "I assume that if the food's bad, I'd be free to change my mind?"

James snorted. "Well, that would probably be a good modification to our tradition, but I don't recall that option. Once the food passes into the house and the question is addressed, the man's fate is sealed, including that of his stomach. All discretion is with the one being courted. It's all up to Susanna now!"

Christian, still holding Susanna's hand, gave out a heavy sigh and shrugged his shoulders. "Oh well, I guess we'll just have to hope for the best. In that case...." He pulled something from his pocket and dropped to one knee, astonishing her. "We have our traditions, too, Susanna. One of them goes something like this." He looked up into her eyes, serious now, and he took her breath away.

He had held out a small box, covered in white velvet. "Susanna Ridge, will you do me the honor of becoming my wife?" He released her hand and opened the box. She gasped. In it was the most beautiful diamond ring that she'd ever seen. She put her free hand down and touched his hair. She swallowed hard, composed herself, running her sleeve across her eyes. She took a deep breath and then, with all the drama she could muster, said, "Christian Gunther, if the food is acceptable, yes, I believe I will marry you."

He stood and swept her into his arms, kissing her for the first time. She felt faint. Any doubts she might have had evaporated like an morning mist under a warm sun. She returned the kiss with a hunger she had never known. James stood watching, feeling a little awkward—but not very much. What he really felt was an insane desire to give a warrior's whoop and dance around the table, but decided that an old man must set an example and try to be dignified.

Eventually, they all sat down to the food. Christian thought it was the best meal he'd ever eaten and told her so to seal the deal. They would walk their paths together. Later that evening, in the quiet stillness out on the front porch, sitting on the swing, she leaning against his chest and holding his hand, said, "I'm afraid for you Christian. You are a white man and I am an Indian woman. People will despise you for marrying me."

He was quiet for a few seconds, and then replied. "No, I'm just a man and you're just a woman, and the people who see anything different than that will never know either of us—and that will be their loss, not ours."

She squeezed his hand and leaned further into his chest. "You are definitely a man, Christian Gunther, a very special one, and I am the woman who will always love you."

Ben and Charlie heard about the engagement the next day. Charlie looked at Christian drolly and said, "You took long enough. Beats me why a girl that pretty waited around for an ugly cuss like you. I'd begin to think that I'd have to raise the subject with her myself on your behalf to force you to action." He grinned. "She's really somethin, Christian! She sure is! You're a lucky man." He shook Christian's hand and clapped him on the shoulder.

Ben McDonald stood back as Christian received Charlie's accolades. Now he came over and hugged Christian close. He choked up. His best friend had finally found his match! He'd begun to doubt that it would ever happen. "Anna and I have hoped and prayed for a long time that you and Susanna would get engaged, but we know you don't form relationships lightly. You are each very special people, with such unique histories behind you. She's a beautiful, dignified, intelligent woman and I think she may prove to be your equal. Charlie's right though. You were so dang slow about all this that we'd just about given up on you! Congratulations, Christian. You have no idea yet how much of a blessing she'll be to you."

Christian smiled and put his arm around Ben's shoulder. "If our marriage comes anywhere near to the quality of yours and Anna's, we'll be well blessed."

They were married in a small, private ceremony at their little house in Jadwin. There were only a few invited guests. Bessie, the maker of beautiful wedding gowns, made Susanna's. There was never a prettier bride, including the tall, stately young woman who served as Susanna's bridesmaid. James proudly gave her away to the only man he'd ever met that he thought worthy of her. Ben and Charlie stood as Christian's best men.

But the proudest guest in the room that day was the Jadwin Postmaster. He valued that wedding invitation more than any other that he ever received in his lifetime. For years, he proudly mentioned it to anyone who'd listen. After all, he and his family had been the personal guests at the wedding of Mr. and Mrs. Christian Gunther!

After the ceremony, the bride and groom left on their honeymoon, heading to eastern Tennessee, to the Blue Ridge Mountains, and then on into North Carolina to a town called Cherokee. Christian had planned the trip as a surprise for his bride. He wanted her to experience the land of her ancestors and, if possible, to meet some of the remaining members of her tribe who had stayed in their homeland. And while it was an unusual thing to do, he had insisted that James Ridge join them on that trip as their personal guide.

Chapter 20

By the summer of 1895, Ben and Anna's family had grown to
five, with three children, ages 4, 2 and 6 months. The first two
were boys, William—named after Bill Chambers—and Daniel.
The youngest was a girl, named Alanna, meaning "darling child"
in Irish. All were healthy and blessed with intelligence and
quick imaginations. Grandma Bessie and Grandpa Jess were
their favorite caregivers when their mom and dad were busy,
which was often, and Bessie's kids were their great pals and
mentors.

Long ago, Anna had reluctantly given up regular teaching,
although she still substituted when she could. But her main job
was working for the Children's Aid Society, tracking the
progress of the orphan train children and intervening in difficult
family situations when necessary.

Missouri Hardwoods, Inc. was booming, with more orders
requested than could easily be filled, even with the company's
increased productivity. Just as Charlie and Ben anticipated,
hardwood flooring had become the company's cash cow,
followed by the production and sale of high quality lumber.

The company now employed or contracted with over 200
workers and was an increasingly important economic driver in
the area. The company's real estate holdings were also growing,
now to more than 10,000 acres of land at any given time. Charlie
still managed that part of the business.

Jess Lough had become the product transportation manager,
supervising the hauling of lumber and flooring products
throughout Missouri and surrounding states by rail and freight.
Now when the itch hit him to travel, he had no trouble scratching

it. He just hopped on a freight train taking the company's products to St. Louis, Kansas City or even Chicago.

He didn't need to worry about Bessie being left alone with children any more. Even the youngest of their kids were in their teens and actively involved in school, including his daughters, which he finally admitted to Bessie had been a good idea. He could never have afforded their schooling earlier in his life, but now his work at the company provided a comfortable living for his family.

Back in the spring of 1891, with encouragement and funding from Emma Mason, Anna had invited all former Orphan Train children, age 18 and older, to a meeting in Jefferson City to discuss further development of the monitoring system for the children placed in Missouri. Anna advertised the meeting statewide. The turnout that first year was modest—only fifty former orphans—but the meeting was a hit and the enthusiasm was high. The group decided to hold the meeting annually. By the spring of 1892, word had gotten out and 200 former orphan train riders participated in the event. By 1895 that number of attendees was approaching 1000.

The meetings, which had become something of a combined convention and reunion, were primarily dedicated to the implementation of the Missouri orphan monitoring system, but also included presentations on broader child and family issues of the day, such as the need for state child labor laws and how to address child abuse or neglect.

Politicians that were sympathetic to the need for a state-funded system to support the welfare of children were featured speakers at many of these events. By 1895 the conference participants also included orphan adults from surrounding states, coming to see how such events were organized so they could do the same thing in their own states.

Anna continued to manage these annual events, and also led the Society's Missouri Monitoring Program for tracking the children placed in Missouri. Increasingly, she became involved in Missouri legislative actions regarding children and families, helping to champion the passage of Missouri child labor laws and those addressing the prevention of cruelty and unnecessary institutionalization of children.

She was called to New York at least twice yearly to confer with Emma and the Board. She never learned to enjoy these trips, although she knew they were necessary for closer communication. When Ben could get away, he joined her, but the flooring business was expanding rapidly and his time was limited.

Anna frequently wrote editorials on needed changes in children's services. The editorials were published in newspapers throughout Missouri and in other states as well, including the New York Times. On three occasions, she was asked to testify before US Congressional Committees. All this exposure caused her to become widely recognized as an articulate expert in the evolving arena of child welfare.

It was inevitable that she would ultimately bump into Missouri State Senator Percival Webster. When they met, he was civil, but cool. Her notoriety was such that he was careful not to attack her work, but he never warmed to her, or she to him.

This was actually not unusual for Percival—called Percy by his closest friends and his mother. Since his mother was dead and he had no close friends left, he was never addressed by that name anymore. He missed the intimacy a little but was okay with it at this point in his life. He'd come to realize that he preferred admiration from a distance.

Webster was from Sedalia in west-central Missouri. His family was well-connected. His father had been a circuit judge in the Western District of Missouri. His mother was also an attorney, which was unusual for the day. His parents had been busy people in their prime. Little Percy had all he needed to live comfortably and succeed, but he wasn't closely bonded to his parents and didn't really have fond memories of his time together with them.

The Senator was a tall, stately-looking man with a long narrow face, hawk-like nose, a large forehead and a massive shock of unruly black hair, which he personally liked the most about his features. The hair reminded people of Lincoln. He had dark brown eyes that could pierce right through anyone who displeased him. He was not exactly a handsome man but his demeanor and physical presence made up for it.

He was an eloquent orator and brilliant debater, and he had a well-formed sense of self-worth. Those who superficially met him, but didn't really know him, which was almost everyone, admired him greatly. He always reminded them of Father Abe. Those who worked more closely with him were not as inclined toward that analogy. He was not a jokester, as Lincoln had been, and he had a volatile temper, which Lincoln didn't. And his ethics were situational, while Lincoln, politically astute, was always guided by his core principles.

Percival joined the family trade and became an attorney—and a very skilled one. He represented powerful people and corporations, and avoided cases involving the poor and downtrodden unless, of course, he was opposing them.

Webster had high hopes of becoming Missouri's Governor, or if the timing was right, a United States Senator, following in the tradition of other famous Missourians. On rare occasions, he even allowed himself to fantasize about a nationwide office. He knew he was capable of it, but he was careful not to express that sentiment publicly to avoid having people think that he was overreaching.

He embraced his causes carefully to build his name recognition. His "causes" were often ones that would raise the visceral reactions of the average voter, even if not based on facts. He felt a little guilty doing that, but thought it necessary when dealing with the common man. He considered the average Missourian ignorant and in need of direction.

Amazingly, while he seldom, if ever, championed any real cause for the "little man", he had become something of an icon to the average Missourian, a seemingly great spokesman for the things they thought they believed in. Chief among his pet causes was halting the flow of unwanted immigrants into his state.

Webster was no fool. He knew the country had been built by immigrants. Now, however, the average Missourian was in denial of this, or at least they felt the state didn't need any more foreigners pouring into the state to compete for jobs and land. Isolationism was the growing sentiment of the day. So, he didn't bother to discriminate among the various immigrant groups coming into his state. For simplicity, he just opposed them all. And the Children's Aid Society's Orphan Train Program was a perfect target in that regard.

He made his opinion on the Orphan Train program widely

known. New York's outcast urchins were a public menace and should be barred from his or any other state. New York should handle its own problems and not try to pass them off as benevolence. Unfortunately, this Anna McDonald and her friends were a distraction from the reality he was creating, and Percival did so hate distractions to his realities.

Anna tried to avoid him whenever she could. But as the years passed, her data and her eloquence became an increasing thorn in his side. Her rather extensive information regarding the children placed in Missouri, backed by researchers at the Universities of Missouri and Columbia University in New York, had yet to uncover even one incident of a child becoming a public menace to Missouri society.

Despite that fact, Anna grew increasingly uneasy, knowing that it would take only one such case to destroy everything the Society had built through the years. To avoid this, she and her organization of volunteers worked tirelessly to increase the number of children being monitored, far beyond those targeted through Columbia University's random sampling process for her state.

Just one bad apple would be all it would take for men like Webster. Just one horrible crime would erase all the good outcomes that her data had repeatedly affirmed. Anna sometimes lay awake in the middle of the night thinking about what that one awful case might look like and how to avoid it.

Chapter 21

Christian and Susanna Gunther, along with James Ridge, who was still healthy and spry despite his advancing age, found their trip to the Cherokee homelands wonderfully enjoyable and enlightening. James discovered distant relatives, now also elderly, who had avoided the great Cherokee roundups of the late 1830s and were still surviving in their homeland, although struggling to do so. The Gunthers and James Ridge also met other Cherokee families as well.

The land and the people in eastern Tennessee and western North Carolina kept calling them back, especially the beautiful Smoky Mountains. They returned to vacation there each year through 1895. Although Susanna was more than a generation separated from her ancestral homeland, she had an eerie sense of déjà vu every time she returned. In roaming the Blue-Ridge Mountains and their foothills, Susanna and Christian quickly realized the terrible loss her people had felt when forced from this beautiful homeland.

The stories about their forced migration were heartrending. Elderly Cherokees, now James' age or older, recounted story after story of the families they knew who were forced to leave loved ones as the soldiers came unexpectedly to rout them from their homes in 1838. They told each story as though it had occurred only recently.

The soldiers, with orders to find the Cherokees and herd them to the gathering camps quickly, appeared unexpectedly at families' homes and gave them fifteen minutes or so to pack what they could carry to begin the trek to the gathering places. More callous soldiers didn't even give them that, driving them out immediately with their bayonets, some of the family members without shoes on their feet or adequate clothing.

Discussions about a migration of the Cherokee nation had been occurring between Cherokee leaders and leaders in Washington D.C. for many months, but nothing had come of it. There was disagreement among Cherokee leaders whether it would ever really happen. That dulled the Cherokee's sense of urgency about when and how it might occur. When it did, no one ever imagined that it would be carried out so precipitously.

Once the powers in Washington D.C. made the decision, federal and state authorities deliberately kept Cherokee leaders in the dark to minimize the risk of an insurrection. They decided to use the element of surprise to minimize resistance, ordering rapid roundups to the holding camps.

One old Cherokee woman told Christian and Susanna of a young mother whose child had died the night before the soldiers came. The body had been prepared for burial and the funeral arrangements made for the next day. But soldiers came that afternoon and forced the mother from her home by bayonet. The child's body was left behind, unburied.

Elderly grandparents, too frail to be moved, were left where they lay with no one to care for them as their families were forced to leave. A man that they talked to, now old, who had been away on business at the time of the roundups, returned to find that his family had vanished and he never found them again. He cried when he told them the story.

The soldiers refused to allow family pets to be taken. Children cried for days about dogs or ponies left behind. All these stories were over fifty years old, but told by people whose voices would still break with emotion as they related them.

Susanna and Christian also obtained many books and Cherokee poems about events before and after the Trail of Tears, including many from people now living in Oklahoma, written and preserved because of Sequoya's Cherokee alphabet. A few were in English, but most were in Cherokee, which James and Sarah had taught Susanna to read when she was a child. Susanna was now teaching the written language to Christian.

Susanna was deeply troubled by many of those poems and stories. When she related them to Christian, he felt shamed by the greed of his own race—particularly the people in Georgia and Tennessee. He came to detest Andrew Jackson and his betrayal of the people who had respected him and were allies in the battles he fought.

More than fifty years after the Cherokee Roundup, most of the Cherokees who had somehow remained in the eastern states were still impoverished. State governments continued to deprive them of their citizenship rights; they could not enter into contracts with whites; they could not vote or serve on juries. They no longer had a defined geographic homeland. Had they been granted a defined reservation, they would have at least enjoyed some self-rule. And the stigma and disrespect meted out to them by their white neighbors continued to sting.

Despite all that, Christian was still amazed at the demeanor of these beaten-down people. They remained noble and deeply proud of their heritage. They had continued to value the education of their children. They weren't impoverished because they were lazy or unintelligent; they were given no opportunities to prosper.

They bore their oppression with dignity. Most Cherokee people carried themselves differently than most of the people he'd met. In fact, many of the whites living around them appeared rough and uncouth by comparison. Christian kept thinking "Such talent wasted!"

In 1896 he decided to do something about it. He was now well-versed in the workings of the lumber industry. The tall forests in the Carolinas and Tennessee were even more plentiful than in southern Missouri. Shortly after the New Year, he asked Susanna, "What would you think about moving to North Carolina to start a lumber business there?"

She was initially speechless. She stared at him, then, almost in a whisper, said, "You'd be willing to do that?"

"Yes, I think so. There's rich timber there, and there's a bunch of good men who need jobs. My guess is that they'd be excellent workers, and very loyal to a company if respected and treated honorably."

Susanna knew exactly which men he was talking about. "But we'd have to leave our wonderful friends in Jadwin!"

"Yes, and that part saddens me, but we could come back to visit regularly. I'm going to talk to Ben and Charlie and see if they'd agree to finance the startup of a business there for a share in the new company. I'll be surprised if Charlie doesn't jump at the deal. He knows the territory. And since I'll primarily use Cherokee workers, there may be some initial resistance to buying our products. I may need to sell the lumber through Missouri Hardwoods."

"Oh, Christian, if we could go back there and help my people, it would be such a wonderful thing! I'd love to give it a try. If it doesn't work out, we could always come back."

Christian smiled. "Yes, we could. I'll talk to Charlie. We'll be reverse pioneers!"

She laughed and hugged him. "Reverse pioneers, huh? Well, it could be true that we'll be traveling to hostile territory and the white natives there may not be all that happy to see us coming. But I have you to rely on, and you have me, and we'll handle whatever comes our way."

Christian talked to Charlie and Ben that week. After getting over the initial shock of the idea of losing him in Missouri, they became intrigued with the idea. That area of the country had better timberland than Missouri, and they had little doubt that Christian could run a profitable company.

They bought into the venture at 25% equity and Charlie offered $50,000 in start-up capital. That could also allow Missouri Hardwoods, Inc. to expand its own markets throughout the East in concert with Christian's operation. If Christian could overcome the prejudice and sell the products directly, great! If not, Charlie was sure he could market the products through his company.

The Schafers, Loughs and McDonalds all saw them off on a tearful day early in March, 1897. It was made easier by everyone knowing that it wasn't a permanent goodbye. They'd see each other at least annually, if not more frequently. But that night, as Charlie lay in his bed, Nellie knew he felt the loss keenly. "You did the right thing, Charlie. And we'll see them a lot."

"I know, Nellie. And from the time he came, I knowed I'd never be able to hold him here fer good. But I'll really miss him. I've never met a man like him before. He was the best I've ever had and I'll never be able to replace him. He's one of a kind."

By the spring of 1898, the Cherokee Lumber Products, Inc. of North Carolina was operating at full steam. Christian primarily hired Cherokee workers, with only a few whites with specialized expertise that he needed in the mix. As he had suspected, the Cherokee workers turned out to be superb.

Within five years, Christian had opened two more mills and employed four timber crews. The lumber they produced was some of the finest in the country. After a couple of years, Charlie's only problem related to the Cherokee Lumber products was that many of his customers preferred them to the lumber he produced in Southern Missouri.

Charlie decided to specialize, using his own Missouri lumber to make most of the flooring products and Christian's lumber for direct sale. Christian had greater access to the taller pines of the Carolinas, which were of higher quality than the Missouri bull pine. Housing construction materials from Christian's company were shipped throughout Eastern and Midwestern United States.

Charlie encouraged Christian to buy every tract of timber that came on the market in his area. When gasoline engines came into use, they extended that reach. Christian paid good prices for the land and was known to be an ethical businessman.

While land was more expensive in the East than in southern Missouri, the eastern forests were also richer and more productive. And the land resold at a higher value, so the same real estate principles Charlie used, worked there.

But Christian's real estate strategy had an interesting twist. He subdivided the land and sold the parcels to his Cherokee workers, with the deeds of sale carefully constructed to protect their ownership. He did this by personally cosigning each deed to make sure it could not be broken.

He also used his personal wealth to make loans to Cherokee families to build their homes, charging modest interest rates, starting his own little banking industry. In addition, he sold lumber for construction at a discounted price to his Cherokee employees. In all the years that he did this, not one Cherokee family ever defaulted on their payment.

Christian Gunther and his company became widely known for its high-quality products and its philanthropic work with the Cherokees. Christian received job applications from Cherokees from throughout the eastern states because of what he did for his Cherokee workers and their families. He had the most committed and talented workforce in the lumber business, including Charlie's operation in Missouri. Charlie loved to visit Christian's mills and always came away envious of his workers.

Susanna and James flourished back in their ancestral homeland. So did Christian. Three children were born to Christian and Susanna—two girls and a boy. They were attractive, inquisitive and intelligent children, and the apple of their father's eye.

Christian and his family came back to Missouri at least twice a year to transact business, but more importantly, to stay connected with the people in southern Missouri. And at least once a year, Charlie and his family or Ben and his family, took time to vacation with the Gunthers in the beautiful Blue Ridge Mountains.

Christian Gunther's company had become a huge success. He became a wealthy man. In doing so, he raised the boats of his Cherokee workers, his community, and his business partners back in Missouri.

Gradually, Christian came to terms with his own demons that had haunted him since childhood, including his father's suicide, and found personal peace. He had become everything Ben McDonald told Anna Murphy that he could be in that mausoleum in a Hell's Kitchen graveyard so long ago, if just given a chance. They all had.

Chapter 22

Jeremy Laminger had been dropped onto the streets of Hell's Kitchen in 1891 by an alcoholic mother whose line of business didn't allow time for a baby. He was taken to an orphanage on the edge of Hell's Kitchen and eventually placed by the Children's Aid Society in 1896 at age five. His new family, Harry and Carla Beasley, lived in Sedalia, Missouri.

Jeremy's was an unusual placement because Harry and Carla had written directly to the Society in advance through their church to ask for a boy between the ages of 3 to 5 years, saying that, if he was healthy, they'd take him, sight unseen. They sent pictures of themselves and their home. They seemed to be the ideal couple to take in a lost child.

It was a long, scary ride for Jeremy from New York to Sedalia. The train was loud and the people riding it seemed hurried and not very friendly. But he'd been told he had a loving mommy and daddy waiting for him and that gave him the hope he needed to get through the trip.

The Society's sponsor riding with the children on this trip, sometimes seemed more impatient with Jeremy than with the other children, maybe because Jeremy had a hard time focusing his attention for very long on any one thing and he didn't quickly grasp the sponsor's instructions, no matter how hard he tried.

But each time it all got too scary, he pulled out the picture of his new mommy and daddy standing in front of the house he'd live in. He hoped they'd understand him better. After all, they wanted him to come to be part of their family. There was a friendly-looking dog in the picture, sitting on the porch, waiting just for him.

In the first year after arriving in Sedalia, things went reasonably well. His new family treated him nicely, bought him new clothes and enrolled him in school. They quickly found that he was behind the other children in his learning and they helped him try to catch up.

He tried hard but never quite made it. At the end of the school year the principal called Jeremy, Carla and Harry in for a conference and recommended that Jeremy repeat the grade. Harry was deeply embarrassed at Jeremy's failure to advance, and that made Jeremy ashamed. Thereafter, Mr. Beasley became more demanding, criticizing Jeremy frequently, insisting that he pay closer attention at school. Carla wasn't as critical, but she seemed less interested in what he did now.

Four years after he arrived, Harry and Carla's marriage was on the rocks. Jeremy watched them fight with a sinking feeling in his stomach that remained with him even when they weren't fighting. He tried to stay out of the way but they seemed angry all the time and he always seemed to become the target of their wrath. Sometimes the conflict got so bad that Jeremy was afraid that Mr. Beasley might hurt Mrs. Beasley.

He begged them not to fight anymore, telling them he would be better and work harder, but that didn't seem to make any difference. They both turned on him and told him to shut up, that this was not his concern. From then on, when they began their loud arguments, he ran upstairs to his room and pulled a pillow over his ears to block the sound.

Just before Christmas in 1900, Harry and Carla told Jeremy that they had decided not to live together anymore and that they were leaving town. He could not go with either of them. However, they said his "uncle", Simon Beasley, would let Jeremy stay with him for a while if he behaved himself and did some chores.

When they told him that, the sick feeling in his stomach grew worse. He didn't' think that Simon Beasley was a nice man. He'd visited Simon's house before on two occasions. It was a run-down shack with lots of whiskey bottles in the yard and two very mean, mangy-looking dogs who did not like strangers.

Jeremy asked if he could take his dog, Brownie, but Harry said that Brownie had never really been his dog and that he would be going away with Harry when he left. Jeremy begged to go along with Brownie, promising to be extra good, but Harry said he just didn't have time to deal with him anymore and couldn't afford to take him. Jeremy looked at Carla with pleading eyes, but she just shook her head.

They threw his things together and took him to Simon's house that very afternoon. Simon told Harry and Carla not to worry, that the boy would do fine and learn to stand on his own two feet under his tutelage. They gave Simon money that they said was Jeremy's school funds for the coming year, and that they'd try to send more for the following year, but Simon and Jeremy both knew that they wouldn't. Jeremy could tell that they were done with him and would forget him quickly.

Simon Beasley was in his late fifties, but hard drinking and unhealthy habits had made him look much older. He had long, greasy hair that came down to his shoulders and only a few broken teeth left in his head, all of which caused him unmerciful pain when he was sober, so he avoided that whenever possible.

He had a rusty old wheelchair that he'd purchased a few years earlier at a farm sale out of town. He found that he could sit in the chair on street corners and ask for money and get enough to support his habits, with a little left over for food to keep him alive. He'd supplemented that by striking up a relationship with an older widow who was a bit more affluent than him. She invited him over to her house regularly for supper and companionship.

To gain sympathy from the townspeople, Simon was careful to always stay in the chair when in public. At home, he used it to sit in, but he walked around the shack handily, without any signs of disability. He smiled to think that he was pulling one over on all those suckers in town.

Initially many of the townspeople realized that the chair was just a pity prop, but after a couple of years, as he began to look more and more emaciated from his drink, everyone came to believe that he really was a cripple. All except Jeremy. He knew better from first-hand experience.

Simon had taken Jeremy in because of the money Carla and Harry gave him and because he'd planned to put Jeremy to work. At least the boy could earn his keep, and maybe he'd have a little left over to help meet Simon's personal needs.

As soon as Harry and Carla left—without even a goodbye for Jeremy—Simon told him that he would not be going to school again and that he would have to get a job to help pay his way. Jeremy said he didn't know how to get a job. Simon said he'd better figure it out shortly or he'd starve to death. Simon sold Jeremy's extra clothes, his books, toys and other possessions to a pawn broker, getting almost nothing from them, but it did pay for his drinks that week.

Jeremy learned to stay away from the shack as much as possible.

Simon's mean dogs chased and bit him every time he ran through the yard to the gate, or back to the shack. He walked the streets of Sedalia during the day, asking people if they needed him to do any jobs. He was able to run a few errands for some of the merchants. Others, who knew Simon and felt sorry for Jeremy, gave him a little money. He took it all home to Simon, hoping that would please him, but Simon always said that it wasn't enough. He said that if Jeremy wanted a roof over his head and food to eat, he'd need to do better than that.

Jeremy tried harder in the coming months, but couldn't find jobs. If he came home with no money, Simon beat him. He would tower over him and hit him across the back and legs with his cane. Sometimes, after harsh beatings, Jeremy just didn't come home at all; but the nights were often cold and he had no place to go for warmth.

He never tried to return to school. He figured the school people would tell Simon and that would make him angry, with another beating to follow. Anyway, his clothes were now filthy and he was embarrassed to be around people. His shoes began to fall apart so he stuffed them with newspapers, trying to make them warmer, tying strings around them to hold them together.

Some adults on the street asked him, in an accusing way, why he wasn't in school. He said he had to care for his sick uncle and wondered if they had any money they might spare. They just looked at him as though he was a loathsome creature and walked away. Most people didn't talk to him at all. They just stared at him and rushed on by or pretended not to see him, like he wasn't really there.

He turned 11 years old in 1902. No one told him what day it was, but Jeremy saw a calendar in a store window and realized that it was his birthday. It didn't matter. There was no one to celebrate it with him. But still, he couldn't help feeling sad. Even at the orphanage they had remembered his birthdays. Now, no one cared whether he lived or died.

Six more miserable months passed. Simon was becoming increasingly belligerent with Jeremy about his lack of success in earning money. Whenever he saw him, he threatened to turn Jeremy over to the Sedalia police as an incorrigible. "I'll have them send you to Booneville, just like you deserve, if you don't start earnin' your keep around here," he repeatedly growled.

Booneville was the toughest youth institution in Missouri for the worst delinquent boys. Jeremy had previously heard the kids in school talk about it. But at times, when Simon threatened it in one of his tirades, Jeremy wondered if it could be any worse there than how he was living now. Simon stopped using the Booneville threat when Jeremy finally responded, "Go ahead and do it. At least they'd feed me there!"

More frequent beatings replaced the verbal threats after Simon realized that words no longer worked. Jeremy's back was black and blue with bruises and open sores where his skin had festered from repetitive beatings.

He had become so weak that Simon's dogs got him down to the ground twice as he tried to run from the door of the shack through the yard. They bit his face, arms and legs, making him bleed, causing more sores that wouldn't heal. Simon watched the attacks with glee from the door and urged his dogs on.

Jeremy was severely malnourished. There was never food for him in the house. Simon said that he personally didn't require it as long as he had his smokes and drinks. But Jeremy knew that was a lie. He saw Simon go to the house of his lady friend down the street nearly every night. Occasionally, when Simon returned from a visit and was feeling particularly mean, he bragged to Jeremy that she gave him plenty of food and sex.

When the hunger became unbearable, Jeremy forged for food in the neighbors' trash cans. He sometimes got caught and was driven away. The Sedalia police paid more attention to him as he got older. Each time they caught him foraging, they would bring him home to Simon and tell him that he needed to take better care of the boy. That would make Simon furious. As soon as they left, he'd beat Jeremy soundly for getting caught.

Jeremy thought about running away, but he didn't know where to go. He was afraid that he couldn't survive alone in the countryside. Instead, he stayed away from the shack as long as the weather allowed, or when he could find someplace else to get out of the cold. Barns were good options. And he was getting smarter about avoiding detection. If milk cows were in the barn, he drank milk directly from their teats.

One particularly cold night, he was sleeping in a barn on the outskirts of town after a particularly hard beating from Simon that morning. He awoke early the next morning and took a little milk from a cow. He'd stayed in that barn before. A farmer appeared out of nowhere and tried to catch him. He was able to get away, but only by tearing out of the farmer's grasp and leaving his coat and shoes behind. He knew that he couldn't go back and ask for them. After that, the winter nights became a lot worse for him.

Jeremy's personal appearance deteriorated even more. The clothes on his back were tattered and filthy; his skin was crusted with dirt; and his hair was long, greasy and unkempt. He was now extremely thin. The sores on his back and legs, and his near-frozen feet caused him to limp noticeably. He was perpetually cold and always had a runny nose that he kept wiping on his dirty shirt sleeve.

Sadly for all concerned, Jeremy Laminger was not one of the children identified through the Children's Aid Society's sampling process. His plight was never known to Anna. But that would change soon, because Jeremy Laminger was the actualization of Anna McDonald's worst nightmares.

Incredibly, another year and dragged by with Jeremy still alive. He turned thirteen and began to grow taller, despite his terrible diet. Out of desperation, he'd learned new survival skills, but he was still a foul-smelling, emaciated apparition, avoided by the townspeople.

He began having violent nightmares that caused him to grow more agitated. He also began to experience blackouts during the day in which his mind shut down and he couldn't remember where he had been or what he had done in the missing time. He still cowered when Simon struck him, but now thoughts—very bad thoughts—began to invade his mind.

On Christmas Eve 1903, Jeremy Laminger finally snapped. He'd gone back to the shack, hoping for a little Christmas mercy from Simon, but to no avail. Simon had been cursing him now for more than an hour. It was obvious that Simon was enjoying it. The house was freezing and Jeremy was running a fever. He felt light-headed and disoriented, depressed and suicidal. He could hear Simon berating him through the fog in his mind, but he was lethargic to it.

Simon, who'd been drinking all day to celebrate, decided that the boy needed a lesson to make him more attentive. He rose from his wheel chair and walked over to Jeremy, who sat with his head in his arms, slumped on the kitchen table. To wake him, Simon raised his cane high and struck Jeremy on the back of his neck, knocking him out of the chair and to his knees. Jeremy smelled the foul stench of drunken breath as Simon leaned down to strike again. That was the last thing he remembered.

To Simon's surprise, the boy stood up and turned toward him, a strange look on his face. Then the boy grabbed the cane and with fearsome strength, wrenching it away from Simon. It was the first time that the boy had ever shown any inclination to fight back. It shocked Simon. He noticed that the boy seemed fixated on an object lying on the table. Simon looked down to see what it was. He saw the old rusty butcher knife with its dull blade and broken handle lying near the boy, and it sent chills up his spine. The boy reached for it. Simon yelled, "Put that knife down!" But the boy didn't seem to hear him.

Minutes later, when Jeremy regained his senses, he was standing over Simon's crumpled body, the butcher knife still in his hand, bright red liquid dripping from the knife onto the floor. Then he saw the same bright color all over his own clothes—and on the table—and pooling on the floor under Simon's body, which lay twisted, his wide eyes staring vacantly up at the ceiling. Simon's mouth was gaping open and the red liquid was oozing out of it and down Simon's neck to join the larger puddle spreading under his body. His face was ghastly and had already turned an ashen-gray color.

Later, in his written report, the Sheriff said that Jeremy Laminger had stabbed the victim in the chest and stomach more than ten times, the number being uncertain, since many of the stab wounds overlapped.

Jeremy, in a daze, tried to drop the knife but it stuck to his hand. He pried it off using his left hand, cutting his palm to the bone as he pulled it away. He stood there for a minute, absently wiping his hands on his pants, but more blood came out and he couldn't get his hands clean.

He staggered out of the shack into the yard. Simon's two dogs, hearing him come and smelling the blood, attacked Jeremy with a vengeance, ripping at his arms and legs as he staggered toward the gate. He didn't really feel pain from the bites, just a tugging sensation.

He wandered toward the heart of town, stumbling along in the frigid air. His hands hurt and blood still dripped from them. He raised them up, hoping the blood would stop coming out.

The people on Main Street, celebrating Christmas Eve, ran the other way as they saw the ghastly, bloody figure appear under the street lights, staggering toward them like a zombie. Jeremy seemed to be reaching his arms out to them, seeking help, but they were afraid to get near him. A man ran to get the Sheriff.

Finally, a compassionate man, who thought Jeremy must have been in a horrible accident, began to steer him toward the doctor's office, getting blood on his own clothing as he did. Then other Samaritans, feeling guilty, tried to help as well.

As Jeremy stumbled along, near collapse, he kept mumbling, "I kilt him. I kilt him." They ask who he killed. But he was confused and couldn't remember Simon's name. "Him! I kilt him!"

They reached the doctor's office and he took control of the

patient. He set about cleaning off the blood to find the boy's wounds. There were huge splinters in the boy's right hand and a deep cut across the palm of his left. His arms and legs were also bleeding and there were many older wounds on his back, where oozing puss had formed. The doctor shook his head. "My God, what has been happening to this boy?"

The doctor began to remove the splinters and sew up the boy's numerous wounds. Still, none of the wounds seemed to account for the amount of blood that had soaked the boy's clothing. Realizing his patient was in shock, he gave Jeremy a sedative, causing the boy to drift off into unconsciousness quickly.

The sheriff and a deputy arrived at the doctor's office. Recognizing who Jeremy was, the sheriff sent the deputy to check out Simon's shack. Jeremy remained unconscious. The sheriff decided that he should wait at the doctor's office for Jeremy to wake up, and for word from the deputy.

The deputy returned in only a few minutes, shaken. He called the sheriff aside and then stayed as the sheriff rushed out. The deputy asked if the doctor had some different clothing for the boy, since the bloody clothing that Jeremy came in with would need to be bagged as evidence.

Four hours later, Jeremy awoke, but was still groggy and confused. The sheriff and deputy were both asking him questions, but he didn't understand what they were saying through his fog. When the doctor allowed it, they carefully helped him dress and took him to the jail, placing him in a warm cell with a cot and real blankets. He fell into a deep asleep that lasted nearly 24 hours.

He awoke again on Christmas night. His mind was clearer now.

He began to weep uncontrollably, his body shaking as though from a hard chill. His breathing was shallow and rapid. It took an hour for him to calm down. The sheriff watched him closely during his episode and didn't try to question him.

Early on December 26th, a reporter from the Sedalia News Leader came by the jail, wanting to interview Jeremy. The deputy had alerted him that the boy was now awake. The sheriff didn't see as to how it could do much harm. Jeremy understood the newspaper man's questions but still couldn't form the words to answer, so he just shook his head and remained silent. The reporter's voice was harsh and unfriendly. Eventually the reporter gave up and left in a huff.

The reporter was a graduate of the MU School of Journalism, talented at his trade and a pretty good investigator. He quickly gleaned what the townspeople knew about Simon Beasley's ward, including the fact that he was an orphan who had been placed in Sedalia by the New York Children's Aid Society. It was all front page news in the Tuesday's edition, under a bold heading.

Sullied New York Orphan Brutally Slaughters Caretaker on Christmas Eve

The article covered the entire front page. What it lacked in objectivity, it made up for in sordid detail. The article fixated on the fact that Jeremy Laminger was a New York Orphan Train transplant, a school dropout, a local vagrant and thief. It described the "controversial" program of orphan placements and quoted hometown Senator Percival Webster from many previously published statements regarding the practice of easterners dumping unwanted homeless urchins into Missouri communities.

It was a dramatic story, even for a wild and wooly trailhead town that had a past of street brawls and shootings, multiple injuries and deaths from strong tornadoes, and hot political controversies in lost competitions with Jefferson City and Columbia as the site for Missouri's State Capitol and the state's major university.

The city's consolation prize had been to be designated as the home of the annual Missouri State Fair, which wasn't such a bad thing in itself, but certainly didn't measure up to being a state capitol or having the state's major university. It could, however, claim the illustrious Senator Percival Webster; and now, it had the notorious Jeremy Laminger.

The Sedalia News and Leader ran stories on the killing each week thereafter, including some special editions that breathlessly followed the developing legal proceedings in the case. Senator Webster was a willing contributor to these articles as the paper rehashed the criticisms to the Orphan Train program. Newspapers in St. Louis, Kansas City, Springfield, Jefferson City, Columbia, Cape Girardeau, Kirksville, Sikeston, St. Joe, and Rolla, as well as numerous other small town weeklies, followed the continuing saga, using the News and Leader articles as their chief source of information.

The Beasley homicide became the most exciting event that had happened in Sedalia in years, and held the promise of a sensational murder trial. The Sedalia News and Leader, spurred on by its illustrious State Senator, wanted the world to know that this trial should be about more than a miscreant beggar boy killing his crippled caretaker.

Missouri's Western District Circuit Court, strongly encouraged by the Pettis County Prosecuting Attorney's office—Sedalia being the county seat of Pettis—and in consideration of the serious nature of the crime, assumed that no one in their right mind would think that the defendant should be tried as an underage delinquent. So it did the convenient thing and ruled that Jeremy Laminger would be tried as an adult. The court did have the good sense to assign its most experienced Judge, a man named Bruce Normile, to handle the trial.

Normile routinely held court in Kansas City, but was occasionally assigned to outstate cases if they were serious and complex. This one fit that bill. Normile was a highly ethical judge who didn't get rattled easily, ran a tight court and handled the press well. Attorneys practicing before his bench knew him to be stern but fair in his judgments. He insisted that the defendants tried in his courtroom be competently represented—particularly in homicide cases.

Shortly after the homicide, the Pettis County Prosecuting Attorney had received a handwritten note from Senator Webster's Chief of Staff. It indicated that the Senator believed this was a case of great importance, and he would be glad to offer whatever modest services he might personally provide, including acting as the lead prosecutor, were that deemed appropriate.

Senator Webster had a reputation as a tenacious trial lawyer and had been elected as the youngest attorney ever to serve as the Pettis County Prosecuting Attorney early in his career. It was where his fame first began to spread. He'd left that office after only two years and moved on to corporate law, making his fortune representing railroads and other major industrial clients. He'd kept those clients after he became a state Senator—which was a good thing since a Senator's pay didn't amount to much in Missouri. But then, becoming a state Senator was never really about the salary as much as it was the influence that the position could wield. And true to form, the position had brought him numerous lucrative clients.

The current Pettis County Prosecutor was not inclined to hard work, nor was he a man who craved the spotlight, so he was more than happy to defer to the Senator and readily agreed that he should serve as prosecutor for the Laminger case on behalf of Pettis County. Senator Webster let them know that he had graciously accepted the role of Special Prosecutor by announcing it to the Sedalia News and Leader.

When Judge Normile saw the announcement, he cursed violently under his breath. He didn't like Webster—thought he was overrated, arrogant and a publicity seeker. His concern about the case increased exponentially. He checked to see who had been appointed as a public defender to Laminger, knowing that that the boy had no personal funds to hire his own attorney. He was notified that the State Public Defender's Office had assigned a "prominent" Sedalia lawyer named Samuel Perkins. Normile knew Perkins well, having attended law school with him. He also knew that lawyer Perkins' main claim to fame these days was as the town's chief alcoholic. To the consternation of the Public Defender's Office, Normile rejected the Perkins assignment outright. Normile's sources told him that lawyer Perkins had been recruited through the personal assistance from Senator Webster's Chief of Staff.

Two weeks later, the Public Defender's Office "regrettably" alerted the judge that his refusal of the appointment of attorney Perkins might be a problem since all other potential defense counsels who had been approached, upon hearing that the good Senator would be the prosecutor, declined the case. Judge Normile then personally tried to find someone from Kansas City who'd take the case but got the same response as the Public Defender's Office.

When quizzed by the Sedalia reporter as to why the trial was taking so long to be scheduled on the docket, Normile snarled, "This case will not move forward until Mr. Laminger has adequate representation, however long that takes."

Privately, Normile knew better. He had a limited amount of time before Webster would request a change of venue—perhaps to Jefferson City in Cole County, where the judges seemed more concerned about the speedy part of a person's constitutional right to a "fair and speedy trial".

By this time the New York newspapers were following the Laminger case closely due to its implications for the Children's Aid Society's Orphan Placement Program. The same New York reporter who had written the long article about Ben and Anna was dispatched to Sedalia to track the case.

He quickly found sides of the story that the Sedalia reporter either hadn't investigated or hadn't reported. His articles gave a more balanced picture, including Jeremy's abandonment by his original foster parents, and the likely abuse and neglect that Jeremy had experienced at the hands of Simon Beasley. Jeremy was described in his articles as "slow in thought." It was not intended as a negative slur, but as an accurate description of Jeremy's intellectual limitations.

The publisher of the Sedalia paper, upon reading the articles in the New York Times, was unhappy that his paper was being "shown up". He called his reporter to the woodshed indicating, from that point forward, he should gather information more objectively if he planned to remain employed with the paper.

As a result, the Sedalia newspaper's articles became more balanced, but the damage in Missouri had already been done. The average Missouri reader didn't understand why the good citizens of Sedalia hadn't already formed a vigilante committee and taken Laminger out of the jail to string him up, saving a lot of hoopla and taxpayer money. It was the fate he obviously deserved as an incorrigible delinquent, a killer and a foreigner— not necessarily in that order. The facts in the papers had already proven that he was guilty as sin, hadn't they?

Chapter 23

Naturally, both Anna and Mrs. Mason followed the Laminger story with intense interest. They surmised, accurately, that this would become *the case* on which the fortunes of the Society's Placement Program would hinge.

Emma read about the difficulty in getting adequate legal representation for Jeremy and knew that such representation was critical, both to his own defense and to the Society's reputation. She considered hiring a prominent New York law firm to handle the case, but dismissed the idea quickly, knowing it would likely add fuel to the fire to send a hotshot Eastern law firm out to the Midwest.

She struggled mightily for a solution. The answer came to her in a flash as she took one of her brisk morning walks. Why not Zachary Lough!? Anna had kept Mrs. Mason informed of Zach's achievements. By 1904 he'd already made a reputation as a rising star among Missouri's trial attorneys.

He was young, but she personally knew how talented he was. He would clearly know what was at stake. The fact that he was an orphan transplant could have huge symbolic value in influencing a jury. His very presence would counteract the notion that all orphan train children were a detriment to society. She immediately contacted Zach and requested to employ him. He, of course, was familiar with the case and readily agreed. The Society wrote the contract to pay his fees.

Lough notified Judge Normile that he'd been retained to represent the defendant. Normile, who'd met Lough previously and knew of his background, was happy to hear it, but asked him who had employed him. Lough told him and Normile was fine with that, although he suspected Webster would make a point of telling that to the jury if he could weave it in at some point. Still, Normile smiled to himself when he found out Lough was representing Laminger. Lough's insertion into the drama would likely make Webster overconfident, since Lough was so young and an Orphan Train kid to boot.

Normile publicly announced Zachary Lough as Jeremy's privately retained attorney and notified Webster, who did in fact, smile broadly when he heard the news. An Orphan Train urchin representing another Orphan Train urchin! How novel and fortuitous!

While Webster attended church to keep up appearances, in the secret recesses of his mind, he often question whether there was an all-seeing God who answered to the whims of every man, rich and poor. He supposed that if God listened to anybody, it would be the brilliant, educated man, created closer to His own image.

Well, maybe it was true after all! Maybe God did guide the fate of brilliant men. How else could one explain these unexpected, serendipitous events that had occurred in his life, like this grizzly murder committed by an Orphan Train urchin in his own back yard? And now, another orphan from New York was the counsel for the defense in the case? How lovely! If this didn't get him the national attention he needed to catapult to a higher office, nothing would.

The Senator had little doubt about the outcome of the trial. The case against Laminger was open and shut; he'd already been tried and convicted by the Missouri Press. Webster doubted if there were twelve adults anywhere in Missouri who wouldn't convict Laminger. A jury trial in this case would be a sure thing. Webster's only fear was that Lough might seek a plea bargain, or try some other method to avoid an open jury trial. That could take away the stage on which Webster needed to perform.

It had taken more than four months to find an attorney for Laminger. Normile allowed four more months for Lough to get familiar with the facts of the case and depositions to be taken. He set the trial date for late August. The citizens of Sedalia, most of Missouri, and even in some parts of New York City, were panting in anticipation.

Shortly after Normile made the defense counsel announcement, the media added the story of Zachary Lough to the saga, emphasizing that he, too, was a transplanted orphan from New York, just as Webster knew they would. They were doing his job for him. They also wrote that Lough was a very young and inexperienced attorney, as opposed to the distinguished and experienced Senator Webster. With the exception of the Rolla paper, the Missouri press rooted for Goliath, and left little doubt for speculation that little David would lose this battle.

The New York press also featured stories about Lough, including quotes from the city's most distinguished banking tycoon, who cautioned the readers to remember that Goliath didn't always win. The paper cited Zachary's exemplary achievements from his humble orphan beginnings to his academic work at Harvard and Yale. They listed the court cases that he had already litigated in his brief law career, suggesting that the good Senator from Missouri might want to think twice about underestimating his opponent.

Zachary met Jeremy for the first time in late April. Jeremy's physical health had improved dramatically with regular meals. Sheriff Dan Blankenship had been appalled at the condition of the boy when first arrested and knew quite a lot about Simon

Beasley, himself a frequent tenant of the jail during his sorry life. Secretly Blankenship sympathized with the boy and figured he'd probably been driven to the crime.

As a wizened old law enforcement officer, he was not unaware that the world would be watching Jeremy's trial closely and he didn't want the boy looking as though he had been mistreated in jail. The jail food was actually good and the Sheriff saw to it that there was plenty, something Jeremy had not experienced in many years.

Emotionally, however, Jeremy Laminger was a wreck. He knew that he'd done an unforgivable thing, even if he couldn't remember actually doing it. His guilt overwhelmed him. He didn't need a jury to tell him that he was a killer and a bad person. When Zachary walked into the cell and introduced himself, Jeremy's first comment was, "I don't need no lawyer. I murdered somebody and I deserve to die." Then he turned his back to Zach and looked out the window of his cell.

Zachary took his time and gently explained that, while no one doubted Jeremy had killed Simon, there were different kinds of guilt. Zachary said that he suspected that the way Simon had treated Jeremy would make a big difference in how a jury would view what Jeremy had done. He indicated that a killer was not necessarily the same as a murderer.

Jeremy didn't understand what Zach meant by "different kinds of guilt" and that "a killer wasn't necessarily a murderer". "I killed him with a knife! There was blood everywhere! I know I'm guilty and I don't deserve no mercy!"

Zach remembered that Jeremy had once had a dog. "Listen, Jeremy, if somebody had a dog that they kept tied outside to a post its whole life, offering it no shelter from the cold or heat, speaking harshly to it, beating it often and starving it to within an inch of its life, and then one day, as that person was about to beat the dog again, it jumped up and bit its owner in the throat, killing him, whose fault would that be?"

Jeremy puzzled over the question and then mumbled. "It'd still be the dog's fault, Mr. Lough, but a master shouldn't treat his dog that way." He remained at the barred window with his back turned to Zach.

"No, he shouldn't, Jeremy, and a man shouldn't treat a boy in his care that way either. I'm not saying that you should have killed Mr. Beasley because of how he treated you, but if people really knew the whole story, they might view what you did differently."

"I don't believe you planned to kill Simon Beasley. And I need to help you understand that to kill somebody doesn't always mean you murdered them. For you to be a murderer of the kind people are saying, you had to plan to kill Simon, and you had to plan out how you'd do it before you actually killed him. Did you plan to murder him?"

Jeremy turned around and faced Zach, puzzling out the question. He shook his head. "I begun to think bad thoughts about him, but I didn't plan on killin him. I didn't even realize that I did it till it was all over and I saw all the blood. I just remember being cold and lonely at Christmas. Then Simon was cursing me and hitting me with his cane. I don't remember anything after that till I saw all that blood."

"Had Simon been drinking that day?"

"Well, yes sir. He drunk ever day. That day was no different."

"Well, Jeremy, if you'll let me, I'd like to be your lawyer so everybody knows the whole story. See, I really don't think you're a bad person. I just think you did a bad thing because of how you were treated."

"Why would you want to be my lawyer?" Jeremy asked suspiciously. "Nobody else did and I ain't got no money."

"I don't need any money from you Jeremy. My firm is being paid by the Children's Aid Society from New York, the same group that helped you ride the train to Sedalia."

"Why would they do that?"

"Because some people think this trial is about more than what you did. Some people think that children from the East have no right to find homes in places like Missouri. There are thousands of kids like you who've been placed in Missouri and other states nearby. Most come to good families. You didn't. But some people—like the Prosecutor—don't believe orphan children should have the right to come to Missouri."

"Is that why you want to speak for me?"

"In part. There are lots of reasons why, actually. The most important one is that everybody, including you, deserves a fair trial. The story of what you did and why you did it needs to be told accurately. Under our country's Constitution, you deserve that. But another reason I'm doing this is to change people's minds about orphan kids."

Jeremy put a hand to his head. "So what I did could keep other orphan kids from finding homes?"

"It could if we let it. I know you feel bad about what you've done, but your case is very important, the most important one I've ever defended, and I need you to help me tell your story accurately, not just for your sake, but for all orphans like you who rode those trains."

"Do all of us who come out here get in trouble?"

"Well, Jeremy, almost every kid makes mistakes as he or she grows up. It's part of learning about life. That can be harder for an orphan kid. But kids placed with good families are allowed to make little mistakes and learn from them. I know that for a fact. I'm like you. I'm an orphan kid too."

Jeremy's eyes widened. "You're an orphan like me?"

"Yes, I am."

"You came on a train?"

"Yes I did. I rode the train when I was about the same age as you were when you came to Sedalia. I went to a little place called Jadwin, and unlike you, I was adopted by a good family. Sometimes, Jeremy, the size of the mistakes you make depends on how you're treated by the people who take you in."

Jeremy looked ashamed. "I was taken in by a family but I don't think they really wanted the likes of me. They gave me to Simon when they found out how stupid I was."

"Well, Jeremy, sometimes adults do bad things too, like taking in an orphan when they aren't prepared to give him a good home. Let's just start from the beginning so I can learn more about what happened to you. Then we'll decide how to defend you."

"You think I deserve to be defended?"

"Absolutely, Jeremy! Everybody does. It's the law."

They talked for six more hours that day, with two very important outcomes. By the time Zachary was ready to leave, he was absolutely certain that Jeremy Laminger had been driven to kill, and Jeremy Laminger began to understand that he might not entirely be the horrible person he thought he was. He was guilty of killing Simon alright, and he'd have to live with that and take his punishment, but he'd begun to understand the difference between being driven to kill and premeditated murder.

Jeremy liked Zachary Lough. Nobody had ever treated him with respect before, or was patient enough to explain things so that he could understand them. Zachary Lough did that and it made him feel better to be treated nice, like he wasn't so bad, or as stupid a person as he had thought.

The jury selection process was easy for Webster. He challenged only two prospective jurors. Surprisingly, Lough challenged only three. Webster exerted his considerable charms on all the prospective jurors. These commoners might just be holding the punch card to the Governor's Office.

He thought Lough seemed to be angling more toward professionals—teachers, ministers, bankers, etc., so he gave preference to the more impressionable salt-of-the-earth farmers, or merchants' wives, whom he believed would be more susceptible to his persuasion. But he was comfortable with educated jurors as well and didn't really care who got selected. He had little doubt that he could sway any Pettis County jury that would be convened, no matter what its composition. His only challenges were to individuals who declared that they could never support the death penalty under any circumstance. He figured their elimination would give Lough heartburn, but if it did, Lough didn't show it.

The trial date finally arrived. The town was jam-packed with reporters and lookers on. Webster assumed that the first day would be a formality. Normile would ask how the defendant pleaded. Unless Lough was an idiot, which Webster doubted, Laminger would plead not guilty by reason of temporary insanity. The Judge would order a psychiatric review and that would be it for the month. That's how Webster would have handled the defense had he been on the other side.

Webster had detailed information regarding how Jeremy had been treated since arriving from New York. He knew Simon was a mean drunk. Giving him a child to care for was tantamount to abandonment. The boy had obviously broken in a rage and committed the crime. Under normal circumstances, he should have been charged with no more than second degree murder. With a very good lawyer—him for example—the boy might even have walked free if his case could be made sympathetic enough.

But that was irrelevant to the larger issue. This boy represented everything bad about the Society's immigrant orphan program. Easterners needed to handle their own social problems and not foist them off on the rest of the country, as they'd been doing now for a half-century. If convincing a jury that this boy was a heinous murderer prevented that in the future, so be it. The sacrifice of one insignificant orphan was a small price to pay. And if Lough tried to play the insanity card, Webster was prepared to trump it.

In fact, Zachary had considered a plea of temporary insanity. He, too, knew that Jeremy had snapped from terrible abuse and didn't realize what he was doing. Even the repetitive stabbings, and what Jeremy did immediately after the killing of Simon Beasley, told him that. Jeremy had finally succumbed to a blind rage caused by terrible abuse and neglect. Yet, even then, Jeremy had never even thought about running away from his crime.

But the insanity plea would be tricky in this case. First, Zach would have to obtain the testimony of a prominent psychiatrist, preferably one from Missouri, and he seriously doubted that any clinician in Missouri would subject himself to Webster's wrath. An out-of-state psychiatrist might be a possibility, but Webster would expect the temporary insanity plea and have a bevy of prominent Missouri psychiatrists, probably from the various state psychiatric hospitals, testifying against it.

Among other things, Webster was the Chair of the Missouri Senate's Appropriations Committee. All state-funded clinicians would know that he could reward their hospitals handsomely if they testified as he wished, or hurt them badly if they refused or did it poorly. And if Zach used the plea of temporary insanity and lost, the outcome could be bad for Jeremy. Temporary insanity was an all or nothing defense. If it failed, Jeremy would likely be convicted of first degree murder, the charge that the Prosecutor's Office had brought against him.

Zach was confident that he could at least convince a jury that this was not a capital murder case. He was surprised that the Prosecutors office had filed those charges. The facts didn't support that level of charge. So, when the court was convened and Judge Normile asked Zach how his client pleaded, Normile was only slightly surprised that Lough responded, "My client pleads not guilty, Your Honor."

A hush fell over the courtroom. Some of the best legal minds in Missouri, and even in New York, had anticipated the insanity plea, smugly informing their respective newspapers as to what Lough would do. Maybe this young attorney was not as smart as people had let on?

Normile hesitated for a just a second too long, then declared that, in light of the plea, the trial would begin on the following Monday. He started to bang the gavel down when Zachary spoke.

"Your Honor, if it pleases the Court, I have a motion related to the jurisdiction of this trial." Zach walked over and handed documents to the Court Clerk. The Clerk, in turn, awaited Normile's instruction.

Normile, stared at Lough and then set his gavel aside. He waived to the Clerk impatiently, "Bring me the motion." The clerk, sensing the rising drama, rushed it forward.

Normile studied the motion for long minutes while everybody waited. Then he handed it back to the clerk and told him to give it to the Prosecutor. As Webster read it, a frown crossed his face.

Normile addressed the court. "There'll be a short recess. Mr. Lough and Mr. Webster, please join me in my chambers. Normile rapped his gavel and exited the courtroom with Webster and Lough trailing close behind. The crowd would have to wait to find out what the new development meant. But it must not be good. They could see Webster's scowl as he exited the courtroom.

The exchange in the judge's chamber was quick and furious. Webster opened fire. "This is a ridiculous motion! He can't be serious! This is an insult to the court! Had he submitted the motion in advance, as he should have, I would have counseled him on Missouri's juvenile statutes; although one would think a person trained at Yale University wouldn't need it."

Zach shot back at Webster. "My client was not represented by counsel when the Western District Court decided to try him as an adult. He was barely 13 when the event occurred. The decision was not made by Judge Normile. I'd like for him to have the opportunity to rule on it."

Webster refused to respond to Zach, instead turning to the judge and making his first significant mistake in his interactions with the judge. "Normile, this is absurd. Straighten the boy out."

Normile's eyes snapped. "Mr. Prosecutor, you will address the Court and Defense Counsel with proper respect or risk contempt."

Webster's face froze and then turned crimson. He realized that Normile was accusing him of stepping across some magic line of court etiquette. "*Pardon me*, Your Honor. I thought we might dispense with formality in the privacy of your chambers."

"We're still discussing the case as a part of a court proceeding, Mr. Prosecutor? You will remember that going forward"

Webster knew he should have said, "Yes, Your Honor, my apologies", but his ego wouldn't allow it. He stared at Normile and nodded slightly, his face still burning. He'd do some damage to this man if he ever had the chance.

Normile turned to Lough. "You have anything more to say in defense of your motion?"

"Yes, Your Honor, there is precedent for juveniles in homicide cases to be tried as delinquents when their actions were driven by severe and chronic abuse or neglect. My motion lists twelve such cases, two of which were tried in Missouri courts. The Western District Court made its ruling even before Mr. Laminger had representation. I saw nothing in the record indicating consideration that extenuating circumstances were in play in this case. I'm confident that we can present ample evidence that Jeremy Laminger was the victim of severe, ongoing abuse and neglect at Simon Beasley's hands. I believe it drove my client to his actions. I believe his young age should have made the court at least consider a delinquency proceeding."

Normile looked at Webster. "Your response, Prosecutor?"

"The juvenile statutes, which I helped to create, and with which I am intimately familiar, were never intended to be used in a crime of this magnitude. It would make a mockery of our legal system if a violent murderer could walk free at age 21 just because he was tried as a juvenile. That's what would happen, and it would be considered a travesty of justice by every citizen in this state."

"Defense Counsel is correct that extenuating circumstances can be considered by a court in ruling on jurisdiction for underage children. However, on quick glance, I'm familiar with most of the cases cited in Mr. Lough's motion. I believe every one of them involved younger children, most age ten or younger, and none of the deaths to the caretaker were anywhere near as violent as this one."

"The public understands why young children, without a full cognizance of right or wrong, could be tried as juveniles, but it would not understand a violent teenager like Laminger getting off that easily. Based on his deposition, I believe Laminger clearly understood what he was doing, and has willingly admitted full guilt for his crime. In police interrogation, he repeatedly indicated that he considered himself a killer. For Christ's sake, the victim was stabbed over ten times! These are not the actions of a child. This would call our whole judicial system into question!"

"Mr. Lough's allegations that Mr. Laminger was abused and neglected have not yet been established in court. It's unproven speculation. Furthermore, being abused doesn't obviate a crime of this magnitude—non-assaultive offenses, maybe, incorrigibility, maybe, running away, maybe; but violence of this nature—never!"

Normile could have ruled against Lough's motion immediately, and probably should have. But it was such fun watching Webster sweat. Had Webster thought it through before getting so flustered, he'd have realized that Normile would be inclined to rule against Lough's motion, if for no other reason than to support the Western District decision and to allow Normile to retain control of the case. There was no real precedent for challenging a jurisdictional decision. Lough would have weak grounds for appeal. But Normile thought that it was a good strategic move on Lough's part.

On the downside, Lough had just divulged the central theme of his defense. That gave Webster more time to adjust his prosecution. "Gentlemen, I'll consider the motion tonight and rule on it tomorrow. Good day to you both." He dismissed them and had the Clerk reconvene the court.

When Normile re-entered the courtroom hushed. "Mr. Lough has submitted a motion for moving this trial from adult to a delinquency proceeding. I will rule on that tomorrow at 1:00 p.m. after considering the motion. Court is adjourned until then." He banged the gavel and walked back to his chambers. A bedlam of noise broke loose behind him.

Normile already knew how he'd rule the next day. He'd make a quick announcement and then proceed immediately to opening arguments. It gave him some satisfaction to think of Webster, fretting about Lough's motion, and not thinking about his opening statements. Normile also assumed that Zachary Lough didn't really expect to win on the motion and would be continuing his own preparation.

Later that evening, Normile sent a runner to find Lough to invite him to judge's chambers. Lough showed up in less than 20 minutes.

"Thanks for joining me, Mr. Lough. Would you like a drink?"

"Water if you have it, Your Honor."

"Nothing stronger?"

"No thanks, sir."

"Why did you introduce the motion? I doubt that you expected me to rule favorably on it. There's no precedent for it. I suspect you know that, or you'd have cited it in the motion."

Zachary smiled. "Yes, sir. I couldn't find any precedent. I'm aware that it was a long shot."

Normile went over to a table to pour himself some brandy. "So, why'd you do it?"

"I think Senator Webster believes he's prosecuting a program, and that the defendant is incidental to the case and can be sacrificed for a larger cause. I believe defending the individual is the larger cause, and that the program that brought him to Missouri is incidental. I wanted to see how he'd react if he thought his chance to prosecute the program in the public eye might be threatened."

Normile grinned and thought, "The boy has balls!" But he said out loud, "And what if you had pissed me off with your motion?"

Lough laughed. "In all deference, Your Honor, from everything I've heard about you, you don't get pissed off easily by defense attorneys trying to defend their clients from a charge of murder."

Normile took that compliment and grinned. "You made Webster sweat a little."

Lough grinned back. "You're making him sweat a lot longer, sir. I expected you to overrule me immediately."

Normile nodded. "Well, I'll rule against you first think tomorrow afternoon, although that's not to be shared. Are you ready for your opening statement?"

Lough nodded. "Yes, sir, as ready as I'll ever be."

Normile started to thank him for coming, but then thought of one more question. "Just as a matter of interest, Mr. Lough, why didn't you use the temporary insanity defense?"

"I was tempted to, sir; my defendant doesn't remember stabbing Beasley at all. He'd been having blackouts for some time before that, probably from a combination of starvation and abuse. But that's basically an all-or-nothing defense, and I assumed Webster would be prepared for it and have the clinical deck stacked against my client. I have another strategy in mind that challenges the level of the murder charge against my client."

Normile nodded again. "Sleep well, Mr. Lough."

"You, too, Your Honor."

Lough left. Normile chuckled after he'd gone. So young and yet so smart! Laminger would get good representation and Webster would probably get more than he bargained for. Normile blew out his lamp and went to bed.

Chapter 24

By one o'clock the town was in a state of high drama wondering how Normile would rule on Lough's motion. The New York paper, while not yet available to Sedalia citizens, had called Lough's delinquency strategy "a bold and unanticipated stroke", although their legal experts speculated that it would be unsuccessful. It had, however, subtly reminded everyone that there were likely extenuating circumstances to the killing and that the defendant was barely more than a child.

At the appointed time, Judge Normile entered the courtroom and glanced at Webster, who looked as though he hadn't slept well. Normile looked over at Lough, who seemed relaxed and calm. Laminger sat beside Lough, decently dressed and quiet, watching the proceedings with interest. Lough seemed to have prepared him well for what was to come.

After gaveling the court to order, Normile quickly got to the point. "The Court rules against Defense Counsel's motion that this trial be conducted under delinquency proceedings. There is no precedent for the challenge. We will now proceed with opening statements. Mr. Prosecutor, are you ready?"

The brevity of it caught Webster off guard. He had expected a lengthier statement from the judge. But then, he'd also expected Lough to use the insanity plea. That would have delayed the opening of the trial at least a month.

He could ask the court to recess for the day or so to give him a little more time to develop his opening statements based on the defense strategy Lough had revealed, but that would make him look unprepared. It also crossed his mind that Normile was subtly setting him up and might refuse his request for delay.

He'd make his opening statement. How hard could it be? He responded quickly. "Thank you, Your Honor. We're ready."

"Then the floor is yours."

Webster whispered an instruction to his assistant, who hustled out. Webster stood and walked over to the Jury box.

"Judge Normile, Ladies and Gentlemen of the Jury, you see before you a defendant who has committed one of the most heinous crimes ever perpetrated in Pettis County. In the course of this trial, the prosecution will show that the defendant maliciously murdered his caretaker, Mr. Simon Beasley, a long time resident of Sedalia."

"As we all know by now, Mr. Laminger is not a long time resident of this city. He's a transplant from New York City, where he was orphaned at infancy by an alcoholic prostitute and then later offered to a gullible family living in Sedalia."

"This crime is defined by its viciousness. The facts will show that Mr. Beasley was stabbed more than ten times in the chest and stomach, the actual count being hard to establish because of overlapping wounds."

"Now, Mr. Laminger's young Defense Counsel over there would have you believe that abuse and neglect caused him to commit the crime, but I offer three points for your consideration related to that."

"First, Mr. Beasley was confined to a wheel chair, the very one my assistant is now bringing into this room." The assistant rolled an old, rickety, rusted wheel chair down the aisle. The leather on its seat and back was torn and crusted, with padding sticking out through the holes. He parked it in front of Webster, who kept it there, leaning his hand on its handles as he continued. "Doesn't it strike you as a wild stretch of the imagination that a person of Mr. Laminger's age, size and mobility was physically abused by a frail old man in a wheel chair?"

"Second, this *alleged* abuser took the defendant into his own home voluntarily when Mr. Laminger's foster parents became disillusioned with the boy's irresolvable deviances. In fact, I am told by each of the former foster parents that the stress from attempting to raise him contributed to the ultimate dissolution of their marriage."

Jeremy swallowed hard and looked down. Zach quietly put his hand on Jeremy' arm below the table, and never changed his expression. Jeremy looked over at him, relaxed a little and returned his focus to Webster.

"Finally, Ladies and Gentlemen, tell me this, how many adolescents have you met that would not complain loudly to everyone around them if they were being abused by their caretakers? Did Jeremy Laminger complain to his teachers? No he did not! Did he complain to the Sheriff? No he did not! Did he ask a minister for help, or anyone else in this city for that matter? Not one person in this town that I could find has ever heard a peep from him about this so-called abuse!"

"Now some of you may have an adolescent at home." Webster's face took on a wearied expression. He shook his head and paused dramatically. "My sympathies to all of you who do." The audience laughed. "I have been so cursed—er, blessed— five times thus far in my life, and I have two more to go—all my own doing, I readily admit." The audience, and even some of the jurors, laughed more loudly this time.

Webster rolled his eyes toward the heavens for effect, evoking more laughter from the audience. "And if I tell any one of my adolescent children that he or she must study a little harder instead of going out with friends, or that she can't have the latest fad in clothing… well, it sometimes evokes dramatics more appropriate to a stage than my humble home."

"And I'll even confess to having been accused of being too old fashioned and, God forbid, even abusive at least once or twice by *my own* children when they disagreed with a decision I made about something they wanted or that they thought they should be allowed to do. Has that ever happened to any other parents in this room, or am I the only abuser here today?" There was more laughter in the courtroom. Normile banged his gavel amiably to restore order, and then nodded for Webster to proceed.

"I've heard, from the testimony coming before me repeatedly in another arena of my professional life"—everyone in the courtroom knew the arena to which he was referring—"that some orphan vagrants who rode the trains from New York City to join our fine families here, have run away, citing all sorts of reasons: from too many farm chores to being bored with the hum-drum rural life that just doesn't measure up to their expectations."

"These ungrateful urchins—that's what they call them in New York, you know—deserted the very families who had rescued them from what we are told is a horrid and dangerous slum life in that Gomorrah on our eastern shores! Perhaps orphan children from that part of the world aren't used to the work our children do as a normal course of life." A few heads nodded in the audience.

"So, if his old caretaker in the wheelchair was all that oppressive, why didn't Mr. Laminger run away? He could have. He, unlike Mr. Beasley, had two young legs to carry him. But he didn't, did he? No, instead, he brutally murdered his caretaker, and on Christmas Eve, no less!"

"So we have to ask ourselves, what was the nature of this '*abuse*' the defendant was supposed to be receiving?" Webster made quotations in the air with his hands to highlight the word abuse. "Was it nagging? Was it yelling? Was it reaching out with a cane from a wheel chair to strike weakly at a youth fully capable of evading such a blow?" Webster stepped back dramatically from the wheel chair, miming what he was saying. "And tell me, Ladies and Gentlemen, what level of abuse would justify a person being stabbed more than ten times?"

"Now, most of us that knew him are aware that Mr. Beasley was not a model citizen. He drank excessively. He wasn't always friendly. He lived in a run-down house. He even allowed Mr. Laminger to drop out of school, requesting that he seek a job instead, since he was not a wealthy man and needed the boy to contribute financially to his own upkeep. He was, Ladies and Gentlemen of the Jury, by all accounts, an old man, with lots of physical ailments, bound to a wheelchair and cranky. Yet, when no one else would give an orphan stray a home, Mr. Beasley stepped up, didn't he."

"Now let's summarize, shall we. We have a frail old man in a wheel chair, who some say was more often drunk than not and, therefore, not physically well coordinated. This same frail man was supposed to have wielded such abusive power over a young, growing adolescent that he forced him to kill in self-defense. Now tell me, how consistent is that with the actual facts of the case?"

"Of what, exactly, was Mr. Laminger afraid? That he would be beaten? A few simple steps backward… and he's saved!"

"Was Mr. Laminger afraid he wouldn't be allowed to leave Mr. Beasley's house? Apparently not, since he came and went freely and often didn't come home at night."

"Did Mr. Laminger fear horrible verbal abused by a weak old man who had lost most of his teeth? What exactly was the threat, that he'd gum him to death? Would the Defense Counsel have us to believe that Mr. Laminger was 'nagged' into his horrible crime?"

"Ladies and Gentlemen of the Jury, even if you are Jeremy Laminger, living in squalor with a weak, wheel-chair-bound old drunk that you hardly knew, would that have driven you to pick up a knife and stab him so many times that he looked like a pin cushion? I think not! And do you know any youth living in Sedalia who would do that? Would you ever expect any of your own children to take such precipitous action, or any of your neighbor's children?"

"Is it not more likely, ladies and gentlemen, that Mr. Laminger, frustrated with his own inadequacies—which sadly, I have been told, are many—built up a long resentment from the admonitions of his caretaker to be more responsible. Is it not possible that Mr. Laminger came to hate Simon Beasley as the herald to his own inadequacies? If that's true—well I'm terribly sorry that Mr. Laminger felt inadequate—but that doesn't obviate his accountability for this horrible crime."

"Perhaps, Ladies and Gentlemen, youth are held by a different standard in the East than in the Midwest. Isn't it ironic that this

'*Orphan Train Program*' commended in some circles, thinks that it is perfectly acceptable to send us a potentially broken and damaged child of an alcoholic mother, rejected and abandoned, and certainly not valued enough by the good citizens of New York City to be kept there?"

"If you have read the New York Children's Aid Society's literature, as I have, you'll see that they claim they are sending orphans—street urchins—for our great benefit. Well, who here today believes that Jeremy Laminger is a benefit to Sedalia?"

"Let me ask you this: how many orphans have we Midwesterners put on a train and sent for relocation in the East? Anyone want to hazard a guess? Would our Midwestern values let us do that? I doubt it. Here in Missouri, we care for our own. And if we were so callous as to try that, would the good citizens of New York generously open their homes, as many of our compassionate families have done? I doubt that too, since they don't even open their doors to their own orphans!"

"Now, I know we have large hearts here in Missouri. It's within the scope of our Midwestern values to take in homeless children. I respect and admire our citizens who've done that, no matter where a child hails from. But there's a larger issue to be considered here. Compassion must be balanced with accountability. Accountability demands that communities take responsibility for their own lost children. And we do no favors to the children of New York when we allow New Yorkers to shun their own responsibilities to the very children they should be helping. Everybody suffers. Unfortunately, Mr. Beasley suffered the most for his compassion. Imagine his physical and emotional pain as he was being attacked and stabbed multiple times by the child he took in."

"Jeremiah Laminger is not a child, as the Judge has so wisely verified by rejecting Mr. Lough's flawed motion—a motion, by the way, which would have made a mockery of our laws and of common sense. Jeremy Laminger committed a terrible crime without just cause and he must be appropriately punished to maintain the fundamental integrity of justice."

"I also believe that Mr. Laminger unwittingly had accomplices implicit in this crime; but sadly, they will not be held accountable by any court of law. Those accomplices are an entire city of callous, irresponsible people who passed their responsibility off on us, at great cost to our legal system and great harm to one of our own."

"Frankly, that is where the real abuse and neglect resides, ladies and gentlemen, not in Sedalia and not with Simon Beasley. And while this court does not have the jurisdiction to hold them accountable, this trial may be a vehicle through a different court, the court of public opinion, to address the accountability now ignored. We don't need more Jeremy Laminger's sent to Missouri to commit horrible crimes like the one that this young man has perpetrated."

"So, yes, I actually agree with my esteemed colleague, young Mr. Lough, that terrible neglect has occurred in the Jeremy Laminger case. But Mr. Beasley didn't commit that crime. The citizens of New York did, and we were the ultimate victims."

"Thank you for listening, ladies and gentlemen. I have unflagging faith in your ability to render a good, common-sense decision based on our Midwestern values. And I will tell you that, in all my years of public service in this great state, not once has a jury of my peers ever betrayed that faith. Good day and God bless each of you as you embrace the sobering responsibility before you."

There was silence in the courtroom when he finished. The audience sat admiring their old lion, their own personal statesman and voice of reason. He had weaved his magic and they liked the tapestry. In the minds of many in the court, the trial had already been decided by the time he finished his opening remarks.

Normile, recognizing that objectivity sometimes demands time and distance, and fearing that the young Defense Counsel might be a bit intimidated by the old lion's skill, gaveled the court adjourned for the day, with the reconvening time set for 9:00 a.m. the following morning.

Zachary Lough was the most grateful man in the courtroom for that decision.

Chapter 25

All rose to the Judge's entry the next morning in a courtroom so packed that there wasn't even standing room. Normile seated the audience and turned to Zachary. "Mr. Lough, you may proceed with your opening statement."

It had been apparent to Normile, who had presided over many such cases, that Webster had scored big points the day before, and even Normile had to admire the work. Webster had not lost any of his oratorical skills. Normile wondered whether Lough could shift the balance back toward his client, or whether this would turn into a stampede for conviction.

Normile was an avid chess player. He knew the importance of a good opening game. That was true in a courtroom trial as well, except that the stakes were higher here. This game could lead to a long stay in prison, or even death, if poorly played.

Zachary stood and walked toward the jury box. He looked relaxed. He didn't hurry into his presentation. He held notes in his hand, looking down at them before he began speaking. They were a prop. He didn't really need them. He'd practiced his opening until he knew it by heart.

"Ladies and Gentlemen of the Jury, Judge Normile, Prosecutor Webster, and all of you in the courtroom today, my name Zachary Lough and it's my duty and honor to represent the defendant, Jeremy Laminger."

Zach looked back at Webster. "I was impressed by Prosecutor Webster's opening remarks and I suspect you were as well." Some heads nodded in the audience and in the jury box. Webster remained impassive, not acknowledging Lough.

"Now the Prosecutor's job in this trial is to paint the most graphic picture of Jeremy Laminger's involvement in the death of Simon Beasley that he can. Yesterday, he showed us he will perform his job admirably."

"But my job is different. I must tell you some things that the Prosecutor will leave out of the picture in his role as prosecuting attorney. My job is to bring balance to the picture. You see, both the Prosecutor and I, by the intended design of our country's great judicial system, must act as biased parties in this trial. If we are honest, we will not pretend otherwise."

"Now the jury's job is far more difficult than mine or Prosecutor Webster's. You must ultimately sort through all the biases and arrive at an objective decision—one of the most important you will make in your lifetimes, because you hold Jeremy Laminger's future, even his life, directly in your hands. And it may surprise you when I tell you this, but from what I already know about this case, I don't think that it will ultimately be a difficult decision for you to make."

"If the Prosecutor and I do our jobs well, we'll shed light on what Jeremy did *and* what drove him to his actions—in other words, his motives."

"Please remember that your decision must address both of those things. First, you must determine what Jeremy Laminger did— the nature of his involvement in Simon Beasley's death— and second, you must determine why he did it if you can, and what that means for the punishment that he receives if found guilty."

"And I tell you without hesitation, that what he *did* seems pretty apparent based on the evidence. But the 'why'—well I suspect that you already know—that's a far more complex question. The Prosecutor will point to certain things that he will say paints a picture of Jeremy's motives. I will point to others. Only you will decide the true picture in the end."

"While most of us yearn for simple 'black and white' answers, as we grow older, we come to realize that it's never really quite that simple. There are all those complicated shades of gray that give subtlety to a picture."

"This is a complex case. It has many shades of gray. The Prosecutor would have you see the picture as black and white. My job is to help you to see those more subtle shades of gray."

"In legal language, we often call them extenuating circumstances. In fact, the Prosecutor himself has already alluded to some of them in his opening statements. Let me tell you a few of the things the Prosecutor said—and didn't say— about these extenuating circumstances, those shades of gray."

"No one in this courtroom doubts that Jeremy Laminger killed Simon Beasley, including Jeremy himself. Black and white, right?"

"So, if Jeremy believes he killed Simon, how could he plead 'not guilty'? Is this just 'a lawyer's trick', to quote from last night's Sedalia paper? How does a man, or a youth in this case, confess to the Sheriff and others that he killed a person and then stand brazenly before you to plead "not guilty" in a court proceeding? A lawyer's trick?"

"I believe that one of the questions that members of the jury will agree on is that Jeremy Laminger was responsible for the death of Simon Beasley. In fact, I believe that will be easy to affirm by the facts of the case—black and white. But that is a very different question than whether Jeremy Laminger committed *first degree murder*, the charge brought forth against the defendant by the Prosecutor's office. As you think about that, you will realize that there are great differences in the guilt of someone who kills on the scales of justice."

Zach had walked over closer to the jury box now and leaned on its rail. On some faces he saw mild confusion. On others, he saw dawning awareness. He looked down at the piece of paper in his hand.

"You see, Jeremy Laminger has been accused by the Prosecutor's indictment of '*murder in the first degree of one Simon Beasley*'. A clear charge, right? Black and white. No allowance for shades of gray in that indictment, is there? Well, as a matter of fact, it is, and it requires clear and convincing evidence for a person to be convicted under that charge."

"Now, all of us know that killing someone can carry differing degrees of guilt and different levels of punishment, depending on the nature and circumstances of the act. But let's just review that for a minute to make certain that we are all absolutely clear about that."

"If you fight for your country and you kill an enemy soldier, is that considered murder?"

"If a man breaks into your home and threatens harm to your family, and you kill him in a struggle, is that murder?"

"If a wife and mother, who has a violently abusive husband, sees him in his drunken state, pick up a ball bat to strike her four year daughter in the head to stop her from crying, so she shoots him with a gun—what kind of killing is that?"

"If a drunken man recklessly smokes in a boarding room bed and starts a fire that kills ten people in their sleep, including some small children, what degree of killing is that?"

"Do any of the above killings meet the legal standard of murder in the first degree? Well, maybe. In a few instances involving the very situations I've just cited above, a jury said it was. In many other such cases, the jury said it wasn't."

"But how could that be! Shouldn't a decision based on the law of the land always result in the same conclusion? Well, the amazing thing about those extenuating circumstances, as seen through the eyes of a jury, is that the verdict can vary from case to case, depending on those shades of gray."

"The Prosecutor says he trusts and admires jury verdicts. Well, so do I. So should you. It's at the very heart of the American legal system that an accused person has the right to a trial by a jury of his peers who considers all the facts *and* the extenuating circumstances and makes an informed, objective decision tailored to the accused person's case."

"It's not a perfect system. Juries can make mistakes, either because of the poor work of the attorneys trying the case, or the biases of jurors. That's why your attention to detail and your objectivity is so critical in this trial. You must see through mistakes that I or the Prosecutor make, and you must overcome your own preconceived notions, to do your job in the manner that our forefathers entrusted to you. It's hard work that we are asking you to do."

"The facts and extenuating circumstances will, hopefully, portray the actions and the true motives of Jeremy Laminger, and the level of punishment that is appropriate. In a civilized society like ours, with carefully crafted state and federal laws defining how a criminal act should be classified and what the appropriate punishment should be, we have clear standards for each."

"Do you know the standard for capital murder? It's the act of killing that we call '*murder in the first degree*' because it carries the highest level of responsibility for a person's death, and therefore, the greatest punishment."

Zach walked backed to his table and lifted a heavy red book, opened it and walked back toward the jury. "These are Missouri Statutes related to criminal proceedings. In the Revised Statutes of Missouri—we often refer to that by its acronym, RSMO—in Chapter 565.020, we read the following definition of murder in the first degree: *A person commits the crime of murder in the first degree if he knowingly plans and causes the death of another person as an act of deliberation.*"

"Now listen to the definition of second degree murder from this same chapter, again RSMO Chapter 565.021: .... *A person commits murder in the second degree if he knowingly causes the death of another person or, with the purpose of causing serious physical injury to another person, causes the death of another person.*"

So what's different between first degree and second degree murder? Really, it's only one thing. In second degree murder, the killer didn't plan out the killing in advance. He just killed on the spur of the moment."

"An example would be that I decide to rob a bank and I am armed. I don't necessarily go into the bank planning to kill a particular person. My gun is simply the threat that gets a teller to give me the bank's money. But as he's giving it to me, the bank's guard walks back into the lobby after having gone to the bathroom. He draws his gun and points it at me. I shoot him and he dies. The killer can reasonably be charged with second degree murder."

"And now Ladies and Gentlemen, listen to this next definition of a different kind of killing, called manslaughter, in the same section of the Statute, RSMO, Chapter 565.023: *A person commits the crime of manslaughter if he causes the death of another person under circumstances that would constitute murder in the second degree under subdivision (1) of subsection 1 of section 565.021, except that he causes the death through negligent action or under the influence of sudden and uncontrolled passion.*"

"*Sudden and uncontrolled passion,* it says. Keep that phrase in mind."

"By now, it may have become apparent to you that, there is a major problem with the Prosecutor's case unless he can prove that Jeremy Laminger *planned* the killing of Simon Beasley in advance—that he deliberated it."

Zach was careful not tell the jury that Senator Webster had insisted on the Pettis County Prosecutor's Office seeking a capital murder charge. He realized that he was walking a fine line when it came to Webster. He didn't want to force the jury to conclude that its beloved Senator had erred in prosecuting the case. That might be a bridge too far for the citizens of Sedalia to cross. They might think they needed to protect Webster more than to reach an unbiased decision about Jeremy Laminger.

"Now the Pettis County Prosecutor's Office decided to press the charge of first degree murder against Jeremy. They chose that standard and they are required by law to meet its legal conditions."

"You didn't choose that level of charge; I certainly didn't choose it; Judge Normile didn't choose it. The Pettis County Prosecutor's Office could easily have pressed for a charge of manslaughter and made this a relatively simple case based on the statutes I just read to you and given what I believe are the facts of the case."

"It isn't necessary for me, you or Prosecutor Webster to address the motive of that decision. All I must do is defend my client against the charge. All you must do—in fact, all that you are allowed to do under the law—is to decide whether the standard of first degree murder is met in this case."

"It should be obvious to you by now that I believe Jeremy's actions fell far short of that standard. Remember the exact nature of Mr. Beasley's death, being stabbed repeatedly with a knife, does not mean that the standard of first degree murder is met. In fact, Jeremy stabbing Simon Beasley multiple times is one of those important 'extenuating circumstances' that could lead you to an entirely different conclusion—that it was *an act of sudden and uncontrolled passion*—might it not?"

"I do not believe that the Prosecutor will be able to prove that Jeremy *knowingly, and with willful intent,* conspired to kill Simon Beasley! Certainly the Prosecutor can speculate that, as he has done in his opening statement. But then, I can speculate the opposite, and neither is proven by the facts."

"Based on my conversations with Jeremy and the information

that I have reviewed, I believe he killed Simon Beasley *from a sudden and uncontrolled passion,* and I intend to prove the cause of that passion."

"*But here is the critical legal point that you must consider in this case.* Even if I can't convince you of all that I believe, the Prosecutor, by law, *must prove by clear and convincing evidence* that Jeremy Laminger knowingly, and with willful intent, planned to murder Simon Beasley, in advance of the act. He must do that, not by speculation, but by hard, cold facts; because, if he can't, then Jeremy Laminger cannot be found guilty as charged under our system of law."

"Speculation does not meet the standard of clear and convincing evidence. In fact, a description of the Statute, written by Senator Webster himself at the time of the passage of the language on capital murder was recorded in his testimony on the floor of the Missouri Senate, and I quote: '*there must be clear and convincing evidence of premeditation to kill in cases of capital murder convictions*'."

"If there is no proof of premeditation, then you cannot find Jeremy guilty of capital murder in the first degree." Zach paused to let that sink in, then repeated it. "It may be easy to prove that Jeremy Laminger killed Simon Beasley, but without proof of premeditated intent, he is not guilty of the charge of capital murder."

"That legal term, '*clear and convincing evidence*' is very important and I want to take a little time to discuss it as it relates to this case. How could the Prosecutor show clear and convincing evidence that Jeremy planned to murder Simon Beasley?"

"Well, if Jeremy told a credible witness *before* he killed Simon Beasley exactly what he intended to do, that could be clear and convincing evidence."

"Or, if the Prosecutor had a letter or some other form of written statement, proven to be in Jeremy Laminger's own handwriting, indicating that he had intended to kill Simon Beasley in advance of the act and how he was going to do it, the standard could be met."

"The Prosecutor might also meet that condition of proof if Jeremy Laminger had told the Sheriff when he was being questioned that he had planned to kill Simon Beasley and how he would do it, with the facts confirming that he did exactly what he said."

"But, you see, unless the Prosecutor has that kind of evidence, he cannot meet the standard of clear and convincing evidence related to Simon Beasley's death."

"Is there clear and convincing evidence that Jeremy *killed* Simon Beasley? I believe that standard can be easily met, including his own confessions that he did, the blood on Jeremy's hands, and what the Sheriff and his deputy saw at the shack. But could you still come to the legal conclusion that the killing doesn't rise to the level of first degree murder? Of course you could."

"Now, let's talk about a few more of those 'extenuating circumstances' the Prosecutor referenced in his opening statement. He asked, '*How abusive can a man in a wheel chair be?* '*Why did Mr. Beasley take Jeremy in, when his foster family deserted him?*' And most important: '*If Jeremy was being abused, why didn't he complain to authorities or run away?*' I believe that the answers to these questions will be relevant to your verdict."

"During this trial I will present facts that address many of the
Prosecutor's questions and that will cast serious doubt that
Jeremy's actions came anywhere near the legal standard of first
degree murder."

Zach turned away from the jury as though he were finished, and
walked toward the Defense Counsel's desk where Jeremy
Laminger sat, listening,. He had almost reached the desk, but
then turned back to the jury.

"Oh by the way, ladies and gentlemen of the Jury, I'd like to
address one more of those extenuating circumstances that
Senator Webster covered in his opening statements." Normile
noticed that Lough had shifted from addressing Webster as the
"Prosecutor" to "Senator Webster".

"Senator Webster raised the question about how appropriate it is
for the Children's Aid Society to send orphan children to be
taken in by Midwestern families seeking foster children. He
indicated that the question is relevant to this trial. While the
Senator is certainly within his rights to disagree with the
Society's Orphan Train Program, I have difficulty understanding
why it is relevant to this particular case, other than it tells us how
Jeremy arrived in Missouri when he was five years old."

"Surely the Senator wasn't implying that all the orphan children
sent to Missouri have killed someone or committed other heinous
crimes. In fact, I doubt that he was even implying that the vast
majority are anything other than honorable citizens of our state,
because that is what they are." Zach walked on over to the desk
and picked up very thick book and walked back toward the jury.
"This is last year's report by Missouri representatives of the

Children's Aid Society, submitted to the Governor and every member of the Missouri Legislature, documenting the status of over two thousand children who rode the orphan trains from New York to Missouri. With the help of the University of Missouri and Columbia University in New York, the Children's Aid Society uses a statistical sampling process to monitor the children placed in Missouri."

"The report, a copy of which was delivered directly to Senator Webster's Office last year, shows that over 99% of these children have thrived with their new families, growing up to become farmers, tradesmen, doctors, attorneys, ministers, teachers, and even a legislator or two."

"I will enter this report as an exhibit for you to review in case there are further questions about the Orphan Train Program, and I'm making copies available to any member of the press covering this trial who so desires it."

"I know about this data because my sister, Anna McDonald, with the help of a large staff of Missouri's adult orphan volunteers and the two major universities, oversaw the development and distribution of this report. She was one of those orphans who rode on an orphan train to Missouri. I am another."

His voice turned whimsical. "Unlike Jeremy Laminger, she and I were blessed by coming to live with a wonderful Missouri family. They gave me the greatest gift I'll ever receive, the gift of my last name."

He concluded. "Ladies and Gentlemen, thanks for listening to my opening statement. I hope it will be helpful as you weigh the facts and make your decision."

Normile allowed a minute or two for people to shift in their seats and whisper to one another as he studied some papers on his desk. Then he gaveled the Court back to order. It was only 10:30 a.m., but Normile decided to give a little more time for Lough's opening statements to settle in. He declared the Court recessed until 1:30 p.m., telling Webster to be prepared to call his first witness at that time. There was quiet, thoughtful discussion among the audience as the courtroom emptied.

Normile liked Lough's performance. As he had watched the reaction of the jury he realized that it was as good as Webster's, but in a different way, and Lough wasn't even speaking to a home crowd. He had come across as thoughtful and down-to-earth, and he was a very good teacher. Normile thought that he'd scored some important points about the validity of the murder charge. It was a good start by both sides.

Zach lunched in a restaurant where townspeople, who'd been in the courtroom audience, were eating. He listened to what they said. People were friendly and respectful to him and seemed to understand his key points about extenuating circumstances and the difference between first degree murder and other forms of homicide. If that was true, he'd gotten what he'd wanted from his opening statements.

The witness portion of the trial began in earnest that afternoon. Webster called the sheriff as his first witness. "Sheriff Blankenship, please tell the Court how you discovered the murder of Simon Beasley."

"Actually, Jeremy Laminger told us. He came into town with blood all over his clothes and hands, mumbling that he had killed someone. On a hunch, I sent my deputy over to Simon's shack and found his body."

Webster winced at the term "shack". "Can you tell us why you had such a hunch?"

"Well, violence is far more often caused by domestic squabbles than not. When I saw Mr. Laminger's condition, my first thought was that possibility."

"So Mr. Laminger told you voluntarily that he murdered his uncle? Was it the first thing he said to you?"

"His words were that 'I kilt him', and yes, that was the first thing he said to me. I asked him who he killed, but he wasn't able to tell me at the time."

"Sheriff, you said Mr. Laminger had blood on his clothes. Can you elaborate?"

"Sure. Jeremy's clothes were drenched in blood. Blood was still dripping on Doc's floor as I was talking to him. He had blood all over his hands, face and feet. We didn't know if it was his or from somebody else."

"When you found the victim, was he still alive?'

"No, he was dead. He'd lost a lot of blood."

"And just for the record, was it apparent that he had been stabbed multiple times?"

"Yes, there were numerous puncture wounds on the front of his body."

"And did Mr. Laminger have wounds?"

"The doc said Mr. Laminger had a number of large splinters in his right hand from the broken knife handle, he had a large cut across the palm of his left hand, and, of course he had the dog bites."

"Can you describe how you think that might have happened?"

"Well, the hand wounds were from the knife handle that either broke when he started stabbing Simon, or was already broken and jagged. It was an old rusty butcher knife. Jeremy said the knife handle stuck to his right hand and he cut his left hand while removing it."

"How much force would you say Mr. Laminger had to use in stabbing Mr. Beasley to cause a knife to stick to his hand."

"I'd say a great deal of force."

"Sheriff, how many times did Mr. Laminger admit to you that he had murdered Simon?"

"Well, he must have mumbled that he killed him ten or more times that day. He signed a statement that he had killed Simon Beasley, and he has told me numerous times in jail how sorry he was that he killed Simon."

Webster, who had taken the Sheriff's depositions prior to the trial, knew that the Sheriff had not been able to establish a clear motive for the killing, or determine if the killing had been planned, so Webster didn't go there in his questioning and he hoped that Lough wouldn't either.

"Thank you, Sheriff. Your Honor, I have no further questions for the witness at this time."

Normile motioned in the direction of Zachary. "Your witness, Mr. Lough."

Zachary approached the Sheriff looking down at notes in his hand. "Sheriff Blankenship, did you keep the clothes Jeremy was wearing when you found him in the doctor's office?"

"Of course. We knew they'd be needed for evidence."

"Beyond the blood, please describe the clothes."

"Well, as best I can recollect, brown shirt and brown trousers."

"Any underwear?"

Webster stood. "Objection, Your Honor. I don't think anyone in this court is interested in Mr. Laminger's underwear."

There was a tittering of laughter in the audience and some whispering. Normile gaveled it down and stared at the audience. "That won't happen again if you plan to remain in this courtroom."

Normile suspected where Zach was going. "Overruled. Proceed, Mr. Lough."

"Please answer the question, Sheriff."

"No, he wasn't wearing any underwear when we got him out of the bloody clothes and there weren't any at the shack. I had to provide underwear from the jail clothes."

"What condition would you say Jeremy's clothes were in, aside from the blood on them?"

"Real bad; plum wore out, actually. There were lots of tears and holes in the pants and shirt. The pant legs were ripped and torn from the dog bites. The clothes were filthy and rotten."

"The dog bites?"

"Yea, Simon had a couple of mean dogs. We had to fight them off every time we went over to the house for any reason. They were particularly vicious on the night we found the body."

"And why do you think the pant legs were ripped and torn by the dogs?"

Webster rose again. "Objection, Your Honor. Defense Counsel is asking for speculation from the witness."

"Sustained." He turned to the stenographer, "Strike the question. Proceed with another line of questioning, Mr. Lough."

"Was he wearing a coat?"

"No, he wasn't."

"I assume the blood was also on his shoes?"

The Sheriff paused. "He wasn't wearing any."

"He wasn't wearing any shoes?"

"No, he had none on. I guess he just ran out of the shack without any on because of what had happened."

"Did you search the shack after you found Simon's body?"

"Yes, of course we did. That's when we found the knife, lying near Simon's body."

"Would you describe the inner rooms and contents in the shack, please?"

"Objection, Your Honor!"

"Overruled. Sheriff, you may answer Mr. Lough's question."

"It has two rooms; just a table and two chairs, a small cupboard and a wash stand in the main room. The other room was Simon's bedroom, with his bed and a rickety chair in it."

"What about Jeremy's bed?"

"He didn't have any."

"Where did he sleep?"

Webster rose again, complaining more loudly. "Your Honor, I must object to this line of questioning as irrelevant."

"Overruled. You may answer the question, Sheriff."

"He slept on the floor, I guess. There was a blanket rolled up in the corner of the main room."

Webster scowled at him and the Sheriff shifted uneasily in the witness chair.

"Where did he keep his clothes?"

The Sheriff paused, thinking. "We didn't find any."

Zach paused. "No other clothing in Jeremy's size in the shack?"

"No, we looked, because we figured he'd be with us a while and would need more clothes. There weren't any at the shack; just some rags and a few old newspapers by the blanket on the floor."

"No coat?"

"No."

"No shoes?"

The Sheriff paused again, thinking, then finally answered, "No, I guess not."

"No underclothing?"

"No, like I said before, none in the shack."

"Did Jeremy tell you he had other clothes stashed somewhere?"

"No."

"Did you ask him that question?"

The Sheriff blushed a little. "No, we did not."

"So let me understand this, Sheriff. You found Jeremy in the doctor's office in a blood-drenched shirt and trousers. He was wearing no coat, no shoes and no underwear, and you found no other clothing or shoes belonging to Jeremy at Simon's shack, or anywhere else later on. And it was December 24th. Is that correct?"

"Yes, that's correct."

"What was the temperature in the shack?"

"Cold. Not that much different than outside."

"How cold was it outside?"

Webster wanted to object—started to rise, but Normile saw the motion and stared him down.

"It was cold."

"How cold approximately?"

"Well the ground was frozen. It was probably 25 or 30 degrees for a high that day and it was night when the murder occurred."

Zach nodded his head. "When you talked to Jeremy in the doctor's office, how did he appear emotionally?"

"Objection, Your Honor! The Sheriff is not a clinician."

"Sustained."

"Sorry, Your Honor. Sheriff, I'm actually asking more about his demeanor. Did he seem belligerent, or frightened, or angry?"

"No, none of those things. He was dazed, almost like he was sleepwalking."

"Objection, Your Honor!"

"Overruled."

Zach again, "Explain what you mean by 'dazed'."

"Well, he had a real dull look in his eyes, like he was somewhere else. I had to keep asking him questions over and over. Then he would look at me like he was surprised that I was there, and like he didn't really know where he was. He would try to answer my questions but couldn't, and then he'd lapse back into that dazed look again. I think he was in shock."

Webster was furious, his face flushed and his eyes shooting daggers at the Sheriff as he rose. The Sheriff avoided looking his way.

"Objection, Your honor! The witness is speculating again."

"Sustained. Sheriff, please remember to keep your testimony to what you observed, not what you speculate!" Normile was firmer this time and the Sheriff's face turned redder.

"Sheriff, I assume you found Simon Beasley slumped in his wheelchair, or perhaps he was lying on the floor beside it?"

"Well, no, not really. The chair was at the end of the table opposite where Simon's body was found on the floor."

"Hmm. So his body wasn't near his wheelchair?"

"No, it was probably ten feet away on the other side of the table."

"How do you think the body got all the way to the other side of the table?"

"I don't know."

"Sheriff, you arrested Jeremy at the doctor's office sometime after discovering Simon's body, didn't you?"

"Yes we did, after we got him some dry clothes and he woke up from the sedative the doc gave him."

"Did you remain in the room while he changed?"

"Of course."

"How would you characterize Jeremy's physical appearance?"

"Your Honor, I must again object!" Webster was almost pleading now.

Normile responded sharply. He was becoming irritated by the interruptions. "Mr. Webster, I know you must, and I know why you are objecting. But please understand that I'm going allow this line of questioning! You can ask the doctor to refute it later if you wish. Proceed with your answer, Sheriff."

The Sheriff had also become irritated with Webster and decided not to hold back. "He was extremely thin, almost skeletal. He weighed a lot less than he does now. He had deep bruises and long scars all over his back and legs, some yellow with age and some fresh and still oozing blood and pus. His hair was long and dirty. We later found he had lice and we had to de-louse him. His finger and toenails were long and filthy."

"So you would say that there is a significant difference between how Jeremy looks now and how he looked in the first few days you incarcerated him?"

"Night and day, Mr. Lough, night and day."

"Only a couple more questions, Sheriff. Did you establish a motive for the homicide?"

"No, Jeremy just kept saying he killed him, but he didn't say why."

"Did you ask him if he planned to kill Mr. Beasley?"

"Yes, we did. He said he never meant to do it, that he didn't remember doing it until after it was already done."

"Did he seem remorseful while he was in jail?"

"Objection, Your Honor."

"Overruled. The witness and his deputy are the only ones who can answer the question. You may answer, Sheriff."

"Yes, he was very remorseful. He felt he'd done something terrible and he cried a lot about it."

"I think that's it for now, Sheriff. Thank you. No further questions, Your Honor."

"More questions for the Sheriff, Prosecutor Webster?" Webster shook his head.

"Step down, Sheriff. Mr. Prosecutor, call your next witness."

Webster called the deputy to the stand and asked him to describe the condition in which he found Simon when he arrived at the shack. The Deputy described the wounds in gruesome detail.

On cross-examination, Zach again questioned the deputy about the general condition of the shack and asked him if he had found any clothing or shoes that would fit Jeremy there. He said he had not.

"Was there any heat in the shack?"

"Not that I recall."

"Then it was cold?"

"Yes, it was cold."

"And yet, neither you nor the Sheriff found any coat or shoes belonging to Jeremy."

"No sir."

"No more questions, Your Honor."

Webster called the school's principal to the stand. He asked him to describe what kind of student Jeremy had been while he attended school. The principal said Jeremy was far behind educationally, slower than other kids his age. Webster asked what grades he had made. The principal said they were all incomplete or unsatisfactory.

Zachary, in cross examining the principal asked, "How supportive were Carla and Harry Beasley with Jeremy's schooling?"

"Well, Mrs. Beasley seemed more supportive than Mr. Beasley. He seemed embarrassed about Jeremy's lack of progress. But neither of them was very enthusiastic in their support."

"Did Jeremy cause trouble in school while he was there?"

"You mean, did he act out or get in fights?"

"Yes, that's exactly what I mean."

"No, he was a quiet kid; more scared and anxious than anything."

"Did he get teased much?"

"Well, yes, some. That's an unfortunate consequence of being that far behind and that bashful."

"Yet he didn't get into any fights?"

"No, as I recall, he just tried to stay out of everybody's way, mainly."

Webster called another witness, a homeowner who had caught Jeremy loitering in his tool shed. The man described Jeremy as a filthy vagrant that he'd caught in the shed twice.

On cross examination, Zach asked, "What did you see him doing when you saw him around your house?"

"Just scrounging around our scrap burner or sneakin into the shed."

"Did he steal anything?"

"He rummaged around and took some of our table scraps from the burn pile."

"Did he steal any of your tools from the shed?"

"No."

"Did he steal anything but scraps of food in your trash container?"

"Not that I recall."

"Thank you. No further questions."

Webster called the farmer who had caught Jeremy in his barn. It was a brief exchange, and Webster was not anticipating much from the witness other than to show a pattern of vagrancy. However Zach's cross-examination caused Webster to regret putting the witness on the stand.

Zach asked, "Can you please tell the Court the circumstances around which you found Jeremy in your barn?"

"Well, I noticed that my milk cow seemed to be giving less milk, and that her bag didn't seem as full as usual on some days. Either she wasn't right or someone was stealin her milk before I got up. So one morning I snuck out to the barn while it was still dark. When I lit the lantern, I found the boy."

"You mean Jeremy Laminger?"

"Yep, it was him alright. I grabbed hold of him and intended to take him in to the Sheriff, but as I reached down for the lantern he tore away and ran. I tried to catch him but I have the gout, and he ran too fast. I shouted after him but he just kept running. He left a filthy coat and a pair of shoes full of holes, stuffed with paper. I burned them after waiting about a month to see if he'd come back for em. They were terrible and I was afraid they might be diseased or infested."

"How long ago was that?"

"Oh, about two months before Simon's death."

"Winter or summer?"

"November."

Webster concluded with his last witness the next day and wasn't happy with his side of the case. Lough had turned almost every witness into a testimonial for how miserably the boy had lived. That was galling since Webster had known from the beginning that it would be Lough's main defense. Webster realized that he'd taken too much for granted and not prepared his witnesses enough. He was irritated with himself. He also realized now that he'd made a serious mistake in forcing the Prosecutor's Office to seek a first degree murder charge. They'd argued against it, wanting to go for second degree murder. Webster now realized that his decision had been driven by his desire to make an example of Laminger to strike a blow against the Children's Aid Society. That had backfired.

Later, he had asked the Prosecutor's Office to find evidence that could prove that Jeremy Laminger had planned to murder Beasley, but they could find nothing. The knife was Beasley's and it was a kitchen utensil. Laminger left nothing in writing about any plans—he could barely write according to school officials. He had no friends or associates to divulge any plans if he had them; in fact, he didn't talk to anyone about much of anything except asking for work or handouts.

This was all very bad. He'd botched this trial. He'd overreached and rested on his laurels instead of working at this case. That was stupid and Lough had made him pay. Lough was smart, but Webster realized that his own mistakes had made Lough's job a lot easier than it should have been.

Webster had four more witnesses ready to testify about the boy's vagrant habits, but he decided not to call them. He rested his case, hoping that he would be able to attack the credibility of Lough's witnesses and gain back some ground.

The trial turned to the defense. Zach first called a drinking associate of Simon's, Ira Fletcher, who indicated that Simon had told him that he was taking the boy in to get the money that came along with him. Webster objected to it as hearsay that could not be corroborated by a dead victim. Normile ruled in his favor and sustained the motion, but the damage was done.

Lough then asked Ira if Simon's drinking habits changed in the two months after the boy had come to live with him. Looking spitefully at Webster, Ira happily replied that Simon had drunk like a fish and flashed some money around during that time. He'd even bought Ira a drink, something he had never done before.

"And where did he get the money?" Zach wondered.

"He said that it was from Jeremy's foster parents, who gave it to Simon for Jeremy's schooling, but I guess that's just hearsay too, ain't it." Ira was looking at Webster and smiling.

Webster, exasperated, didn't bother to object.

"Mr. Fletcher, what else did Simon Beasley have to say about Jeremy Laminger?"

"Objection, Your Honor. Hearsay."

Normile paused a second before ruling. "You know, Mr. Webster, I think I'll overrule you on this one. Proceed, Mr. Lough."

Ira smiled even more sweetly at Webster. He had no reputation to be spoiled or position to protect and he didn't like pompous asses like Webster. "Why yes, Mr. Lough. Simon had a lot to say about Jeremy Laminger. He said he was a no-good parasite who didn't earn his keep. He said he had a mind to trump up some charge and get the Sheriff to take him to Booneville if he didn't start bringin home more money for Simon's liquor. Said he enjoyed beatin the boy. Said it was one of his few pleasures in life. Said he hoped his dogs would tear him apart someday just for the sport of it. Things like that Mr. Lough. That's what he said."

"So I take it that Mr. Beasley didn't express much affection toward Jeremy."

Ira snorted so hard that snot escaped his nose. He got out his handkerchief. "Simon Beasley never expressed affection toward anyone that I ever heard tell."

"Objection!" yelled Webster as the courtroom audience began to whisper to one another.

"Objection sustained," boomed Normile over the tittering as he banged his gavel. "Strike the last statement from the record. Mr. Fletcher, you will limit your answers to the direct questions Mr. Lough asks you, please."

"Okay, Your Honor," replied Fletcher, still smiling sweetly.

"Mr. Fletcher, did Simon ever speak of any birthday or Christmas celebrations with Jeremy?"

Ira snorted again, but then remembering the Judge's admonition, sobered quickly. "No, he never talked of any celebrations with the boy."

"Do you believe that Mr. Beasley was wheel-chair bound?"

Ira laughed loudly at this. "Only in public to get sympathetic donations. Otherwise, he was as good at getting around as you and me when he was out of sight of the good citizens. He got a good amount of charity off that little act. Claimed that townspeople were so stupid they'd fall for anything. Suggested that I find a chair myself. I told him I still had my dignity. He laughed and said dignity didn't buy drinks."

"Thank you, Mr. Fletcher. Your witness, Senator Webster."

Webster tried to skewer Ira on cross examination. "Mr. Fletcher, what do you do for a living?"

"I'm not gainfully employed right now."

"Have you ever been 'gainfully employed' Mr. Fletcher?"

"Sure I have. I was a railroad man in the 70's. Made a good livin then."

"You haven't worked in meaningful employment for thirty years then?"

Zach thought about objecting, but then decided to see how far Webster would go with a witness who had nothing to lose and seemed to enjoy the battle. As Ira started a retort to the 'meaningful employment question' Webster said, "Never mind. Tell us Mr. Fletcher, how much do you drink?"

"A little now and then." Some of the audience laughed out loud. Normile banged the gavel for order.

"Do you drink every day, Mr. Fletcher?"

Fletcher grinned in a lecherous way and said sweetly, "When I can, sir, when I can."

"That's right Mr. Fletcher. You drink every chance you get, don't you? You're a common drunk, aren't you? And how do you expect the jury to believe anything you say about Simon Beasley?"

"Why, sir, Mr. Beasley was a common drunk too," Fletcher smiled back. "Most of my associates are common drunks. Common drunks have little to lose and generally tell the truth more than you sober people do. It's the whiskey that makes us do it. It's harder for us to lie as good as you."

The audience started to laugh, but then glanced at Normile and stopped quickly. Webster realized he might have pushed this too far. He ended his questions.

Zach called the town doctor, Frank Wheatley, to the stand. "Dr. Wheatley, how long have you been serving as Sedalia's physician?"

"Going on 35 years now."

"Did you examine Jeremy Laminger in your office on December 24?"

"Yes, I did."

"And could you describe his wounds?"

"He had large embedded splinters in his right hand, a deep knife cut in his left, long welts on his back and legs, and severe dog bites."

"How hard was it to get the splinters out?"

"They were too deeply imbedded to pull out. I had to cut them out."

"Did you administer an anesthetic?"

"A little. But it wouldn't have mattered. Laminger was in such shock that he didn't seem to feel much pain."

"You looked for other wounds?"

"Yes, of course. Because of all the blood."

"What did you find?"

"Severe dog bites, fresh and old. The boy was extremely malnourished, dehydrated and in terrible condition physically. He had bruises and scabs, old and new all over his neck, back and legs."

"How were those wounds made?"

"By the shape of them, with some sort of long, thin rod."

"Would a cane make those kinds of injuries?"

"It could."

"Objection, Your Honor. Speculation on the part of the Defense Counsel, and leading the witness."

"Overruled, Prosecutor. The witness is an expert on wounds. Proceed with your questioning, Mr. Lough."

"Did he speak to you?"

"He just kept saying, 'I kilt him', over and over."

"The Sheriff said he was 'dazed'. Do you agree with that assessment?"

"Yes, that's accurate. He had entered a state of shock, much as I've seen from victims of serious accidents or assaults."

"Thank you doctor; I have no further questions."

Webster cross-examined. "Doctor, how deeply were the splinters again?"

"All the way to the bone."

"How much force would have been required for that to occur?"

"Considerable force. It probably came from repeated strikes, not just a single blow."

"You mean, Mr. Laminger probably drove the splinters deeper and deeper into his hand as he repeatedly stabbed Simon Beasley?"

"That's likely."

"No further questions of this witness, Your Honor."

Normile motioned Lough to proceed with his witnesses. "I have one final witness, Your Honor. I call Martha Short to the stand."

Martha came forward. She'd been anxious to get to the witness chair. The girls would think she was a celebrity! Martha, in keeping with her last name, was short, squatty, shabbily dressed, with stringy hair and only a couple of teeth left in her head.

"Miss or Mrs. Short?"

"Mrs. Short. I'm a widower."

"Mrs. Short, did you know Simon Beasley?"

"Why, yes, very well. He usually ate supper with me at my house."

"How often, would you say?"

"Almost every day."

"How close were you and Mr. Beasley?"

"Oh, we were very close. He told me that he was going to marry me as soon as he got rid of that terrible boy over there." She pointed over at Jeremy with a short stubby finger that shook.

Webster rose. "Objection, Your Honor. Hearsay." But he had no enthusiasm in his voice.

"Overruled."

"How did he plan to get rid of him?"

"He was starving him out."

"Starving him out?"

"Yea. The boy was a leech. He decided that if he didn't feed him, he'd either starve to death or run away. But he didn't have much hope in the boy running away. Simon said he was too stupid and wouldn't have any idea where to go, so he'd just have to let him starve."

"Did he say he was doing anything else to get Jeremy to leave?"

"Oh, yea. He said that he yelled at him every chance he got and beat him regularly with his cane. He sicced his dogs on him, too, every time he left the house. But the stupid little leech just hung on"—she stared hatefully at Jeremy, who cringed.

She decided to cry to add as much drama as she could to her story. Her voice began to tremble. "He held up my wedding date and now he has killed my Simon! I hope he rots in Hell for all he did!" She started to sob, loudly, but it was poorly acted.

Zach let a little time pass. "No further questions for the witness."

Normile roused himself from his disgust. "Cross examination, Prosecutor Webster?" Webster just shook his head.

Normile looked at Lough. "Is that it, Mr. Lough?"

"May I approach the Bench, Your Honor?"

"You may. Mr. Prosecutor, please join us." They huddled below the bench and Normile leaned over to them so they could speak without being heard. "What is it, Mr. Lough?"

"I'd like for you to clear the courtroom except for the Jury and necessary staff. I want Jeremy to take off his shirt and trousers and show the jury the injuries on his back and legs."

Webster was furious, his voice desperate. "Judge, surely you're not going to grant that request! It's inflammatory! Lough can't prove that whatever scars that the boy has were made by Simon! He could have been in all kinds of fights. He was a low life who roamed the streets, for God's sake!"

Normile stared at Webster for what seemed like forever. Then he curtly dismissed them from the bench. Zach assumed he'd lost his request. But once they had returned to their desks, Normile addressed the audience. "I'm going to need to clear the court for 20 minutes except for the jury, the defendant, the sheriff, the bailiff, the stenographer, and the attorneys for the defense and the prosecution. Everyone else, please leave, now.

The bailiff will notify you when you can return."

The audience left in confusion, looking back over their shoulders and mumbling, shaking their heads as they went. Jeremy looked at Lough, confused. Zach went over to him and explained what he wanted. Jeremy's face reddened and he was deeply embarrassed. He started shaking his head, no, but Zach explained again why it was important. When everyone else had cleared the courtroom, Normile told Zach to bring the boy forward. Jeremy hesitantly complied, with Zach at his side. Webster sat slumped in his chair.

"You may proceed."

"Ladies and Gentlemen of the Jury, for Jeremy's sake, I'm sorry to have to do this. I ask your indulgence. Jeremy, please take off your shirt, undershirt and trousers." Jeremy slowly unbuttoned his clothing, his face a deathly white. He finally stood nearly naked in front of the jury, staring down at the floor.

Zach asked him to turn his back to the jury. When he did, a woman juror gasped and all the jurors stared soberly, sickened by what they saw. Jeremy's back was covered with horrible long, crisscrossing welt-like scars from his neck all the way down his back. Similar scars were also visible up and down his legs, plus long jagged tears in his flesh, some that had healed long ago and others more recent. It was a brutal sight.

Normile gave them a minute and then said quietly, "Thank you, Jeremy. You may dress now."

Once Jeremy was done and seated back at the defense table, the bailiff allowed the audience to return. They looked around the courtroom as they filed in, wondering what had gone on, but everything seemed the same—except for the look on the faces of the jury. All seemed somber and troubled.

Normile called the proceedings to order, but before he could announce the next stage in the trial, Webster stood. "May the Prosecutor approach the bench?"

Normile looked at him quizzically. "Certainly. Mr. Lough, please join us as well."

They huddled again. "What is it, Mr. Prosecutor?"

"I'd like to discuss the possibility of a change in the charge against the defendant. I'd like you to adjourn the court and allow the three of us to discuss this in your chambers if possible."

Normile paused only a second and then said. "Good idea, Mr. Prosecutor. Let's do just that." He announced adjournment until the following day. He, Webster and Zach went into the Judge's chambers.

"What's your proposal, Mr. Prosecutor?"

Webster looked shaken. "I propose the charge be reduced to manslaughter. If it is, and if Defense Counsel and his client agree to that plea, I propose that the Court be given full discretion within the law to establish an appropriate punishment."

"Mr. Lough, your reaction?"

Zach remained impassive. "I'll be glad to bring that proposal to my client, Your Honor."

"Well, then do that, Mr. Lough, and give us an answer in the morning."

Zach explained the proposal in detail to Jeremy that night, indicating that he should still expect punishment for the death of Simon Beasley, but that the punishment would probably be measured in terms of only limited incarceration, depending on what the Judge decided.

Jeremy had been following the trial closely and understood the change. When Zach asked what he wanted to do, he said, "I think I should agree to what Mr. Webster is offerin. I deserve to be punished. I did a horrible thing, but I learned in the trial that it may not have been as bad as I thought. What do you think? Should I agree to Mr. Webster's offer?"

"I think so, Jeremy. Whatever punishment the Judge decides to give you for a manslaughter charge should be fair. Once we find that out, we can talk about your future."

"You think I deserve a future?"

"I definitely think you deserve a future, and I've got some ideas about that for you, but I want to see what the Judge says first."

The next morning, Lough told Normile and Webster that his client was prepared to plead guilty to the charge of manslaughter, would waive further need for a jury trial, and would rely on the Court's judgment as to an appropriate punishment.

When the Court was called to order, Judge Normile explained that the Prosecuting Attorney had submitted a proposal for the lesser charge of manslaughter, that the defendant had agreed to plead guilty and waived a jury trial on those conditions. Judge

Normile thanked the jury for its time and set the sentencing date for the following day. The Court was adjourned. Some of the jurors smiled at Jeremy on the way out, which surprised him and made him feel good.

That night, Normile called Zach Lough back to his chambers once more. "Well played, Mr. Lough! You presented an excellent defense for your client."

Zach permitted himself to smile. "Thank you, Your Honor. But in all honesty, the case wasn't very hard to defend. Senator Webster overreached."

"You're right, Zachary, but I've seen cases far easier to defend than this one lost by a poor defense counsel. Your case wasn't hard on its face, but it was made more difficult by the press and the intervention of Senator Webster. In the end, it was obvious, even to him, that justice didn't support what he wanted to do to Mr. Laminger."

"You were right. He was trying to prosecute a program and the defendant was incidental. That was a major mistake on his part and you deflected that in your opening statements. I thank you for your good work in my court."

"Now, as to the disposition of this case, let me ask you something. If I were to remand Jeremy Laminger to your supervision, would you and your sister, Mrs. McDonald, be able to handle that and give Jeremy the positive support he needs to get on with his life?"

Zach smiled. "Judge Normile, I assure you, we could do that."

"Thank you, Mr. Lough. It's been a pleasure to have you in my court. Have a restful evening."

Zach left Normile's chambers. He wasn't sure whether he walked or floated out.

Anna McDonald had been in Sedalia for some time now, quietly following the trial from Zach's reports each evening, but not in the audience at the trial for fear that she could become a distraction. Now Zach insisted that she come to the sentencing hearing the next day. He was pretty sure what Normile would do and he wanted Anna to be there to meet Jeremy.

The next morning, at the sentencing hearing, Normile addressed Jeremy. "Mr. Laminger, I want to make sure that you understand that what you did was a terrible thing. You took a human life and that is not an acceptable response despite what was happening to you. Do you understand that?"

Jeremy swallowed hard and nodded. "Yes, sir, I understand that and feel awful about what I did. I never did ever hurt anybody or anything before this."

"Thank you, Jeremy. I believe you. I also believe horrible things happened to you that caused you to react the way you did. Now, by law, the punishment for manslaughter could range from two years in prison to considerably longer. Given the circumstances surrounding your offense, I'm sentencing you to the minimum—two years confinement—with allowance for the time you've already served in jail awaiting and during your trial. That's about a year."

"I'm also allowed to grant probation in cases in which I believe there is no public safety issue involved. On the condition that you agree to the supervision of Mr. Lough or his designee, I'm going to substitute probation for the remainder of your time served." Jeremy looked over at Zach, a little confused. Zach smiled and nodded, patting him on the arm.

"But hear me well on this, Mr. Laminger, during that probationary period, should you become involved in any delinquent behavior or crime of any kind, I will rescind this order and you will serve full jail time. Do you understand that?"

"Yes sir, I'll be good."

"Mr. Lough, do you accept responsibility for Mr. Laminger during his supervisory probation?"

"I do, Your Honor."

"Mr. Prosecutor, any objection?" Webster shook his head.

"Very well then. I've already written the order for all of you to sign. This trial is concluded."

Webster left quickly, refusing to comment to the press. Anna came forward to meet Jeremy. Zach introduced them and told Jeremy that he would be returning with them to where Anna lived. He told him that her husband, Ben McDonald would give him a job and a place to stay. Anna told him that, were he interested, she would personally help him finish his schooling.

Jeremy thanked her and said he would really like to try, but that he wasn't a very good student. Zach laughed and told him that he should wait and see, that Mrs. McDonald was a very good teacher.

They boarded the train that afternoon out of Sedalia. Zach and

Anna were glad to be going home. Jeremy was elated to have a chance to start his new life with people who cared about and had respect for him.

Webster headed to his office to catch up on his law practice. He was angry with himself. He'd allowed his ego and ambition to blind him and Lough had made him pay dearly. Lough was mature for his age and Webster admired how he'd handled himself, although he wasn't about to tell him that.

But he eventually did, when Lough joined him in the Missouri Senate and became the closest thing Webster would have to a friend during his remaining years in the Senate, the highest level of public service he ever attained in his long career.

Chapter 26

Zach returned to his law practice after the trial and Anna to her work. Charlie and Ben's business was booming, a reflection of a healthy state and national economy. Ben and Anna added two new rooms to their house in Jadwin to accommodate their growing family.

They assumed the family was complete now, deciding not to have additional children because the last childbirth had taken a heavy physical toll on Anna. She still looked healthy, but she was chronically fatigued as she tried to manage her busy schedule of work, substitute teaching, and raising her family. She hid it well. Only Ben and Bessie knew of her occasional exhaustion. But Ben had begun to worry about it and admonished her to slow down a little.

Three years passed. Anna was increasingly sure that there was no pregnancy risk. But she had miscalculated. In August 1906 she became ill with what she thought was a stomach ailment. The nausea lasted a week. It struck her hardest in the mornings but persisted at some level throughout the day. Then, just as quickly as it had come, it went away and she returned to normal.

But by mid-September, she began to suspect that her symptoms had not been illness-related. Her menstrual cycle was disrupted and she began to have the same feelings in her body that had accompanied her prior pregnancies. She decided not to tell Ben and worry him until she was sure. By early October, she was sure.

Ben fretted over this pregnancy more than any other. He just had a premonition that something wasn't right, but there was no evidence to justify his concern. Anna was actually doing better now than in her prior pregnancies. After that initial sickness, she felt strong and healthy, actually better than she had in a long time. She told him to relax, that it was just another one of God's little miracles for them.

But from November through January, the pregnancy again became difficult. The cramps, nausea, and exhaustion returned in full force. Her condition was not helped by the work she had to do to prepare for the largest yet annual conference of Missouri's orphan train placements, with more than 2,000 attendees coming.

Her physician gave her pills to increase the iron in her blood, but could think of little more to do for her. She refused home rest and was still traveling throughout Missouri in her monitoring activities. She did watch her diet carefully and rested when she could, but she had so much to do that simply couldn't be avoided.

But by late January her symptoms were so severe that she finally had to stop working and take bed rest. She and Ben traveled to St. Louis to see an obstetrician, named Sara Rogers, to determine why this pregnancy was so difficult. After examining Anna, she told them she was concerned with the baby's weak heart rate and erratic movements. She warned them that it might be difficult to keep the baby alive to birth unless Anna took complete bed rest. She sent numerous medication instructions to Anna's local physician in Salem and placed Anna on a richer diet. Anna had not been gaining enough weight for the pregnancy.

Anna despised the bed rest, but Ben policed her like an army sergeant. He developed an unshakeable anxiety about her mortality, terrified at the thought of losing her. He never told her so but she could see it on his face, so she reluctantly tried to accommodate him.

Her freedom from work gave her time to write to legislators and advocates throughout the State regarding her concerns about yet another bill introduced in the Missouri Legislature to halt orphan placements. The same bill had been introduced three years in a row now and each year it had become more difficult to defeat it.

Her efforts, and those of other opponents, were not enough this time. The bill narrowly passed both the House and Senate and was sent to the Governor's desk in March, 1907 late in the eighth-month of Anna's pregnancy. Ben made a mistake and didn't tell her of its passage for fear that it might increase her anxiety and worsen her condition, or that she'd try to go to Jefferson City to talk personally with the Governor's Office.

Anna's immune system had grown weaker since January and she experienced respiratory problems and a continuing low-grade fever. Dr. Rogers finally prescribed more powerful medications even though it presented some threat to the unborn child. Rogers began to worry that they might lose both Anna and the child during childbirth. Now, Anna was actually beginning to lose weight, which was a very bad sign in a pregnancy.

Finally, in late March, fearing Anna's wrath if the Governor signed the legislation prohibiting the immigration of New York orphans to Missouri without her knowing it, Ben told her of the passage of the bill. When she heard, she was furious and lashed out at him in ways she'd never done before. He understood the anger and let it pass.

Anna immediately wrote the Governor, appealing to him to veto the bill. Her letter arrived with only one day remaining for the

Governor to veto it if he was going to. Otherwise, it would automatically become law.

Governor Joe Folk, a Democrat, had won his first term only three years prior after a hard-fought campaign with his long-time Republican rival, Senator Percival Webster. The odds had seemed to be against him. Webster had a strong political machine behind him and a lot of industry money. Theodore Roosevelt, also a Republican, was still in the White House and his popularity was contagious. Roosevelt had sent letters to the larger Missouri newspapers, endorsing Webster.

But an earlier sensational court trial in Sedalia had resulted in some negative publicity for Webster. He was widely considered to have botched his handling of the prosecution, and even accused of trying to railroad a terribly abused child. That, and Webster's aloofness, weakened him just enough for Folk to defeat him. Governor Folk knew all about that trial and the role that Zach Lough and Anna had played. He considered himself a personal friend of both Anna and Zach.

The Governor hated the legislation. It was reactionary and sensationalist, and was insulting to the thousands of orphan immigrants already successfully integrated into Missouri's social and economic structure. He also knew that it was a strong priority of Webster's.

He wanted to veto the bill as much as any that had ever been placed before him, but the Senate was holding hostage some of his own high-priority legislation that he needed to pass. He'd already decided that he'd have to punt on this one, holding his nose and leaving the bill unsigned, allowing it to become law. He had informed Webster of this, who was pleased and agreed to support the release of the Governor's to the Senate floor for a vote.

It was at that point that Folk got Anna's letter. He read it with consternation. She had eloquently stated the case against the bill in both ethical and human-impact terms. He talked to his wife and his advisors. His Director of the Department of Health and Welfare privately thought the bill should be vetoed, but suggested it would not be wise to do so because of sure retribution from Webster.

The Governor's wife said he would have to follow his own conscience. She was a friend of Anna's and could not advise him in an unbiased manner. All of his advisors told him that he had to be pragmatic; that there would be significant loss to his credibility if he did not get his priority bills out of the log jam that Webster had created.

Folk went personally to see Webster again. No one except them knew what they discussed, but afterwards Webster expressed public anger with the Governor and accused him of reneging on a deal. The following day, the governor vetoed the bill and lost his major legislative priorities for the year.

His wife told him she was proud of him. His advisors reminded him of the damage to farmers that would be caused by the loss of his agricultural legislation. The agricultural advocates were disappointed in his leadership. They vowed that he would not win another statewide office. He didn't.

Anna sent him a warm letter of appreciation. He wrote back, hoping her remaining pregnancy would go more smoothly and that she would have a healthy baby. The Governor's good wishes were not to come true. The pregnancy continued to be hard right up to the day of the delivery.

The preacher came by frequently to visit Anna and Ben. He knew they were anxious about the pregnancy. They told him they were praying for the miracle of a healthy, normal baby. He said, "I hope your prayers are answered, but the miracle you pray for may not always be the one you get."

When the baby was born, Anna nearly died from a loss of blood. She was semi-conscious for a full day. When she finally came to and was able to speak, she asked Ben how the baby was doing. She saw sadness on Ben's face. "It's a boy. The doctor doesn't know how he's doing yet. He had a terrible time getting him to cry at the birth. He's very small. We won't know for a while if he'll live, or how much he is affected, but we think there will be handicaps."

Anna knew something was terribly wrong the first time she held the child. He was listless and unresponsive. She cried herself to sleep that night. And, in fact, there were many things wrong with their son, Bobby. He lived, but was very slow to respond as an infant. He was weak and sickly for the first six months of his life. He nearly died of infections in his tiny lungs numerous times. The doctor told them that he would be significantly mentally and physically handicapped all his life and suggested it would be best to institutionalize him. They declined, preferring to keep him at home if they could.

Bobby didn't start to crawl until age three and he took his first troubled steps at age five. At age six, he tried to say his first words, but they couldn't understand what he said.

But there were so many things right with Bobby McDonald. He had an amazing shock of coal-black hair from the day he was born. He had big brown eyes that seemed to stare right into the souls of anyone who paid attention to him. And he was an amazing little fighter. Every time it looked as though an infection would take him, he overcame it and lived to fight another day.

By the time he was six months old he could begin to focus his eyes. From that point forward he watched his mother's every move with intense delight squealing and squirming in excitement every morning she came to get him. He smiled nearly all the time and cooed when people picked him up. He seldom cried, and then only briefly. He finally learned to walk, and then to run in an awkward gait. The doctors had been sure that would never happen.

His little hands were drawn and palsied, but by the age of five, he loved to bang on the toy piano that Ben had purchased for him from St. Louis. He was in the middle of everything. He drove his older brothers and sisters mad with his antics, making them laugh all the while. He was the family's clown and he liked the role.

He was intellectually disabled and never learned to speak clearly. There was no such thing as speech therapy in southern Missouri at the time. Had there been, perhaps Bobby might have been able to make a little progress, but Anna doubted that it would be much better than it was. She did what she could but his speech patterns were dramatically affected by his disability. So verbal articulation was not his primary method of communication.

This eventually became evident to all who attended the Jadwin Church of Christ. Long before he could construct a sentence, he was singing as loudly as his little lungs would allow, right along with everyone else, only just a bit off key and in a language that only he could understand. It was a shock to visitors, but the regular members soon got used to it. Anna and Ben never "shushed" him. The truth was that the singing got livelier at the Jadwin Church after Bobby began raising his little voice to the Lord.

He loved everybody, and everyone loved him back. As a child he gave big slobbery kisses to anyone who would come close enough to allow it. He did master the word "love" pretty well by the time he was seven. Grown men and women, who'd forgotten how to say that word, had it said to them without reservation, and they happily returned the favor.

Anna and Ben grieved at times over the condition of their youngest son, but never in front of him, or to anyone else. They knew Bobby would always be disabled, or "unique" as Zach phrased it. He wouldn't be able to run swiftly or do well in school like his favorite Uncle Zach. But he could make everybody laugh at his antics and bask in the warmth of his love. That was enough for him

Sometimes the miracle you pray for is not the miracle you get.

Chapter 27

In 1909, the New York State Legislature did what Senator Percival Webster never could. It ended the orphan train movement by passing the most progressive child welfare legislation in America, establishing a new state agency for child and family aid. The Society's Rural Relocation Program was no longer necessary. A sophisticated foster and residential care system was being established to take care of orphaned and abused children in New York, by New Yorkers.

The Society had lobbied hard for this legislation for many years under the leadership of the irrepressible Emma Mason. First introduced in 1905, it had taken four long years to be perfected. Its passage represented Emma's finest hour and marked the true beginning of the shaping of government-directed child and family services in America. Within ten years, an additional twenty-five states would pass bills patterned after New York and Massachusetts statutes, including major child labor reform.

Two other important variables had contributed to passage of the bill. First, the great immigrant waves of the 19th Century were over. New York City was no longer the primary entry point of immigrants into the United States. Second, the American economy was recovering from the Roosevelt Recession and Americans were feeling good about themselves. With more federal and state tax revenues coming into the coffers, orphaned and abused children became the "cause célèbre" of the decade.

The Children's Aid Society sponsored another major celebration in New York to mark the passage of the legislation, again attended by thousands. Nellie Taft, the wife of the newly-elected President William Howard Taft, had even agreed to attend. She and Mrs. Roosevelt had long been admirers of Emma Mason's work.

First Lady Taft was a charismatic woman who was not satisfied to be a wallflower wife in Washington D.C. She was a champion of women's rights, particularly the right to vote. She had talked her reluctant husband into running for the office of President when all he really wanted to be was a U.S. Supreme Court Justice. And she had committed to Emma that she would turn her attention toward the cause of disenfranchised children when her husband was elected.

But on May 17, 1909, Nellie Taft suffered a major stroke that left her unable to speak. She would not be able to attend the event. So she had President Taft send his and her most trusted advisor and eloquent spokesperson, Major Archie Butt, in her place. The event was also to be attended by numerous other dignitaries from New York, Washington D.C. and many of the states that had taken in Charles Loring Brace's little street urchins.

Mrs. Mason had written Anna and Ben to insist on their participation in the celebration, along with Zachary's. She wanted them there a week early to show them the dramatic new programs now opening to orphan children in the city. Ben, Anna and family arrived on July 4th just in time to participate in a spectacular Independence Day celebration sponsored by the City, including a fireworks display unlike anything they had ever seen.

Mrs. Mason had offered to have Bessie and Jess come along to help with the children, who now ranged from their older teens to little Bobby. She'd met them on a recent visit to Jadwin and had floated the Current River with them.

She paid full costs of travel and a per diem for all the happy travelers. It was the trip of Jess's lifetime. He was as giddy as the children. Bessie had her hands full containing them as Anna and Ben met with Mrs. Mason on matters related to the Missouri Monitoring Program.

It was a whirlwind week. Anna and Ben saw beautiful new orphanages and group homes built with both private and public funds. They talked to a large group of foster families who told them about their training and their excitement for taking children into their homes.

Archie Butt joined them in their review of the new programs. Despite his strange name, Ben and Anna found him to be one of the noblest, kindest and most talented men that they'd ever met. In their short time together they struck up a meaningful friendship. Archie was the Chief Attaché to President Taft, loyal, incredibly diplomatic, mature far beyond his age, and a wonderful speaker. He represented First Lady Nellie Taft well, giving the most inspiring of all the speeches at the conference.

Emma Mason was the closing speaker at the 1909 conference. She did a good job.

"Our world has changed dramatically since 1854, when a young preacher viewed the devastation of Hell's Kitchen and decided that he, personally, had to find a way to make a difference. In those terrible days, 30,000 homeless children roamed those dirty, dangerous streets. Now, little more than a half-century later, because of what he inspired, few children have to experience that fate." Applause broke out as the audience stood to acknowledge her declaration.

When the crowd had quieted, she continued. "I am, of course, referring to Reverend Charles Loring Brace, now passed from us. But while he was here, he touched the lives of thousands, young and old alike, including me. I know people in this room who probably would not be alive today except for his intervention."

"Reverend Brace was a poor preacher, and I don't mean economically!" The audience laughed. "He only spoke eloquently on one topic. But that did not belie his passion. He was as fearless as a mother grizzly when it came to his street urchins. While New York City's citizenry collectively averted their eyes, he focused the world's attention on this one great cause. When the best minds of the city said, 'It's a terrible tragedy, but it is just too complex and difficult to be overcome', he said, 'tell that to the little-three-year-old who'll die tonight, alone in some alleyway, trying to find warmth!' He changed the world, one child at a time. And one at a time, he rescued over 150,000 homeless children from the horrors of our city's mean streets." Another long standing ovation broke out.

"But the Reverend Brace's work is not yet done. We have come to learn that the needs of vulnerable children across this country are far too great to be met by a single individual or organization. It will require the collective power of our federal and state governments to address the magnitude of the problem that exists. Today celebrates a major turning point in our history, in which states and the federal government have embraced that role. I wasn't certain I would live to see this day, and I feel deeply blessed that I have."

When Emma finished her speech, Archie Butt came forward again, surprising Emma—it was definitely not on the agenda— and presented her with the United States National Humanities Award, the highest honor in her field of service. She received a standing ovation that lasted a full five minutes from the crowd of 12,000, who'd been tipped off and stayed around for the special presentation. For the first time in her life, Emma Mason cried in public.

It was late Thursday afternoon when Anna, Ben, Jess, Bessie and the children boarded the train to return to Missouri. Zach had returned to Rolla a day earlier. Emma wept for the second time and hugged them all closely before they boarded. She had a premonition that she might not see them again.

She was correct. She died six months later at age 76 on one of her brisk morning walks, presumably thinking about some new strategy for all the vulnerable children of America, all of them hers.

The last great founding champion of the Children's Aid Society had passed. She was mourned nationwide, and most acutely in a little out-of-the-way community in southern Missouri, where she had visited twice to meet the people and float down the Current River with Billy and her closest Missouri friends.

Shortly after Emma's death, Archie Butt also made a trip to Jadwin to visit with his friends. He just needed to get away from Washington D.C. for a while. The stress between his two great political mentors was increasing. Archie was a close friend of the Tafts, but he had previously been Chief Attaché to Theodore Roosevelt, and was a close friend of the Roosevelt family. In fact, that's how he'd first met William Taft, who was a prominent member of the Roosevelt Cabinet.

Unfortunately, after Teddy Roosevelt orchestrated William Taft to succeed him as President, and after returning from a year-long sabbatical in Africa, he became disenchanted with Taft, who was gentler and less combative than the former President. The tension grew and Roosevelt decided to try to unseat Taft, creating a major schism in the Republican Party and putting

Archie squarely in the middle of the feud between his two powerful friends. The conflict between the two men finally went public, although Taft had tried desperately to avoid it.

Theodore Roosevelt kept trying to persuade Archie to abandon Taft, but he politely refused. Although he knew Roosevelt was, by far, the more charismatic and action-oriented of the two men, he believed Taft to be the more noble, and with the truer heart.

In letters to Anna and Ben, between 1910 and 1912, Archie related his unceasing effort to reunite the two old friends, fearing that their conflicts would result in an irreversible rift, not only between the Roosevelts and Tafts, but also within the Republican Party.

In 1912, while Archie was away in Europe vacationing, Roosevelt publicly attacked Taft in a way that Archie knew was disingenuous. He was in the fourth week of a six week European trip when the news of Roosevelt's actions came to him. He feared that Roosevelt's attack could crush Taft's spirit, so he cut his vacation short to return to Washington D.C. as quickly as he could. He booked passage on the first ship leaving port from Europe. It was a big new luxury liner and he had to pay a lot of money for a last-minute ticket, but he felt he had no choice. The name of the ship was the Titanic.

Archie never made it home. His loss at sea saddened the thousands who knew him, including the Tafts and the Roosevelts. Nellie and William Taft felt as though they'd lost a son. And, in a quieter part of the world, Ben and Anna McDonald both wept.

When the stories of the Titanic's survivors were told, one man stood out in particular for his heroic efforts to save the passengers as the ship sank. That was Major Archie Butt, the young man who had spoken so eloquently at the Children's Aid Society's Conference in 1909, and who had so admired the three dynamic orphans from Missouri that he'd come to know.

Chapter 28

The years flowed by for Anna and Ben like the crystal waters of the Current River. The McDonald children thrived, grew into adulthood and married. With his increased share of the profits, Ben invested in land and owned more than 2,000 acres of woodlands in southern Missouri. Both the McDonald and the Schafer families kept in close contact with Christian and Susanna and their family in North Carolina, often traveling there on vacation. Christian and Susanna also came back to southern Missouri at least once a year on business as Charlie, Ben and Christian continued to grow their companies.

Their collaborative companies were among the first to convert from steam power to the combustible engine in the operation of their mills. Horses were still used for the logging, but the transportation of the logs to and from the mills was now greatly speeded by the use of trucks.

It was an especially good time for Anna. She had passed childbearing age and remained healthy and vibrant. While not quite as slim as in her early years, the few pounds she added fit her well. She now appeared to be a graceful and dignified middle-aged woman to all except Ben, who still saw her as much the same girl he had found again in that little one-room school house so long ago.

Anna assisted the Children's Aid Society for a few more years after 1910, but each year that responsibility diminished. Now her primary attention was focused on the reform of Missouri's own human services systems. She, along with other key Missouri leaders, like the recently elected state Senator from District 16, Zachary Lough, was influential in the passage of child labor laws similar to those of New York.

The Jadwin community remained small, although Anna's old elementary school was enlarged, and a second teacher added. Jess continued to sit on the Jadwin School Board, as he had done for more than 30 years.

Jess and Bessie were empty nesters now and traveled more. Both enjoyed good health. They had a marvelous time on their trips to the great Rocky Mountains, Yellowstone National Park, Yosemite and the Grand Canyon, taking some of their grandchildren with them each summer. Only occasionally would Bessie resist Jess's vagabond instincts and request that they just stay home and relax in the place she still loved the most.

In the spring of 1910 they traveled to Niagara Falls and didn't return until mid-summer. They both claimed it was their second honeymoon, laughing and explaining that their first was a canoe trip down the Current River, staying in a tent at night.

By late 1910, that huge old oak tree in the center of the Lough meadow had begun to show signs of dying. Jess hated the thought of that because he knew it was still Anna's favorite spot next to her bluff on the Current River. The tree was void of all leaves by the summer of 1915 and was fully dead, with broken limbs littering the ground around it. It had now become a safety hazard. Jess worried that the bigger limbs might fall on his cattle or horses, since they still congregated under it on rainy days out of habit, although it could offer them no protection anymore.

Jess saw Anna walking down the road toward his house one September day and went up to meet her. They stood at the edge of the meadow, looking sadly out at their old friend that had provided such wonderful shade and peace for both of them. It was the last representative of the old growth forest that had once dominated Jess's land. He looked over at her and said gently, "I've gotta cut it down, Anna. It's gettin too dangerous for the cattle to be around and I'm scared that some kid will try to climb it and get hurt."

She nodded, tears forming in her eyes. "I'll have Ben give you a hand." They walked on down to the house in silence, hand in hand.

The next day, he decided not to wait for the weekend when Ben could join him, although he knew that felling a tree of that size would be tricky and realized that someone probably should be there with him when he tried. But the lean of the tree was an easy one to read and he was sure it would fall in the direction he anticipated. He began cutting it on the morning of what would become a hot September day. By noon, the temperature approached 90 and the air was heavy with humidity. He felt himself overheating and began to work more slowly.

But the tree had fallen exactly where he thought and he had already began cut much of the lower trunk into stove-length sections that he would later split before hauling the wood to the house to stack for drying.

He became a little light headed and his sweating slowed, which he knew could be trouble. He decided to stop and return to the house for lunch with Bessie and to take a short nap. He complained to Bessie over lunch about not feeling well. She told him that he should wait until it cooled down, that the tree couldn't hurt anyone now, but Jess was stubborn and decided he should do a little more that day. He promised that he would take it easy.

By late afternoon, he'd cut the largest branches from the trunk, some as big around as most tree trunks themselves. Now it got trickier because of the tree's massive weight putting immense pressure on the remaining branches, frequently pinching his saw blade no matter how careful he was. Those limbs also tended to snap unpredictably as they were being cut. He finally reached the smaller treetop branches by about 4:00 p.m., over 60 feet up from the tree's stump. He was hot and feeling a little light headed again. He decided he'd stop after cutting one more branch.

As he leaned low to saw into that branch, he felt a stabbing pain on the back of his neck, and then another. Instinctively, he reached up to grab at the angry insect that had stung him. It clung to his hand and stung him again as he brought it away. He saw the yellow stripes on its streamlined body and recognized it as a yellow jacket, the most vicious little warrior of the wasp family. A yellow jacket's sting could be more painful and dangerous than any of its insect peers, and since it didn't leave its stinger behind, it would sting aggressively and repeatedly.

Unlike most bees, yellow jackets nest underground, and so their nest is not as easily detected. Many Missouri farmers, plowing new ground, encountered these aggressive insects and usually regretted it before they got away. Yellow jackets attack in swarms. When their nest is disturbed, they will follow a victim up to a quarter-mile to inflict their revenge. Jess had seen horses and cattle run right through fences when attacked by a swarm of yellow jackets.

Realizing what he'd stumbled onto, he tried to quickly back away, certain there was a nest nearby that had been damaged by the fallen tree. But he was in the middle of the thickest part of the tree's upper branches, with some still attached to the trunk and other cut ones bunched up around him. As he tried to escape the mess, his foot caught in the tangle of limbs and he tripped. His momentum worked against him, making him fall hard, hitting the back of his head on a protruding limb as he did, and stunning him.

But far worse, he had landed right by the disturbed opening of the large yellow jacket nest that had been punctured by a jagged, broken tree limb. The insects swarmed him immediately. The stings quickly brought him to consciousness and he tried to get up. By the time he got his legs under him, the yellow jackets were all over him, stinging his face and hands and penetrating his clothing. He tried to scramble away from the tree, fighting them off with his hands, but he didn't get far. With one last hope, he dropped to the ground and tried to lie still, hoping they'd give up, but they just kept stinging.

Bessie waited until 5:00 p.m. before becoming worried enough to make her way up the lane. At first she didn't see him because he was on the opposite side of the fallen tree. But she saw a few of his tools near the trunk of the tree and knew he wouldn't leave them willingly.

She walked around the tree and discovered his swollen body, now nearly unrecognizable. Yellow jackets were still darting in and out around him. She put her apron over her head and ran to him, grabbing his arms and pulling desperately. She was able to drag his body about 50 feet from the tree before the stings forced her to run. She waited a few seconds and then ran back to him, pulling him on down the gradual slope of the field toward the house. She didn't know whether he was still alive.

She endured the stings again, but this time she was able to pull him far enough that most of the yellow jackets returned to their nest. Thankfully, Anna and Ben were coming down the lane to deliver a package. Spotting Bessie, they rushed over to help. They were shocked by what they saw.

As soon as they got Jess to the house, Ben rushed out to summon the doctor from Salem. It would be two hours before he could find him and get him back to Jadwin. Meanwhile, Anna and Bessie bathed Jess and applied cold compresses. His breathing was labored and shallow. He began to groan and move a little, but could not open his swollen eyes. He kept mumbling something, but they could not make out what he was trying to say through his badly swollen lips.

Upon arriving and surveying the situation, the doctor gave Jess a heavy dose of sedative. His body relaxed and he floated off into oblivion. They kept him sedated for three days while the swelling slowly subsided. Bessie fed him liquids with a spoon and fretted about his inability to take food. On the fourth day he opened his eyes. The swelling had subsided considerably but the skin on his face, neck and hands were still splotched in angry blackish-blue colors.

He smiled when he saw Bessie, but the smile only covered half his face. The other side drooped and one of his eyes no longer seemed to focus. He tried to talk to her, but his words were not understandable. He kept trying to tell her something, growing louder with each try until it exhausted him, the panic evident in his eyes. He lay back on the pillow and tears ran down the side of his face. Bessie squeezed his hand. He could respond reasonably well with one hand, but his other arm hung limp, no longer in his control. He looked at it, then at Bessie, and shook his head sadly.

She remained positive, telling him he would be fine when the venom finally left his body, but she knew better. The doctor had told her that a combination of the heat and the massive amount of venom from the stings had caused a stroke. His chance for full recovery was small.

He lay two more weeks in that condition. The dark bruises on his skin gradually receded to yellow and then faded away, but the damage from the stroke was lasting. One side of his body was totally paralyzed. He had trouble breathing. Bessie stayed by his side the entire time, even during the nights, holding his good hand. He would occasionally stroke her hair as she slept fitfully in a rocking chair, leaning her head on the bed beside him.

Bessie figured out some elementary communication signals for food, water and for going to the bathroom that his scrambled brain could understand. She decided that having him with her, even in a crippled condition, was worth whatever work it took to help him recover as much as he could. But Jess was terribly depressed and frustrated with his mind and body. He cried often, and when he did, it broke Bessie's heart.

Bessie was beside herself with guilt after the accident. She was convinced Jess would still be fine if she'd just insisted that he wait to cut up that tree after the first frost and cooler weather. The yellow jackets would have hibernated, or at least have been less active. Jess wouldn't have gotten overheated. All she had to do was to insist he did not go back out to work that afternoon.

She finally confided her guilt to Anna, who found her sitting alone in the parlor one evening after Jess had gone to sleep, weeping quietly. Anna took her in her arms and said, "Bessie, Jess wouldn't have listened to you. He was a strong man and he would have insisted on clearing that tree once he felled it. Sometimes fate just plays a hand and we can't really control it. I don't think you could have stopped what happened. Accidents always involve events that we might easily have changed if we knew they were going to happen, but we never can know. That must be left to God's will."

Bessie wasn't entirely ready to accept Anna's consolation, but it helped. Eventually she came to grips with her guilt. She wished with all her heart it hadn't happened but she didn't own it anymore.

On Monday of the third week, Jess developed pneumonia and his health declined rapidly. He was having difficulty breathing and was slipping in and out of consciousness. Fluid was building in his lungs and he was too weak to cough it out. The doctor summoned Ben, Anna and Zach to the farm along with all the other children, now grown.

Near the end, Jess relaxed and seemed somewhat better. He looked at all them and smiled as best he could. He formed the word "love" awkwardly and took each of their hands in his good one. Then he went to sleep with Bessie at his side and he never woke up again.

The funeral was a somber, painful affair for the family and for the broader Jadwin community. Jess had many friends and admirers and no real enemies. He had been such a positive, vibrant part of the community. Family and neighbors brought food to the Lough house and sat with Bessie for two days, trying to give her and the children some comfort, trying to find comfort for themselves. Jess was interred at the Jadwin cemetery.

Bessie had difficulty recovering—but perhaps not quite as much as Zach. Jess had been the father he never had and the best friend of his life. For days, he caught himself weeping uncontrollably at odd times and finally had to take time off from his work. He came back to the Lough farm for two months and spent the time with Bessie, continuing the chores Jess would have done. He took long walks with Anna. Gradually the pain settled to a dull ache that would remain with him for many years, particularly each time he returned to Jadwin. He had difficulty going to church on Sundays because the graveyard was just across the lane, in plain sight of the church door.

One of the first things Zach did when he came home was to take out the yellow jacket nest. He carried a five gallon can of kerosene up to the hole. It was still a warm day and the yellow jackets were in the air, but he didn't care. They stung him as he poured the kerosene down the hole and over a 20 foot circle all around it. He stepped back a small distance and lit a match as angry yellow jackets continued to sting him. He felt their stings, but he didn't run.

He dropped the match to the grass and the flames slowly spread to the edge of the hole and then dropped down in. Soon a great geyser of fire shot up as though it were a living thing. The yellow jackets left him and desperately flew back toward their hole until their wings caught fire, and they fell to the ground to be consumed by their own little version of hell that Zach had created for them. None of the yellow jackets survived.

Zach stood silently, watching the fire for more than an hour, tears streaming down his face. Finally he turned and walked back home where Bessie was waiting to place ointment on the stings that she knew he'd have. Time was the only salve for the pain he felt inside.

Bessie was a strong woman. Everyone could see it. She recovered—outwardly. She had too many children and grandchildren to quit on life. She seemed to be her same old self, laughing with friends and family, caring for grandchildren, helping sick neighbors, and cooking her trademark large Sunday dinners. It continued to be a lively place at Thanksgiving and Christmas. The Lough children still came home on Sunday. Jess's departure would not change that. Anna came to visit her almost every night for the first six months after Jess died, until Bessie told her she didn't need to anymore and that she should be with Ben and her own family.

By all accounts she had handled the loss very well. She willed herself out of self-pity and depression. Her family marveled at her strength and talked about how well she'd adjusted. Bessie was a marvelous actress during the daytime.

No one saw her nights. She lay in her bed and thought of him before she went to sleep. She prayed to God that she would see him again someday. She could not shake the feeling that a large part of her had left the earth. She was now only half-whole. For years she would hold Jess's pillow in her arms until she fell asleep.

She was a fastidious woman, that Bessie. Jess had often accused her of taking the trousers and shirt right off his body to wash them before he even got through the door. But she never washed that pillowcase again. The pillow, those fading family pictures and her memory were all that was left of the man she'd loved more than life itself for nearly as long as she could remember.

Chapter 29

Ben brought a puppy home to Anna a few months after Jess died.
He was on a business trip in Rolla and a man brought puppies
into Sam's office asking if he could display them for adoption.
They were beautiful little fuzzy-haired, pure-bred Labs. One
chubby little fellow climbed out of the box, turning it over as he
did, scattering puppies all over the floor. He sauntered over and
looked up at Ben with an expression that made Ben laugh.

Sam said, "Why Ben, I think he's adopted you!" The puppy kept
looking up at Ben, trying to wag his little tail but wagging his
whole rear instead because the tail was too small to function as
he desired. Anna's continuing sadness over the loss of Jess had
thrown her into a funk. She tried to shake it but life just felt a
little gray. So Ben had brought the pup home, hoping it would
cheer her up.

Ben, questioning his own sanity, loaded the dog into his car. The
McDonalds already had a bevy of pets at home, from cats to
turtles, snakes, lizards, and for a long while, Rascal, the
honeymoon raccoon, until he had died of old age.

The dog was at least as stubborn and as much of a troublemaker
as the raccoon had been, getting into everything he wasn't
supposed to. He was fearless and had an insatiable curiosity. He
would argue with any family member or any other pet that got in
his way, even though he was only a few weeks old, still fuzzy
haired and puppy fat.

If scolded, he would scold back, barking and growling at his
accuser and looking up defiantly. That endeared him to Anna.
She would start laughing just watching him waddle jauntily into
a room. By six months of age he'd destroyed every piece of

clothing he could find left unattended around the house and a few good shoes as well. He was noted for sneaking into clothes baskets to perpetrate his crimes.

He "talked" to the family every day. He really did seem to be trying to form words. He would inflect his barks, yips, whines and growls, and he would become frustrated when the humans never quite seemed to get what he was saying. By the time he was a year old he was the absolute master of the McDonald household.

She called him Rascal2, and it was clear that she was his human, and his alone, as related to other animals around the house. And all other humans were just bystanders to be tolerated. Everybody could see that it was the Rascal2-Anna show. When he sensed Anna's sadness, he did his best to cheer her up with his goofy antics.

As a pup, he would come up to her in the evenings as she sat on the porch and whine until she picked him up; then he'd place his head on her chest and his front paws up to her neck, watching her with his big soft eyes. He always stayed in her lap as long as she'd let him.

She was the only one who could correct him without him becoming defiant. He tried to follow her everywhere, including to school when she substituted, where he would wait all day until she was ready to go home. He watched over her with a protecting eye. They had formed an unbreakable bond.

In the autumn of 1916, Ben began his usual process of cutting wood on weekends in preparation for the winter, even though he knew that he should have just hired it delivered. He liked the mindless achievement the work provided, and the direct use of the saw and axe. He would often take Bobby with him, and sometimes, Anna, as he cut the standing dead timber from the wooded areas of his own property and on the Lough farm.

One clear crisp Saturday morning, he, Anna and Bobby loaded into the truck for the short trip to the woods not far from Bessie's house. They began cutting by 7:00 a.m. and were half loaded by mid-morning.

Ben began to cut down a red oak tree that had died the previous year. It had long heavy limbs snaking out in every direction from its trunk. It wasn't entirely clear to him which way the tree would fall because of the angle of the ground and the influence of the weight of the upper branches, so he widened the notch on what he hoped was the correct side of the trunk. Felling trees was a tricky business and required caution. He alerted Anna and Bobby to stand back as he went to the other side and began to cut through the trunk toward his notch.

He had sawed nearly all the way through the trunk to the notch, but the tree hadn't begun to lean, and wasn't pinching his saw blade yet. It was going to be one of those balancing trees that timber men hated. It made him nervous and he cut slower. He paused to make sure Anna and Bobby were far enough back and out of the tree's range. Rascal2 sat patiently beside Anna, her hand on his head.

Ben returned to his cautious sawing. He hadn't gotten far when the tree suddenly shifted the wrong way, pinning his saw tightly in the crease of the cut. It was definitely not going to fall in the direction of the notch. He started toward the wagon to get wedges when he heard a loud cracking noise as the final wooden strands on the trunk gave way. The tree leaned further. It would fall sideways to his cut and would damage the saw unless he

372

could get it out.

Anna recognized the trouble but was not worried. The tree was coming toward them, but away from Ben, and they were far enough back that the tree's top couldn't reach them. She'd seen Ben pull his saw loose many times just as a tree leaned far enough to release it.

But suddenly, as the tree leaned further, finally pulled toward the earth by its gravity, a squirrel, previously unnoticed, panicked and jumped from about halfway up the trunk to the ground, exactly in the direction that the tree was falling. Rascal2 saw it at the same time Ben did.

Ben yelled for Anna to grab the dog, but it was too late. Rascal2 was off in a flash toward the falling tree, intent on catching the squirrel. Instinctively Ben ran toward the dog to pull him away. He reached Rascal2 and grabbed him in a single motion, turning to get them both out of harm's way. He almost made it.

He looked up as he ran, trying to gauge his best direction of flight. It was going to be close. With Rascal2 in his arms he dived as far forward as he could trying to get out of the line of fall of a heavy limb that protruded far out from the trunk. He felt its crushing blow as it smashed across his lower left leg. He heard the sickening sound of bones breaking even before he felt much. It instantly reminded him of the sound of Christian's arm that night in Hell's Kitchen when he'd rescued Anna. It didn't hurt for a few seconds and he began to hope that the leg that the limb had fallen across wasn't too badly damaged. But then the pain came and he knew better.

Anna came wading through the branches to get where Ben and Rascal2 lay. Ben released the dog, and Rascal2 sprang up unharmed. Then Anna saw the branch across Ben's leg. She went to the other side of the branch and was sickened to find his lower leg bent sharply at an odd angle, still under the weight of the massive limb. She knew that she would not be to pull him free.

She looked around frantically for the crosscut saw and found it still lying near the base of the tree stump. Thankfully it had not been broken. She looked into Ben's face. It was white and beaded with sweat.

"We'll not be able to pull you from under the tree. I think your leg is badly damaged. We are going to have to saw this limb to relieve the pressure."

Ben tried to remain calm but his breath was coming in short stabs and he was faint and sick to his stomach. "Okay, do what you think is best." He lay back on the ground, his face now totally void of color, fighting unconsciousness. Anna yelled at Bobby to run to Bessie's house and get her. Then she awkwardly began to cut the branch near the trunk, a foot or so below Ben's leg.

It took her a few minutes to cut through the limb enough to free him. The saw kept getting pinched until Ben told her that she needed to drive a wedge into the opening she was cutting.

She kept glancing at Ben to see how he was. As the limb finally came loose from the tree, the main trunk made ominous snapping sounds and slid toward Ben. Anna grabbed him and pulled him from under the branch and out of harm's way.

Getting free of the branch gave Ben some relief, but it also allowed him a better view of the leg. It was crushed about eight inches below the knee with bone sticking through skin. It was bleeding profusely so Anna tore her petticoat and tied a tourniquet just above the crushed area. The bleeding diminished and then slowed to a trickle.

Bessie and Bobby came running up. Ben could not bear to move on his own. He told them they would need to find cedar and cut thin poles to make a leg brace. The cedar was plentiful there and Anna and Bessie quickly cut the pieces.

"You're going to have to straighten the leg," said Ben, grimacing. "I may pass out. If I do, just go ahead and straighten the leg quickly and then place the poles along the leg and tie strips of cloth around them to keep it straight." Anna and Bessie nodded.

Ben reached forward and grabbed a small limb that protruded from the trunk about two feet past his head. He nodded. Bessie held on to his upper leg and Anna took the lower leg and moved it slightly. He cried out. She stopped. Panting, Ben said, "You'll have to do it quickly, no matter how much pain I am in. It'll be better that way." Anna grimaced and nodded again.

Taking a deep breath, she took the lower stump of the leg firmly in both hands and jerked it in line with the upper leg. He cried out and lost consciousness. She finished pulling the leg straight and felt bone scraping bone as she did. Chills ran up and down her spine like when some kid would make a loud screeching sound on a chalk board. Bessie tore four long strips from her undergarments and tied them as Anna held the splints.

They pulled the truck as close to Ben's body as they could. Anna instructed Bobby, "We have to load daddy onto the back of the truck. It will be hard but we must do it before he wakes up. Grandma and I will get his shoulders and you help with his legs.

You must be careful with the one that's broken. Can you do that?" He nodded, his eyes wide with fear. She patted him on the shoulder and told him it'd be alright, that daddy would be fine.

With Anna on one side, Bessie on the other and Bobby struggling with the legs, they loaded Ben onto the truck bed. Bessie held him and Anna leaped into the truck, taking Bobby with her. They got him to the house and into the car. Anna drove as fast as she could to Salem, but it was an hour later by the time Ben got full medical attention. He was awake now and in considerable pain. The doctor cut away the pant leg to survey the damage. The bones in the lower leg had been crushed and were not salvageable.

He gave Ben some ether to put him out and then turned to Anna. "I've got to remove this lower part of the leg before gangrene sets in." She could see the damage for herself and nodded. The doctor called for his nurse and asked Anna and Bessie to sit in the waiting room. He easily cut the rest of leg away, cauterizing arteries and veins as he went.

Recovery was slow and painful, but Ben never complained. If he mourned the loss of his leg, he never said so. After the first two or three days, he began to feel better, to eat heartily and joke with Anna about pirates, asking how she and Rascal2 would feel about a parrot.

When the swelling subsided the doctor took measurements of Ben's stump. As he was doing so, Ben told the doctor that he was grateful the tree hadn't crushed his knee. The doctor agreed that it would have been much more of a handicap had that occurred.

Rascal2 knew that Ben had been seriously hurt and somehow sensed that he might have had something to do with it. He stayed by his bedside throughout his recovery. Every hour or so he would get up and place his head near Ben's hand or attempt to lick his face.

Ben began to get around the house on crutches and eventually ventured outside. Rascal2 still remained at his side, careful not to cut in front of him or interfere with his crutches. When Ben finally received an artificial leg from Chicago and made his first painful steps, Rascal2 walked proudly beside him.

Full recovery took two months, after which Ben returned to work. He never let the artificial leg interfere with his activities during the day, but during the first six months after the injury, he was very glad to get home to rest at night.

Only in the evenings after supper, in his favorite easy chair, would he take off the artificial leg. He refused to use a crutch. When he retired for the evening, he walked on his knees from his easy chair to his bed, developing hardened calluses on his knees that never went away. Once he was used to the artificial leg, the people who didn't know Ben well never realized that he had the handicap. Those who did only noticed a slight limp.

His main frustration with the accident was that he was no longer able to play baseball as well as before. Prior to the accident, he had excelled at that sport. He'd played shortstop for the town team. He had extremely quick reflexes, sure hands and a powerful arm.

After the accident his teammates suggested that he take up pitching, which he did, and became successful at it. His only real problem was that he couldn't run the bases well or field his position easily. Out of courtesy, opposing teams generally didn't try to take advantage of him by bunting, and they allowed him to substitute a runner without leaving the game once he reached first base. He hit a lot of long singles during those years. He continued to play baseball competitively until age 50.

Chapter 30

By 1917 a massive war had been raging across the European front for nearly three years. President Woodrow Wilson had hoped to keep America neutral, as was the general sentiment in America, but that became impossible as the German fleet indiscriminately sank American ships. American entry into the "War to End all Wars" became inevitable. It was a tardy entry, barely in time to bolster the Allied cause.

President Wilson initially called for volunteers to fight, and mobilized the nation's industry to war production. But only 73,000 men heeded the call voluntarily. Wilson needed one million men in the first six weeks alone. Something had to be done to get the necessary manpower.

Congress responded quickly, passing the Selective Service Act in June, 1917, requiring registration for potential draft of any American male between the ages of 21-31. Unlike previous wars America had fought, no form of bounty or substitution was allowed.

The Selective Service Act of 1917 brought the reality of the war to all parts of America, including Jadwin, where families like the McDonalds and the Schafers had sons of drafting age. Charlie's and Nellie's sons registered but were not called up. Anna's and Ben's two sons also registered. Bill, the oldest, got lucky and was not drafted. Dan was not so lucky.

Dan had graduated three years earlier from the University of Missouri with a degree in business finance and was already working in a management position for his father and Charlie. Both were enthusiastic about his talents and believed that he had a bright future in the company.

Dan had married Margaret (Maggie) Allen in 1913, whom he had met at the university. Maggie, originally from a small town in northeast Missouri, had little trouble adjusting to life in the Jadwin area. In 1914 Dan and Maggie had their first child, a little girl, that they named Marie.

Dan adored Marie and she worshipped her daddy, almost from the beginning. Their special bond was apparent to all who knew them. And from the time she could barely walk, she loved the waters of the Current River. She would stay in the river until her little lips turned blue and she shook all over, after which Maggie would have to drag her out, with Marie resisting all the way. From the first day they took her to the river, she had absolutely no fear of the water and learned to swim by age 3. Dan was so proud that he gave her a nickname, calling her his very own little Otter.

Marie was little more than three years old when Dan had to leave for service in the army. It almost killed him to go. While leaving Maggie, his parents, his job and his friends was difficult, he could handle that. But it was Marie that he didn't know how to say goodbye to.

On the night before he left, he took a walk with her to try to explain. "Otter, Daddy has to go away for a while."

Otter looked at him with her big brown eyes. "You mean like when you go to work, Daddy?"

He shook his head, trying to hold his emotion. "No, this is different than Daddy's work. I have to go far away for a while to help keep our country safe. I have to go to a place called Europe, and it's a long way off, farther even than Indiana, where Great

Grandma and Grandpa Emily and Jake live. In fact, it's across a big body of water called an ocean, so I'll have to be gone a long time."

She looked up at him, troubled, "Will Mama have to go, too?"

"No, honey, mama will stay here with you while I'm gone. It's just me that has to go."

Marie's lip began to quiver and she grabbed her daddy's legs. "But I don't want you to go, Daddy. Please don't go. Tell somebody else to go keep the country safe. You stay with me and Momma and keep us safe."

Ben's heart was breaking. "I can't Otter. It's not just to keep the country safe that I have to go. It's to keep you and Momma safe too. And Grandma and Grandpa, and everybody you know. But I promise that while I'm gone, Grandpa Ben and Grandma Anna will help momma keep you safe until I come back to you."

Marie began to cry. "No daddy, you stay here and keep me safe. I don't want you to go away."

Dan picked her up and held her tight as she cried. "Daddy wishes he could, but he can't. But I promise you that I'll write you as often as I can, and I'll send you presents, and I'll think about you every day. I love you, Otter, more than anything in the world. And I'll come home to you just as soon as I can."

It didn't appease her. She cried herself to sleep that night. He had to leave at 5:00 a.m. the next day to get to Rolla in time to catch the train with the other draftees. He was afraid it would hurt her too much, so he didn't wake her up to say goodbye. He boarded a train in Rolla for the East, where he quickly completed a basic training program, then another for officer training. Before he knew it, he was aboard a ship headed to France as Second Lieutenant Daniel McDonald.

Dan wrote to Maggie and Marie every day during training and on the boat. At least once a week, he also enclosed a letter to his mom and dad. He bought little gifts whenever he could and sent them back to Marie.

As soon as he reached France, he and his Company were transported to the front line in the Argonne forests of northern France. They suffered from the miserable weather in the region, often wet and cold, from the bad food, and their wet feet that were always freezing as they stood in ankle-deep mud in the trenches.

Sometimes they suffered from the tediousness of boring, endless days, knowing full well that those days could swiftly be broken by the sheer terror of donning face masks to avoid mustard gas, fierce battles that they would be ordered to fight to push the enemy back a few hundred yards, or when the enemy tried to do the same to them. They watched their buddies die in all sorts of gruesome ways as they stood next to them in the bunkers or ran through the woods.

Dan was wounded twice as he crawled into no-man's land to pull his fallen troops across barbed wire barriers and back to the safety of the bunkers. Fortunately or unfortunately, depending on one's perspective, his wounds were not serious enough to allow him to leave the front or go home.

Back at home, Marie would watch for the mail carrier every day and run to him to receive letters or packages from her daddy, which her momma would stop and read to her as soon as she brought them in the house. At first, her waits were always rewarded, but then her daddy's letters didn't come every day and her momma had a hard time explaining why. Then the letters came only one day a week, then once every two weeks.

Marie still waited every day at the mailbox, but she began to be afraid that her daddy was forgetting about her. Her mommy tried to explain that daddy was in a dark, cold forest and sometimes his mailman couldn't pick up the letters he'd written her every day, but that they'd come if she'd be patient. But she was only three, going, on four, and it was really hard to be patient.

Early on, his letters were optimistic and descriptive about where he was and what he was doing. He explained things carefully and simply, hoping Otter could understand what he was saying. But later, as the letters became more infrequent, they began to hint at the suffering that he and his troops were experiencing on the front lines. He told Otter that it was very cold there, colder than in Jadwin, and that he had to work hard to try to stay warm. He told her he had very cold feet, and that when he got home he wanted her to heat him some water so he could soak them and get them warm.

On a particularly blustery day early in 1918, somewhere along a rapidly moving battle line at the edge of northern France, he and his Company of men were ordered into a bloody engagement of little note except for those who survived, and for the families on both sides who would receive the notices about those who didn't. Confusion had reigned that morning among the Allied command. They had ordered an advance that made no sense to those on the ground. Dan and his men were ordered forward too soon and became isolated from their support lines, and were eventually surrounded by German troops.

They held out for three days until they ran out of ammunition. The remaining Allied troops had been pushed back and could not save them. A lot of men in the Company died, including the Company's captain, leaving Dan in charge of the men that were left. When their ammunition, gave out, he made the difficult decision to surrender, hoping to avoid his men being massacred. But he feared that he was consigning his men to death anyway, because he'd heard that being taken to a German prison camp meant slow starvation or being gassed. His Company was moved to an internment camp not far inside the Belgium border.

It was in February that his letters to Otter stopped altogether. And it was in March before Maggie found out why, when she received the dreaded letter that she'd seen other wives and mothers get. Billy handed it to her with a sad, sympathetic look. She didn't want to open it there in front of him, so she waited until she got to Anna's and Ben's house and they opened it together.

Dear Mrs. McDonald:

We regret to inform you that your husband, Lieutenant Daniel McDonald, is missing in action. We have reason to believe he has been taken prisoner by the German Army as he and his Company were involved in action near the Belgium border.

Please be assured that the War Department is making every effort to communicate with the German authorities regarding the plight of the American prisoners. We are hopeful this will result in the release and return of your son and other brave Americans being held by the Axis powers.

Sincerely,
Major Anthony Wiles,

She cried and that scared Marie, but Grandma Anna held Marie and told her that her momma was just having a bad day and that everything was going to be okay. But Otter was smart and knew it was about what was in that letter.

"Was that a letter from my daddy?"

"No dear, it wasn't."

"Was it about my daddy?"

Anna hesitated. Marie's eyes widened. "It was about my daddy, wasn't it? Did my daddy die like Sally's daddy did?"

Anna held her close, trying not to cry. "No, the letter didn't say that your daddy died. It just said that he got lost in the woods and that they are looking for him."

Marie didn't say anything more. She went to her room and closed her door softly. That night, she refused to eat. In the following days, she was listless and sad. She seldom spoke. But she still waited every day at the mailbox until Billy came by. But he never had a letter from her daddy.

Amazingly, the internment camp environment was not as bad as Dan had feared. In fact, it wasn't much worse than when they were in the bunkers on the front lines. The Germans had set up a makeshift tent village surrounded by high barbed wire fences with armed guards patrolling the exterior at all hours. The nights were bitterly cold, but at least Dan and his men were dry.

There was barely enough food to keep them alive, but the

German commander, a man named Eric Schmidt, was not cruel and offered what food and medical supplies he could. Some of the men still died from their prior wounds, but Schmidt allowed the Americans to bury them and hold their funeral ceremonies.

Back in Jadwin there was an outbreak of scarlet fever. It hit the children ages four through eight the hardest. One of the children it hit was a little girl named Marie McDonald. It started with a sore throat, then the spiking fever, then the red rashes on her face and body.

Otter didn't seem to have the strength to fight the disease. She grew increasingly listless. As the fever got worse, she called for her daddy for days, even while she was fitfully sleeping, tearing Maggie's heart out. She tried to comfort her. "When you get better, Otter, Daddy will come home."

"But I need him now, to get better".

She kept calling his name. But Daddy didn't come.

Marie McDonald died in late March, 1918 and was buried in the Jadwin cemetery after a sad funeral in which everybody wept and called her name.

In the summer of 1918 Allied forces overran the area where her daddy was a prisoner of war. Schmidt refused a suggestion from some of the German guards to execute the prisoners, both from a sense of humanity and because he knew that Germany would eventually lose this war and face post-war scrutiny related to the atrocities it committed.

On the day the camp was about to be overrun, Schmidt called Dan to his office. Dan was shocked when he heard him speak perfect English. "Lieutenant McDonald, our sources tell me that we're surrounded and will soon be overrun by your Allied forces. We could attempt to repel them when they reach the camp, but it would be futile and cost lives unnecessarily. I also believe our prisoners of war would be in jeopardy during such a conflict. I don't know whether I can control what some of my men might do in a battle in which they think they will die."

"So, I have a proposition for you that I'd like you to discuss with your colleagues. I propose that we surrender our arms and trade places with you. You can fly a white flag over the camp and get word to your advancing forces that you are in control. In return, I must have your word of honor that your men will not harm my men, and that you will do your best to see that they are protected as your Allied forces overrun us. We have little time to finalize this so I ask that you decide as quickly as possible."

Dan respected Schmidt, fully realizing that he and the other prisoners had been treated fairly. They shook hands and Dan was rushed back to confer with the officers of other companies being held at the POW camp. All readily agreed to the offer, knowing they had nothing to lose.

Quietly, each officer called his company together to explain the proposal and to stress that no German soldiers were to be harassed or hurt in the transfer. They selected their most experienced and reliable men to form guard units once the transfer was completed. With preparations finished, Dan notified the German guard who promptly took him back to Schmidt's office, where final negotiations were quickly completed.

The transfer went surprisingly well. The Americans, British and French were allowed outside the barbed wire fences to establish their guard. As they began the exchange, they began to hear the big guns of the Allied invasion drawing closer and knew they needed to act quickly. In a brief, hurried ceremony, Schmidt surrendered his weapon to Dan and the German troops stacked their guns by the barbed wire gate as they hurried inside.

A large white flag was raised over the camp and the officers commissioned a small platoon of American, British and French soldiers to find the nearest Allied forces and inform them of the Camp's location and status. That group reached allied lines within thirty minutes. By evening, Allied forces had marched into the camp to the cheers of the former prisoners of war.

The German prisoners were treated fairly, as promised by Dan and his fellow officers. Later that evening, Dan asked permission to go speak to Schmidt privately. He offered him a smoke, which Schmidt took willingly, expressing his thanks.

"I ought to be the one thanking you. I deeply appreciate how you treated us and for your willingness to exchange places."

Schmidt smiled sadly. "I wish that same sentiment would prevail when I get back to Germany, but it won't. Some of my men are still angry with me and will make sure that everyone knows what I did. It will be viewed unfavorably.

"I'm sorry to hear that. You probably saved a lot of men's lives today."

Schmidt shrugged and took a drag on his cigarette.

"I'm curious, Major Schmidt. Why did you single me out from among the officers to negotiate?"

Schmidt smiled. "You are American. You entered the war a lot later than your British and French counterparts. You were less likely to be bitter, or hold grudges. I had no way of knowing for sure, of course, so I was taking a calculated risk. Also, I watched your communication with your colleagues. You carry yourself well and are respected by your own men and those in other Companies. You looked to me like a leader. That's all."

Dan thought about it and nodded. "Thanks for telling me. Good luck when you get home."

"You, too, Lieutenant. Who knows; if I survive, maybe I'll come back to America and we will meet again someday."

"Come back? You were there before?"

Schmidt smiled sadly. "Yes, I was a student at your Massachusetts Institute of Technology. I was trained as an engineer."

"So what were you doing as a POW camp commander?"

"I didn't agree with how my country was executing the war. They decided to punish me."

"Ah, I see. Well, I'm writing my home address here." He handed Schmidt a piece of paper. "I work for a good company. If you make it to America, we could use a guy like you. Look us up."

Schmidt looked at the paper, smiled sadly and said, "Thanks". Then he returned inside the wire.

Daniel McDonald made it back behind the Allied lines and picked up a large stack of letters that had piled up from his family. He got to the one that told him Marie was very sick and his heart sank, and his stomach churned. He opened the next and found that she had died. He wept for a week.

Dan returned to Jadwin as a bona fide war hero. He resumed his work with Charlie and Ben and did a terrific job, but he was a different man than the one who had left. War kills some men and leaves others alive, but there is often collateral damage.

Dan and Maggie had another child, a son, within ten months after he returned. He was proud of his son, but afraid to get too close to him for fear that something would happen and he wouldn't be there to comfort him. Collateral damage.

He was a wonderful, kind dad in most ways, but he seldom hugged his son, and as the boy developed, Dan couldn't help but think about Otter at almost every milestone the baby reached— the first time he crawled, the first time he walked, his first words. The boy loved him, but sensed that his daddy was a little distant. Collateral damage.

For years, Dan spent a lot of his spare time maintaining the cemetery at Jadwin and caring for Otter's grave. Collateral damage.

When Dan's firstborn son grew up, and he had his own daughter, it took him years before he learned to tell her he loved her or hug her freely. She worshiped her dad, but grew up uncertain of his true feelings for her. Collateral damage.

Eric Schmidt returned to his home town in Germany. It was in ruins. One of the men he had commanded at the prisoner of war camp had come from there, too. He publicly accused Eric of being a traitor for letting his prisoners of war go and not killing

them when he had the chance. With the stigma, Eric couldn't'
get a job, even with his superior skills as an engineer. Collateral
damage.

Eric's father was mortified at his son's weakness and let it be
known publicly that his son was a coward. Eric fell into a deep
state of depression and ultimately took his own life, unable to
cope with the disappointment of his family. Collateral damage.

Back in Jadwin, Dan refused to talk about his wartime
experiences to anyone. He occasionally thought about Eric
Schmidt, who'd probably saved his life, and wondered how he'd
fared when he returned home. He hoped to contact him
someday, or thought perhaps Eric might look him up if he ever
came back to America. But he never did.

Chapter 31

In January 1925, at age 54, Anna was forced to reduce her work schedule because of a nagging illness. It started with chronic back pain and discomfort in her lower abdomen. Initially it was just annoying, but eventually it became worrisome when the pain increased, her appetite decreased and her weight began to drop.

In early April, Ben insisted on taking her to the doctor in Salem, who was immediately concerned with the symptoms. By that time, she'd lost 20 pounds. During the examination, the doctor felt something hard in her lower abdomen and she winced when he pressed down on the area. The mass that he felt, coupled with her weight loss and diminished energy caused him to refer her to a specialist in St. Louis as quickly as it could be arranged. The specialist, named Robbins, was connected with the new, prominent Barnes Hospital, a teaching hospital associated with Washington University.

Anna and Ben boarded a train to St. Louis on the following Friday morning for what was billed to the kids and Bessie as a "long weekend" in the city. Only Charlie knew the real reason. But Bessie was skeptical because she knew of Anna's weight loss, her exhaustion and her recent visit to the Salem doctor. She kept asking Anna what the doctor had said but received only vague answers about Anna just being run down.

Ben and Anna reached the city in time for an early lunch on "the Hill", the traditional Italian section of St. Louis, and then grabbed a cab to the hospital for their 1:00 p.m. meeting with Dr. Robbins. He was a pleasant, rotund man and seemed highly competent. He greeted them amiably and chatted informally, quizzing them about their family and life in Jadwin as he examined Anna. His childhood had been spent in a similar community across the river in southern Illinois. He had Anna describe her symptoms. He had already reviewed her medical records and the Salem doctor's preliminary diagnosis.

He asked Anna to change into a hospital gown and continued the physical examination. He felt the lump in her abdomen, drew some blood and requested a urine sample. He asked them if they could remain in St. Louis until Monday while he analyzed the results of his tests and talked to colleagues. He assured them he could give them more information by that time.

Anna and Ben, realizing that the condition was potentially serious, agreed to stay. They made reservations at a hotel near Forest Park, the same one that their family had used when they visited the 1904 World's Fair. As they walked in the park that afternoon, Ben chuckled about how young they had been when the World's Fair was in town.

On the spur of the moment, to relieve the stress of waiting, they attended a production at the Fox Theatre and then finally retired to their hotel room. They talked far into the night, speaking optimistically about the future and assuring each other that the illness was likely not that serious, each knowing that they really feared the opposite. In the wee hours of the morning, they finally turned out the lights. Ben only dozed, lying by her side, listening to her breathing and feeling the rhythm of her heart. On Saturday, they explored the new exhibits at the St. Louis Zoo. On Sunday, they toured the Botanical Gardens, then retired early and finally slept from the exhaustion of waiting.

Early Monday morning they walked the wide paths of Forest Park again, holding hands, then went to their scheduled appointment with Dr. Robbins. Neither had been hungry enough to eat breakfast.

They arrived at the hospital a little early but Robbins was already there and invited them into his office. His face was grave. "Anna, you have a large growth in your abdomen that's pressing against your stomach and kidneys. That's why you're experiencing the pain and lack of appetite. You have probably read about such growths in the papers. It's a cancer, and unfortunately it's a life-threatening condition. If left unattended it'll spread and ultimately attack your vital organs. It's an invasive growth that overtakes and negatively restructures the healthy cells in your body."

The doctor stopped and waited for their questions. Ben and Anna looked at each other. He took her hand. Ben, his voice taut, asked, "Is there a cure?" He was subconsciously squeezing her hand until it hurt, but she didn't tell him so or withdraw it.

"Not an easy one," said Robbins. "We're still in the early stages of understanding how to treat cancer, although I believe people have been afflicted by it for ages. We generally recommend surgery to remove the growth, followed by a long period of convalescence with as little stress as possible. There have been some cases where this treatment has worked and others where it hasn't."

"If we remove it and it doesn't reappear in your body for five years, generally, we consider you cured. However, I must warn you that there's a lot we don't yet know. I strongly recommend that you undergo surgery as soon as possible. The good news for you is that the growth is in a region of the body that isn't life threatening or too complicated to operate on, and that will make the operation easier and the recovery quicker."

"One more thing, Anna; you'll need lots of bed rest and will probably have to remain in St. Louis for a significant period of time after the surgery, certainly throughout the summer, for additional tests and monitoring. And you must free yourself from as many stressors as possible as soon as you can. I strongly recommend that you suspend all work for at least a year."

He watched her catch her breath. He felt badly that he couldn't be gentler, but she needed to understand the gravity of the situation and accept a changed lifestyle for at least a while. "I'm sorry to spring this on you all at once, Anna. I know it will be difficult to give up your work, but your health is the most important thing to concentrate on for a while. You're in a very serious fight for your life."

She nodded, still silent. Ben asked a few more questions, including how soon the surgery could be scheduled. Dr. Robbins said he had a colleague that he wanted to assist who was away and would return later in the month. He would schedule it as soon after that as possible. Ben and Anna agreed. After further instructions, they left for the train station and the long ride home.

The surgery date wasn't far off, forcing Ben and Anna to tell Charlie, Bessie, Zach and their children about the illness and the scheduled treatment. The family was shocked and sobered by the news. Bessie assured Anna that she'd pray for her and that God would take care of her. But when Bessie returned home, she wept. In Jadwin, everyone knew the frailty of life and that God didn't always restore people to health just because they asked.

Ben took a leave of absence from work, with Daniel taking over for him. Ben and Anna rented a nice two-bedroom furnished apartment near Forest Park and moved to St. Louis during the week before the surgery. Charlie promised to watch over the house in Jadwin. He, Nellie and Bessie would also take care of Bobby until Ben and Anna were able to have him join them in St. Louis or they got home. Bessie insisted that she be allowed to come to St. Louis during the week of surgery, and Anna gladly accepted her request.

Anna checked into the hospital two days before surgery for additional tests and preparation. Ben stayed with her throughout and refused to leave at night despite her admonition that he go to the apartment and get some rest. The hospital staff also insisted that he leave because of their protocols, but he refused. The impasse was finally broken by Robbins, who approved his stay.

On the night before the surgery Ben, lying close to her, whispered, "When we beat this thing, Anna, I think you and I should travel. We've never really done that because of our work and Bobby. Bessie can watch over him and it's time you and I splurge a little. Where would you like to go?"

She brightened, drawing his hand to her heart. "I want to go home, Ben"

He was confused. "Okay, if that's what you want, we'll just go back to Jadwin and spend time together there."

"No, that's not what I meant. I want to go home—to Doolin—in Ireland."

"Oh, I see! Well, that would be terrific! Let's go to Ireland. I've always wanted to see where you came from."

She smiled and nodded. "Yes, something for us to look forward to."

The surgery was long—longer than even Dr. Robbins had expected. There was more internal bleeding than he anticipated. Ben feared that the longer time was a bad sign and was beside himself as he, Bessie and Zach waited for word. It was four full hours before Robbins came out to the waiting room, looking tired, to talk to them.

"She's doing as well as can be expected. A person loses quite a bit of blood during surgery and we are giving her transfusions now. She's stable. We cut out a growth about the size of an apple from her abdomen. It was complicated. The growth was more invasive than we thought. I'm hoping that we got it all, but we just won't know for a while. She needs lots of rest now."

Robbins told Ben that they would bring Anna back to her room in a few hours after she awoke and was out of immediate danger, but that she would be groggy for the next 24 hours, which would be a blessing because of the inevitable pain. He said he'd stop in to see them each morning. Ben thanked Robbins for his work.

He stayed at Anna's side for the first three days of her recovery until it was apparent that her strength was returning and her pain subsiding. Then he went to the apartment and passed out, physically and emotionally exhausted, sleeping for twelve solid hours.

Two weeks after the surgery Anna looked remarkably well. Her appetite had returned. In fact, she was ravenous all the time. Her complexion was no longer ashen. Robbins, stopping by early in the third week, was delighted with her progress. Anna and Ben were teasing and laughing and her face was flushed. All her vital signs were strong.

Robbins already knew much of the history of these two

remarkable people from the Salem doctor, and recognized the unusual bond between them that seemed far stronger than most married couples experienced, certainly stronger than his own marriage, which was always stressed by his work. He admired these two wonderful people and hoped that he and his colleagues had given Anna and Ben many more years together. But he wasn't confident. The type of cancer that Anna had was known to be aggressive.

As they rode the train to Rolla, they talked about the time they'd have together on the cruise and the tour of Ireland. They were to arrive at the port of Galway, then travel to Doolin to spend two weeks with her relatives. After that, Ben had hired a guide to take them to other notable places on the Emerald Isle that had been recommended by her cousin, Connor, before sailing back to America. She was elated at the thought of returning to Ireland and visiting with relatives she hadn't seen since she was a young child.

When they arrived home there was a large crowd of well-wishers awaiting them, the most important of which was Bobby. He cried and hugged them repeatedly, telling them each time how happy he was that they were home.

When the last guests had gone, Anna sighed contentedly and walked through her house, looking at each room and item of furniture as though she was being reunited with old friends. Bobby followed her everywhere, jabbering excitedly about his adventures at Charlie's house.

Anna had regained her full strength by Thanksgiving. It was an especially poignant occasion for the Loughs, Schafers and the McDonalds at the big family dinner held at Bessie's house. Zach gave the blessing prior to the meal. As they all joined hands, standing around the table, he said, "Lord, we have much to be thankful for on this special day, including this sumptuous meal. But we especially thank You for bringing our Anna back home to us safely. She is our treasure. She is our greatest Thanksgiving gift. May we be blessed with her presence for many, many years to come."

There were loud "Amens" all around the table that day, followed by much celebration and laughter. These family gatherings seemed more special now somehow. They'd lost Jess. They'd feared losing Anna. They remembered anew that life was fleeting and not to be taken for granted.

Chapter 32

Ben and Anna remained at home through the Christmas holidays and then watched the earth's winter mantle finally give way to one of the most beautiful spring seasons anyone could remember. It was an omen of better things to come. It was so warm by late April that Anna, Ben, Bessie and Bobby spent a number of pleasant days at the Current River.

Anna and Ben were to leave for New York in June. There they would board a cruise ship to Ireland. Bobby was upset when they told him that they were not taking him on the trip, but Ben promised to take him on the next one and Bessie bribed him with numerous promises of things they would do while Ben and Anna were gone, including what kinds of food they'd eat—all of which were his favorites.

Ben indicated that he wanted to travel to Jefferson City first to pay their respects to their friend, former Governor Hyde, who had only recently left office and, according to Ben, had been ill. Ben said that Hyde had insisted that they come up as soon as Anna was sufficiently recovered. There was also supposed to be a striking exhibit in the Capitol that Ben wanted to see featuring Missouri Native American artifacts that would ultimately be exhibited across the country over the summer. Anna thought it a bit odd, but Ben seemed to have his heart set on the side trip and she really didn't mind. It had been a while since she'd seen her friends in Jefferson City.

They arrived in Jefferson City on the fifth of June. Former Governor Hyde met them at the train station, which hadn't changed much since her arrival there on that Orphan Train in 1884. Anna was a little surprised that Hyde looked so healthy. She asked him how he was feeling. He looked puzzled for a second, and then tried to recover the slow uptake. "Oh, yes! I'm feeling much better now. Actually, I'm as healthy as a horse. Thanks for asking."

Hyde took them to a good Jefferson City restaurant for lunch. Zach surprised them by showing up to join them even though the legislature had been out of session for over two weeks. Anna was surprised to see him. She knew he was extremely busy with his law practice, but Zach indicated he happened to have some residual legislative business in Jefferson City that day.

After lunch, they rode over to the State Capitol to view the new Native American Exhibit. They climbed the stairs from the basement and walked down the hall to the first floor rotunda, where Hyde said the exhibit began.

Jefferson City boasted one of the most beautiful state capitols anywhere in the country. The Rotunda was jam-packed with people, all sitting in chairs, or standing around chatting. She recognized many of them, including a few of her legislator friends. She wondered why they were still there. They should be back in their home districts. Maybe they were attending the same meetings as Zach.

But as she looked around and saw who was there, she began to smell a rat. She looked quizzically at Ben and Arthur Hyde, both of whom had innocent expressions on their faces. Hyde asked her to come with him to meet somebody and quickly headed toward the stage on the north side of the Rotunda under the two grand staircases leading up to the second floor Governor's Office. As she followed Hyde, the audience suddenly hushed and everyone stood and began to clap. She knew then that this alleged review of an exhibit was a set-up.

Hyde left her at the foot of the stairs, asking her to wait a second, and then he bounded up to the podium. The audience continued to applaud. He smiled and waved them down. "Oh, hush; I know it's not for me, so sit down!" They laughed and quieted.

"Thank you for coming to this very special event today. I have a proclamation here, signed by the Speaker of the House, the Senate Pro Tem, Governor Baker"—he paused for effect, grinning broadly—"and me!" The audience laughed and applauded.

"The words on this Proclamation were written by the Honorable Senator from the 16th District, who has considerable personal knowledge of its subject. It's a joint resolution, passed, unanimously by both the House and Senate little more than two weeks ago."

"Now I admit that Senator Lough would have been more eloquent in the reading of the proclamation. I've heard him speak on many occasions and I know that he's a better orator than me." He took on a look of crestfallen embarrassment and paused for effect until the laughter and catcalls subsided.

"But the Senator from Phelps and the husband of our honoree, and even my own lovely wife, have long been aware that I have held a crush for the person we're honoring today since I was very young. So I have usurped the privilege of reading this proclamation to her as Governor emeritus. Anna, please think of this as the love letter I could never write you at age 13!"

She pretended to frown, and shook her finger at him as he raised his glasses to his eyes and, cleared his throat.

A Joint Proclamation of the Missouri House and Senate

Be it Proclaimed:

"Whereas, in November, 1884 Anna Murphy, as one of a party of orphan children from New York City, came to the fair State of Missouri at the tender age of 13, shortly after the tragic passing of her mother and father and her rescue from the streets of New York City's Hell's Kitchen by another street urchin who would eventually become her cherished husband;

And Whereas, she brought with her another physically frail orphan boy of only five years of age who would live to become the author of this proclamation;

And Whereas, she completed her high school education in exemplary fashion at the age of 16 years, passing her teaching examination shortly thereafter and becoming a distinguished elementary school teacher in the small south-central community of Jadwin, Missouri;

And Whereas, in that role, she sculpted the education of students as skillfully as any of the great masters of stone and clay, enabling them to become successful farmers, doctors, lawyers, engineers and other noteworthy professions, including a State Senator from District 16;

And Whereas, she has also monitored and supported the welfare of thousands of orphan children immigrating to the *great state of Missouri from the City of New York, and has served for more than 35 years as one of the nation's most eloquent voices for the advancement of its troubled children;*

And Whereas, her deeds shall live on immortally through all the children and families she has touched, and through their descendents;

And Whereas, she commands the enduring admiration and respect of Presidents, Members of Congress, Governors, State Legislators, and most important, the families and children in her state and across the nation, for whom she has advocated so well;

Now Therefore, the members of this Missouri General Assembly in concert with the elected officials undersigned below, do hereby proclaim our everlasting appreciation for the invaluable contributions of Anna Murphy McDonald to Missouri and the nation, and do hereby proclaim this the fifth day of June, of the year of our Lord One Thousand Nine Hundred and Twenty Six, as "Anna Murphy McDonald Day" and order that this Proclamation be widely distributed to the general public for purpose of honoring her notable achievements.

When the reading was concluded, he held the elaborately written proclamation up for all to see. The audience rose in a standing ovation and turned their eyes toward her. She glanced over at Ben, standing off to the side by one of the Rotunda's massive pillars, smiling. He blew her a kiss and nodded.

Hyde motioned toward her. "Mrs. McDonald, I have been asked to convey the audience's sincere request that you respond to this proclamation. Would the Senator from Phelps please escort our honored guest to the podium?"

With that, Zach, who'd come up beside her, took her by the arm and led her up the stage's steps, smiling broadly, a look of intense pride on his face for all to see.

Once at the podium, Anna deliberately looked over at him and gave him a disapproving frown for all his deception. He sobered, like one of her elementary school students caught in a mischievous act, and looked contrite. But she couldn't hold her stern countenance and began to grin at him. Her mind flashed back to that little crippled boy who had accompanied her on her first trip to Jefferson City. She reached over and hugged him tightly. These two formerly unwanted orphans, joined by bonds that few would ever understand, stood before an enthusiastic audience as it continued to applaud. He tried to step back but she held his hand and would not allow him to leave.

When the audience finally stopped applauding, she spoke. "Governor Hyde and all of you distinguished members of the audience, I am overwhelmed and rendered nearly speechless by this proclamation and the honor it reflects…Nearly, but not quite." The audience laughed.

"Of course, I have absolutely no prepared comments since I was not informed of the nature of this occasion and badly misled as to its purpose, something your former Governor, my husband and my little brother will pay dearly for when the opportunity arises!" The audience laughed again.

"If Governor Hyde, who allegedly had an adolescent crush for me when he was 13, really loved me half as much as he claims, he would not deceive me in this manner. And I must tell you that his deception was poorly played. He was a great Governor, but I fear he might not be as worthy as an actor. I was told by my husband that Governor Hyde had been ill, might be at his last breath, and that his dying wish was for me to come see him. But when I arrived, he looked quite healthy and seemed to have forgotten that he was supposed to be ill." Hyde's face mimed a woebegone expression behind her and he put his hands to the sides of his head, causing more laughter from the audience.

"How do I respond to this? Well, let me begin by indicating that the wording of this Proclamation would certainly merit at least a grade of "C", were its author still under my tutelage." She stared at Zach who pretended to look down, embarrassed and shaking his head. The audience laughed again.

She became serious. "My life has been a series of amazing contrasts. For every personal tragedy, there was a corresponding miracle. And in the whole, I have been blessed beyond measure. Zach and I were embraced by a wonderful Missouri family at a time when we needed them most. Their love was, and will always be Missouri's greatest gift to us. And I can't tell you how many times that I have awakened and looked over at my handsome husband, who really did literally save my life, and thought that I must be living in a fairy tale."

"Now you have added this wonderful honor to my memories." She held the framed plaque up to her heart and hugged it. "I thank you for that from the bottom of my heart. Your recognition means more than you will ever know."

She paused for long seconds, trying to control her emotions, the audience waiting, many eyes misting. Then she concluded.

"Our work must go on. It must never end. It must transcend our lives and our times, because we must never, ever squander the amazing potential of even one child, no matter how weak, disabled or poor that child might be."

"Because we will never know which of these children might be a Zachary Lough, or a Ben McDonald, or Christian Gunther, who most of you have never met, but who saved both my life and my husband's, and who may be the best of us all. It is on their behalf, and on behalf of all orphaned children that I accept this proclamation. Thank you, and as one of Charles Dickens' most beloved characters would say, God bless us each and every one!"

She hugged the former Governor and then Zach—him for a very lengthy time—and made her way down from the stage, spending the next hour receiving well-wishes of hundreds of friends in the audience.

Finally, emotionally and physically spent, she sought her rock, waiting patiently for her in the shadows at the side of the Rotunda. He kissed her and held her for a long minute. Then Governor Hyde and Zach whisked them off to the train station to begin her journey home.

Chapter 33

The train ride to New York was pleasant. That mode of travel had improved dramatically since her lonely trip to Missouri in 1884. Ben, sparing no expense, had purchased first class tickets that included comfortable sleeping compartments. They reached New York on the day before their steamship left for Galway, Ireland. They spent the night in a hotel and arrived at the cruise ship at 10:00 a.m. the next day.

Anna was amazed at the massive size of the ship. It was over 500 feet in length with huge boilers at its center and multiple passenger levels. They boarded and stood for a few minutes on the deck, looking down at the dock and the bay. Memories of her father and mother flooded back as she recalled the time they, too, had stood on the deck of a much smaller ship as it entered the bay to a New York City port. They had all been so optimistic on that day. Her throat caught at the thought of the excitement of her parents, and of their subsequent fate.

This trip across the North Atlantic was uneventful and relaxing, taking only a week, just as advertised. Upon their approach to the Irish coastline she spotted the spectacular Cliffs of Mohr, towering 700 feet straight up out of the sea off the starboard side of the ship.

Ben laughed at her as she became increasingly excited, grabbing his arm and pulling him along the ship's rail. The cliffs looked exactly as she had remembered them. Ben, who had never even seen pictures of the Cliffs of Mohr, was awed by their sheer height. Off the boat's port side lay the Aran Islands that Anna had visited as a small child.

And then the boat passed very near the little inlet of her family's hometown of Doolin as it made its way on up to Galway Harbor. Anna was beside herself. Ben couldn't stop laughing as she ran from one side of the ship to the other, taking in sights that she had never expected to see again. He finally grabbed hold of her and suggested that they move up closer to the bow so they could view both sides without exhausting themselves. She laughed and agreed, her eyes shining. He had never seen her so radiant as the wind whipped her hair across her face.

They arrived in Galway and were met by Anna's first cousin, Connor Murphy, the eldest son of her uncle. Connor now owned the Murphy family farm, handed down to eldest sons for at least six generations.

The minute Connor saw her, he ran to her, picking her up and whirling her around like a child. He said he could never forget little Aine, one of his favorite childhood playmates who'd left for America, now so long ago. He laughed delightedly as he twirled her, telling her that he'd feared that he'd never see her again.

When Anna and her mother and father had departed for America, Ireland was still devastated by the potato famine that had occurred 20 years before. The land could not sustain any but the eldest son and his family, so her father had chosen to migrate to America, and Connor's father had inherited the farm. It had been a heartrending decision for her father. He loved Ireland.

"My daddy said his brother, your daddy, was the best of them all—bigger, more handsome, wittier, and more talented than anyone in the family. It broke his heart to see them go. And your mother…well now, my dad said, that there was no more beautiful lass on the whole Island. I remember her too, even now. She sure seemed a beauty to me then, though I was nearly as little as you when ya had ta go." Connor stopped speaking and hugged her again, squeezing the breath right out of her, and told her how very sad he was that her momma and papa had passed so quickly after getting to America.

She hugged him back, fighting back her tears. She'd written Connor occasionally and told him of what had transpired in her life. His father, Michael, had lived to a ripe old age and had died only recently, leaving the land to Connor.

Connor was a strikingly handsome Irishman. Ben thought he looked just like a movie star. He had a shock of thick reddish-gray hair that curled naturally around his head. He had bright, twinkling green eyes bordered by thick salt and pepper eyebrows and a square jaw with a large dimple in the middle. He could have made the ladies swoon anywhere in the world. He still looked to be in good shape, with broad shoulders and a solid waistline. He had a senatorial voice. On seeing him, Anna was shocked at how much he looked like her father.

It took them little more than an hour in Connor's car to wind their way around the back side of Galway Bay to Doolin. Childhood memories flooded back to her with each mile they drove. For Ben, it was all new. The Irish landscape was like nothing he'd ever seen, pristinely beautiful and rugged, with stone fences and picturesque stone cottages everywhere.

Those stone fences, looking hundreds of years old. They bordered the very edges of the roads and ran up the steep valleys, dividing the farms all the way to the top of the distant ridges, dramatically outlining the vast deep-green landscape. All the stone cottages, with their thick thatched rooflines, looked as though they had come right out of a storybook. In a few places, along the distant ridges, he could see what looked like tall castle ruins or ancient fortresses.

There were cattle and sheep everywhere—more sheep than cattle. Ben had never seen such pastoral beauty. How could anyone ever bring themselves to leave this place? The rich emerald green of the sloping countryside provided sharp contrast to the deep blue ocean below. These unbelievably rich colors, framed by the dark stone fences that formed great triangles and went on forever, created the most spectacular landscape that he had ever seen.

Although it was June, the weather was cool in Ireland, no more than 50 degrees Fahrenheit at the height of the day. The wind blew briskly, creating whitecaps along the shoreline of the bay as they made their way around to Doolin.

Doolin was a small seaside village, famously known for its Irish music and the River Aille, bordering the village, draining the rain from the slopes of the Burren to empty it into the sea less than a mile beyond the town. It was typical of many coastal villages of Ireland's Connemara area.

The Murphy family lived only a quarter of a mile west of and above Doolin, bordered on all sides by the ancient stone fences standing over four feet high, consisting of large black and gray flat stones, stacked widely at the bottom and narrowing to a single stone at the top.

Connor's car speeded blithely along those rough, extremely narrow, roads within what seemed to Ben to be an inch or so of the stone walls, so close that it made his heart race and his stomach churn. Connor didn't help it any by seeming to drive very fast, talking all the time, expressing himself with a free hand. The proximity of the fences and the narrowness of the road may have made the speed deceptive, but it was still intimidating to Ben. Anna didn't seem to mind it at all. She sat in the front seat with Connor, laughing and talking just as fast as he did, and pointing out all the places she knew.

Throughout their time in Ireland, Ben had butterflies everywhere they drove, particularly when passing a car or horse and cart coming from the other direction. Each time that happened, Ben was absolutely sure that there was no way the vehicles could ever get past each other—but they always did, their passengers waving friendly greetings as they slipped by. And to make it all worse, the Irish drove on the wrong side of the road! Actually, it was just the British driving system, but it certainly felt like the wrong side of the road to Ben.

When they arrived at the Murphy farm, Anna and Ben were greeted warmly by at least twenty Irish families of the larger clan, some of whom still fondly remembered Anna's mom and dad. They all wept and hugged Anna and Ben as though they were long lost prodigal children just come home—which, in her case, was absolutely true! Ben was struck by the warmth and friendliness of these people despite the ravages of the famine, their country's horrible economy, and their long, bitter struggle with the British for Home Rule that had finally bred a civil war, just-concluded, over the partition of Northern and Southern Ireland.

Anna and Ben spent two full weeks with Connor and his family, reveling in the cool Irish air that felt and "tasted" so clean. It was unlike any other air Ben had ever breathed.

Anna was an entirely different person here. She was always smiling and laughing frequently, and loud. If she had appeared sophisticated and slightly reserved at times to the people of Jadwin, and even to Ben on occasion, she had now morphed into a spunky, bonny Irish lass on her own turf.

The culminating event of their visit with Connor occurred only two days before they departed from Doolin for their broader tour. It was then that they hiked from his farm, all the way up to the top of the Cliffs of Mohr, a four and a half mile trek up steep terrain from near sea level, along centuries-old pathways that meandered precipitously close to the edge of the cliffs. It was unparalleled for its scenery that changed dramatically every few hundred feet.

As they traversed those ancient pathways along the rugged coastline, the deep blue Atlantic Ocean smashed violently into the base of the cliffs below, just as it had for eons, making a dramatic booming sound and sending sparkling spray high into the air along the cliffs.

The action of the waves against the cliffs had carved massive stone ledges more than 100 feet wide near the cliff bottoms. Each giant wave crashed up and over those ledges, then drained reluctantly back into the ocean.

Far ahead, where the cliffs rose to their highest point, they could see that the massive waves had carved out giant stone towers that looked like tall castle buttresses rising up from the ocean. It was sculpting on a grand scale, far beyond the architectural capabilities of mankind that had created these unimaginable masterpieces.

The pathway steepened as the cliffs rose higher. It ran along the very edge of the cliffs. Everyone on it was whipped by fierce winds screaming up the face of the cliffs, forcing the people to lean forward if they were to make progress.

Everywhere, the view was awe inspiring, each new vista more beautiful than the one before. If they tired of looking at the sea, or needed to turn their backs to the wind for respite, they could scan the steep, emerald hillsides sloping above them for a mile or more, with those stone fences that seemed to run to infinity, and the fat cattle and sheep grazing lazily along the hillsides.

Anna never tired of viewing all those little stone cottages dotting the landscape, many now in ruins, or the tall fortress ruin standing prominently on the hillside just above Doolin that had once protected her ancestors from marauders of the sea.

The wind, on which the gulls and puffins rode with such grace, playing in the updrafts, always blew in gale force this high up, pushing fiercely on them as they climbed. Anna's face had a healthy glow, and her hair, now shining with a reddish tint in the bright sunlight, streamed almost straight out when she turned to the wind. Ben had forgotten, or perhaps had never fully understood, how much her beauty had been shaped by her heritage.

The party stopped frequently to huddle together for Connor to point out special sights that even Anna didn't recall. Below them, Ben guessed 200 or 300 feet down, Connor pointed to the huge rock ledges over which massive white waves broke and said, "That's where we went fishing as young men at low tide, and we still do it to this day. I seldom go down there anymore personally, because of my advancing age, but even I still do it on occasion."

"And over there, on that wide ledge where waves have cut out that big bowl that you see that looks like a swimming pool, that's where I swam on the warmest days every summer. You might think it too cold in Ireland to do that, but down there at low tide, with that black rock catching the sun, the water in that pool warms very quickly, and I tell ya now, there's no pool in the world as good as that one." As he spoke, the wind tugged at his hair and whisked his words away. His handsome face gave him the appearance of a god as he regaled them with one story after another about the ledges below.

"Connor," Ben shouted, "how on earth did you ever get down there to fish or swim?!"

Connor gave out a mighty laugh and motioned Ben a little closer to the edge. With the violent wind blowing, Ben became even more nervous as he inched over to Connor, who was bending down to point out a narrow rock ledge four feet below him at the very edge of the cliff. "Look here now, Ben." He was pointing to a spot in the middle of the ledge.

Ben saw a large metal "O-ring" attached to a rod that disappeared into the rock. "You see, our ancestors, so long ago that we don't know who did it, drilled a deep hole in the rock just the size of that rod and drove it in. I was told that it goes down at least four feet, although how they know that now, I cannot tell. It has bonded into that rock and will never be pulled out by man or wind."

"We just put ropes through that O-ring and drop over the cliff. There's nothin to it really, although the climbing back up can be a chore. If you'd come in August, I'd take you down. It's not really hard, you see. Every boy worth his salt learns the trick by the time he's ten. The water's cold—really cold—when you're fishing and the spray hits, but there are really big mackerel waiting to be caught down there, and the pools get so warmed by the sun as to be almost hot. I tell you, it's a great relief to swim after fightin with the fish for hours!"

Ben shook his head. "You're all just plain nuts!"

Connor laughed and clapped him on the shoulder. "That we are, Benjamin me boy; that we are! You gotta be a little crazy to live in Ireland, lad."

A half mile on up the trail, they came to a wide, flat stone bench with sea grass surrounding it as high as Anna's waist. They were now about 400 feet above the breakers. The view of the bay was panoramic, over ten miles wide here. They could see the Aran Islands across the bay. Doolin lay in the distance to their right and far below. Fishing and ferry boats crawled across the water, bobbing in the waves like toys in a bathtub, some making their way to and from the mainland and the Aran Islands.

Connor stood on the ledge looking down at the wide bay. He grew silent and didn't speak for long minutes. They went silent as well, realizing there was something about the place that bade reverence.

Finally he spoke. "There's a lotta sadness here lads and lasses— a lotta sadness. You see, it's here that the Irish families of countless generations have come to wave goodbye to their fathers, daughters, sons, brothers, sisters and cousins as they left for Australia, or Canada, or America, or God only knows where else, knowin full well that the odds are strong that they'll never see em again. We still do that."

"We waved goodbye to you and your mum and daddy right on this spot Aine, so long ago. Do you remember it now? Do you remember us up here sendin you our last goodbyes? I remember that we ran all the way up from Doolin to get here before your ship passed out of the harbor below. We ran as hard as we could up that path to say our last goodbyes."

She searched her memory, recalling that sad day. Then she turned back to Connor, her tears being whisked away by the wind. "Yes, yes, I remember. We were on the deck of that little ship, looking up at the Cliffs when Daddy pointed up here and exclaimed, 'Your grandpa and uncles and cousins are all right up there on that bluff waving goodbye to us, Anna. Let's wave back at em. We might not see em again'. I remember it well, Conner. I waved for you that day, too. Could you see me?"

"No, missy, you were too far away, but we waved just the same as if we could, sendin our love and hopes for a better life for you and your mum and dad." He bowed his head and looked away. "I'm so glad that the good Lord answered our prayers for you, and sorry he couldn't for your mum and dad. But, I'm surely glad you finally came home to us, Aine." His arms embraced her in a powerful hug, tears in his eyes. She wasn't sure if the tears were just for her or for all the Irish who'd left the island before and after her.

They all stood there for a while longer, silently, honoring those who had left and those who'd watched them go. That knoll had hosted centuries of tears, but it was less than a heartbeat in its own history.

They climbed again, higher and higher, the vistas ever changing along the face of the cliffs and at the edge of the deep sea below them, with thousands of gulls and puffins hanging effortlessly in the updrafts, along sides of the cliffs. They were so high now that they could no longer hear the sea crashing against the bottom of the cliffs below. All they could hear now was the fierce wind roaring up the side of the cliffs of Mohr.

They came upon a crystal stream no more than ten feet wide, dropping down from the steep hills above and spilling over the cliff's edge in what should have been more than a 500 foot fall to the sea. But the water never made it even half-way down. It was met by that gale-force wind, catching it in mid-air, overcoming its gravity and pushing it back up past them in a great misting spray to the fields above, from where it had recently come, and from where it would eventually join the stream again, to flow down to the cliff's edge and over again, repeating the cycle until it finally evaporated on the green grasslands above, creating their deep, glistening color.

At the very top of Mohr, 700 feet above the sea, they were overwhelmed by the wind and mesmerized by vista as they looked out over the ocean, the westernmost point of where the island met the sea. Below them, spectacular stone towers that looked like castles stood alone, in the water, a hundred feet out from the cliffs, shaped and reshaped by the roaring waves. In a hundred thousand years, or perhaps a million, their bases would erode and they would collapse into the sea; but for now they stood majestically, some over 200 feet high, yet still dwarfed by the cliffs behind them.

Ben had never seen anything as wild and beautiful as the Cliffs of Mohr, nor would he ever see anything in nature that spectacular again, even America's Grand Canyon, because it didn't have the wild ocean and the violent wind to interact with its massive cliffs.

Exhausted from the four mile climb, they rested and had lunch before making their way back down the path to Connor's little farmhouse on the steep hillside that slanted down toward Doolin and that timeless sea.

Ben and Anna finally left Doolin and headed for Kilarney to the south. It was the town that served as the gateway to the beautiful Kilarney National Park, and further south, to the Ring of Kerry. Anna didn't have the chance to see Kilarney as a child, so it was new to her too. But her mother and father had told her of it so often that she knew what to expect. They stayed at the Lake Hotel, at a beautiful site on the north end of the lower Kilarney Lake with the ruin of a small castle nestled beside the lake. That was the view from their window.

She and Ben took carriage rides throughout the national park, visiting the beautiful Muckross Abbey, the Franciscan Friary of Irrelogh, founded in 1448 by Daniel McCarthy Mor. The Abbey was surrounded by ancient trees, some of which dwarfed the large courtyards of the Abbey. It was the most beautiful and haunting man-made structure they would see in their visit to Ireland.

They also visited the Muckross House, a 65 room mansion built in the mid 1840s by Henry and Mary Balfour Herbert, on a peninsula between Muckross Lake and the Lough Leane, two of Kilarney's beautiful smaller lakes. Henry had desperately wanted to impress the British Empire, so he did extensive, and expensive, refinishing of his mansion to lure Queen Victoria for a visit in 1861. He had hoped that her visit would result in the house becoming a tourist attraction and make it profitable.

But the Queen's stay was not a pleasant one. She didn't like the place, or Kilarney, or Ireland in general, considering it a primitive and backward country. She was supposed to stay for the summer but she left after only two days, in a snit, to check into a hotel in the city and wouldn't leave her hotel room until she could head back to Great Britain later in the week. It ruined Henry's plans and the bad publicity bankrupted him. Arthur

Guinness had purchased it in 1899, and eventually gave it to Ireland as a public monument.

Ben and Anna took a guided tour of the 100 mile circular route of the Ring of Kerry, a beautiful coastal region that took two days to encompass. The valleys were steeper, higher and longer than those of Doolin's Connemara.

They saw a phenomenal sheep dog herding exhibition that awed Ben. The dogs responded to the whistles and other signals from their master more than a half-mile away as they herded the sheep from the high slopes to the sheds below.

They stayed at a quaint little inn at Waterville on the night of their excursion and then traveled the rest of the way around the Ring of Kerry along a steep coastline overlooking deep valleys that seemed miles in length, running down to the ocean. Their guide was a man named Dennis, a knowledgeable historian of the Ring of Kerry.

On a slope overlooking one of most rustic and longest valleys of the Ring, they saw numerous ruins of stone cottages scattered below, with their ancient stone fences dividing the farmland all the way up to where they stood, miles above the sea. But they saw no cattle or sheep, and no people. Ben asked Dennis why.

"Ah, Ben, this is the abandoned valley. In 1840 it was teeming with people, but then twenty years later, the potato famine hit and thousands starved. Eventually everyone left the valley—not one soul remains in all those farms you see below. You probably don't know it, but Ireland had a population of eight million in 1840. Then the famine hit and our country's population dropped to 4 million—its level of today. We lost half our population to death or immigration in less than 50 years. Here, we lost everybody."

Ben looked confused. "I don't get it, Dennis. I've heard that the potato famine was devastating. But how could losing a single crop cause four million people to disappear? Look at that seacoast down there. It looks very accessible from the valley, and I heard in Doolin that the Atlantic Ocean fishing is spectacular. Why didn't the people turn to seafood?"

Dennis smiled ruefully and said, "Ah, what a good question that is now! You see, Ben, none of our families in this part of Ireland were landowners. We were just tenants on the land. The owners were all rich barons from London or Paris or some other fancy European city. For them, the land was just an investment. A good many of them never visited their holdings here."

"But they all had a uniform policy, strictly enforced, to protect their assets from theft by us Irish peasants, who they never trusted and desired to keep in line. They gave us all little plots of land to grow vegetables for our survival as long as we followed their rules and maintained their land. But we weren't allowed to fish in their waters, you see, or to slaughter their precious sheep or cattle, or use their land for our own needs."

"Their laws were strictly enforced in a very simple and effective way. If an Irishman was caught fishing in their waters or harmin their animals, he received a one-way ticket on a boat to Australia. Not him and his family, mind you now, just him. His family was left behind to starve."

"We always lived on the edge of poverty, no matter how hard we worked. And then the blight hit us and it tipped the scales. A father would get desperate watching his wife and kids starve, so he'd try to sneak down and catch a fish or two to keep em alive."

"The overseers watched this closely and were in collusion with the police. You can see a long way in this land. Even if a man was successful one or two times, they'd ultimately catch him and convict him quickly putting him on that boat to Australia, our penal colony without walls, to make an example of him and stop it from becomin a wholesale problem."

He shrugged his shoulders in the way that Ben had seen many Irishmen do, sort of a resignation to the whims of capricious gods. "Maybe we'll recover someday, I don't know. It's a poor country that we live in and I doubt that'll change. We have only the rocks and the beauty of the land for resources. If our children want to succeed beyond scrabble farming, they won't find a good future in Ireland. So they migrate to America, or Europe, or Australia or to Canada. Not many to Britain, you see. We don't like them so much, nor they us."

"Tis great beauty and friendship that you'll find on this island, but not much more." He finished his explanation and became morose for a brief time. Anna and Ben didn't question him further. They took in the beautiful scenery and reflected on all the ghosts below.

At the end of their stay in Ireland, Ben and Anna boarded their ship home. Their return trip was also uneventful. But it was now apparent to Ben, and probably to her too, that Anna wasn't the same person who'd left New York three weeks earlier. She'd found her true roots and a great peace had come over her, one that would stay with her throughout her remaining days.

Ben was not changed as much as Anna, but he'd found something very special too. He'd become friends with a courageous, fatalistic, downtrodden, but still great, civilization, clinging to their lovely island rock as best they could, because it defined them.

And somehow, in seeing all that, he came to know his wife in an entirely new light, although, if asked, he wouldn't have been able to explain why at the time. But it was really quite simple and he'd fathom it much later. On that lonely island, he'd come face to face with the forces that had shaped her, long before she was ever born.

Chapter 34

They kept their promise to Bobby in the following year and traveled with him to the American West. Surprisingly, he turned out to be a delightful traveling companion. Every new scene excited him. He'd jump up and down and yell out at each new vista or natural wonder, amusing them and the strangers around him.

He would frequently run up to a stranger and babble, while pointing at something he wanted that person to see. While no one besides Anna, Ben or Bessie could decipher exactly what he said, it was apparent that he loved what he saw and wanted to make sure they saw it too. His enthusiasm was infectious. He even made them see beauty they'd missed, or had taken for granted, giving them a fresh perspective through the eyes of a special child.

Neither Anna nor Ben ever tried to curb his enthusiasm or his communication with the strangers around him. He didn't know that it was "improper" for a person with his limitations to converse with people like everyone else did. On the long train rides, he built friendships with the train personnel and most of the passengers who rode with him. Those who acted aloof or not interested never bothered him. He'd just go to the next person.

In succeeding years, they returned to Ireland twice, taking Bobby with them each time, reuniting with Connor and his family, as well as others in the extended Murphy clan. They traveled throughout Ireland, touring Connemara, Waterford and all the way to Dublin on one trip and north to Belfast and its unique coastal regions in the other. They had no trouble visiting the north of Ireland, despite what the Irish called "The Troubles" between the regions.

Each time, Anna came away renewed. Ben began to think about buying a summer home there but didn't mention it to Anna yet.

In the autumn, winter and spring months, Ben still worked at the flooring business, which continued to thrive as the nation's economy boomed. He and Charlie had groomed a number of younger staff, like Dan McDonald, who now oversaw day-to-day operations, freeing the two partners to focus on new markets and product lines. They now shipped those products throughout the United States, and even to Europe.

Anna remained at home, spending her time with Bessie, or working on numerous landscaping projects she'd envisioned around her house. Bessie was always an optimistic, willing partner in Anna's domestic adventures.

Anna was asked to sit on the Jadwin School Board but declined. She rarely provided consultation for the Children's Aid Society now, but did consult for a few states where child welfare legislation was still in doubt. She declined travel and limited her work to phone conferences or written correspondence. Charlie's Company had installed a phone line at its headquarters. Anna used it for conference calls when it wasn't tied up with the lumber business. She refused financial stipends for her work, choosing to serve as a volunteer.

Zach came to visit Ann as often as he could to seek advice or just to get away from the increasing pressures associated with his work and service in the Missouri Legislature. He and Anna were even closer now, finding their time together increasingly precious.

And always, there was Bobby. He was inquisitive beyond the limitations of his intelligence. He wanted to learn to play an organ like the one at the Baptist church, so Ben purchased a used upright organ. Bobby spent hours every week banging away at the keyboard, learning to pedal with his stiff feet to generate the air that made the sound.

Surprisingly, he had a pretty good ear for music and shocked everyone who heard him by playing songs they knew. He'd practice over and over, frequently hitting a wrong key as he was learning the song, or because his hands were so stiff. When he did, he'd shake his head dramatically, sighing heavily, and start the song all over again, no matter how close he was to the end.

But most of all, Bobby wanted to learn to ride a bike. Amazingly, he could balance himself on one and roll downhill, but unfortunately, he was never able to grasp the pedaling of the bike or how to use the brakes. That meant that, while he could coast in a straight line, turning corners was an adventure that usually ended in spills. The only way for him to stop was to coast down one hill and partway up the next until the momentum of his bike slowed enough for him to step down. Then he'd turn around and coast the other way.

For a while, Anna worked with him every day until she finally resigned herself to the reality of his limitations on two-wheelers. So Ben purchased a three-wheeler and, with much repetition, taught him how to move his feet properly to turn the pedals, and how to use a hand brake. Bobby was elated and rode his bike along the road in front of the McDonald house daily. That created a hazard for the trucks and cars passing down the lane. Anna fretted that he might get run over someday. But the traffic was all local and everyone knew to look out for him near his home. They enjoyed his friendly greetings as they crept around him.

Anna remained in good health throughout their travels. It had now been more than five years since her cancer had been treated. Dr Robbins grew less wary each year, increasingly confident that they had gotten all the cancer cells. Her weight remained constant and her appetite good. Her skin had retained its glow and she looked younger than her age. Those stress-free years were wonderfully pleasant for her and Ben.

Ben was delighted with her health. The nagging fear haunting him during the first three years after her operation gradually receded. Their travels to Ireland and throughout the West were some of the most enjoyable times of their lives. He looked forward to many more of those peaceful years once he fully retired, which he was contemplating soon.

Without Anna knowing it, he had contacted Connor to ask him to look for a summer home for them in Ireland near Doolin as a surprise for her. If Connor could find a suitable place, Ben had authorized him to act as his agent and sign a contract for it.

Chapter 35

Anna contracted a cold that lingered in the spring of her sixth year after the operation. It settled into her lungs and she couldn't seem to clear them. As days turned into weeks, she didn't improve, and the old fears that Ben had laid aside came rushing back to haunt him. Then Anna began to run a low-grade fever and lost her appetite. The color left her face. She and Ben went to the doctor and he prescribed medication, indicating he wanted to see her at least weekly until the condition resolved itself

But by early May, it hadn't, and they had to cancel a vacation to the West. By early June, she began to cough up blood in her mucous and Ben insisted on a trip back to St. Louis to see Robbins. They stayed there while he ran numerous tests. After Robbins reviewed the results, he gave them the prognosis.

He took her hands in his and said, "You probably have already guessed by now Anna that you're not just fighting a cold. The cancer has returned, or perhaps a new cancer has developed, we're not sure which. In either case, it has attacked your lungs this time and we don't think we can operate."

"I don't have any good treatment choices for you. I've actually heard that some doctors are experimenting with certain chemicals in low doses that are commonly thought of as poisons, but we simply don't have enough evidence to know if they will work. If you want me to explore that option, I will."

Ben and Anna sat silently for a few minutes as Robbins waited for the questions. But neither asked them. Tears came to Ben's eyes, but strangely, Anna didn't react in that manner. Instead, she smiled at Robbins. "We've fought well together, haven't we, Dr. Robbins? You gave me some of the most wonderful years of my life. How much longer do you think I have?"

Robbins choked a little and had to clear his throat. "I can't tell you exactly, but not long I'm afraid. Once a fast acting cancer settles into the lungs, it is usually a matter of months, certainly no more than a year."

She said she didn't need him to explore the experimental chemicals. They returned to Jadwin. They had driven their own car to St. Louis this time instead of riding the train. She leaned against Ben and slept most of the way, his arm around her shoulders. Once home, Ben informed the family.

Anna craved rest and slept often now. Ben remained near her at all times. In the better periods, when the coughing abated, they talked, reminiscing about their lives, their family and their travels together. One day, when she seemed half asleep, she said dreamily, "Do you remember the size of the cliffs, Ben?" He knew what cliffs she meant and said yes. "Well, that's the size of my love for you." Then she drifted off to sleep again.

Near the end, they talked of their coming separation. Ben, who had tried to be strong, just couldn't do it anymore and broke down. She smiled and took his hand. He sobbed, "I don't think I can go on without you, Anna."

She nodded slowly and smiled again, "Yes you can Ben. You'll have all those wonderful memories to keep you company, and you'll have Bobby. He'll always need you. Promise me you'll care for him as long as you can. He would be so lost in an institution. Our children will support him if he outlives you. The doctors already told us he shouldn't have lived this long, but I don't think they really know. He'll live much longer with your love."

She paused, out of breath, "So promise me, Ben, that you'll remain steady for him. In return, I promise you that I will always be with you while you live; and if Bessie's right, we'll be together again someday and won't ever have to worry about separation again."

She rested a minute and then continued. "One more thing, Ben; I know it'll be seen as unusual for Jadwin, but I want you to take my ashes back to the Cliffs of Mohr and release them by that little river that falls over the bluff but can't reach the sea. Can you do that for me?" He nodded his head and then put it down to her chest, weeping. She held him as best she could and ran her fingers through his hair.

Christian and Susannah came from North Carolina to see her two days later. She had weakened even more. Susannah held her and wept. Then Christian came up and took her hands in his, trying to smile. She was so very weak that she could only smile faintly, her eyes nearly closed. "Well, Christian, did we?"

"Did we, what, Anna?"

"Did Ben and I do enough to justify you giving up everything in Hell's Kitchen to save us?"

He smiled. "Anna, you'd already done that by the time Ben and I arrived in Jadwin. It's the thing I'm proudest of in my life, that I was able to help you and Ben that night. It always will be."

She smiled and nodded and drifted off to sleep.

Christian and Susannah stayed, visiting her for short intervals and, more important, helping to comfort Ben, the children and

Bessie. It was apparent that Anna would not be with them much longer. She became weaker with each passing hour. She passed in and out of consciousness. The family gathered, knowing the end was near.

Late in the evening, when she and Ben were alone, a moment of clarity came to her. She awakened with a start and looked at him. She smiled and then whispered. "You have no idea what an honor it's been to be your wife." He took her in his arms. She closed her eyes and sighed, resting quietly; and then she drifted away.

Chapter 36

Anna Murphy McDonald's body lay in repose at her home for two days to give the visitors from all over the state time to pay their respects. Then, Ben, Christian and Susannah and Zach accompanied the body to St. Louis, where she was cremated. Her ashes were placed in a beautiful wooden urn that Charlie had commissioned to be made from burled oak. All of them then accompanied Ben to Ireland. He was grateful. He wasn't sure he could have made it alone. Bessie kept Bobby, who continued grieving, broken-hearted and inconsolable.

They returned to Galway, where Connor met them and took them to Doolin. After a day of rest, they made the trek up to the stream. Connor and his family, along with Christian, Zach and Susanna, stayed back as Ben made his way to the stream's edge, just above where it dropped over the cliff. The spray on the wind, coming back up the cliff, surrounded him.

He opened the urn and raised it to the heavens, then slowly turned it sideways, letting the wind sweep her ashes away. They rose and mingled with the mist, swirling up along that long green slope. The mist moistened the ashes, adding substance and gravity. Halfway up the slope, she settled into the soil of her homeland, joining her ancestors.

Ben gave the urn to Connor as a memento. It was empty now and there was no reason for him to keep it.

Two days later, they traveled back to Galway to catch the ship home. Christian and Susanna left them at New York, catching a train to North Carolina, promising to come back to Missouri for a long visit after he'd had a little more time to recover. Ben and Zach made the sad ride back to Missouri together, glad for the company but speaking little, each lost in his own sorrow.

Two days after Ben arrived home, it was a Sunday. The family had gathered at Bessie's for lunch, including Ben and Anna's children, now adults with children of their own. Late that afternoon, Ben was restless and took a walk. He hiked up through the meadow to the big dead stump of the tree that Anna had loved so much. He sat on it and wept. It was peaceful there and he felt more connected to her. His heart ached till he thought it would break and he wasn't sure how he'd ever be able to go on.

He'd been there about an hour when he heard the footsteps. He looked up and saw the chubby boy fighting the weeds to get his little legs through, coming Ben's way. It was one of his grandsons, the five-year-old cherub of his daughter who had married one of Charlie's sons—the kid who liked to play checkers.

The little boy finally made it to him and then tried to climb up on the stump, but couldn't. Ben lifted him up. He sat down by his grandpa and didn't say anything at first. Ben didn't feel like speaking either, but, for some reason, he didn't mind having the boy there. Finally Ben broke the silence. "Why'd you leave your cousins? They're probably playing and having fun. Grandpa just needed to get away for a little while."

"I'll go back soon, Grandpa, but I wanted to make sure that you're okay."

Tears began to stream down Ben's face. He hated crying in front of the little boy, fearing that it would scare him, but Ben wasn't okay. He'd never be okay again. He was ashamed of himself— to weep in front of a child like that. But the boy just reached over and patted Ben's lower back with his little hand without saying anything, looking down the meadow toward the house.

Then, after a while, the little boy said, "My momma says you and Grandma were together almost ten times longer than I am old." He held up both hands and spread his fingers, looking at them, trying to puzzle it out. "You had Grandma for a real long time, didn't you Grandpa."

The child's observation startled Ben. How long it been? She'd lived to age 61. My God, the boy was right! They'd known each other for 48 years and had been together for 45. He smiled sadly, looking down at the boy and then he said, "Not really, son. It was only just a moment in time."

The boy looked confused, but was smart enough not to question his grandpa. Ben stood up and hefted the boy onto his shoulders. It felt way high up to the boy, like maybe a hundred feet, because his grandfather was a giant. He was a little scared. He put his hands on his grandfather's big head with its shiny gray hair to steady himself.

Ben turned toward that little house out on the peninsula and the family that she had loved so much.

Epilogue

I never knew my grandmother very well. She died when I was 5. I do recall her funeral as one of those disconcerting events of my early childhood, when everybody I knew was sad and I realized for the first time that I was supposed to be sad too. But I can still see her face through the haze of my childhood memories and she seemed very pretty to me then. Now, aided by old family pictures, I realize that I was right all along—she really was a beautiful woman.

I was fortunate enough to come to know my grandfather well. He became my most cherished friend during the time his and my life intersected. When I think of him, which is often, I still marvel at that, since he was in his late fifties on the day I was born. But to me he always was, and will always be, ageless.

He died at age 93. It was the hardest funeral that I ever attended, and in his and my other grandfather's large families, I have attended many. But His death was the first one that hurt so badly that it brought me to thoughts of my own mortality.

Before that though, he and I had come to be something more than just grandfather and grandson. That closeness evolved in an odd way, I suppose—over a checkerboard.

I wasn't much over 4 years old when we started playing. Later, Grandpa would come to live with my family in the winters, along with Bobby, my disabled uncle. Grandpa and I would play checkers at every opportunity and for as long as possible at a sitting.

I remember my mother frequently chiding us both on a Sunday

evening, insisting that we put the checkerboard away and get ready for church, which always started at 6:00 p.m. That meant that we had to leave at 5:30 p.m. for reasons I never understood, since the church building was only a ten-minute drive away. Grandpa and I would inevitably still be playing at 5:15, when she would begin harassing us in earnest.

I think maybe I was one of the few people he knew that loved the game as much as he did. Nothing will ever quite match those days of my childhood, frowning over a checkerboard, trying to beat my grandfather—except maybe some of the chess games that I have played with my own daughter and son when they were young.

Grandpa was a very good checker player, and of course, as a child, I was not. But I learned—often through losses that were painful to my pride—and I gradually improved.

He never really tried to teach me. We just competed, over and over again, until I got better and could give him a decent battle. In those days he always won, but never gloated or said anything bad to me. I liked learning by watching his moves and how he laid his traps. If he ever took one checker more than me, I was a goner. But as years passed, my skill grew and his inevitably diminished. I began to win more. I could tell he hated that, and yet enjoyed it at the same time. By watching what he did, I'd become a worthy adversary, the student learning from the master. In his late years, I was his equal perhaps, maybe even better for a short while, but only in checkers—never in life.

Long before his death, I had realized he was a very special man. Not because people said that he was, but because he just was. Though his body aged, his mind never did. I don't recall him ever being bitter about his age or complaining about his frequent health problems. He never spoke out against the stupidity of the younger generation. He adjusted easily to our rapidly changing world. His life had spanned from horses to rocket ships and he was at ease with it all.

He was never judgmental, that self-perceived right of every old person I've ever known other than him and Grandpa Schafer. He was not rigid or petty. To me, he seemed noble in his quiet ways, a characteristic that I, sadly, did not inherit from him.

Looking back, I believe that he must have been lonely during all those years that I knew him, but he never spoke of it, save once, when he was 89 and allegedly dying in a hospital.

To this day I'm not certain exactly why he was so different. Sometimes I've wondered if my view of him was so colored that I made him something he wasn't—sort of my own mythical legend. But when I talk to others who knew him, they remember him in much the same light as I do.

As a child, I heard stories about him and my grandmother, how they were abandoned to the streets of a place called Hell's Kitchen in New York City. At the time I first heard it, I thought that was a very bad name for a town. He never told me those stories directly and my family was characteristically understated about it. We were taught to avoid thinking about things that might make us feel special. Praise was rare in my family. Doing the right thing for its own sake was more highly valued.

I suppose my grandfather could have been called physically disabled, although that would have been a gross mislabel. He had lost part of his right leg in an accident long before I knew him. A hollow wooden leg took the place of his real one and he walked with a slight limp—more so in his late years.

In the evenings he would take the wooden leg off to relieve the pain. It never fit comfortably and so he used a heavy, woolen sock-like thing over the stump of his leg. When he went to bed he would always "walk" on his knees from his easy chair to the bedroom. I never once saw him use a crutch.

Despite his artificial leg, we kids considered him a terrific ball player. The old people said that he actually was when he was young. Watching his quick hands as he snared hard-hit balls back to the pitcher's box—the position he always played with us—I could see how that may have been true.

But even those hands were mangled by the time I knew him. In various milling accidents over the years, he'd lost a thumb and forefinger on his left hand, and his pinky and ring finger on his right. He didn't complain, although he did use the missing thumb as a prop for jokes on his grandchildren and great grandchildren when they were toddlers—including me. He'd see a little boy or girl busily sucking a thumb and he'd call them over to his chair and stick out his big hand with its missing thumb. Then, with a woebegone expression, he'd say, "that's what'll happen to you if you keep sucking your thumb as long as I did. It'll just melt away!"

The kid would invariably stare at his big hand and touch the place where the missing thumb should have been, and then inspect his or her own little thumb closely and run away, looking back at him in shock, wanting to mistrust what he said, but not sure they should.

He had a series of heart attacks during the years I knew him, starting not long after my grandmother died. I spent a number of nights with my mother at his house, sitting up, trying to help him through his pain. The heart attacks were the main reason he came to live with us, particularly in the winter months. Two or three times the doctors were sure he'd die, but he always recovered. Ultimately, in his late eighties, he lived full-time in a trailer parked next to our house, just across our driveway.

In the end it was a stroke that got him and I wished it had been a heart attack instead. He lived three terrible weeks after that stroke. Although he was conscious and knew us, he couldn't move the right side of his body, or talk, or help himself to the bathroom.

Once, during that awful period, I set up the checkerboard pretending to try to help him pass the time—in reality, just wanting one last game. But his mind was too scrambled and it frustrated him, so I put the board away forever.

He had a fierce, quiet will to live that was evident after the heart attacks, and even after the stroke. I think the task of living was a mandate for him, although I'm not entirely sure why. He had great faith in God and believed in an afterlife for those who deserved it, with a reunion of passed loved ones. I never got the idea that dying frightened him much. As he advanced into his later years, I know that life was not that exciting to him anymore.

Perhaps his will to live was inspired by his concern about Bobby, worried about who would take care of him after he was gone. But he needn't have worried. Next to my grandfather, Bobby was the most revered person in my large family and was well cared for throughout his time with us. Bobby was our family's very own Peter Pan. While his body aged, his mind never did. Unfortunately none of us could be his gang of "Lost Boys" for long because, unlike him, we did grow up and lose our childhood spirit. So he'd turn to the next generation of children in our family to find more playmates.

Through those years that he remained with my grandfather, and then with us, Bobby fundamentally reshaped our family's perspective about what was important in life. While we were trying desperately—and generally unsuccessfully—to change him to be more like us, he changed all of us to be just a little more like him. As I think back on it now, I believe that Bobby's disabilities were just a disguise that he used to help us understand what was really important.

With his severe disabilities, I suppose that it would have been easy for his parents to institutionalize him, but I'm told that they never seriously considered it. And those of us privileged to know Bobby gradually came to understand that "disabled" is a word that has different meanings. For him it was some physical and cognitive limitations. For many of us, the disabilities were more serious. We lost our ability to see life's little excitements and got hung up on material things. He never bothered to worry about that.

Sometimes, as a teenager, I was embarrassed to be seen in public with him, something I regretted later, particularly after he died at age 70. He still looked young for his age up to the day he died, with mostly coal black hair and very few wrinkles. It's a mystery how he managed that.

Even now, I can't think of my grandfather without thinking of Bobby. I'm sure my grandfather's life would not have been as special had Bobby not been in it, and Bobby's certainly would not have been nearly as rich without his father and mother.

My grandfather and I didn't really talk that much during our times together. He was not a talkative man. And I couldn't talk when we were playing checkers. The competition was so fierce that I had to focus all my concentration on the game. But on rare occasions we talked, first as grandfather and grandson, and eventually—and I know this is odd, considering our age differences—as close friends.

I particularly remember that time when he was 89 years old and in the hospital after yet another one of his heart attacks. The doctors had decided that the old man's time had come and hadn't bothered with much treatment or pain medicine for him. Pain was just something the doctors expected one to bear in those days to avoid the possibility of addiction. I suppose it never occurred to them that, since they thought he was dying anyway, the idea of addiction was somewhat ludicrous. It was one of the few times that I saw him visibly shaken.

But one of my cousins was a nurse from Texas and she came up to take charge of the doctors, as only strong nurses can. Since they couldn't intimidate her, they had to listen, knowing that she would not be fooled. So they reluctantly started some treatment and pain medicine and, to their embarrassment, he began to recover yet again.

I spent a lot of time with him during that episode. For some reason, during those days, a particular memory from my early childhood flashed through my mind of that day when I followed him to a meadow and talked with him about his life with my grandmother shortly after she had died.

He was very sad that day—so sad that, even as a young child, I could read it on his face. I remember trying to comfort him by telling him that he and Grandma had been together a long time. But when I said that, he looked at me in a funny way, almost angry-like, and I was afraid that I had displeased him. Then he smiled sadly and told me he was with her for only "a moment in time". I didn't understand what he meant then, and perhaps I still don't fully, but it makes a little more sense to me now.

If we are lucky, we get the opportunity to know our ancestors before they die. Generally, we waste it because we have no idea how much of a blessing it really is. Too often, we see them as those aged, frail caricatures of people that might once have been relevant, but no more. We speak to them in our patented "old person" voices that they probably find ludicrous. But they generally play along because there's little else to do with that sort of naïveté, and they probably think it's nice that somebody stops to pay a little attention to them.

Everybody flashes by them with very little eye contact and no time to talk except to deliver some trite statements before hurrying on with their busy lives. Age seldom makes old people stupid. They can still read sign language and they know that most people who visit them would usually rather be somewhere else. But every one of them I've ever taken the time to know, inevitably tell me that, looking back, their lives flashed by far too fast—just brief moments in time.

Their stories would be so interesting if we could have seen their real lives, not the ones disguised by old age. Rich or poor, famous or not, they often had special stories to tell. Lots of people said that my grandfather and grandmother were very special, and I also knew that my Grandpa Schafer was a marvel at business. And once I met their close friend, Christian Gunther, when he came to spend the month with my grandfather after his wife, Susanna, had died. He was supposed to by the hero who saved both Grandpa and Grandma McDonald's lives. But he was very old at the time and brokenhearted, so I hurried on and didn't talk to him much.

It's easy for those kinds of people to become myths. My family tended to make them more than they probably ever really wanted to be, even to the point that they became cartoonish to us. That's really too bad. That separated them from us and discounted their humanity. They were just people who happened to do exceptional things—things they probably wouldn't even have considered that exceptional as they were occurring.

And I have also learned that the richness of the quality of a life is not limited to how important a person was. I came to know my great grandmother, Bessie, and she was this incredible person, even though she was never a noted public figure. From the stories of my grandfather, I learned that she and my great grandfather Jess, who died years before I was born, were the real reasons why most of the stories about Uncle Zach and Grandma and Grandpa McDonald are even known in Missouri. And then, of course, there was Bobby, who taught my extended family more about living and loving than any other person I know.

Even the "common" people who lived before us—especially the common people—help to shape our lives in ways that we will never fully understand. We look at all those faded pictures in old family albums—snapshots of the ghosts in their moments in time—and we never know all that they did to help shape us. The tapestry of their lives colors ours, as ours will those who come after us, for both good and bad. It's life's pattern.

To understand what Grandpa was telling me, I had to mature enough to come in touch with my own mortality—by losing him. And all of my family understood it better when we lost Bobby. *That* was a very hard funeral for my family to bear. He was our last true link to Ben and Anna.

One afternoon in that St. Charles hospital, as Grandpa and I sat looking out his hospital window, a train crept along the Missouri River bottom at a great distance, like some slow-moving mechanical snake. It curved and stretched itself out along the river as its smoke drifted back in long wispy strands. His face changed and his eyes took on a haunted look as he watched that train, and for a few seconds, I lost him to the past. Then he returned to me and stared at me in a way he'd not done before. "When I pass on, I want you to have a bundle of letters that I keep in a safe at home. Your mother will know where they are."

"Okay, I'll ask her when that time comes, but I hope it will be a long way off."

He smiled at me sadly and I realized that he didn't share that wish.

I didn't inquire what the letters were about at the time. He'd have told me if he wanted to. But I know now. I still have those letters written so long ago. They are, in fact, my most prized possession.

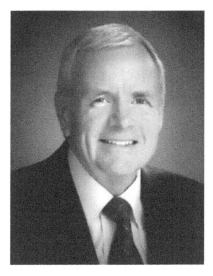

Keith Schafer was raised in south-central Missouri in a rural area near Licking, which is 22 miles from the little Jadwin community featured in his first two books. He is a member of a very large extended family from that area that includes the Schafer and the Lough clans. In his professional career, Keith held a number of executive positions in state human services agencies, where he first learned of the New York Children's Aid Society Orphan Train program and its impact on the history of Missouri and surrounding states.

Made in the USA
Monee, IL
20 February 2021